# Cherokee Storm

## Also by Janelle Taylor

*Shadowing Ivy*

*Haunting Olivia*

*Watching Amanda*

*Dying to Marry*

*Don't Go Home*

*Not Without You*

*Night Moves*

*In Too Deep*

*Lakota Flower*

Published by Kensington Publishing Corporation

# Cherokee Storm

## Janelle Taylor

ZEBRA BOOKS
KENSINGTON PUBLISHING CORP.

ZEBRA BOOKS are published by

Kensington Publishing Corp.
119 West 40th Street
New York, NY 10018

ISBN-13: 978-1-61664-507-6

Printed in the United States of America

# Chapter 1

*Great Smoky Mountains*
*June 1756*

"I want to die in my bed, not murdered by heathen savages."

Shannon O'Shea glanced from the older woman to the willows lining the creek a hundred yards away. It wasn't that far, and the cow was thirsty.

"Scalped or worse . . ." Hannah Clark threw another branch on the campfire and trailed off ominously, leaving unsaid all her earlier lurid predictions of torture and rape by Cherokee war parties.

"Take that animal to water, Shannon." Nathan Clark scowled at his wife. "And you hold your tongue, and stop scaring her." He heaved the wagon tongue off the ground, lifting it high enough for Shannon to lead the milk cow out of the enclosure. "Go on, girl. Doubt you'll be scalped between here and the creek with Drake to stand guard."

Shannon nodded, knotting her shawl against the damp. She'd forgotten how chilly these mountains could be in June. Dark clouds hovered over the mountaintops, and she could smell the coming rain. Funny how the familiar sounds and scents all came rushing back to her, after so many years away.

"You waitin' for the second coming?" Nathan's meaty arms bulged under the weight of the wagon tongue.

Shannon shivered, despite the thick wool of her new shawl. She had to admit the tale the white fur trappers had related this morning about being attacked by Cherokee made her nervous. After a month on the trail west, they were still three days' journey from her father's home. She wouldn't feel safe until she felt his strong arms around her again.

"Storm's moving in fast," Nathan chided. "Cow don't drink tonight, she don't give milk tomorrow."

Shannon tugged on the halter rope. The spotted cow rolled her eyes and planted her front feet in the mud. "Come on," Shannon coaxed. Of all the cows she'd ever tended, Betty had the worst disposition. She was stubborn, she kicked, and she'd hook you with her broken horn if you weren't careful.

Thunder rumbled in the distance, echoing down the long valley. Tree branches whipped and groaned overhead; leaves swirled and danced around the wagons. Sand and grit blew against Shannon's face and arms.

Hannah shook a thick finger at Nathan. "You'll rue the day you didn't listen to me."

"I rue the day I ever did. I said I was sending Drake to watch over her. Drake! Where'd you get to?"

Hannah's shrill voice rose to a high-pitched whine. "A bucket of milk ain't worth a girl's life. How you gonna explain to Flynn O'Shea you sent his girl out to be massacred for—"

"Cherokee ain't stupid!" Nathan roared. "Six wagons, ten men, and fifteen good rifles. Sneaky devils want no part of us. Leave the girl to tend that cantankerous beast and me worry about Indians." He slapped a hand on Betty's bony hip, and the cow charged forward, tossing her horns and slinging mud through the air with all four hooves. "Drake!" Nathan bellowed again.

Shannon dodged the cow's rush and dashed ahead, holding tightly to the halter rope. Intent on hanging on to Betty without being trampled, she didn't notice Nathan's oldest son until she slammed into his broad chest.

Drake chuckled and wrapped his big arms around her, trapping her in his embrace. Somewhere in the process, he grabbed the cow's rope and yanked Betty to a skidding halt.

"Drake?" Shannon inhaled the mingled scents of damp wool, tobacco, and saddle oil. It had to be Drake. Drake had worn a blue shirt today . . . or was that his twin brother? Drake and Damon were identical, making it nearly impossible to tell them apart, even to their father. They even sounded alike. "You are Drake, aren't you?"

Pale blue eyes narrowed with mischief. "Maybe. Had I knowed you wanted me this bad, I'd of come when Pa first yelled. What's he want now?"

Shannon ducked under Drake's rifle and wiggled out of his embrace. She liked him well enough, despite his outlandish notion that she'd marry him before Christmas. "He wants you to walk to the river with us. Watch out for hostiles."

"You take care!" Drake's mother shouted from within the circle of wagons. "I'll not have my oldest scalped for cow nor woman."

"Mind your own business, Ma," Drake yelled back.

"Can we just go?" Shannon asked. "Betty needs her water before the rain starts." She didn't care for the way he spoke to his mother. She thought it was disrespectful. Hannah Clark was a rude woman, but Drake was her son. He should have better manners.

*Janelle Taylor*

Drake tilted his head up and raindrops splattered across his broad face. "Rain's already started, I'd say. And most cows don't melt in a little rain, or is this one special?"

"Funny."

He flashed her a devilish grin. "Damon and me were just—"

"Drake!" His mirror image appeared around the corner of the nearest Conestoga, also wearing an identical blue homespun shirt. "Jacob wants us to help pull that wagon wheel so he can grease the axle."

Drake glanced down at her. "You certain you need my protection?"

"Go ahead," she urged. "I'll be fine. It's not a hundred yards to the creek. They can see me from the wagons."

"Reckon that's so."

Shannon looked back at the cow and shook the lead rope. She could swear the animal was giving her the evil eye. "Go." Betty mooed, lowered her head, and began to trot toward the water.

The creek bank sloped down to gravelly shallows. No more than fifteen feet across, the rocky stream was icy cold and so clear, Shannon could see silvery fish zipping along the bottom. When the cow began to drink, Shannon bent and splashed handfuls of water on her face.

Without warning, lightning crashed a short distance away. To Shannon's left, a tall pine tree quivered and burst into flames. The stench of sulfur choked her as she stumbled back, slipped on a mossy stone, and fell on her backside in six inches of water. Betty bawled and leaped straight in the air, ripping the lead rope out of Shannon's hand. She grabbed for the rope, but couldn't hold the panicked animal. The cow splashed through the creek, struggled up the far bank, and plunged into the thick undergrowth.

"Whoa! Whoa! Betty, come back!" Shannon didn't

hesitate. All she could think of was how valuable a milk cow was and how much trouble she'd once gotten in when two hens at the tavern had gone missing. Surely, if she lost Betty, her father would have to pay her worth in hard coin. Swallowing her own fears and oblivious to the rising wind and rain, she waded through the icy water and raced into the forest after the panicked animal.

Blackberries and wild grape vines tangled around Shannon's legs and tore at her cap. Needles of rain stung her face and blurred her vision. Thunder rolled and boomed overhead. "Betty!" she called. "Betty!"

The thicket opened into a shadowy glade sheltered by towering oaks, and directly ahead, the print of a cow's hoof stood out clearly on the thick moss. Shannon glanced back over her shoulder, but a wall of green leaves obscured the creek. She wondered if she should go back for help.

A roll of thunder nearly drowned out the cow's bawl of distress. Shannon circled a tree trunk wider than a covered wagon and caught sight of Betty no more than fifty feet ahead. The rope dangled enticingly from the animal's halter. "Easy," Shannon soothed. "Easy, girl. Good cow." Branches overhead swayed in the wind, and huge drops of rain filtered through the green interlaced canopy overhead.

Betty stood motionless until Shannon was almost within reach of the trailing line, then leaped forward over a rotting log, and scampered away. For five minutes, perhaps ten, they played a game of cat and mouse until, just as Shannon was about to admit defeat, Betty's rope caught between two rocks. "Got you!" Shannon cried.

Caught, the cow uttered a plaintive moo, raised her tail, and voided her bladder. Shannon dodged the yellow stream and considered strangling Betty with her own lead line. Muttering dire threats, she wrapped the rope around one wrist. If she followed her own footprints on the forest floor, there was no chance of losing her way back to the creek.

Shannon knew that her plan would have worked if it hadn't gotten so dark that she couldn't see the ground under her feet . . . or if every oak tree hadn't loomed as black and shapeless as the one beside it. Or if the downpour didn't make it impossible to distinguish an oak from a chestnut.

When the moss under her feet became gravel and ragged tufts of grass and the trees became smaller, Shannon realized she was lost. Teeth chattering, she leaned against the cow and fought back tears. No one from the wagons could find her in this storm. She'd be out here in the cold and wet all night, and the longer she wandered, the farther she might be from camp. If the lightning didn't strike her dead, she'd freeze before dawn.

Abruptly, Betty yanked back on the rope and started walking up an incline. Having no better idea, Shannon didn't try to stop her. Animals had a good sense of smell, she reasoned. Maybe Betty could find the way back. The stream and a warm fire might be just beyond those—

Another bolt of lightning lit up the woods, half blinding Shannon and raising the hair at the nape of her neck. Betty fell to her knees then scrambled up and charged toward a black void in the hillside, dragging Shannon after her. One shoe came off as Shannon threw up her arms to protect her head. The rope cut into her flesh painfully and then came loose as lightning struck a second time even closer. Betty plunged into what appeared to be the mouth of a cave. Shannon regained her footing, stumbled into the shelter of the overhanging rock, and sank to the dry floor.

She could hear the cow's hooves clacking on stone, but had lost sight of the animal when she careened around a pillar of rock and vanished into the depths of the cavern. Grateful to be out of the storm, hands and knees raw from being dragged, Shannon curled into a ball and caught her breath. The muted sound of rain and the absence of the biting wind soothed her and did much to restore her nerve. All she had to do was sit here until daylight, and someone would find her.

Images of bears and mountain lions nudged the corners of her mind and she pushed them back. If any wild beast had taken shelter in the cave, the cow would have smelled it. Nothing could hurt her here. She kicked off her single remaining shoe, drew off her soaking shawl, and wrung out the water.

Gooseflesh rose on her arms, and she rubbed them vigorously in an attempt to stave off the chills that shook her body and made her teeth chatter. Her skirt was as wet as the wrap. She stripped off the woolen gown and her stockings, leaving only her shift and petticoats. They were wet too, but she could hardly sleep on the cave floor as naked as an egg without even a blanket.

She peered out into the night. She could smell smoke, hear the faint crackle of fire. Was it possible that the woods were on fire? Oddly, the scent seemed to be stronger at the back of the cave. She ventured to the far corner and looked around the rock pillar that hid the passage to the deeper section of the cavern. She gave a small gasp of astonishment and took several steps down the natural incline to the inner chamber.

Fire! But how . . . a shadowy figure raised a head beyond the flames—not a cow, but a horse. Curiosity became fear as Shannon realized that the fire couldn't have come from the lightning. She clapped a hand over her mouth to stifle the cry that rose from her throat and turned to run. And for the second time that day, she smacked into the hard muscle and sinew of a man's chest. And for the second time, she found herself trapped in powerful bare arms.

Fierce black eyes glared into her own. Eyes set into a copper-hued face, high cheekbones, and rugged features that might have been hewn from granite.

*Cherokee!* Terror lent her strength. She kicked and struggled to get free, but he crushed her against his naked flesh.

"Quiet, woman."

Tears blurred her vision. "Let me go!" she repeated as he lifted her off the floor and carried her effortlessly back toward the fire. Her voice rang high and frightened in her ears. This couldn't be happening. "No, please . . ." Was she going to die here and now?

Hannah Clark's warnings of rape and torture curled down Shannon's spine and made her knees go weak as milk. She balled her hands into fists and struck at her captor's face. If she died, she would die fighting.

"Peace, Mary Shan-non. I am not your enemy."

As suddenly as he'd seized her, the Indian let her go. She half circled the fire and backed up until she felt the cold stone wall block her escape. Mouth dry, eyes wide, she stared at him.

Cherokee. Her heart sank.

Even on the far side of the fire, he towered over her—a Cherokee warrior at the height of his power, painted for war with twin streaks of black paint adorning each cheek. A single eagle feather dangled from hair as dark and glossy as a raven's wing and fell unbound below massive shoulders. Beaten silver rings pierced each earlobe, and a single band of silver encircled one bulging bicep. A ribbon of tribal tattoos ran from collarbone to hip to knee on his right side, a decoration revealed in all its glory by the expanse of honey-dark skin, lean belly, and muscular thigh.

Fear shimmered through her—utter terror and another emotion that she didn't dare name. Buzzing rang in her ears and spots danced before her eyes. Where was her shame? Her throat tightened and she felt blood rush to her face. She couldn't tear her gaze away from him.

Nothing covered the Cherokee's raw nakedness but a twisted cord of rawhide around his lean waist, a loincloth that did little to conceal his obvious sex, and a pair of high, beaded deerskin moccasins. Tall and broad shouldered, he seemed more dream than flesh-and-blood man. . . . But no ghost who invaded her dreams had worn both a sheathed hunting knife and a steel Cherokee tomahawk strapped to his waist.

"I won't hurt you, Mary Shan-non."

His deep voice echoed off the limestone ceiling and walls. "Maryshannon . . . Maryshannon . . . Maryshannon."

English. He was speaking English, accented, with an almost musical cadence, but she could understand every word. She sucked air into her chest and the buzzing noise receded. How did he know her name? "Who are you?" she stammered.

"Men call me Storm Dancer, but you knew me once when I wore a different name."

She shook her head. "No. I don't know you. You're a stranger."

His thin lips turned up in a faint smile. "Are you sure?"

"Please. Let me go back to my friends. My father is a friend to the Cherokee. He will pay—"

"It is as you say. Flynn O'Shea is a good friend to the Cherokee." He touched his lips with two fingers in a graceful gesture. "Among my people, we call him *Truth Teller.*"

"And he will pay well for my safe return." Shannon straightened her shoulders and tried to force her voice to calm. If she could keep him talking, reason with him, she might live to walk out of here as untouched as she'd entered. She took another breath. "How do you know who I am?"

He made a click with his tongue that might have been amusement. "You don't listen. But I should have remembered. Once an idea lodged in your head, you did not give it up easily."

She shook her head. "I'm sorry. I—"

"Have you forgotten the boy who taught you to catch trout with your bare hands? To ride a pony astride without bridle or saddle?"

Otter? She looked at him again. Once, long ago, when she was small, a boy had come often to her father's trading post with his uncle, an important man called Winter Fox. He'd been older than she by a few years, not many, young enough that her mother hadn't forbidden them to play together. Other children had visited the post from time to time, but Otter had been her only real friend. But Otter had been a shy, gentle boy, slender as a reed with a quiet smile and tender hands. This savage warrior couldn't possibly be . . .

He folded his arms across his chest. "Now you remember."

"Otter?"

He retrieved a blanket from the edge of the fire and approached her with slow, measured steps. "You are cold, Mary Shannon. Warm yourself."

"No," she said stubbornly, clinging to reason. "You can't be my Otter."

When she flinched, he followed and draped the blanket around her shoulders. "Long ago I was," he said. "But his time is past."

Emboldened by his kind gesture, she sidled past the horse's rump. In the far corner, a second horse stood nose to nose with Betty. With a shock she realized she knew these animals. The white trappers who'd stopped the Clark party early this morning had ridden these horses—the men who'd warned them about the raid by hostile Indians. This man, whoever he was, was at least a thief, perhaps even a murderer. Her fear flowed back twofold.

"Please, if you'd just let me go."

He took a stand between her and the entrance. "Do you want to die?"

Her heart hammered against her chest, blood ringing in her ears. "You said . . . you promised you wouldn't hurt me." Tears welled up and rolled down her cheeks. "You promised."

"Do you think Flynn O'Shea is the only man who speaks true?" His question rang hard and aggrieved. "You are my guest, Mary Shannon. Out there lies danger. I will keep you safe by my fire until morning."

She swallowed the lump in her throat as thunder boomed and rolled across the mountain peaks. Alone with a nearly naked stranger, a barbaric tribesman with skin of dusty bronze . . . Safe? And her clad only in shift and stays, how could she be safe with him?

"Come." He bent and added another log to the fire. "Warm yourself." The words were soft, but commanding.

"The horses . . ." she dared. "You took them from—"

He nodded. "I did."

"And the men who rode them?"

His sloe-black eyes glittered in the firelight. "This is Cherokee land," he murmured. "The enemy of the Cherokee can expect no mercy."

# Chapter 2

A twig snapped and the flames flared, casting grotesque shadows on the wall and ceiling. A bone-deep chill radiated out from the pit of Shannon's stomach, and she couldn't help shivering. He'd as much as admitted he'd stolen the horses and murdered the men who'd ridden them. He was right. If he ever had been her friend Otter, it was long ago—replaced by a cold and heartless killer . . . a man who could use her as he pleased and discard her without a shred of conscience.

She wasn't a coward, but she didn't want to die. Still, if she had to, she'd do it with dignity. She wouldn't give him the satisfaction of begging for her life. And she wouldn't make it easy for him. She'd fight as long as she drew breath.

"Please," she said, trying not to show how frightened she was, "I'm cold. Could I have my dress? It's out there." She pointed, but he'd already ducked around the wall of rock that concealed the inner chamber from the cave mouth. Before she could take two deep breaths, he was back, her dripping garment and stockings in his hands, beads of rain streaking his hard features and bare chest.

"You cannot wear these," he said.

"Yes, I can."

She reached for them, but he shook his head and draped the wet garments over a saddle on the far side of the fire. "You were never such a fool, Mary Shan-non. If you put them on before they dry, you will be even colder."

"Don't call me that," she protested without thinking. Her mother had only used her full baptismal name when she'd been in trouble for some childish mischief. Moreover, it was what the orphanage matron, Mistress Murrain, had called her when she'd beaten her for breaking the rules. *Mar-ry Shan-non—Mar-ry Shan-non!*" And each taunting syllable had brought another slash of the leather strap and more mocking ridicule from the other girls. "I go by Shannon now," she finished, her voice dropping to a whisper.

"Shan-non."

His soft Cherokee struck an unfamiliar chord, piercing her defenses, and unfurling a bright ribbon of excitement deep inside her. Tears welled in her eyes and she blinked them back. "If you let me go, I won't tell anyone I saw you," she bargained.

"And I am to let the daughter of Truth Teller walk out into the storm to be struck down by *anagalisgi*, the lightning, or eaten by *yona*, the black bear?" He motioned her to sit down on the floor of the cave, fumbled in a leather bag, and tossed her a patty of what looked like corn bread. "Eat. You are too thin."

Why was he offering her food? Did he think she'd fall into his arms for a morsel of bread?

"Eat, woman. Are you simple?"

Reluctantly, she nibbled at the cake. It was sweet and laced with dried berries. And after the first bite, her stomach growled, reminding her that she'd had nothing since mush and weak tea at dawn. Ravenous, she consumed the last crumbs.

"Good." He indicated the cow contentedly chewing her cud. "There is milk to wash it down. No?"

Shannon dropped the blanket on the cave floor and did as she was told. She squirted warm milk from the cow's teats into her mouth and drank until her belly was full. Then she glanced at him.

He shook his head. "Milk is not for the *Tsalagi.*" He didn't have to translate. She remembered that that was the word that the Cherokee used to describe themselves. *Tsalagi* . . . the people. He dropped into a sitting position and held out his palms to the fire. "Warm yourself."

She returned to the fire, more conscious than ever of her state of undress, and wrapped the blanket around her again. By the cow's foot had been a jagged stone half the size of her hand. She held it now, concealed from him. It was a poor weapon against a tomahawk or the long rifle leaning against the far wall, but it was something. She was no light skirts, and she'd fight him with every ounce of her strength if he tried to have his way with her.

"Where is your other moccasin?" He indicated her bare foot. "I saw only one at the cave entrance."

"My shoe? I lost it . . . in the storm." Desperate not to sound foolish, she added, "The cow tried to get away. I couldn't stop to find it."

"I see." He pulled a wicked-looking knife from the sheath at his waist and began to sharpen it with a stone. Firelight flashed on the surface of the steel blade.

"I'm not afraid of you." When he looked doubtful, she repeated the lie. "You don't scare me."

"You are a poor liar, Mary Shannon."

"I'm not . . ." She trailed off, knowing that he was right. She was terrified. Even the air in the cavern seemed charged, as though lightning would strike them at any second. The tension made it difficult to breathe . . . to sit still. "Your uncle . . ."

She stopped. This wasn't Otter; he couldn't be. He was the liar. "Otter's uncle is a great man among the Cherokee. He will be angry if you hurt the only child of his good friend."

He fixed those black eyes on hers. "Have I hurt you, woman? I have given you shelter from the storm, fed you, and covered you with my only blanket."

"You haven't hurt me," she admitted. At least, not yet. "But you're holding me against my will. And . . ." Her gaze strayed to the knife in his hand. "You murdered those men in cold blood."

He shrugged. "So you say."

"You killed them, didn't you?"

"Go to sleep. I will keep watch."

Not a chance, she thought. If she closed her eyes, who knew what he'd do? She curled her bare feet under her and pretended to drift off. The smells of the crackling fire, the warm familiar scent of the animals, the rain falling steadily at the cave mouth all conspired to lull her into a false sense of security. She was determined to watch for his attack, but as the minutes became hours and he continued to sit there, her resolve faltered and slumber as deep as death claimed her.

"Shan-non."

Her eyes snapped open and she sat up abruptly, startling the cow who snorted and shook her horns at the nearest horse. Shannon uttered a small gasp and tried to remember where she was.

"It is morning," he said. "The sun has risen and the rain has stopped." He held out a woven basket smaller than her fist. "Have you thirst?"

Her hand trembled as she reached for the object. He was so close she could smell his damp hair and skin, an unfamiliar woodsy blend of earth and forest . . . foreign but not unpleasant. As she took the basket, his lean fingers brushed hers and her heart raced at his touch. She drew in a deep breath. "What is—"

"Water from the spring. Drink."

She obeyed and found the liquid cold and sweet, so different from the well water at Klank's tavern that it seemed impossible both could be the same substance. She drained the cup to the last drop. "Where did you get this little basket?" she asked. It seemed fashioned of leaves and twigs, but it was watertight and light as duck down.

His bronze features remained expressionless, but his eyes narrowed. "It is nothing. A skill my aunt taught me when I was . . ." He hesitated, searching for the word. "A cub."

"A small child," she corrected. Had she lost her mind that she would concern herself with precise words? The man was nearly naked. His muscular legs were long and powerful. One bare thigh bore three great ivory scars that started at his hip and ran down the outside of his leg halfway to his knee. Only one animal could leave such a mark. She'd not been so long in the East that she didn't recognize the damage a bear's claw could do.

"Yes," he said, tapping the single ornament that hung from a string of rawhide at his throat. "I was foolish enough to meet *yona* as he woke hungry from his winter's sleep."

Shannon swallowed hard. The necklace bore a bear's claw, so large that simply looking at it made shivers run down her spine. "A big bear," she murmured.

He shrugged. "An old warrior bear, strong and wise." He touched the claw lightly. "Veteran of many battles."

"But you escaped."

He shook his head. "No. *Yona* killed me."

Her eyes widened in astonishment before she saw one corner of his mouth twitch in amusement and realized that he was teasing her. "You said you were a cub," she ventured. "Do you have some power over bears?"

"I was born to the Wolf Clan of the *Tsalagi*. A cub is a young one, no?"

"Yes, but—"

"A cub and a child the same."

"Your English is very good, but a cub is an animal and a child is a human."

"So you believe."

Unwilling to argue the point with him, Shannon looked down at the vessel cradled in her hand. The weaving was simple yet beautiful. She wished she could make something so useful out of twigs and leaves. Strange to think a bloodthirsty Cherokee warrior might create such a thing . . . for her.

Otter had brought her small gifts whenever he'd visited the trading post. Once he'd given her a doll fashioned of wood and leather with real hair from a horse's mane. She remembered how she'd loved the doll, even though it had no features. Where the eyes and mouth and nose should have been was only smooth buckskin. Otter had explained that only the Creator could make a human. The Cherokee sewed no faces on their children's dolls. Odd, but charming.

But this wasn't Otter, she reminded herself. Now that she wasn't quite so frightened, she could see that this man wasn't ugly. This morning, the war paint had vanished, leaving only those high cheekbones, the proud nose, and that honey red-brown skin. The fire had died to embers and she could no longer see his dark, fierce eyes, but she felt the intense power of his gaze.

"Can I go now?" she asked him.

He stepped back and allowed her to pass. She snatched

up her dress and yanked it over her head. It was wrinkled but almost dry, and she felt confidence returning as soon as she was decently covered.

"I have to take the cow."

He shrugged. "Did I not tell you I don't drink milk?"

"She belongs to the Clark family. I'm responsible for the cow," she babbled. Hope surged in her chest. Was he really going to allow her to walk out of here unharmed? She took hold of Betty's dangling rope and pulled the troublesome animal after her. This seemed too easy. After all her fears, was he really just going to allow her to walk away?

When she reached the mouth of the cave, the sun was so bright that she had to shield her eyes from the glare. The storm that had made the woods so forbidding had transformed the forest into an Eden tinted with every shade of green. Birdsong echoed from branch to tree-top, and a rainbow of wildflowers adorned the thick carpet of grass and moss.

Her one shoe lay where she'd discarded it, but the other was hopelessly lost. She'd have to find her way back to the camp in her stockinged feet. How she would replace the shoes, she had no clue. Worn though they were, the footwear had been her only pair.

"Come on, Betty," she urged, pulling at the cow's lead. She wanted to get away as quickly as possible—before he could change his mind. At least she wouldn't have to return without the Clarks' cow. She knew she'd be blamed for getting lost and—

A rifle shot rang out nearby. A flock of crows flew up in alarm, and a blue jay rasped an urgent warning. Shannon shouted, "Here! I'm here!" Then started as the Cherokee appeared beside her.

"Go." He waved toward the forest.

She started down the slope, tugging Betty after her. "Over here!"

Suddenly Drake and his twin brother stepped from the trees. Damon shouted, but his words were drowned by the sound of horses' hooves on the stone ledge behind her. Drake aimed his rifle toward the cave.

"No!" Shannon shouted. "Wait, he's not—"

The gun roared.

The Cherokee shoved her to the ground. "Stay down!" He turned and vaulted onto the back of the black horse, leaning over so far that nothing showed but one leg and moccasined foot and a single fist tightly gripping the animal's mane. With a cry he drove his mount down the stone-strewn incline directly toward Drake and Damon. The second horse followed half a length behind, running full out, tail and mane flying.

Drake struggled to reload. Damon raised his rifle to fire, but the black horse was almost on him, and he had to leap aside to avoid being trampled. Damon's foot tangled in the undergrowth and he sprawled full length on the ground. Shannon screamed as the black horse's hooves came perilously close to his head.

At the last instant, the animal leaped over Damon's fallen body and plunged into the woods. The other horse veered left between the brothers and galloped after the mounted Cherokee.

Cursing, Drake got off a second shot, but the slug missed the target by yards and struck the trunk of a massive oak, sending bark spraying into the air. Shannon got to her feet and ran to Damon's side. "Are you hurt?"

Damon sat up, blinked, and rubbed his left knee. "I'm all right," he managed. His rifle lay a few feet away, the stock splintered where a flying hoof had struck it.

"Damn it to hell," Drake swore. "I had him in my sights. I could have—"

"He didn't hurt me," Shannon protested. "You shouldn't have shot at him."

Drake scowled as he took in her bare legs and wrinkled dress. "You look like . . ." His face reddened. "Did he—"

"No. He didn't touch me. I got caught in the storm. We spent last night in the cave together, but—"

"You spent the night with him and lived to tell about it?" Drake set his jaw in that stubborn way he had and his eyes narrowed.

"The storm was terrible," she explained. "I didn't know he was in the cave when—"

"I know those horses." Damon cut her off. "Same exact ones those trappers were riding. He's a horse thief."

"They're all horse thieves." Drake took hold of her arm and peered into her face. "You're certain he didn't do more? Didn't force you to—"

"He didn't touch me," she repeated. She was struck by how different Drake smelled than the Cherokee. Not worse, necessarily, but different.

Damon frowned. "It'll be hard to expect folks to believe that."

"It's true." She brushed the dirt off the front of her dress in an attempt to make herself more presentable. Damon's close call had shaken her, but she realized with icy certainty that it hadn't been Damon she'd been worried about. She hadn't wanted either of the Clark boys to hurt the Cherokee. Horse thief or not, he'd been good to her. She'd wanted him to escape.

She glanced into the forest, her gaze automatically locking on the spot where Storm Dancer had vanished into the trees. *Storm Dancer.* Not just a Cherokee, but a man unlike any she'd ever known. Gradually, her heartbeat slowed to normal, and she realized that Drake was talking to her . . . evidently expecting an answer.

"I heard of a woman taken by the Cherokee three

years ago in western Georgia." Damon rubbed his knee. "When they got her back, she was big with child and stark raving mad."

"Look at me, Shannon," Drake said. "Are you certain he never—"

"Must have," Damon said. "Them Cherokee are randy as goats."

"No!" she insisted. "How many times do I have to say it?"

"Father will want more of an explanation than that," Damon warned.

Drake touched her cheek. "People will believe that—"

"I can't help what they think. He didn't hurt me. He gave me food and a fire."

"Are you telling me the truth?" he demanded.

"Of course."

"Why would he do that?" Damon asked. "He just stole those horses, probably murdered and scalped those trappers. Why wouldn't he have his way with you?"

"Enough of that talk," Drake said. "You heard her. He didn't use her. Probably planning something worse. Torture or—"

"Burning at the stake," his brother supplied. "They say the squaws are the worst. Peel a man's roasted skin like an apple."

"Stop." Shannon put her hands over her ears. "I don't want to hear any more."

Drake grimaced. "But you will," he said. "And Ma will be the worst."

# Chapter 3

Back at the wagons, the families gathered excitedly around the three of them while Drake told of their encounter with the Cherokee horse thief and Damon's near escape from being trampled. The men were all armed with rifles. All the settlers talked at once. A baby shrieked, and Betty the cow mooed. Ada Baker kept shouting over and over, "Lord be praised. Lord be praised."

Most of the women were asking questions, except for the twins' mother, Hannah. She stood in silence, arms locked over her ample bosom, and mouth pursed in disapproval as her husband climbed up on a wagon seat to make himself heard above the din. "Quiet down, everyone," he said. "Let's get this story straight, Damon. You say the Indian fired at you first?"

"Yep," Damon said.

"You didn't tell me that!" Hannah cried. "You could have been killed, boy."

Drake scowled at her. "Hush your mouth, Ma!"

"Mind how you talk to your mother!" Nathan admonished.

Damon came to his brother's side. "How are we goin' to tell what happened with all these women yammering?"

"The Cherokee didn't shoot at anyone," Shannon corrected. "Damon's mistaken."

Nathan hushed her with a raised palm. "You'll get your chance, girl. I'm asking my son."

"Can't say who fired first, Pa," Damon said. "It all happened fast. Shannon screamed and—"

"The trappers we met up with yesterday," Drake interjected. "The horses they were riding . . . The Cherokee had them. He was just about to ride off with them and Shannon when we caught up with him."

"That's wrong," Shannon argued. "He said I could go. He let me take the cow and—"

"He hit her," Damon said. "Knocked her flat on the ground."

"That was after Drake took a shot at him," Shannon explained.

"I said I'd get to you," Nathan reminded her. "My boys are saying their piece."

"We need to set off after him," Drake said. "Now, while his trail's fresh. Let him get away with murder and thievery and half the Cherokee nation will be at our throats."

"Teach him a lesson," Damon agreed. "Hang him from the nearest tree."

"'Course, we ain't sure there was a killin'," Jacob Baker pointed out. "He could've stole the horses and left them fellars alive."

"Don't matter," Ben Taylor said. "We hang horse thieves in Virginny. Guess that's fair for white or Injun."

"Not to mention what he did to this poor girl."

Shannon whirled on Cory Jakes. "He didn't do anything to me. He gave me food and water, and he let me go. And you don't know if he stole the horses or not. He might have—"

"Them men might have given the horses to him—as a present," Ben Taylor suggested, and then laughed at his own joke. "He's a thief, all right. Probably got their scalps curing over a fire right now."

"Ain't there a bounty on scalps in Penn's Colony?" Drake asked.

"Injun scalps, not white," his father answered.

"'Course, with dark hair, it's hard to tell white from red," Abe Link pointed out.

"Might be he was planning on ravishing Shannon, then murder. I'm for going after him," Drake said. "Who's with me?"

A few voices rose in agreement before Nathan's angry bellow cut them off. "None of you is going into these mountains after a Cherokee. Too dangerous. We got the girl back, and she says she's not harmed. We got my milk cow back. Time enough to reckon with that Indian."

"Pa," Damon pleaded. "We can't let—"

"You listen to your pa," Hannah said.

Drake glared at her. "Ma, stay out of this!"

"You heard me," Nathan said. "I'm not about to risk your hair or anybody else's in this party over some trappers or their stolen horses."

A dog began to bark and two more took up the chorus. Men looked to their weapons and scanned the trees anxiously.

"Glad to hear at least one of ye has a lick of sense," came a hearty voice from beyond the wagon circle. A stocky white man clad all in buckskins stepped into the clearing. "Call off your hounds, Nathan Clark. Be there a decent cup of tea to be had at your fire?"

The Irish brogue was as thick as pea soup, but Shannon would have known it anywhere. She'd heard it often enough in her dreams. "Da!" she cried, flinging herself at him.

Nathan laughed. "Lower your rifles, boys. It's Flynn O'Shea."

Suddenly shy, Shannon stopped a few feet from her father and looked up into his face. He was older than she'd remembered, his Gaelic features more lined and weather-beaten, his dark beard heavily sprinkled with gray, but his eyes were as blue and merry as ever. "Oh, Da," she murmured. "I've missed you so."

"Give us a hug, darlin'." Tears glistened in his eyes. "Dead or lost to me, I thought ye."

She didn't remember running the last few steps into his arms, but suddenly he was hugging her tight, and she was crying so hard she couldn't speak. "Da . . . Da," was all she could manage.

Her father produced a wrinkled but clean linen handkerchief and wiped her eyes. "'Tis a sight you are, darlin'." He handed her the handkerchief, and she saw that it was her mother's, monogrammed with elegant cursive letters, M. E. B. The handkerchief had been part of her dowry, sewn for her grandmother, Mary Eileen Boyd, who'd been born to the gentry, the Boyds of Shannon Grove in Limerick. Mama had been so careful to pack all that remained of her linens when she'd left Da. This handkerchief must have been left behind by accident.

"Blow that little nose." Da patted the top of her head. "You're bigger than when I saw you last, but still no taller than my shoulder. The spitting image of your mother." He released her and turned his attention to Nathan. "So why are the lot of ye as jumpy as fleas on a griddle? Shawnee on the warpath?"

"Not Shawnee." Drake pushed through the circle of men. "Cherokee. Shannon was kidnapped and held captive for—"

"I was not kidnapped," she protested. "I just got turned around in the dark."

Nathan's expression hardened. "More to it than that, Flynn. Held against her will, she was. All night."

Drake and Damon took positions on either side of their father, arms folded, feet planted, as alike as a pair of bookends. "Ask her," Damon said. "Cherokee buck held her prisoner all night in a cave. God knows what would have happened if we hadn't found her just as he was fixing to ride off with her."

"It wasn't like that," Shannon said. "I was caught in a thunderstorm and took shelter in the cave. A man was there—a Cherokee brave. It's true he wouldn't let me leave until morning, but the lightning was fierce. He didn't hurt me."

Her father looked thoughtful. "A Cherokee, you say?"

Drake nodded. "A horse thief."

"He said his name was Storm Dancer." Shannon balled up the handkerchief and tucked it into her pocket. "He fed me, Da, and he gave me his blanket. He had every chance to do harm to me, but he didn't." She glared at Drake. "He has it all wrong. The Cherokee said he knew you. Said his people call you Truth Teller."

Her father glanced toward the cook fire. "My throat's as dry as last year's corn fodder. I'd not say no to a cup of real China tea, if it was offered. I've been drinking naught but sassafras tea for a month."

"You know this Indian?" Nathan asked.

Shannon remembered the war paint that had streaked Storm Dancer's cheeks, but she didn't speak of it. There would be time enough to tell her father when they were alone.

"Known him since he was a sprout. Winter Fox's nephew. Cherokee take big stock in their mother's kin. Hardly speak of their father's." Her father smiled at her. "Remember how I taught you the Cherokee claim the bloodline through the mother's side?"

Hannah Clark sniffed. "A heathen notion."

"Uncivilized," agreed Ada Baker.

"Some do say so, mistress." Da grinned. "But the upshot is that no babe is born on the wrong side of the blanket, so to speak."

"No bastards, you mean?" Drake asked.

"Hush that talk in front of your mother," Nathan chastised.

"As if I don't hear worse from you every day," his wife retorted. "And it speaks of bastards in the Good Book so it's no sin for the boy to mention it."

"No illegitimate children," her father soothed. "For each babe does know its own mother."

"What of this Cherokee?" Nathan demanded. "You know him well? My boys saw him with horses that white men was riding just that morning. He's a horse thief for certain, probably a murderer."

Her father appeared to consider the question. "Could be he lifted those horses. A wild one is Storm Dancer according to Winter Fox. Got a following among the young men, too. It's hard for the tribal councils to control their hotheads, what with the French and the English competing for recruits among the Cherokee. Both sides offer bounties to fight for them."

"So you agree he's a danger," Drake said.

"Didn't say that. Known the boy since he was knee high to a beaver. Never had him steal so much as a stick of candy from my store. But he might have gone hostile. I'd watch my stock if I were you. But don't take any shots at him or any other Cherokee unless it's him or you. Cherokee are bad about seeking revenge. You kill one of them, they'll kill two or three of you in turn. They carry a blood feud worse than the Scots. Best you stay on the right side of the Cherokee if you're going to live in these mountains."

"Maybe they'd better live like honest white men," Nathan said. "Or get out of this territory."

"Not likely," her father replied. "Cherokee been here since the days of Noah and the Flood. You'll not pry them from this land in your lifetime or your grandbabies'."

Seventeen-year-old Alice Clayton twittered as she offered him a tin cup of hot tea.

"Much obliged." He cupped the mug in his hands and inhaled the aroma with obvious delight. "Cherokee are honest for the most part." His eyes narrowed. "But they live by their own code. Twenty-odd years I've lived in Cherokee territory, and I've called many friends and a few enemy. No better friends . . . and no worse enemies." He took a sip and smiled. "Excellent tea, miss. Excellent."

Alice blushed and scuttled back to her mother.

"You know where to find this Storm Dancer?" Drake asked. "You can help us hunt him down?"

"Yes, and no, lad. Chances are he's somewhere in these mountains. As for sticking my nose in and leading a search party after Winter Fox's sister's boy, I'd sooner lead ye all straight to the gates of hell."

"Maybe you been here too long, Mr. O'Shea," Damon ventured. "You've forgot the color of your own skin."

"It's white, when I've scrubbed off the dirt, but I know the Cherokee. I take to hunting down Storm Dancer, the lot of ye and my own family are as good as dead." He swallowed another sip of tea. "And dead in ways ye don't want to think of, let alone bring about."

Tangled in vines, Shannon struggled and cried out.

"Shannon, darlin', wake up!"

She opened her eyes to find her father peering anxiously into her face.

"Be ye sick?" He laid a calloused hand on her forehead. "You're cool. No fever. Like as not, you're worn to a nubbin from all this travel."

Embarrassed, she sat up and threw off the blanket. Not vines or briars, just the blanket she'd tangled in. The two of them were alone, camped in a hollow under a spreading beech tree. They'd sat up late last night talking and looking up at the stars. Da named the constellations for her as he had when she was a child.

Shannon could smell porridge bubbling on the campfire. They'd left the Nathan Clark party the day before yesterday. Her father was eager to get back to the trading post, and she was more than ready to be with family, rather than the Clarks and their friends. Too long, she'd been the outsider, the orphan who didn't belong. It was strange to be with Da again, but wonderful. So why had nightmares troubled her sleep?

Not nightmares, she admitted to herself, a single dream . . . a dream that seemed so real she could swear she smelled the wild scent of the man who'd haunted her. She inhaled deeply, trying to compose herself. But the dream remained, so vivid that she felt her cheeks grow hot in shame.

She'd been bathing in a forest stream, naked, her fresh-washed hair wet and hanging loose around her shoulders. Heavy fog surrounded the creek, so thick that she couldn't see the banks. The water was warm, so warm that steam rose in tendrils into the moonlit sky. The woods were still and quiet, except for the occasional hoot of an owl and the chirp of insects. Peaceful . . . relaxing . . .

Until Storm Dancer invaded her solitude . . . her privacy. . . . One moment she was alone and the next he was there, standing in front of her, huge and magnificent in the moonlight . . . standing so close that she could feel the warmth of his breath. He must have been swimming, because beads of water rolled off his honey-bronze shoulders and down over his chest. Moonlight glinted off the planes of his face, revealing the penetrating black eyes and rough-carved cheekbones.

Startled, she'd wanted to run, but her feet seemed to have turned to stone. She couldn't move, couldn't draw breath or raise her arms to protect herself. No longer a life-and-blood woman . . . but a statue unable to utter a single sound.

For what seemed an eternity he stared into her eyes. And then he spoke her name. "Shan-non."

Sweet sensations of light rippled through her. Her lips, which had been stone, parted and softened. She became aware of the thud of her heart as Storm Dancer stepped even closer. He reached out and touched her hair, lacing his fingers through the damp weight of it, stroking and murmuring her name.

Then he lifted a section of her hair, bent, and pressed his lips to her throat beneath her left ear. She still could not move, but she felt an inner trembling radiate from his kiss, sending her heart into free fall.

He trailed slow caresses to the hollow of her throat and lower still, until she felt her nipples harden to tight buds and heat throb at the apex of thighs. "Shan-non," he whispered. "My woman. Do you know how long I have waited for you?"

Wherever his lips touched, she came alive. Her skin tingled, and blood coursed through her veins. He raised his head, bringing his mouth to hers, tracing her bottom lip with the tip of his tongue, making her open to receive his kiss. His lips were firm and smooth, his tongue as soft as velvet, his breath sweet as orchard honey.

She groaned softly as their kiss deepened and she grew light-headed with the sheer joy of it. His fingertips moved over her throat and bare shoulder, caressing. Long fingers massaged and stroked her naked skin, moving down until he found a breast and cupped it in his hand.

She realized then that her legs and feet were muscle and bone once more. She could have fled, but she no longer wanted to . . . not when his thumb circled and teased her nipple until the aching grew to a pulsing need. And not when he lowered his head and drew the hot bud between his lips and suckled until she screamed with pleasure.

He'd drawn her tight against the length of his naked body, and she'd felt the heat and length of his swollen phallus. They'd stood there, skin to skin, lips to lips, his long hair wrapped around them for what seemed for-ever, before she caught one of his hands in hers and moved it to touch her in her most intimate place.

Abruptly, the dream changed, and she was running through a black forest. Undergrowth tangled around her legs and slowed her wild dash. Storm Dancer was running too. She could hear his feet hitting the ground, but she didn't know if she was running toward him or away from him. Her heart raced, and she screamed as the vines entrapped her.

Shannon closed her eyes, ashamed of her thoughts, not wanting her father to read what might be revealed there. Where had such shameful fantasies come from? She'd kissed boys, certainly, enjoyed it, but she'd never allowed herself to be touched . . . never willingly let a man touch her breast or took pleasure in it. She knew what happened in the sex act between a man and woman. No girl who'd served at a tavern could help but see the acts of raw lust or playful coupling. She'd had her share of slaps on her bottom or pinches from over-friendly customers, but she'd objected violently to being touched against her will.

How could she conceive of such shocking behavior with a man? With a Cherokee? With Storm Dancer? She tightened her hands into fists and tried to ignore the damp heat between her legs, proof that the dream had excited her in ways that made her blush.

"Are you all right, darlin'? You gave me a fright."

"Yes, yes." She got to her feet. "I'm fine, really." She was fully dressed in her one spare dress. She'd taken off only her shawl and her shoes before she curled up in the blanket by the fire last night. "Just a bad dream." She pretended to laugh. "I was caught in a briar patch."

Her father handed her a cup of tea. "I had Nathan buy me a stock of tea back on the coast. No milk. None in my pack and none back at the post. I don't keep a cow."

She smiled at him. "I don't mind. I've had all I want of cows. Stupid creatures. And Betty—that's the Clarks' animal—was the most cantankerous I've ever laid eyes on. It was her fault I was caught out at night in the storm."

He knelt by the fire and spooned out porridge into a bowl. "Eat up. We've a good four hours' ride ahead of us to get home, longer if the river hasn't gone down. I had to ride downstream to a crossing coming to meet you. Cost me nearly half a day. All that rain coming down out of the mountains."

Shannon reached for the porridge. To her surprise, it was flavored with dried apples, nuts, and cinnamon. "Delicious."

"I'm glad ye like it. Oona will be pleased."

She glanced up at him. "Who?"

He concentrated on his cup of tea. "'Tis a surprise I've been meaning to share."

Now he had her full attention. "Oona?"

"Learning that your mother had passed makes it easier, but I'll not hide the fact that I've taken a companion."

"A partner? You have a partner?"

"Not exactly." He stared at his shoes.

Not shoes, Shannon corrected herself. High, fringed leather moccasins with fine beadwork. She'd assumed he'd traded with the Cherokee for them, but Oona was a woman's name.

"When your mother left me, I knew she wasn't coming back," he said softly. "I'm a man as any other, and I tire of my own company."

"You've taken a wife?"

"Not exactly," he hedged. "For I thought I had one, ye see. A sinner I may be, but I do respect the laws of the Holy Church."

"You live with a woman?" she demanded. "Out of wedlock?" What kind of woman would agree to such an arrangement, she wondered. "Is she Irish?"

"Best you wait until we get home and see for yourself. She's been all aflutter waiting for ye to get here. You'll be the best of friends, I promise."

She stared at him in disbelief. She'd thought it would be just the two of them, that she'd have all of his attention and love after so long being parted. She hadn't expected to be the outsider again—the stranger in another woman's kitchen.

"Trust me, darlin'. In no time at all you'll love her as I do."

# Chapter 4

The sun was directly overhead when Shannon's father stopped to rest on a fallen log. She was footsore and tired from climbing the mountain, but she would have rather bitten her tongue than admit it. She wanted to get home as quickly as possible, and she had no intention of telling him that the used shoes he'd purchased for her from Ada Baker were two sizes too big. Shannon had stuffed leaves in them, but the rough leather had rubbed blisters on her heels that stung with every step she took.

"I should have brought the horses," he said. "You're not used to so much walking. But the fastest way home is cross-country, rough for the horses—hard on their legs and hooves. I thought we'd make better time on foot."

"I'm fine, Da, really."

"Can ye not bring yourself to call me Flynn, as others do?"

"But you're my father. It doesn't seem respectful."

"It's been so long since we've been together. When you call me Da, I think of you as a child." Moisture welled in his eyes. "You're far from that, me girl. You're a woman grown. Flynn will do fine."

"If it pleases you."

"It does. I've not been a proper father in years, but I'll try to make up for it. I promise."

"And I'll try to be a good daughter."

"You've done nothing wrong. The sin, however deep, is my own."

A comfortable silence settled between them. Overhead a blue jay scolded a circling crow, and Shannon stared up at it. There were so many birds. When she was young, her father had taught her to identify them by their alarm calls and songs. Even now, tired and aching, the sweet music soothed her, and she strained to see glimpses of the different species in the foliage.

Her father . . . Flynn . . . offered her a biscuit and dried meat wrapped in corn husks. "It's rabbit," he explained. "Oona smokes and dries it, then pounds it to flour and mixes it with berries and bear fat. It's a winter staple for the Cherokee." He supplied the Cherokee word, but no matter how she tried, she couldn't pronounce it correctly.

He chuckled. "It will come back to you. Cherokee is hard. Not so hard as Gaelic, but tough for adults to learn. You spoke both languages when you were a tot. In time you'll remember."

"Is it important? That I speak Cherokee?"

"If you want to be a help at the trading post. Not many of my customers will admit knowing English. Storm Dancer speaks it and French as well. His uncle sent him north to a mission school. But most Cherokee and Shawnee speak only their own tongue. Cherokee is a kind of poetry. Do you know how many ways they have to describe rain?"

She nodded. "I'll do my best to learn, Da."

His eyes narrowed. "Flynn."

"All right. I'll try to remember. I want you to be glad you brought me here. I don't want to be a burden."

"That could never be. My worry is that I've ruined your chances of a good marriage. There are few prospects for a white woman, even a beautiful one, in these wild mountains."

"Fewer still back East for an indentured girl at a rough crossroads tavern. Most of the barmaids ended in disgrace with big bellies and no husband. Not that they were wicked, just lonely and unlucky." Shannon nibbled her lower lip thoughtfully at memories of the indignities she'd had to endure during those years at Klank's. "This is my home. With you. This is where I want to be, where I belong."

Her father touched her cheek. "Put the bad times behind you, daughter. 'Tis my shame. It's a man's duty to protect his children."

"It's not your fault," she protested. "You didn't know—"

"I should have." His eyes glistened with moisture. "It was selfish of me to bring your mother out here. I should have done better by her. Tried harder to please her."

A lump rose in Shannon's throat. "She shouldn't have left you."

"It's just that I never fitted in back there. Never could hold a decent job. Seemed like walls were always closing in on me so that I couldn't breathe. Out here . . . in these mountains . . ." He choked up and Shannon dug her grandmother's handkerchief out of her pocket. He blew his nose and then wiped his eyes with the back of his hand. "These mountains are the closest to heaven I'll ever get."

She squeezed his hand. She'd wanted to hug him, but she was suddenly shy. She couldn't remember her father ever crying before. He'd always been strong and hearty, too tough to show emotion. Had the years changed him so much?

"We were never really matched. She came from gentry stock, fallen on hard times, and my own father was an outlaw hanged for stealing a pig."

"Was he guilty?"

"Guilty as sin, but the pig saved us from starving. It was a bad time. Too much rain ruined the crops. We lost our farm and had to take to the road like tinkers."

"How old were you?"

"Old enough to watch him hang. But Da said he wasn't sorry. It was worth it." Pain flickered in his gaze. "He was an unlucky man, but he had a good heart. I'd like to think that the Lord took pity on him, a sinner or not."

"I'm sure He would."

Her father nodded thoughtfully. "I hope so."

"Hadn't we better move on?" she suggested.

"Right you are. It will be easier traveling this afternoon. We go downhill, cross the river, and follow a pass through the mountains. If we don't camp tonight, we can be home by midnight. If you're up to it?" He forced a smile. "You're certain you're all right?"

"Right as rain," she said. *Hours of walking to go yet?* She groaned inwardly. All she wanted to do was take off these shoes, curl up, and take a nap.

"The thing is, darlin', all that rain. The river was fierce when I came through before. We can save half a day by using the crossing below. And if we walk down the mountain and find it too high to wade or too swift to swim, we've got to climb up again."

Shannon exhaled softly. Retracing their steps was a dreadful prospect.

"What I'm thinking, is to leave you rest here, go down alone, and take a look-see."

"Leave me alone?"

"You'll be safe as a nun's soul," he promised. "See that clump of bushes there? You crawl in out of sight, quiet as a fawn laying low and waiting for its mama."

She averted her eyes, not wanting him to see how afraid she was to be left behind. "Bears?" she ventured. "Mountain lions?"

Her father chuckled. "This time of year, they're more afraid of you than you are of them. You don't want to walk up on a mama bear, understand? No sense of humor at all when they've got young ones. But you mind your business and old *yona* will do the same. As for the painters—mountain lions—they're shy. Hate the scent of a human. I'd not leave you if I thought harm would come to you."

She nodded. "All right." The thought of a rest seemed better and better. If she took off her shoes, the blisters might not hurt so much when they had to go on. "I'll wait here."

He smiled. "That's my brave girl."

"You're certain you'll be able to find me again?"

Da's smile became a wide grin. His teeth were still whole and white, the teeth of a much younger man. His smile hadn't changed. "I know this country, darlin'," he assured her. "I haven't been lost in more than ten years. The devil and all his fiends couldn't stop me from coming back for you."

At first, she lay awake straining to hear every sound in the woods, every bird whistle, every chattering squirrel, every insect drone and buzz. She'd been so tired, but once Flynn's erect figure had vanished through the trees, she hadn't been able to hold back her distress.

Suppose that rustle of leaves was a poisonous snake? Weren't there wolves in these mountains? Suppose her father fell and broke his leg and couldn't get back? What would she do if she found herself truly alone?

Gradually, common sense took over. Weariness settled over her like a warm cloak. She unlaced the heavy shoes and pulled them off, sighing with relief. Hadn't her father explained that she was perfectly safe? Didn't he know this country as well as any white man? She would be reasonable and rest as he'd told her. And when he got back, she could continue on without complaining or slowing him down. Her eyelids were heavy. She yawned, laid her head on her arm, and drifted off.

The dream seized her and drew her down.

*It was no longer daylight, but night. A canopy of glittering stars arched overhead. She could smell sweet spring grass and wild strawberries. . . . She could hear him murmuring her name as his strong hands stroked and caressed every inch of her body . . . as he cupped her breasts and teased her nipples to taut excitement.*

*She groaned, arching against his touch, reveling in the sweet sensations that flashed through her, igniting an incandescent heat between her thighs. His mouth lingered on hers. He tasted of ripe strawberries.*

*She inhaled deeply, seeking more, wanting more, wanting all of him. She tossed her head, hunting for him, needing him, not wanting the throbbing waves of pure joy to stop.*

But they did stop. Abruptly, she could no longer feel his touch.

With a small cry, she opened her eyes. Where was he? Where was her secret lover? Where were the stars and the velvet bowl of night sky? Bright rays of sunlight pierced her hiding spot. She gasped and squinted against the glare. Stunned, she withdrew her hand . . . fingertips moist from her own inner folds.

No phantom lover . . . she'd been touching herself . . . pleasuring herself. Her own fingers had stirred the sexual yearning in her body. Hesitantly, she reached down to rub her swollen flesh. She should have felt shame, but the urge was overpowering.

How many times had she found release in the dark of the night by such action? Better to fulfill her woman's need quietly under the covers in her own bed than to be a man's plaything. If there was sin, she would pay for it. But surely, such a thing was only a small sin.

Tentatively, she stroked the moist button deep inside her woman's folds. It felt so good . . . so good. But she needed more. She had never known a man, but she could imagine what the act between a man and a woman might be like. Imagined it well, she had to admit to herself, if she was honest. How else could she conceive of the feelings a man might evoke . . . and not just any man.

Storm Dancer.

Impossible. Her pulse quickened. Her breaths came faster. She gritted her teeth, imagining his hands on her, his voice whispering in her ear, letting her fantasies run wild. And all the while, she continued to massage and stroke her inner flesh until she was rewarded by small spasms of pleasure that spread outward through her body and seemed to resonate through her bones.

She sighed, letting her eyes drift closed in contentment.

"Mary Shan-non, what would your mother say?"

Her eyes snapped open and she cried out. He was here, not a dream lover, but flesh and blood. Shannon clapped her hand over her mouth as Storm Dancer's face and form materialized out of the surrounding foliage.

He was there! Within arm's reach. Spying on her— watching as she . . .

She scrambled out of her bed of leaves so fast that

she tripped and fell headlong into his arms. "You!" she cried. "Why—"

Storm Dancer stood her upright, stepped away, threw back his head, and laughed and laughed until she felt her face grow hot and she smacked him hard in the chest with a balled fist.

"How could you?" she shouted.

Tears of laughter rolled from his eyes and streaked his cheeks.

"Stop it. Stop laughing at me."

"Such games are for girls," he managed, between roars of laughter. "Women need more."

Shame dissolved before anger, and she looked frantically for something to hit him with. All she could find was a pinecone. She threw that as hard as she could. It bounced off his forehead, and he laughed harder. She rushed at him, pounding him with both fists.

He caught her and brought his mouth down to hers. For the briefest instant, it seemed that lightning flashed between them as he moistened her lower lip with his tongue and nibbled it gently. She trembled as he lowered his head and nuzzled her neck.

Her breath caught in her throat. Her heart crashed against her ribs. Her hands fisted and opened, tightened and opened helplessly. And, somehow, without knowing how or why, she was touching him, running her fingers over satin smooth copper skin, reveling in the heat and hard, rippling muscles.

Time stopped. Black spots danced behind her eyelids. She drew in a great gulp of air, and reason flooded her. What was she doing? How had a dream become real?

"Let me go. Please," she begged.

"Mary Shannon."

Her name on his lips turned her bones to butter. "No, this is wrong," she protested. "I can't . . . You can't . . ."

He let her go and stepped back. She stumbled and almost lost her balance. She looked into his eyes . . . his beautiful dark eyes, and almost plunged into damnation. She could fall into the depths of those eyes . . . fall and fall forever.

"No," she repeated stiffly. "My father—"

His bronze chest rose and fell as he drew in air. "Truth Teller should never have left you alone," he said stiffly. "This is no place for a woman alone. Not a Cherokee woman . . . not a white woman."

She backed away, putting distance between them. She fought against the urge to fling herself back into that strong embrace, to catch that red-gold skin between her teeth and taste the salt that must glisten there. She tried to ignore the tingle of her nipples, the sensation that her breasts were swollen and tender, the feeling that she was more alive at this moment than ever in her life. She fought lust as she had never fought it before.

"He will be back," she said. "Da . . . my father. If he finds you here—"

"He will be glad that it is me and not another." Again, Storm Dancer's deep, soft voice sent shivers down her spine.

"Why are you here? Why did you follow us?" she demanded. She wasn't afraid of him. What had happened between them was wrong, but it was as much her fault as his. She had to make sense of this. She had to make what was wrong right.

She wondered if this was the dream . . . if she would awaken under the Clarks' wagon or in her own bed in the attic of the tavern.

"I brought you a pony," he said. His smooth features hardened. His eyes darkened and he was suddenly a stoic savage again. "You are not used to walking so far. The river is too high to cross. You should ride."

"A pony?" she echoed. "You brought me a pony?" She

stared at him in utter bewilderment, wondering if she'd heard correctly. "Another stolen horse?" she said, regretting the accusation the instant the words rolled off her tongue.

He scowled. "Tell your father not to be careless. There are Shawnee in these mountains. Tell him that it may not be a place that he can live anymore." Storm Dancer turned and walked into the forest.

She stared after him. Was he a ghost? One minute he was there—the next, he was gone. She realized that she was standing in bare feet and looked around for her shoes. They were no longer in the leaves where she'd left them. In their place was a pair of butter-soft woman's moccasins with a design of wild strawberries stitched into the leather. She laced them up and took a few tentative steps.

Why had Storm Dancer followed them if he meant them no harm? Why had he taken her shoes and replaced them with—

The snap of a twig jerked her from her reverie. She heard a snort and the branches parted. A brown pony with a large head, one blue eye and one brown eye stepped into the clearing. The animal's legs were short and thick, the hindquarters solid and heavily muscled. Except for the size—just under thirteen hands—she guessed, the pony appeared much like a draft horse.

"Storm Dancer? Where are you?"

No answer.

The pony snatched a mouthful of grass. It wore no bridle. Instead, a braided leather rope encircled the animal's nose and looped loosely over the neck. Red and blue beads were woven into the heavy mane.

"Storm Dancer," she called again. "Where did you get him? I don't want a stolen pony. I won't ride it. I'll leave it here for the wolves to eat."

The pony raised his head and stared at her through thick lashes. She put out a hand to it. "I don't want you," she said. "This is ridiculous. I can't accept—"

"Who are you talking to?" Her father moved into the clearing and glanced around. "Where did he come from?"

Shannon noticed that Da was breathing hard and his face was red. Small gray lines tugged at the corners of his mouth, and his eyes were heavy with fatigue. "Are you all right?" she asked.

He set the butt of his long rifle on the ground and leaned on the barrel. The pony looked at him and swished his tail. "How did you come by this beast, darlin'?"

She told him. Not everything, not everything by half, but enough. "I told him I didn't want it. It's probably stolen, isn't it? And why is he following us?"

Her father shook his head. "Hard to say. Storm Dancer's a Cherokee. Long as I've known them, ate with them, wintered with them, I don't know them. They aren't like whites. Might as well be a different breed of animal. Not less than a white man, you understand, but different— blood and bone different." He paused. "I've seen a Cherokee, Listens to Thunder, by name, decide to die. Why, I can't tell you . . . some point of honor, I couldn't make head nor tail of."

"Was he an old man?"

"Nope, no older than you and hale and hearty as a spring calf. Listens to Thunder just sits down, wraps himself in a blanket, and starts to sing his death song. He was cold as a landlord's heart by morning. Just willed hisself to die."

"That's crazy," she said.

"No, that's a Cherokee. No telling why Storm Dancer brought this animal for you, but it would be an insult to refuse his gift. You'll be glad enough to ride by the time we reach the post."

She shook her head. "I'm not a good rider. I haven't ridden since I went East."

"Comes right back to you. You'll see, darlin'. Bad news is, the river's up. I was afraid it might be. No crossing here, not for a week. And we need to get home."

"But if the pony is stolen . . ."

"Not likely. Not when he gave it to you. He wouldn't be above lifting a horse or two from an enemy. That's part of their code. But this is a mountain pony, Cherokee bred, most likely. See those short legs. Tough and strong little animals. Too small for most men to ride, but just right for you."

"I walked from Virginia," she said stubbornly. "I can walk home."

"It's not safe to leave Oona or the post alone too long. We'll go a lot faster if you just do as I say."

"Storm Dancer wanted me to give you a message. He said there might be Shawnee in the area."

Apprehension clouded her father's eyes. "Then we'd best make tracks." He glanced down at the moccasins on her feet. "If I didn't know better, I'd say he was courting you, girl. You'd best take care not to lead him on. No telling what—"

"I've not led him on." It was unfair. She'd told Storm Dancer . . . Guilt rose in her chest, and she nodded. "I wouldn't," she said. "I know better."

"Enough said." Da shouldered his pack. "Hop on, darlin'. And don't fear this pony will lose his footing and tumble off the mountain. They're more cat than horse. He'll carry you safely home."

Home. She'd been traveling so long to get there. Would it be as wonderful as she remembered? "Is she there? Oona?"

"She is."

"Will she resent me?"

"Oona?" He smiled. "Not her. A better heart never beat in a woman. You'll see. She'll be a second mother to you. And you'll be a help to her." He ducked his head, then flushed as he raised his gaze to meet hers. "She's wanted a child of her own for years. And now, God willing, our prayers will be answered."

Shannon looked at him in confusion. "You mean . . ."

"I do, darlin'. She's with child. You're going to have a new baby brother or sister. Isn't that wonderful?"

Reserved and stone-faced, the Indian woman turned her back on Shannon and stooped to turn the flat corn cakes baking on an upturned iron skillet in the fireplace. Embarrassed, Shannon glanced around the snug cabin and then back to her father. He hadn't seemed to notice the frost in the air when he'd introduced Oona to his only daughter. And he hadn't mentioned that one side of his companion's face was horribly scarred.

Oona was younger than Shannon had expected, perhaps thirty. It was difficult for her to tell the age of Indians. Oona's hair fell to her waist, black, and thick, and glossy. She would have been a beauty if it wasn't for the disfigurement. Shannon wondered how she had gotten the terrible injury.

"What do you think of my Mary Shannon? Is she as pretty as moonlight on the river?" her father asked the Indian woman.

Oona's spine stiffened. She dipped hot liquid from a kettle suspended over the coals and brought him a steaming pewter mug of something that Shannon couldn't identify. It smelled of herbs with an underlying hint of willow bark.

Da settled into a leather-and-wood high-backed chair by the fireplace. "You can see I've added on since you last were here," he said. "Three rooms and the loft now. Oona and I sleep through there in the end room with the second fireplace. When I found out that you were coming home, I built another room just for you. It's smaller than ours, but snug. You'll be warm in winter."

"Thank you," she murmured. A bedroom of her own was a luxury she'd never imagined. When she was tiny, she'd slept in her parents' bed, tucked securely between them, and when she was older, Da had traded for a bearskin, and her mother had made a thick pallet for her on the floor between the big bed and the wall.

At the children's home, she'd slept under the eaves with dozens of other orphans, and they'd called her a liar when she'd boasted of sleeping on a bearskin at home. Later, when she went into service, there were always three or four girls sharing two lumpy beds in the attic chamber at the tavern. Hot in summer and freezing at winter—she'd never known anything else since her mother had taken her away.

And now, at last, she was home again. It didn't seem real, after so many years of dreaming about this place. But now that she was here, nothing was as she'd expected. Salty tears scalded the backs of her eyelids but she refused to let them fall. She stood there, stiff and doll-like, bone-tired in a dirt-stained dress and Indian moccasins, while her world slowly cracked and dissolved around her.

Da was growing old, and he had a new wife. Not even a wife, Shannon reminded herself. He was living out of wedlock with Oona. And as shocking as that realization had been, his woman wasn't Irish as Shannon had assumed by her Irish name. She was Indian, dark-skinned, and foreign. Worse, it was clear to Shannon by the expression in her flashing black eyes that Oona didn't want her here.

This strange woman had a life with Flynn O'Shea that didn't include a long-lost daughter by a first wife. Da and Oona were expecting a child. How could her father think they could all live together as though they were a family?

Had she come so far to find she was still an unwanted outsider?

# Chapter 5

The sun was well up when Shannon threw open the shutters in her room the following morning. She was shocked at the time. She'd had every intention of rising early the morning after her arrival and helping with the household chores. She was used to working at the tavern from before dawn until bedtime, and she didn't want her father or Oona to think her lazy. But the long hours of travel had taken their toll, and she'd slept much later than she'd wanted to. She hoped tomorrow she'd wake earlier and make a better impression.

Feather ticks made her bed as soft as a cloud. No wonder she'd slept as soundly as a child. Although the addition Da had built to the cabin wasn't large, there was space in her room for a cherry poster bed, a brassbound mahogany chest, a butterfly table, and a small mirror. The bed had been fashioned of local wood, but the other pieces had been her mother's and had originally come from Shannon Hall in Ireland. And although the bed was handmade and not made by a craftsman, some- one had taken the trouble to carve a garland of beech leaves twining around each post.

The scenery from her open window was so beautiful

that it brought tears to her eyes. Wooded mountains fell away into the distance, and below in the valley a rocky creek wound its way through a flower-strewn meadow, the racing water as white and frothy as meringue on a lemon pie. High above the creek, an eagle soared, wings spread wide, proud white head etched against a cloudless sky as vividly blue as Mary's cloak.

Reluctant to break the enchantment, but well aware that she couldn't avoid Oona's disapproving glare, Shannon hurriedly dressed, twisted her hair into a knot, and splashed cold water on her face. Had she dreamed of Storm Dancer at all last night?

She touched her bottom lip, remembering the taste of Storm Dancer's mouth. It had been despicable of him to spy on her, and if she should be ashamed of touching herself for pleasure, his behavior was worse. What man worth his salt would take advantage of a woman in her weakest moment? And when she'd confronted him, he'd laughed at her. It was mortifying.

What had happened later—when she'd allowed him to kiss her—was a greater mistake. It could never happen again. If her father guessed that she'd permitted an Indian to kiss her, he'd be furious, perhaps angry enough to send her away.

Storm Dancer was Cherokee; she was a white woman. Their worlds were too far apart to allow such intimacies. What was wrong with her that she could be tempted by the man? She'd never believed herself to be a saint, but she hadn't thought she suffered from the sin of lust.

She would have to return the pony. Keeping such a valuable gift from Storm Dancer was out of the question. Explaining where it had come from would be impossible. It had been an act of kindness for him to loan her the animal, but Storm Dancer would have to take it back.

Surely, her father would see the reason in that. She would talk to Da about it after breakfast.

But when she stepped into the main room of the cabin, the keeping room, containing the kitchen and sitting area, she found it empty. It was obvious that Da and Oona had already eaten without her. Breakfast bowls and cups were drying upside down on the trestle table, and a pan of flatbread hung on a hook at the back of the fireplace. Someone, probably Oona, had set a place for her at the table: a bowl of porridge, a pewter mug of peppermint tea, and a handful of berries waited. The porridge was cold and the tea unsweetened. Shannon nibbled at the berries, grabbed a piece of flatbread, and went outside.

The trading post consisted of the house, a fortlike, log, two-story structure that served as the store, a stable, another smaller cabin that provided shelter for passing customers, and several lean-to storage sheds. Da had cut down all the trees around the buildings except a few large ones, and erected a ten-foot palisade of upright logs sharpened to points on the top around the entire compound. There was a double gate reinforced with iron hinges that Shannon had rarely seen closed when she was a child.

Today was no exception. The doors to the post enclosure stood wide and welcoming, and the narrow Dutch door to the store was open. Three horses stamped impatiently at the hitching post in front of the store. Da's pack of dogs milled by the step, eyes keen, ears pricked, alert, as if waiting for a command. When they saw Shannon, they trotted over and surrounded her, sniffing curiously and eyeing her flatbread. She'd noticed the hounds last night, but none were those she remembered from childhood. They seemed well behaved, as Da's dogs always were. *Flynn's* dogs, she corrected herself.

"No begging," she said, lifting her bread out of reach of a lean, black and tan bitch with one ragged ear. Shannon was hungry, and she intended to eat it herself. As she crossed the yard, curious to see who was in the store, she heard the faint tinkling of bells. Oona came around the corner of the house leading the pony that Storm Dancer had given her. "Good morning," Shannon said.

Oona acknowledged Shannon's greeting with a quick nod that set the tiny silver bells in her pierced ears jingling and handed her the animal's rope. Shannon passed her uneaten bread to her other hand and took the pony's lead.

"Water." Oona motioned toward the hard-packed path that led away from the cabin. "Spring is—"

"I know where the spring is. I grew up here. Remember?" Shannon had fetched water for her mother as long as she could remember. The source of drinking water and the pretty glade around it had been her favorite spot as a child. Da had nearly convinced her that there were Irish fairies living at the bottom of the pool, and she'd spent long warm afternoons lying in the grass looking for them.

"Good," Oona said.

"Did someone come to trade this morning?" Shannon asked, although it was obvious they had visitors. She didn't think the horses in the yard belonged to white men. Only one horse wore a saddle, and that was a crude affair of wood and hide. "Are they Indians?"

Oona stared at her for long seconds, and Shannon wondered if she would answer her question at all. She was a tall woman, almost as tall as Flynn, and slender with delicate hands and a graceful walk. She was younger than Shannon had thought last night, probably no more than twenty-five.

Today, the Indian woman had braided her blue-black hair

into a single thick plait, and she was wearing moccasins and a blue cloth dress that fell just below her knees. The garment was loose and shapeless, but the seams were neatly stitched and bright red beads decorated the hem and neckline. In the daylight, Shannon could see the scar on Oona's cheek better, and it was evident that the disfigurement was the result of an old burn, long since healed.

Oona brushed her cheek with her fingertips. "It frighten you?"

"No, of course not." Shannon tried again. "Who do the horses belong to? Do we have customers?"

"Cherokee come to buy powder." She held up three fingers. "Ghost Elk, Runs Alongside Bear, and Gall." At the last name, Oona grimaced as though she'd bit into a sour plum, then placed her hand on one knee and took several limping steps. "Gall," she repeated, and spat on the hard-packed ground.

Shannon wanted to see the Cherokee customers, but it was clear that Oona expected her to tend to the pony's needs first. And above all, Shannon wanted to end this uncomfortable conversation. Nodding agreement, she led the pony away from the cabin toward the main gate.

Oona picked up a bucket and held it out. "Water for house."

"Yes, of course. I can do that." Again, Shannon felt awkward, uncertain. What was her place here? Did her father's common-law-wife expect her to obey her as she might her own mother? Or was she to act as an unpaid servant? It wasn't the chore that offended her—she wanted to help. It was Oona's unfriendly manner.

The pony stretched out his neck and neatly snatched the flatbread from Shannon's hand. Oona chuckled. "He's a thief, that one."

"We'll have to teach you better," Shannon said. "If you

stay." She had to admit that there was something very endearing about the animal. As Flynn had promised, the pony had carried her uphill and down, across creeks, and through thick woods without ever missing a step.

The pony plodded after her as she led it through the entrance. She followed the worn trail through trees that had grown taller since she'd last seen them, around a bend, and up a slight incline, her heart feeling lighter with each step. Everything smelled as she remembered it. This felt like home.

As she circled a massive outcrop of rock and entered the hollow where the spring flowed out of the hill, she stopped short. Someone was there ahead of her. A slight figure in a fringed leather shirt and leggings was kneeling at the pool's edge. By the Cherokee turban and ink-black hair, she supposed the stranger must be an Indian.

The boy glanced up and raised one palm in greeting. Immediately, she saw that although he was not very tall, he wasn't a child.

"You are Truth Teller's daughter." The stranger took a step, limping heavily on one leg that was shorter than the other. "Welcome home. Your father is glad to have you here."

Shannon walked forward to meet him. "You must be . . ." She tried to remember the names of the visiting Cherokee Oona had mentioned. "Gall?"

"Yes, yes." He laughed merrily, and she saw that that the young man's eyes were not brown like all of the other Indians she'd ever known, but light gray. "I am Gall. And you are Shan-nan."

In contrast to Oona, Gall was small and light-skinned, not much taller than she was. His dark hair fell to shoulder length, topped with a red and yellow turban, and his fine-boned face as soft and pretty as a girl's. "I'm pleased to meet you," she said, extending her hand. "And it's Shannon."

Gall clasped her fingers stiffly and shook her hand up and down. "I hope you will not be lonely here," he said. "There are no white women near." His English was good, less accented even than Storm Dancer's, but higher pitched and slightly lisping. Shell earrings hung from each dainty ear, and his hunting shirt bore a pattern of white flowers stitched along the neckline.

The pony pushed past her to sink his nose deep into the pool and drink. "I hope my father has what you need today," Shannon said.

Gall studied the pony. "I know this animal. His name is Badger. He belongs to my mother's friend, Corn Woman. Where did you get him?"

"Someone gave him to me. A Cherokee," she explained, stumbling over her words. "A man named Storm Dancer gave him to me."

Gall looked dubious. "If you say my cousin gave you this pony, I must believe you. Truth Teller's daughter would not lie. But how do you know Storm Dancer? He is not a friend to the whites."

"He said he was a friend of my father. No," she corrected. "He said his uncle was. Winter Fox. I thought . . . Is Winter Fox your father?"

For the first time, the amusement faded from Gall's gray eyes. "No, he is not. I am the son of Luce Pascal, called Big Pascal. It was a joke, you see, because my mother says he was not so tall as me. My father, this Luce Pascal, was a French trader of furs, but he went back across the sea when I was a child, and I do not know if he lives or not."

"I'm sorry."

He shrugged. "It doesn't matter. My mother is

*Tsalagi*—Cherokee—so I am Cherokee. You see? Among our people, it is the mother who matters."

"It's what my father said." The pony finished drinking and began to munch mouthfuls of new grass beside the pool. Shannon scratched his withers. "But with us . . . the whites . . . a father means everything."

"So I have been told." He limped to the other side of the pony and smiled at her over the animal's back. "I will ask my mother's friend if her pony has wandered, or if she sold him to my cousin."

"I would appreciate that."

"Badger is a mischievous pony," he continued, "always getting into the green cornfields and knocking down the smoking racks. She might have sold him." He pulled a burr from the pony's hide. "I would be your friend, if you want."

She nodded. "I'd like that."

"Good." He hesitated. "But you must take care with my cousin. Storm Dancer is . . . How do you say it? His head is hot?"

"A hothead?"

"Just so. The high council of the Cherokee has voted to support the English, not the French, but my cousin argues against the decision. It is a bad thing to do. We are a people of law. But Storm Dancer will not listen to reason. He goes his own way. I think he may take the French silver to fight against your people. And if he does, other foolish young men will follow him."

"He could have hurt me, but he didn't."

Gall pursed his lips. "My mother says he is dangerous and will lead us to war. My mother is a wise woman. Take care, Shan-non. My cousin wears two faces. If he gave you this pony, he had a reason. I only hope that Corn Woman sold him. It would be a bad thing if you had a stolen *Tsalagi* pony. People would not understand."

"I agree. I didn't want to accept the gift, but my father said it would be an insult not to."

"Maybe a worse thing to keep it. Among your people, do women take gifts from men?"

"Small things, impersonal. Not expensive things like a horse." She could see that the conversation was becoming too complicated. "You could return the pony for me."

He sighed. "I can not. We travel west, away from Corn Woman's village. And I do not want to make my cousin angry with me. He is not a man you want angry. This is between you and Storm Dancer, I think." He tilted his head and peered into her face. "You are a pretty woman, I think, even if your skin is too pale. Your hair is like corn silk. I have never seen a woman with yellow hair. Are many of your tribe like you?"

"Some." She brushed a stray lock away from her face. His manner had been so open and friendly, she hadn't expected the conversation to turn personal. And there could be no doubt that his gaze was more than casual. He was staring at her in exactly the same way as the Clark twins did when they thought she wasn't looking.

"Mary Shannon!"

She turned at the sound of her father's voice. He and two Indian men were walking down the trail toward the pool. The Cherokee were leading the three horses. She could see that the animals wore heavy packs. "Here, Flynn."

He smiled at her. "Runs Alongside Bear, Ghost Elk, this is my daughter," he said. And then to her, continued, "I see you've already met Gall."

"Yes," she answered, "and he tells me that he is a cousin of Storm Dancer."

Ghost Elk frowned and said something to his companion in his own language. Runs Alongside Bear, a stout, middle-aged man with a wide band of red cloth tied around his head, kept his features immobile.

Her father's mouth tightened, and then he chuckled with a forced sense of heartiness. "These men tell me they speak no English. They are some of my best customers." He turned and repeated his words in Cherokee. "But they are good bargainers."

"Very good," Gall said.

"*Oui.*" Ghost Elk signed with his hands. "No Englaise." Ghost Elk was older than Gall but younger than Runs Alongside Bear. He was short and muscular with a broad face and three dots tattooed down his chin.

"Don't bet on it," her father said with a wink. He shook hands with each man in turn and presented them with a small cloth bag of tobacco as a gift. "Next time you come, I'll try to have that red cloth."

A few more pleasantries were exchanged in a mixture of English and Cherokee, and then the three Indians mounted and rode off through the woods. Before they vanished into the trees, Gall turned and waved at her, and she returned the wave.

"Best not to mention Storm Dancer to anyone," Da said quietly. "He's not in favor with the council according to Ghost Elk."

"Gall said that this pony belonged to his mother's friend, a woman named Corn." She took hold of the animal's halter. "I feel guilty about keeping him. Gall thought . . ."

"Don't put too much stock in what Gall says. He's half-French. Cherokee are devious, but a half-breed is worse." Her father shook his head. "Gall is way too talkative for a Cherokee. He pretends to be a harmless fool, but I think he's far from it."

"Da." She stared at him. "It isn't like you to judge someone by the color of their skin." She thought with a start that men would label Da's child with Oona that name—*half-breed*. She wondered if it was fair to bring an innocent baby into the world where it would never truly belong to white or Cherokee.

"It's not the Indian half I worry about in Gall," Da said. "It's the French half. The boy's never done me wrong, but I never feel quite easy with him. Oona don't think much of him, I can tell you." He turned back toward the house.

Leading the pony, Shannon fell into step beside him. "I gathered that much—that Oona didn't like Gall." She kept thinking of the baby, her new brother or sister. Would it look Indian or Irish? She vowed to love it, no matter. A mixed-blood child would face prejudice from all sides and would need all the champions he or she could get.

"Oona's a pretty good judge of character," her father mused.

"I don't think she likes me."

"Give her time. Oona doesn't know you. She's never known any white women. She's just shy."

"I hope you're right." Shannon didn't think it was shyness . . . more like jealousy. "I want to. . . Oh, I forgot the bucket of water." She glanced back. The bucket was lying where she'd dropped it near the spring. "Can you take him? I'll get the water."

"Come back to the store after you fetch the water, and we'll get started. I want to give you the prices on our bestselling trade goods. Some things are locked up for safekeeping." He pulled a rawhide cord from under his shirt and showed her a key. "I do the trading for powder, shot, and steel hatchets."

She nodded and walked back toward the pool. She was eager to learn all about the business. Buying and selling goods had always interested her, although she'd had little chance to develop her skills at the tavern. She didn't want to be a burden on her father.

She picked up the bucket and carried it to the spot where clear water rushed and bubbled out of the rock. She rinsed out the container and began to fill it, conscious of the tranquility and beauty of this spot. How many times in the past years she had wished she was here . . . a child again without worries or fears . . . an only child who knew how much she was loved by both her parents.

It seemed to her as if the trees were bigger here than in Virginia . . . their branches more massive . . . the leaves greener. Even the sky seemed larger . . . higher . . . the blue more intense. She closed her eyes and drank in the familiar scents of the warm rock, the lush moss, and wildflowers spilling down the hillside. Maybe her father was right . . . maybe this was the closest either of them would ever be to heaven.

Sighing, Shannon opened her eyes and held the bucket under the spring until the water reached the rim. Why, she wondered, had her mother never fallen in love with this unspoiled wilderness? Why had she longed for the dark, crowded streets of her native—

A voice tore her from her reverie.

"I have thirst. Will you let me drink from your spring?"

She whirled around on Storm Dancer so fast that water spilled down her dress. He stood only a few feet behind her. "What are you doing here?" she demanded.

"What were you doing with Gall?"

"We were talking. And what business is it of yours?"

"You should stay near your father when he is here. Gall can be dangerous for a woman."

She glared at him, refusing to be intimidated. "He said the same of you."

Amusement twinkled in Storm Dancer's eyes, as if

he knew some secret, but wouldn't explain it to her. That infuriated her. Was it some joke on her?

She clutched the dripping bucket to her chest, making it a solid barrier between them. "It was good of you to let me borrow your pony," she said, "but you can take it back now. I don't need him anymore."

A muscle twitched at the corner of his thin lips . . . lips that had thrilled her only yesterday. "Why would I take your pony? He does not belong to me. He is yours."

Had she forgotten how tall he was? How she had to tilt her head to look into his fierce black eyes? How broad his chest? His lean muscular body? He could break her in those strong hands . . . hands that had touched her so gently. She shivered, despite the warmth of the sunshine. "I don't want him," she lied. "He's . . . he's ill-mannered. And his gait is as rough as a mule's."

He shrugged. "Then eat him. He is fat."

"That's savage. We don't eat horses." Her voice sounded high and foolish in her ears. Thoughts tumbled in her head. She had to get away from him. If he didn't let her pass, she'd shout for her father. He'd come and see that Storm Dancer was here. He would make him go away.

"Horse meat is very sweet." Storm Dancer reached out and caught a lock of her hair. He rubbed it between his fingers. "So fine."

She stepped back, yanking her hair free, splashing more water down the front of her dress. "Your cousin said that he knew this pony, that it belonged to a friend of his mother's."

"Yes, Corn Woman. I traded a bear for him."

"You killed a bear?"

His eyes gleamed with amusement, but his words, when he answered, were solemn. "This is not the time for hunting bears. They are thin and sour in summer. When the snow flies, in the Trading Moon that you call

November, I will track *yona* and bring him down. I will take the rich meat and the thick winter bearskin to Corn Woman. It is a good trade."

"I don't want you to kill a bear for me, and I don't want your gifts. I want you to leave me alone."

His expression hardened. "I would do that, but I cannot."

"I don't understand."

"It is not a good thing, that we should come together. It means trouble."

"Yes, exactly," she agreed. "Not a good thing. So go away. Go, and don't come back."

She tried not to stare at him. Today, he wore a short open buckskin vest, fringed and decorated with porcupine quills, over a short leather kilt and high moccasins. Six inches of muscular chest gleamed bare between the fringed seams. She fought the urge to caress that copper skin, to move so close that her thighs would press against his naked ones.

He touched her face, lightly grazing her lips and chin with his long fingers. The bucket fell out of her grasp, splashing them both. Her senses reeled, and she shuddered, conscious only of her pounding heart, of the bright sensations running through her veins.

"Please . . ." she begged. "Don't . . ."

His almond-shaped eyes pierced her. "I thought of you many times since you go away to the East."

"I never thought of you," she lied.

"You did," he corrected. "Your spirit calls to mine. It always has."

"No, that's not possible."

"When I first saw you as a woman grown, it was in teeth of a great storm."

"At the cave."

He nodded. "In the strike of lightning. It was a sign."

"No, it wasn't. I was chasing a cow and got lost. How can that be a sign?"

"Shan-nan!" Oona's voice. "Shan-nan!"

"I have to go," she said. "Please, let me go."

"Then your spirit must cut the bond between us." He stepped aside and she dashed down the path without looking back.

Oona waited at the bend in the trail. "Your father is asking for you," she said. "Why did you not come?"

"Tell him that," Shannon said, suddenly breathless. She pointed back along the path toward the spring. "He's here. Storm—" She glanced around. He was gone. "He was there," she insisted. "Storm Dancer was here."

"I do not see him," Oona said.

"No, he's not here now. But he was. Don't you believe me?"

"I think you play with fire, Shannon O'Shea."

"What fire?"

The Indian woman's sloe eyes narrowed. "Storm Dancer is not for you. Do not meddle with what you do not understand."

"I'm not meddling. Don't you understand? It's him. I've done nothing wrong."

"You did not bring the water. I need water for the house." Oona brushed past her. "I will fetch it."

Frustrated, Shannon stalked toward the cabin.

"He is a prince among the Cherokee," Oona called after her. "A great one."

"I don't care," Shannon flung back.

"And he is promised to another."

"He's nothing to me! Nothing." But even as she shouted the words, she knew she was lying. And she knew because her stomach knotted and she could see that the sunlight had gone out of the morning, leaving all the brilliant greens and blues and browns of the forest muted and gray.

# Chapter 6

A week passed, and then two, as Shannon eased into the daily routine of her father's trading post. She became accustomed to the luxury of sleeping in a bed and having a room all to herself without being awakened by someone snoring or the stench and tinkle of another woman using a chamber pot inches from her head. If she heated water at night, she was free to drag the big copper washtub into her private space and bathe from head to toe with real soap.

A handful of beeswax candles hung in a leather case on the wall near her window. Shannon could read by candlelight with ease instead of squinting until her eyes ached, as she had for so many years. At the tavern, where she'd been apprenticed since she was thirteen, the only light after dark was a fireplace or tallow burning in a smoky Betty Lamp. And, to her delight, Flynn had given her the silver-backed antique hand mirror that her mother—afraid it would break—had carried from Baltimore every step of the way over the mountains from the coast when they'd first come to Cherokee territory. Shannon could gaze into the precious mirror as often as she liked, squint her eyes and imagine she could see her mother's beloved reflection staring back at her.

Shannon felt like a princess in one of her father's old tales. Each morning, Oona prepared a hot breakfast for the three of them, and Shannon was encouraged to eat as much as she wanted. She could put honey on her hot-cakes and stir fresh berries into her porridge. No one tossed leftover scraps retrieved from tavern customers' plates into a pot of soup for her to share with the other serving girls, and no one watched to see that she didn't take a second helping of bread. And after she and Flynn and Oona had eaten, he would take her to the store to teach her the art of trading.

Soon she'd realized that the post's account book was a mess. Flynn was repeatedly making errors in his arith-metic, and his handwriting was so bad that often he couldn't read it. Was that *"8 trade mirrors"* or *"no trade mirrors"*? Zero pairs of French scissors remaining or nine?

And the picture darkened once Shannon began taking inventory of glass beads and trinkets, clay pipes, cheap cloth, men's hats, and bottled medicinals. It was obvious that the store had far too many boxes of those frivolous items gathering dust on the shelves, while the trade goods the Cherokee seemed to desire most, such as steel knives, hatchets, needles, powder and shot, were in short supply.

Worst of all, Shannon found lists of customers who bought supplies *on ticket* and never paid with the prom-ised furs or gold nuggets. Some debts went back a decade, and others were simply written off. Shannon had even discovered sales of gunpowder or knives that were marked *"no charge."*

In theory, the isolated trading post was a solid business. No other store existed for days in every direc-tion, and her father had enjoyed the friendship of the prosperous Cherokee nation for many years. But the account books proved that Da had made less profit every season for the past five years. And the money he'd paid to buy her indenture and pay her passage west had cost him most of his savings.

When Shannon questioned him about the problems, he laughed off her concerns, saying that she was like her mother, thinking she could teach a rooster how to crow. He knew the Cherokee, he insisted, and he knew his trade. Some customers might be slow to make good on their promises, but in the end, most would honor their obligations. As for the items he'd given away, the recipients were on hard times and needed assistance rather than a debt. That was the Cherokee way, and to live among the people, he was expected to adopt some of their ways.

In those two weeks, while Shannon struggled to understand her father's business sense, they had no visitors. And although Storm Dancer continued to invade her dreams and her pulse became erratic every time she went to the spring to fetch water, she saw no sign of him in the flesh. Neither she nor Oona told her father about Storm Dancer's visit that first morning. At least, Shannon assumed that Oona had kept her secret, because Da said nothing to her about it.

And as for her lustful dreams, they were most disturbing . . . so lascivious, that an unwed maid should be ashamed of knowing such behavior between a man and woman existed, let alone being party to it in her mind. If her bedroom door hadn't been barred from the inside and her window too small to admit a grown man, she would swear that Storm Dancer had been with her in her bed every night. She would swear that Storm Dancer had licked and nibbled and kissed every inch of her body from the crown of her head to the tips of her toes, and that she had eagerly done as much to him.

She wondered if she were bewitched. Was she too weak to resist the temptation of her nightly fantasy orgies? If she couldn't banish the dreams, decency should have compelled her to try to stay awake, to sit late by the kitchen fire, refuse to lay her head on her pillow and give herself over to her wicked imagination. Instead, to her shame, she welcomed them . . . seeking her bed early and savoring the licentious memories the following day.

And worse, after she'd gone to bed, in the moments before she fell asleep, she would touch herself . . . rubbing her nipples until they tingled . . . massaging the mound where her nether curls sprang . . . sliding her fingers into her woman's cleft until she shuddered with pleasure.

Usually, her dream lover came to her in her soft featherbed within the four posters, but sometimes the two of them sought out secret places in the mountains. There, they would swim naked in the creeks or race hand in hand into an enchanted hollow where wild strawberries and violets grew thick and the air smelled of perfume.

There, with trees for walls, sky for a roof, and thick moss for their bed, Storm Dancer would sprawl on his back and she would fling herself on top of him. They would kiss and fondle, tease and play until desire would not be denied. Then, wet and eager for his love, she would spread her legs for him and he would enter her.

She had never known a man, yet in her dreams she was wanton. In her dreams she cried out with passion and urged him to plunge deeper ever deeper inside her. In her dreams, she not only touched his sex but fondled . . . even kissed it as it swelled and lengthened. It was her shame and her glory, and she had to accept her bold nature or believe herself to be a wicked and sinful creature.

Did other decent women have such dreams? Never had she longed so much for her friend Anna from the orphanage. She could have asked Anna anything, told her any secret, knowing that Anna would never judge her, never mock or reproach her. But Anna, dearer than any sister, was lost to her, and she was alone. There was no one to ask, least of all her father's disapproving woman.

Oona might not have told Shannon's father about seeing Storm Dancer with her at the spring, but that was her only kindness. No matter how Shannon tried to fit in, the woman remained as distant and disapproving as she had been the first night they'd met. She rarely spoke, rarely smiled, and almost never sat still. Even after supper, when Flynn would stretch out in his chair before the fire and smoke his pipe, Oona sewed or ground corn kernels into flour, or worked on her baskets.

Shannon had never seen a woman work so hard. After a full day of cleaning, cooking, washing, and tanning hides or smoking meat or fish, Oona would weave intricate reed baskets to sell at the store. The dyes she brewed herself from forest plants and minerals, and she decorated the containers with beautiful geometric designs, beads, and feathers. So tightly woven were the seams of Oona's baskets, that some would hold water. Shannon had offered to help one evening and been firmly rebuffed.

Oona's eyes had widened in shock at the suggestion. "Never. Two people cannot make a basket," she said, making a hand sign that Shannon had come to understand would ward off evil. "Each basket has a spirit," Oona whispered. "If two women try to weave the same one, the basket spirit will wither and die."

"I could learn," Shannon suggested. "You could teach me, and I could weave my own basket."

"You are too old," the Indian woman dismissed. "My mother taught me when I was a child."

"I'm hardly in my dotage. Two of us could make twice as many baskets, and—"

Flynn stood up, frowned first at her and then at Oona, and walked out of the cabin without saying a word. All three dogs trailed after him. Oona uttered a sound of amusement and bent over the basket in her lap.

Shannon threw down her book, followed her father outside, and found him leaning against a porch post, tamping down the tobacco in his pipe. "Da, I mean Flynn, I—"

"Settle it between you. I won't take sides between my womenfolk."

"She hates me!"

"She doesn't."

"I'm not welcome here."

"I don't believe that." He drew on the pipe until the tobacco glowed red. "Oona's got her funny ways, certain. She won't even let me touch her baskets until they're done. Superstitious as a Galway Bay sailor."

"I just want to be of help."

"Aren't you putting my accounts to right? And didn't you find those playing cards I've been missing for over a year? I've had three customers wanting a deck, and couldn't find them."

"Cherokee play cards?" One of the hounds nosed her ankle, but she paid the bitch no heed.

He chuckled. "No, not them. Great gamblers are the Cherokee, but they prefer their own games of chance. I'm meanin' His Majesty's finest from Fort Hood. Only three days away by horseback. I get soldiers every couple months, pockets heavy with shillings. And they'll pay dearly for fresh cards."

"Da, when I was young," she replied, "I remember you saying that a trader had to be fair, and he had to be friendly. But most of all, he had to be a good business-man. If you give away your profits to the Indians, the sale of ten decks of playing cards won't save you."

He sat down on the porch, let the dog curl around his ankles, and dug a piece of smoked meat from his pocket. He fed the treat to the hound and stroked the animal's head. "Maybe I did say that," he agreed. "I thought that way then, but after you and your mother left, I realized there was more to life than turning a coin. Family, and conscience, and friendship matter more to me now. Knowing I might be a better father to the babe comin' than I was to you, that's important."

"You could end up old and poor, Flynn." She sat down beside him.

"I've been poor before, and there's worse things."

"Worse than going to bed hungry? Worse than seeing your mother go into a pauper's grave because there's no money for a church funeral?"

"That too?" He sighed. "I didn't know that useless uncle of yours denied her a proper burial. I'm sorry."

"She wasn't buried in holy ground, just a weedy field near the river."

"Oh, child. How did you bear it and you only a little lass of nine?"

Shannon's throat constricted. "She had a priest, Da. I ran to the church and brought one back when she was dying. Uncle whipped me for it later. Said I cost him money to pay the Father, but it eased her, I think—to have the last rites."

Flynn stroked her hair with a rough hand. "She was a lady, your mother. She married me because . . ."

"Go on," she urged, certain he would say they fell in love despite their differences.

"It's no tale for you, darlin'. They were hard times."

Not harder than the orphanage, she thought, but couldn't say so. Better for her father not to know that she'd awakened one morning when she was eleven to find the girl next to her dead, her body frozen stiff and eyes staring. Better that no one knew that a rat had chewed her friend's fingers to the bone.

"Your mother never went without food or a place to lay her head, after we married," her father continued, unaware of her own dark memories. "You see, darlin', the man she'd wanted had died before they could be wed and she thought she was with child."

"My mother?" Shannon was shocked. How could that be true? No more modest woman ever lived. Could she have been intimate with a man out of wedlock? A man other than her father?

"It didn't matter to me."

"You mean . . ." Shannon's breath caught in her throat. Was he going to tell her that he wasn't her father? "What happened to the baby?"

He knocked out the remaining tobacco in his pipe and rubbed out the coals with the heel of one moccasin. "She got her courses the week after we were wed. She hadn't been in the family way after all."

Relief made her knees feel weak. "So there was no child?"

"No, and none for us for years. It was a mistake between us," he said. "She never forgave me for not being him—the man she'd loved and lost."

"She never loved you?"

"I like to think she did, after a fashion, after we wore smooth the burrs. She loved you, though. Never think for a minute she didn't."

"She shouldn't have taken me away from you."

"Ah, no, you can say that. But how can you tell a mother not to cling to her only chick? We made a mess of things, but you're the best of us both."

"And you care for Oona, don't you?"

"God help me, I do. It's been my fortune to have two women both better than me."

She leaned close and hugged him. "I'll try harder to get along with her."

"Good girl. She'll need you with the wee one comin'. She's like a walnut, my Oona. Hard on the outside, sweet and soft on the in."

It was on the tip of Shannon's tongue to say what a good job the Indian woman did of hiding her sweeter side, but she didn't. She sat there beside him and watched as the moon rose higher and the stars blinked on, one after another until the sky was adorned with glittering diamonds and most of her resentment at Oona had drained away.

That night, the three of them stayed up longer than usual. Da was cleaning his rifle, and Oona's head was bent low over a tiny pair of moccasins she was sewing for the baby. When Shannon finally went to bed, the hands on the mantel clock showed quarter past ten. And when she went to her window to close and lock the shutters, she found a life-sized wooden bird lying on the wide sill.

"Storm Dancer? Are you out there?" she called softly. The little bird was beautiful, each feather and curve perfect. It was a wren, carved of cedar and sweet smelling. It was so lifelike, she almost expected it to take wing and fly out of her hands. "Storm Dancer?" she called again as she peered into the darkness.

From somewhere she could just make out the faint

melody of a flute. She shivered. She knew that sound from childhood, remembered her father telling her that it was a courting song. She drew in a deep breath. Oona was right; they were playing with fire.

He was out there—she knew it. She cradled the little wren in her hands as memories of another gift enveloped her. She hid the wooden wren under her pillow and padded barefoot into the kitchen. The fire had died to coals, but she didn't need light. One stone on the hearth was always loose.

Shannon knelt and eased the stone free of its rocky bed. Beneath, wrapped in oiled cloth, she'd kept her treasures when she was a child: a blue stone that she'd been certain had been magic, a crumbling bit of red silk ribbon, a silver penny, and a carved cedar wolf so small it could fit into the palm of her hand.

Moisture blurred her vision. She raised the wolf to her nose and sniffed. Could she still smell the cedar? She was certain she could. So long ago . . . She'd been seven, and it was her birthday. Her mother had promised her a cake and new ribbons for her hair for her Saint's name day, but when the day had finally arrived, there had been important guests, a British officer and so many soldiers that they'd filled the compound. Her parents were busy, and when she'd tried to remind her mother that it was her special day, Mam had scolded her. Instead of presents, her mother had told her that she was too old for such nonsense. Couldn't she see that the water pail needed refilling?

Shannon had told herself she wouldn't cry, not then, not now. She'd taken the bucket and trudged, barefoot as she was now, down the path to the spring, her heart so heavy with self-pity that it was a wonder it didn't burst through her chest. Her special day that she'd waited for had come, but no one had time for her, and no one cared.

No one but her friend Otter.

He was waiting for her at the spring, sitting on his spotted pony and smiling that slow, sweet smile of his. He'd remembered her birthday, and he'd carved the little wolf for her. She held up Otter's gift and her throat constricted. It was a boy's gift, crudely made. The animal's head was too big for the body, the tail too short, and the eyes too large, but she loved it all the same. He'd made it for her, and she cherished it.

Storm Dancer hadn't forgotten her. Today wasn't her birthday, but she'd been feeling low . . . struggling to rebuild a bond with her father . . . trying to fit in to his new family. Storm Dancer had remembered the wolf he carved for her and he'd made the little wren to lift her spirits. He might not be the sweet boy she'd known years ago, but he would never harm her. For the rest of it, the way she dreamed of the man Otter had become or her own wanton feelings . . . she had no answer. She had only herself to blame.

She only knew she wanted to see him now . . . to press her body to his, and feel his warm breath on her face. No, not wanted. Wanted was wrong. She *had* to touch him, *had* to know that he was real and not just something she had conjured out of the depths of her being.

She wrapped her precious treasures and put them back in their secret spot. She settled the stone in place and scattered ashes over the top so no one would notice that the stone had been removed. Then, she crossed the worn board floor and slipped out into the cool night.

She had to still this restless yearning that swelled inside of her. And if it meant her downfall . . . her shame . . . nothing mattered but pressing her mouth to his, breathing in his breath, and feeling the throb of his heart against hers.

# Chapter 7

How had Storm Dancer gotten inside the locked trading post compound to leave the wren? And how, Shannon wondered, had he gotten out again without alarming the dogs? The little carved bird was real—not a figment of her dream. He'd been here, and she had to find him.

She didn't go to the main gate, the one that stood open in the daytime and was barred tonight. She chose the narrow door that opened behind the cabins, wide enough only for a single person to go through, only if they were small in stature or ducked low.

Flynn called it the postern gate, and this too was barred with three heavy wooden crosspieces set into iron brackets. In case of an attack by hostiles, the small gate provided almost as formidable a barrier as the front entranceway. The hinges to the postern were mounted on the inside and the door disguised, so only someone familiar with the passageway would know that it wasn't part of the stockade fence.

Moonlight illuminated the meadow, but no matter how hard Shannon stared, she could make out no silhouette of a man. She had been certain that the flute music had come from this side of the compound. Now, the flute was silent and she no longer could be certain of the direction. Which way to go?

"Storm Dancer," she ventured. Her voice rang loud above the chirp of insects. A great horned owl hooted, but no copper-skinned warrior strode through the knee-high grass.

Thoughts of the great gray wolves that ranged these mountains made her shiver. As a child, she'd often heard them howling on winter nights. Less seen but even more deadly was the lone puma. The big cat could strike without a sound, slash her mortally with razor-sharp claws, and devour her before she could cry out. She'd never seen a living mountain lion, but Cherokee had come to trade for their hides, and she'd seen one hunter whose face and arms had been scarred by the claws.

Shannon knew she had no business outside the wall at night. What if a French patrol or a Shawnee war party chanced by? She should go back inside before it was too late, but she couldn't. . . .

Storm Dancer had been at her window. He had brought the carved bird. He must have known that she'd come out to him. What game was he playing? Did he realize what his presence had done to her? Could he be so cruel?

She turned around and then around again. She called his name and waited, straining to hear the bone flute again. Another owl on a far hillside answered the first; rabbits and small creatures rustled in the grass, but no tall man strode from the forest to meet her.

She waited. Gradually, her anticipation became disappointment and she turned back toward the compound. If the wren wasn't there, under her pillow where she'd hidden it, she'd know that she was dreaming again. But when she had slipped through the doorway, rebarred the gate, and entered the cabin, she found Storm Dancer's gift where she'd hidden it in her bed.

It hadn't been her imagination. He had come and left her the wren.

Dreamless, she slept that night with the wooden bird locked in her fingers. It was still there when she woke, and she tucked it into her traveling case, beneath her undergarments, before going to the keeping room to start breakfast. She was first up for once, and by the time Oona entered the kitchen, journey cake was browning on the baking stone and the oat porridge was bubbling.

The Indian woman went to the fireplace, peered into the kettle of porridge, stirred the bread batter to check the consistency, and lifted the lid of the teapot to smell the brew. Only then did she glance at Shannon and nod. "Good," Oona said. And, "You have added willow bark to the China tea leaves."

Shannon smiled. "Yes. I thought it would make the tea last longer. And willow bark will ease your morning stomach." She had heard Oona being sick in the morning and guessed that her pregnancy was a difficult one.

Oona nodded her approval once more. "There will be little difference in the taste. You know about willow?"

"And wintergreen. When I was little, Da used to brew them for my bellyaches."

"Truth Teller is wise. Most whites do not want Indian medicine." Oona took three mugs from the shelf and poured tea. "They would rather suffer than believe that a savage might know something about healing they don't."

Shannon used a flat wooden tool to turn the bread. "Ignorance makes people afraid. A woman at the tavern where I was indentured burned her arm and legs making soap. It was so bad that they called a doctor for her. He bled her and smeared the burns with tallow."

Oona's dark eyes flickered with interest. "Did she die, this woman?"

Shannon swallowed against the constriction in her throat. Mable had screamed for four days until her voice gave out. The stench was so bad that the mistress had her carried to the barn. "The burns sickened and fever took her." But not soon enough. . . .

"Snakeroot is good for burns." She touched the scar on her cheek. "Both a tea and a poultice for the burns."

Shannon nodded. It was strange how she rarely noticed Oona's burn anymore. "Once, when I was small," she said, "I burned my finger on a nail I pulled from the fire. Da crushed violet leaves into a paste, and it took away the hurt."

"Violet is good."

"Yes, and so is cattail root. I wish I knew more about healing."

"There are other plants my mother taught me," Oona admitted. "She was a powerful medicine woman. Many sick and injured came to her door."

Shannon nodded, and Oona went on. "Gold thread makes a fine yellow dye, and the roots of squaw flower are good for a woman in labor. If you want, I will show you when to gather them and how they are to be used."

"I'd like that," Shannon said. If she knew about Indian medicine, she might prevent the death of someone, perhaps even someone she loved, like her dear friend Anna.

"That's what I like to see." Her father came out of the bedroom and joined Oona at the table. "The two of you getting on as family should."

Shannon brought the first plate of journey cake to the table. When Oona rose to help with the rest of the breakfast, Shannon held up her hand. "No, please, let me. I've been a guest here long enough." She went back for the kettle of porridge. "It's going to be a fair day. I saw three does at the spring."

"Three is a lucky number," her father agreed. "Like the three of us at table." He chuckled and bowed his head to offer the morning prayer.

Shannon slid onto the bench across from the two of them. She and Oona might not be the best of friends, but a small crack had opened. With luck, things between them would improve. They were alone so much of the time that being at odds with each other would be terrible. Perhaps the native remedies would prove the means to narrow the breach between them.

It was late afternoon that day and Shannon was scrubbing the hearth stones when her father shouted to her through the open door.

"Leave the bucket and change your apron," he said. "We have a guest."

She glanced back at the stones. Only a quarter of the hearth was left to do, but obediently she rose from her knees and wiped her hands on her work apron. "Shouldn't I finish here first?"

"No, darlin'." He grinned at her from the doorway. "Someone has come to bring you a gift. Go fix your hair and pinch your cheeks or whatever you women do to entice us. Step lively now." He hesitated. "And say nothing about Oona."

"Oona? Why?"

"Her being Indian. 'Tis not something I brag about, having her here."

"Are you ashamed of her?" It was true that her father's woman hadn't welcomed her into their home, but if he didn't mind sleeping with her, why did it matter what others thought of their relationship?

"It would be bad for trade if some white men knew of it. Not that it's any of their affair."

"All right," she agreed. "I won't say anything. But who is it that's come?"

"You'll see soon enough. T'will please you, I'm sure."

Puzzled, she did as he bade her. She washed her face and hands, removed the apron and donned a spotless white one, pinned up the stray tendrils of hair that had fallen loose around her face, and fastened her mother's cameo brooch at her throat.

The first thing she saw when she stepped onto the porch was the cow tied to the hitching rail. Not just any cow, but the devil's own horned minion, Betty. Her heart sank. Not Storm Dancer come to see her, but one of the Clark twins. It had to be. Why had they brought the damnable cow here?

She knew the answer. She simply didn't want to accept it.

"There she is," her father called. "There's my girl."

Drake Clark came out of the store and doffed his wide-brimmed hat in greeting. He was wearing the same blue shirt he'd worn the day Betty had run away and she'd gotten lost in the woods. His sandy blond hair was damp and he seemed even more solid than when she'd seen him last. "Miss Shannon."

"Drake." She nodded. She'd forgotten how good-looking he was.

Drake grinned and thrust out his chest.

*Cocky as ever,* Shannon thought. "What brings you here?"

"He brought you a fine present," Flynn said. "This cow. What do you say to that?"

"No, thank you. I don't . . . I mean . . ." She took a breath and tried again. "I'm honored," she said, brushing at an imaginary wrinkle in her apron, "but I can't accept such an expensive gift." What was a cow worth out here? More money than she wanted to think of. But she didn't want a cow, and she didn't want this one. She'd never been fond of milk. "Your mother," she began. "Betty belongs to her."

"Ma's got enough cows to tend. 'Sides, I paid her for Betty fair and square," Drake said, striding forward. "Thought we have five milk cows and you none. We got more than we need. And a woman needs a cow for butter and such."

"I'm sorry. I can't . . ."

Drake's brow furrowed. "I'd be obliged if you'd accept the animal. If I recall, you make a fine bread pudding."

"Of course, she will," her father said. "Come on into the house and take dinner with us. I want to hear all the news. Is your family settled in?"

Drake brushed against Shannon as he stepped through the doorway, and for an instant, he pressed his body against hers. She gasped as excitement made her pulse quicken. Damn the man. He was too forward by far. Still, something bold inside her was stirred by his presence.

Fixing her with a self-satisfied look, Drake crossed the kitchen and settled himself at the table. Shannon glanced around for Oona, but the Indian woman had obviously made herself scarce. It was up to her to whip up a meal that wouldn't shame Flynn's hospitality.

"Ma sent butter and a side of bacon," Drake said. "And another envelope of tea leaves. Can't abide the stuff myself, but she said you favor it."

"That I do," her father proclaimed. "As any self-respecting Irishman would."

Shannon took down cornmeal, honey, and salt from the shelf. She'd put corn bread in the iron spider to bake and added vegetables to the stew Oona had served the night before.

"Drake's got his own place," Flynn said. "A cabin and two hundred acres more or less of prime valley land."

"I got a good cabin with a root cellar dug underneath and barrels of salt pork and cornmeal stowed for the winter," Drake said. "It's good farming country. If I work hard, I'll do well."

"I thought this was all Cherokee hunting ground," she said.

"Not Green Valley," her father explained. "It's a far sight from here. The Cherokee consider the mountain and valley cursed. The Cherokee don't hunt there, and they don't camp there."

"Superstitious nonsense," Drake said, "but good for us. My pa bought more than two thousand acres off an Indian chief for next to nothing."

"He bought it from a half-breed Creek Indian who was no more chief than I am." Da chuckled. "Cherokee don't sell land. They think it's like air, a gift from the Creator. A man can't own it any more than he can own the rain."

"One Indian's the same as another to me," Drake said. "And Pa's got a deed that will stand up in a white man's court."

"It is good land," Flynn agreed. "You'll do well, so long as the war don't sweep over these mountains. If it does, we'll all be blown away like last year's dry leaves."

"If war comes, we'll give the Frenchies what for," Drake boasted.

"Doubtless," Shannon put in. Drake echoed his father when it came to politics, and like most men, he was always eager to fight, rather than find other ways to settle disagreements.

"And I'm claiming more upland acres, good for grazing." Drake folded his arms and leaned back. "Pa's raising beef for Fort Hood, but I've a mind to breed horses. Good horseflesh is rare out here and more folks comin' all the time. Reckon I'll be needing a helpmate soon."

Shannon pretended not to hear. The morning before, Oona had found a clutch of duck eggs near the creek. It wasn't often that they had eggs, and she'd saved them for a special treat. Shannon decided to add them to the cornmeal mixture with some of the butter and the salt and honey.

She didn't look at Drake, but didn't need to. She could feel his gaze on her. It was obvious that he'd come courting, and she wouldn't have been human if she hadn't thrilled a little to the thought. No matter how well she tried to hide it, she wasn't immune to his charms.

Drake cut a fine figure with his broad shoulders and clear blue eyes. He had a way about him, and he was all man. No wife of his would ever have to worry about a roof over her head or food in her belly. . . . No wife of his would lie awake in her bed pleasuring herself.

On the trip out from Virginia, Drake had made it clear that he was interested in her. At first, she'd believed it was just that he was trying to see if he could get under her skirts, but even after she'd put a firm stop to that, he'd kept watching her. She hadn't wanted to encourage him. She'd hoped that once she left the Clarks, he'd turn his attention to the Clayton girl. Alice was only seventeen, but settled, more ready to be a married woman than she was.

As for herself, Shannon wasn't looking to be a wife, at least not anytime in the near future. She'd been a servant for so long that it pleased her to be beholden to no man—other than the respect and duty she owed her father. She beat the eggs harder.

Drake was a handsome man, decent, and hardworking. A woman could do a lot worse. Other than having a hot temper, being somewhat of a braggart, and having no understanding of the Indians, Drake had no real fault in him that Shannon could find. He'd make Alice Clayton a good husband.

But not her. At least, she didn't think so.

Shannon's years working as a barmaid had given her a distrust of men. Most men, married or not, fathers or not, were always on the lookout for an easy roll in the hay with whatever woman they could catch. And most men were all too quick to tell a wife to hold her tongue or mind her children. She had opinions, and she would be hard-pressed to keep from speaking up for herself. Even Oona, who seemed smart enough, was quick to jump when Shannon's father asked for something. And Oona never contradicted him. That kind of wife Shannon knew she could never be.

As she assembled the meal, she listened to what Drake and Flynn said, but she didn't directly enter the conversation. She kept expecting Oona to join them, but she didn't, and Flynn made no mention of her absence. Shannon wondered if it was the Clarks he was hiding Oona from.

"You keep a sharp eye out for hostiles," Drake said as Shannon slid the hot pan of corn bread on the serving platter. "You 'member those trappers we met on the trail?" He glanced at Shannon. "Ones said their mounts was stolen?"

"Yes," she murmured. "I do." She ladled out bowls of stew to each man. Drake's hand clamped down on hers, pinning it to the table.

"Amos Tyler, he come out from Virginia with four wagons three days behind us. Found what was left of them. Dead as dead can be. Scalped."

She pulled her hand free.

"Not ten miles from where they left us," he continued.

His gaze challenged her as he stuffed a chunk of corn bread in his mouth and chewed steadily.

"Bad luck," her father said. He tasted the stew. "Good. You added something, didn't you?"

She nodded, unable to find words. The trappers dead. Scalped. Had Storm Dancer killed them? Cold dread seized her. Was she a fool to think she was safe with Storm Dancer because they'd been friends as children?

"That renegade did it, certain," Drake said. "Murderin' bastard. We should have finished him when we had the chance."

*You tried,* Shannon thought. *But Storm Dancer outfoxed you and your brother.* "You don't know it was him," she said.

"Who else?" Drake asked. "Plain as plain can be. If Pa hadn't stopped us from goin' after him, this would be over and those trappers would be alive today."

"He's smart, your father," Da said. "Not much chance of catching a Cherokee in these mountains. And there's no way of tellin' who killed those men. Could have been allies of the French or other trappers."

Drake shook his head. "White men don't scalp."

"Don't be so sure," Flynn replied. "Who do you think taught the Indians the custom? Heard it all started during King Philip's War, up Massachusetts way."

"Don't know about that," Drake said.

"If it was other trappers, what better way to turn suspicion away? Scalps bring a bounty in New England, so I hear."

"All the same, if that Storm Dancer crosses my sights, he's a dead man," Drake insisted.

"Don't say that," she said. "You can't condemn him when you don't know he's done anything wrong."

"I don't hold with that talk," Flynn said. "I've known him since he was a boy, and I've never known him to do a dishonorable thing. Not that he couldn't kill if it came to that. I just don't see him murderin' without good reason."

Drake shook his head. "It's time the Cherokee moved on, pack and parcel. This land's too good for them. Decent folks will be comin' in, tillin' the soil, and raising livestock. God-fearing folk."

Flynn spread honey on his corn bread. "Mind that talk. You shoot a Cherokee, any Cherokee, and you may as well stick your head in a hornet's nest. More trouble than you can imagine. Stick to raisin' your livestock, Drake. You'll live longer."

"I'm of a different opinion, Mr. O'Shea, but I didn't come to argue with you. I came to ask your permission to walk out with your daughter."

Flynn glanced across the table at her. She glared at him. "You're always welcome here," her father said to Drake. "But Shannon's been on her own for a long time. You two will have to come to an agreement between you."

"I'd be a good provider," Drake assured him. "Shannon's caught my eye, and what I take a fancy to, I usually get."

"Do I have any say in this?" Shannon asked.

"You'll come around," Drake said. "'Cause you'll soon see, the life I can offer you is too good to resist."

Drake spent the night at the post and left for home at daybreak. Shannon was relieved to see him go. She couldn't deny that he was an attractive man and that his family was well-off by frontier standards. She was so used to being dismissed as a bound girl, good for nothing but bed sport, if a man could persuade her—which none had.

It was natural that she was a little flattered by Drake's offer. If she'd been inclined to marriage, he'd be a good choice. And, the longer he was nearby, the more difficult he would be to resist. There was a high price to pay for keeping her independence . . . maybe too high.

And then there was Oona. Shannon had worried about the Indian woman. Where had she gone over-night? Was she safe?

Her fears turned out to be for naught, because Drake was gone no more than half an hour and the Indian woman came into the house and began her daily chores.

"Why did you go?" Shannon asked. "Are you all right?"

Oona shrugged.

"I don't understand. Why did you have to leave?"

Oona put a finger to her lips. "It saves trouble."

Shannon shook her head. "It's not right that you—"

"It is our way."

Shannon reached for her leather apron, but her father motioned to her. "I've a mind to ride out to the nearest village and do some trading with Split Cane's people. I thought ye might care to go along and make your acquaintance of some of the women."

She glanced from him to Oona.

"Go," the Indian woman said. "I will watch the store."

"I'd like that," she said. It would give her a chance to spend time with him alone. They had so many years to make up for. And it might give her a chance to ask him how he could live with Oona and want to hide her from whites. It seemed shameful somehow, and unlike the father she remembered, the man who chose his own path, regardless of what others thought.

They took the horses, and Shannon found herself once more astride Badger's broad back. The way was downhill for the first few miles, but they made good time. The pony had no trouble keeping up with her father's sorrel gelding, even though the horse had longer legs.

"Are you of a mind to accept Drake Clark's offer?"

Flynn asked when they'd stopped by a nameless creek to water the animals. "He's a good catch."

"So he seems to think."

Her father sat down on a rock and filled his pipe with tobacco. He was dressed all in buckskins, and if it hadn't been for his merry Irish eyes, he might have looked like an Indian himself, Shannon thought. Maybe he was, in a way. Maybe this wild country changed you.

"You're of an age to take a husband."

"Drake Clark doesn't treat his mother with much respect."

"According to Nathan, she's not an easy woman to live with."

"You'd never let me get away with sassing my mother."

"No, I wouldn't," Da agreed. "But Hannah raised him and his twin brother. If he's lackin' in respect, the fault's hers. Have you any real objection to Drake—other than that?"

"I like him well enough, I suppose." More than that, if she was honest. He was a lusty man, and her own strong nature responded to that. But, she wondered, would having a good husband in her bed be enough?

Once married, she would be trapped into a way of life where she'd have few choices. Nathan Clark didn't hesitate to slap his wife when he was angry. Most men did as much. Would Drake treat her the same way? And if he did, could she submit to him as a wife was supposed to? As the law gave them the right?

She glanced in her father's direction. "I don't know. I'm not sure I know Drake well enough to make a decision like that."

"He has a temper, that's true enough."

"Like his father."

"Who wouldn't with the shrew Nathan's married to?"

She chuckled. It was true: Hannah Clark was an

unpleasant woman, but . . . maybe she had good reason. She was a hard worker, and she didn't seem particularly appreciated by either her husband or her sons.

Shannon's pony thrust his nose deep into the water, swishing his tail as he drank. On a branch nearby, a wren hopped and chattered. The sun was warm on her face, and she felt lighthearted . . . truly happy.

"Don't think to wait for a love match, me girl. Few white men cross our path out here, let alone princes on unicorns."

"No? And I thought the mountains must be full of them," she teased.

"I felt that way about your mother. Like she was something shining out of one of the old stories. When I first laid eyes on her, the sun was gleaming off that golden hair of hers—like yours, it was. She was a sight to behold, with a waist a man could circle with his two hands."

Shannon picked up a stone and tossed it into the creek.

"A grand passion it was, at least for me. Is that what you're waiting for, darlin'?"

"No, it's not that. It's just that I'm not certain I want any husband," she admitted.

"Hush your mouth. What way is that for a beautiful young woman to talk? Of course, ye want a husband. And a houseful of babies."

"Maybe someday. I would like children." She tossed another stone into the creek and watched as ripples radiated out from the spot where the pebble landed. "But if I do decide to marry, I want to choose with my head rather than my heart. Love isn't always enough. You felt that passion for my mother, and it ended with you both miserable."

The sorrel horse nosed at Shannon's pony, and Badger nipped at the gelding. "Here now," Flynn admonished, separating the two animals. "Best we'd get back on the trail," he said, swinging up into the saddle. "We've a ways to go yet." He glanced back over his shoulder at her. "When you talk like that, you sound like your mother. But I know you. Deep inside, you're like me. When lightning strikes you, you'll follow the right man to the ends of the earth."

"I guess we'll just have to wait and see about that," she answered.

"Aye, so we will, darlin'."

"What about Oona?" she ventured. "Do you feel that way about her? Did lightning strike?"

He laughed. "More like a good rain after a long drought. She's good for me."

"What about her? Do you make her happy?"

He glanced at her and frowned. "You didn't like it— that I sent her away when Drake came."

"No, I didn't. Why, Da? Are you ashamed of her?"

"A little maybe," he admitted. "She's not white."

"But she's good enough to have your child."

"Drop it, girl. 'Tis between the two of us."

"But—"

"It's our way, and it suits us. Stay out of what isn't your affair, Mary Shannon."

"I just—"

He held up a callused hand. "We'll talk of this no more."

Frustrated, she kicked her heels into the pony's sides. He broke into a trot and pushed ahead of the sorrel. The old saddle that her father had altered to fit Badger had seen better days, but Shannon was glad to have it. It wasn't a side saddle, but since she was a novice rider, it was easier to keep her balance with the aid of stirrups.

The meadow that stretched ahead of them was knee-deep in grass and ablaze in color from the wildflowers that grew in abundance everywhere: black-eyed Susan, orange-yellow jewelweed, white May apple, Fairy Wand, and bloodroot, as well as vast tangles of purple rhododendron, so large that they had to follow deer paths around and through them.

It was hard to stay angry with her father with such beauty all around her. And, it was almost as difficult to realize that he had human failings. She thought that his treatment of Oona was unfair, but maybe it was their business and not hers. She'd have to talk with Oona about it sometime when her father wasn't around. It could be that Oona was uncomfortable about whites and preferred to leave. That would be something to ask. For now, she'd do as Da wanted and not discuss it with him, but she couldn't forget it, and she would pursue the matter later.

They rode for hours, down hollows and up slopes, along creek beds, and climbing mountainsides so steep that they had to dismount and lead the animals. How her father found his way through the thick forests of old trees with leaves so thick that sunlight couldn't penetrate, Shannon couldn't imagine, yet he never seemed to hesitate.

"Not far to go now," he promised when they'd topped yet another hill and descended into a steep valley. "About another two to three miles as the crow flies."

"I wish I was a crow," she said. Her bottom ached and her legs were stiff. They'd stopped to drink three times, but she was parched, and her stomach was growling from hunger.

"I've pushed you hard, haven't I?"

"No," she lied. "I'm fine."

Finally, as long shadows faded into dusk, Flynn reined in beside a huge beech tree. "We'll wait here," he explained. "Hold tight to your pony. You can step down." Once she'd gotten off the pony, he fired his rifle in the air. "Just to announce our presence," he said. "Not that they don't know we're here."

"I haven't seen anyone." She looked around. Ahead and to the left was a rolling cornfield, but there was no one in sight. "Are you sure there's a camp here?" She was worried about her father. There were dark shadows under his eyes, and he looked tired.

"You'll see."

Minutes passed before an owl hooted from the trees. Flynn put a fist to his lips and gave a good imitation of the same bird's cry. Seconds later, a Cherokee youth dropped down from a tree branch fifty feet away. He walked toward them, and Shannon immediately saw that he walked with a limp.

"Is that . . . Gall!" she called. "It's good to see you."

"And you, Shannon O'Shea." He approached and shook her father's hand vigorously. "You make good time," Gall said. "Three Spears saw you when you crossed Old Woman Creek. Have you come to trade or just to trade stories?" He smiled. "We will feast this night to welcome you."

"I'm lookin' forward to it." Flynn motioned to the pony. "Might as well scramble up again. The village is about a mile away."

Gall led the way downhill to a wooded area. They followed a barely visible trail through the trees to a rocky river. Shannon looked longingly at the fast-moving current. She was hot and sweaty and would have traded her best ribbons for a chance to wash and cool off.

Others apparently had the same idea. Gall led them past a group of young boys, as bare as God had made them, frolicking in the shallows. When they caught sight of Shannon and her father, they shouted and pointed, then dove in and swam out into deeper water.

A few yards away, several young women were bathing

infants. One round-cheeked girl with skin the color of honey, barely sixteen, glanced shyly at Shannon, smiled, and then hid her face under a fall of midnight-black hair. Shannon waved at her.

The path snaked around a sharp bend in the woods before opening into a mossy hollow. Two Indians, a man and a woman, were just emerging from the river. Gall and her father, deep in conversation, didn't seem to notice.

Shannon gasped. The woman, hair unbound around her shoulders and falling to her hips, wearing not a stitch of clothing, stood knee-deep in the water. Shamelessly, she made no effort to hide her full naked breasts or the dark curls between her legs. She stared at Shannon, then turned and said something in her own tongue to her companion behind her.

Laughing, the man plunged forward, caught her by the waist and threw her over his shoulder. She screamed playfully and pounded at his back, but he paid no heed. Instead, he waded out of the water, carrying his prize.

Hot blood scalded Shannon's cheeks and she averted her eyes, but not before she recognized the slattern's partner. It was Storm Dancer in all his glory. He was naked as a jaybird, tattoos wet and glistening, his swollen sex visible for all the world to see, and his arms wrapped around a beautiful stranger.

# Chapter 8

Suddenly seeing what she was seeing, Shannon's father grabbed her arm and spun her away from the river, pushing his horse between her and the shameful display of unclad flesh. "Sorry I be, that ye should see such," he said, clearly embarrassed. "'Tis their heathen way." He glanced at Gall. "No offense meant." He quickened his pace, hurrying her along with him.

Gall shrugged and rushed to keep up, limping badly. "Your ways are as strange to the *Tsalagi*, Truth Teller. Are not all men and women made the same? Do not the white men take joy in their lovers and make babies in the same manner as we do?"

"Not something we talk about," Flynn said. "My unmarried daughter is rightly modest." He glanced back over his shoulder at the river. "We think that such matters should be kept private."

"It's all right," she protested. She could feel the rush of blood scalding her cheeks and throat.

The sight of Storm Dancer naked had been a shock, but she didn't feel shame so much as indignity. She'd seen bare breasts among the Cherokee when she was a child, but this woman was clearly a common jade to flaunt her body, exposing herself to anyone passing by. Shannon knew that some indecent women gave themselves to men, usually for money, but she'd never imagined that whores existed among the Cherokee.

Once, she'd seen her mistress whip a kitchen slut out of the tavern on Christmas Eve for plying her trade with two drunken coach passengers. The three had made a comical sight. The wench, hair unbound, barefoot, and clad only in shift and bodice, had shrieked her innocence as she ran.

One of her companions had been beer-bellied with skinny legs and a jiggling backside, and the other, a bearded and bespectacled reverend, as tall and disjointed as a beanpole, wearing nothing but his boots and hat, and clutching his Bible. The guilty men's willys had bounced like tiny, pink sausages as they fled through the crowded public room, clutching their garments and packs amid the jeers and laughter of the other guests.

Those men had looked nothing like Storm Dancer. Far from being an object of amusement, he'd been almost frightening, blatantly male, as powerful as a stallion. Shannon swallowed, trying to rid her mind of the image of his muscular chest and hard, red-bronze arms and legs . . . of his beautiful water-sheened skin and the all-too-certain proof of his virility.

She had not known that a man could be so well-endowed.

"Shannon?"

Suddenly she was aware of the smell of cooking fires and the bark of village dogs. With a start, she realized that they'd reached the settlement. Ahead of them, in a natural hollow, spread dozens of substantial log-and-bark structures. Indian men and women left their chores, waved, and hurried toward them. "I'm sorry, Da," Shannon said. "What did you say?"

She had forgotten how large a Cherokee settlement could be and how sturdy their round, windowless houses and peak-roofed open shelters were. Other than their outlandish mode of dress, or undress, the people looked as well-fed and prosperous as those in the frontier settlements she'd passed through on her journey west. Perhaps these Cherokee were healthier than the whites. Even older men and women here seemed to have all their teeth, and there were no hollow-eyed children with runny noses and sores around their mouths and eyes.

A shy little fairy of a girl wearing only a tiny kilt, peeked out from behind a tree and stuck out her tongue, making Shannon laugh. Next, two naked boys, no older than five or six dashed out from behind a frame with a deerskin stretched on it to dry. The boys stopped short to stare at her. One pointed at her hair, and the other backed up, wide-eyed.

"They've probably never seen a white woman," Flynn said, "least of all one with fair hair. The boy with the woodpecker feathers and beads in his hair is trying to convince his friend that you're a ghost."

"They're adorable," she replied. More and more Cherokee came to greet them, most with smiling faces. But not all seemed glad to see them. Several young men scowled and hung back, whispering among themselves, and one elderly woman with long thin braids and a face like a dried apple threw up two fingers and in a shrill voice called something that clearly wasn't pleasant.

"That is Tumbling Water, the oldest woman in six villages. She says you are evil. She makes a sign to ward off witches," Gall explained.

"I'm no witch," Shannon protested.

"I will tell her," Gall said, "but I don't think she will believe me."

There was a murmur from the crowd and heads

turned. A gray-haired woman wearing a feathered cape and carrying a carved walking stick came out of one of the larger round houses. People moved aside to give her room, and Shannon knew instantly that the plump lady with the erect carriage and solemn expression was someone of importance.

"Be on your best behavior," Flynn murmured, proving her deduction correct. "That is Split Cane, headwoman of the village."

Split Cane had gray hair gathered into a queue at her neck, shells in her ears, and a necklace of bear claws dangled between her sagging breasts. Her leather skirt was very short, barely reaching midthigh, and she wore no garment at all above her waist.

Nudity, Shannon thought, was obviously common among the Cherokee.

Feather Blanket smacked Storm Dancer's bicep as hard as she could with a tight fist. "Take your eyes off Truth Teller's pale daughter," she said.

He pried her loose from his shoulder and tossed her into the water. She came up laughing, and he grasped her around the waist again and lifted her high. "What makes you think I was looking at her? Maybe I was watching my cousin Gall."

"Gall?" She wrinkled her nose. "That one is not worth a flea on a dog's back. You were staring at the woman with the yellow hair. Don't you believe that is an unnatural color for a human's hair?"

"Hadn't thought about it."

"Liar."

He pulled her close, and she wrapped her bare legs around his waist. "Do you dare to call a warrior a liar?"

She leaned against him and nibbled at his lower lip.

"You might fool some, but not me. I know you too well." She leaned back in his arms. "She is trouble, my friend, far too much trouble. You would be better to make your match with Cardinal and be done with it."

"There is time." He kissed Feather Blanket and carried her to the far bank where she'd left her kilt and moccasins. "Neither of us is in a hurry."

"The women will not be satisfied until you have fulfilled the prophesy. You are the chosen one and you must do your duty to your people as Cardinal must." Feather Blanket wrung the water out of her hair, tied it back with a leather thong, and fastened her fringed doeskin skirt around her hips. "Come to my lodge later when Corncob is sleeping. I will make you forget the yellow-haired woman with skin like river clay."

He patted her pretty bottom. "You are insatiable."

She laughed. "Yes, I am." She ran honey-colored fingers over her woman's mound in an open invitation to tarry longer. "Have I tired you, mighty warrior?"

He ignored her teasing. "And there is nothing to forget. Shannon O'Shea is nothing to me."

Feather Blanket chuckled. "Shannon? You know her name? If you truly believe that she means nothing to you, you are more of a fool than I think you are."

He smiled at her. "Most men are fools when it comes to women, aren't they?" He drew her into his arms and nuzzled her neck. "Friends?"

"If you come to me tonight, we are friends. Otherwise, I will think less of you and find another to warm my blanket."

He caught her chin in his hand and raised it so that he could press his mouth to hers. Her tongue brushed his and she wiggled out of his arms. "There are none like you. And as soon as you see the back of me departing this village, you will tumble another man."

She laughed again, her amusement as clear and sweet as a silver bell. "You know me too well. Save your flattery and your strength for Truth Teller's daughter. Although I doubt her thighs will be as soft and sweet as mine."

"Enough of her."

"Deceive yourself, if you will," she answered, "but I know the look of a man struck by lightning. Take care, Storm Dancer. If her father sees you sniffing around her, he will fill that empty head of yours with cold lead."

He turned away from her, donned his own leather kilt and vest, and strung the strap holding his blowgun over one shoulder. Snatching up his knife, sheath, and belt, he strode away without another word. The truth of Feather Blanket's words burned like live coals in the pit of his belly, and he could protest no longer.

Shannon O'Shea had caught him in a web of sorcery. She haunted his dreams and sapped his will. Not even Feather Blanket's charms could break the spell. He had cheated her even as he'd driven his swollen shaft deep into her cleft . . . as he'd poured his seed into her womb and spanned her thrusting hips with his hands. He had shared the dance of love with Feather Blanket but in his mind it had been Shannon's flesh he had embraced, her mouth he had kissed, and her he had given his life fluid to.

Feather Blanket was right. Nothing good could come of his longing for Truth Teller's yellow-haired daughter. He was promised to Cardinal. He could never offer Shannon his protection . . . his promise to love only her so long as they each lived.

He had been lost in thoughts of her when he'd gone to her father's house and wooed her with his bone flute. He had wanted her so badly that night, wanted to hold her, to whisper his longing into her ears. But then reality had hit him with full force in the worst possible way.

An owl had flown up almost under his feet and hovered within arm's length—a white omen of doom. Surely, no owl of blood and flesh but one of fog and spirit, a ghost owl, promising disaster and death for them both if he continued on his heedless path.

Still, he had not departed as the owl surely wanted. He had lingered, watching Shannon from the shadows, feeling the pull of her heart to his. Only after she'd returned to the safety of her father's compound had he mounted his horse and ridden for this village, where he could find wise counsel. . . . Where he could drown his desire for one woman in the arms of another.

But she had come after him. As certain as rain after rolling thunder, Shannon had followed him to this place of sanctuary. She had seen him with Feather Blanket, and she knew that he had been intimate with her. For an instant, their gazes had locked. The invisible tie had not severed. He wanted her more than ever . . . more than honor . . . more than duty.

He must possess her or die.

The village welcomed Shannon and her father as if they were family, pressing fresh-cooked meat, Indian bread, sweet berries, and gourds of honey water on them until she couldn't eat another bite. Women gathered around her, touching her hair and chattering to her in a mixture of English and Cherokee. A few words and phrases seemed familiar, but for the most, she had to communicate with smiles and gestures.

One young girl tugged at Shannon's hand and repeatedly entreated her to come with her. Shannon glanced at her father who seemed deep in conversation with Split Cane and an older man. Da still looked tired, and she hoped that he'd have an opportunity to rest before nightfall. "Flynn, excuse me. What does she want?"

"Dove is inviting you to bathe with her." He wiped the sweat from his forehead. "It's a warm day, and you've ridden a long way. The Cherokee are great ones for washing."

"Should I go?"

He shrugged. "If you like. There are things I must discuss with the elders, once the formalities are out of the way."

"Is it safe?"

"Aye. No one will harm you, and no men will dare spy on your bath. As guests, we're safer than the Holy Father in Saint Peter's Chapel. Dove is Split Cane's favorite granddaughter. I've known the colleen since she was a sprig."

"All right." She turned back to the girl. She wasn't as young as Shannon had first thought, perhaps thirteen or fourteen, and very pretty with slanting almond eyes and hair like black satin. Petite, Dove stood no higher than her own shoulder.

"You come?" Dove asked. "Come . . ." She seemed at a loss for the right word until the six-year-old boy with the woodpecker feathers and beads in his hair wiggled forward through the throng of onlookers.

"I make the talk," he proclaimed. "Woodpecker has the good English."

"You do," Shannon agreed, chuckling. "Are you called Woodpecker?"

"He is!" the boy said, speaking of himself in the third person. A wide grin spread over his face, and she saw that he was missing a front tooth. "He be Woodpecker!"

"I am happy to meet you." Shannon took his extended hand and shook it. Please tell Dove that I will come with her to wash."

It was true she needed a bath. Her arms and legs were dusty from the trail, and her fingers sticky from the honey water. She imagined what her hair must look like. She'd always liked to be clean. At the tavern, her mistress had chided her for how much hot water and soap she used.

Odd, how the Cherokee and whites had different ideas about morality and personal hygiene. These Indians had an unusual smell, almost a musty scent. Not unpleasant, but different from her own kind. But with all the women and men, she caught no odor of body sweat other than what her father emitted.

Dove smiled shyly. "You come," she repeated.

"Now come." Woodpecker tugged at Shannon's hand.

She rose from the ground, stretched the kinks out of her legs, and followed the two, trailed by a troop of chattering children and adolescent girls. The village was as lively and fascinating as Shannon remembered a Cherokee settlement her father had taken her to when she was young.

Most of the Cherokee lived in sturdy round houses in extended family groups, but in warm weather, as it was now, most slept in what appeared to be long, open sheds. Kettles of stew hung over cooking fires at every hearth, and children—who were rarely scolded for any mischief—ate when and where they pleased. The homes were scattered, not arranged in orderly lines as in towns back East, but the hard-packed paths were swept clean of trash, and all seemed in order.

Here, two women were weaving baskets; there, an old man was teaching a younger one how to glue the feathers on darts for a blowgun. And just to the left, in front of a cornfield, a group of young boys were playing with a ball sewn of deer hide. She knew it was deerskin because the ball still had the hair on it.

"Is my house," Woodpecker said, pointing to a circular

dwelling that looked exactly like the others. "My mother is best cook in all world. Woodpecker got brother and sister, but Woodpecker be olderest boy. Soon Woodpecker be big enough to go to warrior house."

Shannon remembered her father explaining that boys stayed with their mothers until nine or ten when they joined other youths in a young men's house. There they would be trained in hunting and tracking skills by the mother's brothers, and sometimes, their own fathers. While the boys studied the art of hunting, toolmaking, and fishing, the girls remained under their mothers' wing, helping in the gardens and learning to cook and care for babies, weave baskets, tan hides, sew, and dry food for the winter.

"Woodpecker's mother be Paint." He stuck out his chest. "Paint be best clan."

Shannon knew that the Cherokee divided themselves into seven clans, but she could remember only Wolf, Deer, and Bird. If Woodpecker was a Paint, then there were three more. One clan, she thought, might be Holly. When a Cherokee couple married, the man made his home with her family, but the children took their mother's clan at birth. No one married into his or her own clan. And Da had said that the children, home, and all personal belongings, other than a man's hunting and fishing gear, belonged to the wife.

"What clan be yellow-haired ghost?" Woodpecker demanded.

"I'm not a ghost. And my name is Shannon O'Shea."

The boy puckered up his mouth. "So what clan be Sha-naan-O-Say?"

"Irish, I suppose," she replied.

He nodded. "I-nish. Be all I-nish have skin like fish belly?"

She could barely suppress a giggle. "I suppose we do."

"Poor I-nish. But Woodpecker like all same." He reached up to touch the end of her braid. "Pretty ghost hair." He stopped and pointed through the trees to the river. "There be bath place. Woodpecker wait."

"Yes," she agreed. "You may wait here for me." She followed the gaggle of chattering girls down to a secluded pool in the bend of the river. There were already two women there washing their hair.

Dove pulled at her skirt. "Washy. Washy," she ordered.

Dutifully, Shannon stripped down to her shift and waded into the water. It felt heavenly. One of the girls produced a small basket containing a paste that Dove scooped out and made motions of rubbing in her hair. "Wash my hair with this?" Shannon asked.

When Dove nodded, Shannon sniffed it. The mixture smelled of pleasant herbs, and mixed with water it produced a healthy lather. Glancing around to make sure there were no men watching, Shannon gave herself over to the luxury of an all-over bath where she didn't have to first heat and then carry buckets of hot water.

Soon Shannon was joined by several of the adolescent girls, and one young woman a little older than Dove. It had been a long time since Shannon had enjoyed the company of females close to her age. Even with the barrier of language between them, she enjoyed herself, swimming, splashing, and laughing with the group.

Sometime while Shannon was bathing, Dove washed her skirt, bodice, jacket, and leggings and spread them on the rocks to dry. Since Shannon couldn't put her own garments back on and her shift was soaking wet, she allowed the girls to dress her in a fringed leather skirt and cape. The skirt came halfway to her ankles, immodest by white standards, but positively severe for the Cherokee.

Woodpecker was waiting for them on the path. He led the procession back to the village center, all the while talking up a storm to Shannon in fractured English. "Dancing we must be. Good thing to eat. Much happy for friend Truth Teller and Sha-naan-O-Say of I-nish Clan. *Tsalagi* make welcome. Yes?"

"Yes, the *Tsalagi* do make welcome," Shannon replied as she joined her father again. Flynn rolled his eyes when he saw the Indian garments. Shannon shrugged. "Mine are wet," she whispered.

She didn't mind, really. The buckskin was soft, softer than the wool or linsey-woolsey she was used to. Having no bodice and confining stays was a relief. Woodpecker had called her pretty, and she felt pretty. Her borrowed clothing matched the soft moccasins that Storm Dancer had given her.

She had seen no sign of him since she and her father had first arrived at the camp—neither Storm Dancer nor the naked slut who'd been playing with him. Not that she wanted to see him. It would be far too embarrassing. Best he keep far away from her . . . better for both of them.

The welcome celebration went on for hours. Darkness fell, but still the bowls and platters of food continued to appear before Shannon and her father. Women brought soups and stews and all manner of corn dishes; grilled fish, rabbit, and squirrel contended with venison, duck, and roasted goose for their flavor. Best of all, Shannon loved the chunks of dripping honeycomb and baskets of wild berries. She ate until she could eat no more, but still the Cherokee offered course after course of their best.

Men played drums in the shadows, some drums large as washtubs, others so small that Shannon could have spanned them with her hands. Turtle shells and gourd rattles, flutes, and tinkling bells added to the ancient rhythms. Dancing began with the children and spread to their elders. Women danced in long undulating lines, weaving in and out of the firelight, followed by young men who whirled and stomped as the music quickened and took on a primitive throbbing cadence.

Finally, when it seemed to Shannon that she could not keep her eyelids open another minute, families began to gather their little ones and retire to their sleeping places. Dove came out the shadows and took Shannon's hand.

"Come," she said. "You make sleep. Mother lodge."

Shannon glanced at her father.

"Go on, girl. You'll be safe enough."

And so she was. Dove led her to an open shelter and a soft bed of pine boughs against the back wall. Already women and children were dropping off to sleep around them, and the house fire had burned low. The night air sweeping down from the mountains was refreshingly cool and Shannon snuggled down under a fur coverlet.

Sleep did not come. Through the wall of woven branches, she could see stars, diamond bright against a velvet sky. The crackle of the fire, the soft breaths of the women around her should have lulled her, but instead, she found herself remembering Storm Dancer as she had seen him, proud and naked, water dripping from his crow-black hair.

And when she heard the first faint strains of a bone flute, she thought she was dreaming. The tune was the same as the one she'd heard from her bedroom window, high and poignant . . . touching the secret places of her heart and bringing tears to her eyes.

Reason told her to stay where she was. Nothing good could come of leaving the sanctuary of the women's shelter. Outside the glow of the firelight she risked unknown perils.

The flute called to her. . . .

# Chapter 9

Time passed . . . perhaps an hour, perhaps less. Shannon couldn't be certain . . . could no longer trust her own judgment. All that while, the flutist played on, the high, sweet notes seeped through her consciousness, and deeper still, into her very bones, weaving an enchanted web that entangled and seduced her.

The haunting melody seemed at once the saddest thing she'd ever heard and the most hopeful. It should have been foreign to her ears, yet, she felt a kinship to the refrain from someplace long ago . . . before she was conceived in her mother's womb . . . perhaps before the first wanderers set foot on Irish shores.

Yet, reason told her that she could not weaken. She must resist the mysterious call of the flute. If she weakened, if she left this shelter and walked into the night, her life would never be the same again. Anything might happen in the magical fastness of these mountains on such a night when the sky seemed vaster and the stars closer and more brilliant than ever before.

Her heart raced; she could hear the pulse of blood in her head as she fought the inevitable. Storm Dancer was out there waiting for her. Once in every woman's life, a woman had to do something wild and crazy. If not tonight, now, at this instant, she suspected she would regret it for the rest of her days.

Slowly, Shannon pushed back the warm fur blanket and rose to her knees. The shelter was quiet, the silence broken only by the sounds of steady breathing. Beyond, the camp, the surrounding fields, and the forest were as still as if painted on a canvas. She got to her feet and cautiously crept past the women and girls, circled the fire pit with its glowing coals, and stepped onto the path that wound between the dwellings.

Outside, fog lay in thick white ribbons, hiding the ground, muffling and distorting each sound. Even her breath—her hesitant footsteps on the hard-packed street—echoed eerily. The moon, a huge, ivory crescent, glowed with an intense radiance, laying mounds of spun sugar through the village and giving a dreamlike quality to the night.

The flute continued to emit the crystalline, enticing notes. . . .

Her breath caught in her throat. Her mouth was so dry she could hardly swallow. Perhaps the music wasn't real, she argued with herself. Perhaps she was dreaming. She'd dreamed of Storm Dancer before, hadn't she? She pinched herself hard and winced when it hurt. If this wasn't a dream, if she was awake, how could her sense of perception be so altered? She'd had nothing to eat or drink that would cloud her judgment.

To her left, she heard the sleepy voice of a mother soothing a restless infant, and from the shelter on her right, the hushed laughter of lovers. No dogs barked; no guard barred her way. If this was a dream, it was the most real she'd ever known. What harm could it be to seek out the musician?

And if it wasn't . . . If it wasn't a dream, her recklessness could cost her everything dear to her . . . her father's love . . . her reputation . . . Flynn O'Shea would never countenance such a sin. He would disown her . . . send her away at the least.

But the siren song of the flute would not be denied. . . .

Trembling, she followed the sweet music out of the village, across the ball field, and through a garden where the fresh tilled earth felt soft beneath her moccasins and green tendrils of squash plants wound around miniature cornstalks. As she reached the far end of the cultivated field, she could hear the river, gurgling, splashing over mossy rocks, and smell the primal scents of forest and lush vegetation.

Abruptly, the flute went silent. Shannon stopped, glanced around, peering into the dark trees shrouded in mist. Her eyes widened. Her heart skipped a beat. Where was he? Where had he gone? Had he vanished as he had before on that other night she'd been so bold?

"Storm Dancer?" she called softly. The fog swallowed her words, drowning them in a sea of white condensation. "Where are you?"

Fear curled in the pit of her belly. Hair prickled at the nape of her neck. "Storm Dancer," she cried again.

"You should not be here."

Tingling joy flooded through her veins. He was here. She wasn't dreaming. "You shouldn't have called me." She turned around, trying to see him, but the fog was disorienting. She wasn't certain which way she'd just come or where the river lay.

"But I did," he answered.

"And I came."

He appeared out of the mist, not two arms' lengths away. "I play what is in my heart. I didn't call you."

"You did." She could make out the features of his face in the moonlight. He seemed a man carved of granite.

She fisted her fingers at her sides to keep them from trembling.

"Why did you follow me to this village?" he demanded. "I came here to forget you."

He moved closer still, looming over her. She could feel the warmth of his breath on her lips. "I didn't know you were here. My father brought me."

"This can not be."

"You must believe me." She extended an open hand to him. "I didn't know you were here . . . in the arms of your woman."

"Feather Blanket is not my woman."

The air sizzled with energy, exactly as she'd felt that night at the cave when lightning struck around her. "I saw you," she protested. "I know—"

"You know nothing." He seized her and dragged her against him. His mouth crushed hers, hard fingers tangled in her hair. She opened to him, reveling in the sweet, hot taste of his tongue. The earth dropped away beneath her as she clung to him and their kiss went on and on.

When he finally pushed her away, she staggered back. Her senses reeled.

"You see what this is?" Anger rang in his voice. "It can not be."

"Because you are Cherokee and I'm not."

"The color of your skin means nothing to me."

"It does to most people." She knew what her own kind thought of Indians—heathen savages—hardly better than animals. She knew that he was right, that it could not be. A white woman did not go with a Cherokee. It was unheard of; it went against all civilized law and belief.

"Whites. Not true men. The Cherokee hold all men and women to be children of the Creator."

"That must be true. A loving God couldn't make us all and love only some."

"If I could, I would defy them all. I would make you my wife and take you so far into the mountains that no whites would ever come to claim you."

Her heart leaped. She knew it was impossible, but it thrilled her to hear him say it. "I've never wanted a husband," she said. "Any husband."

He nodded. "Good, because I can not make you mine. I am promised to another."

Her knees felt weak. "It's true then. The beautiful woman I saw you with?"

"There is nothing between us but friendship."

"You can tell me the truth. I know what I saw," she flung back. "You lay with her."

"She has nothing to do with this."

"Nothing?"

His tone grew hard. "Feather Blanket's husband is dead. She takes her pleasure where she finds it."

She took another step toward him. She could smell him now, all woods and wild mountains. The scent was heady. "And she found it with you?"

"I hoped her arms would break the spell you've cast over me."

"It's not me who cast a spell. Since we met in the cave . . . I can't stop thinking about you."

"This is wrong."

She took another step and brushed her fingers across his lips. "I know—but why does it feel so right?"

"Shannon . . ."

"We both know there's only one cure for this sickness."

"What do you want of me?"

"Shhh." She pulled the fringed Cherokee garment over her head and let it fall to the ground. "Can't we have one night? Tomorrow, we can pretend it was a dream. We can be what they want us to be." Shamelessly, she untied the skirt and, naked, opened her arms to him.

With a groan, he swept her up in his arms. Her head fell back, her hair trailing almost to the ground. She felt his lips against her throat, and desire shot through her. She arched to lock her hands behind his neck.

"This night," he said. "This night. No more."

"This night," she repeated. "Our night."

He carried her into the forest. Low-growing boughs brushed her head and arms. She buried her face in his chest as he began to run with her. "Trust me."

"Always," she said. She didn't care. To be here, in his embrace, that was all that mattered. Yesterday . . . tomorrow . . . nothing mattered but this moment.

Storm Dancer slowed and climbed a steep slope. "Here," he said. He lowered her to her feet and clasped her hand. Lifting a heavy pine bough, he led her into a small, round shelter, only half enclosed. Moonlight streamed through the open walls.

"What is this place?" she asked.

He silenced her with a kiss, and pulled her down onto a wide, soft bed of the softest furs she had ever felt. She shivered in the night air, more with apprehension than cold. "I will warm you," he said as he cast off his own garments.

In seconds, they were lying breast to breast, arms and legs intertwined, light and dark hair tangled together. She tilted her face and kissed him, and all doubts fled. This was where she belonged, where she had to be. Of all the men in the world, this was the one God had intended her to find.

Powerful hands stroked and caressed her body, cupping her breasts, and sliding down to cup her buttocks one after another. Sweet hot kisses sent spirals of bubbling excitement to her core. She clung to him, savoring his lean, hard fingers, and the thrust of his hips against hers.

His sex was hot against her thighs, and he brought her hand down to touch him. "Are you sure?" he asked.

Her heart thudded as she closed her fingers around him. He groaned in pleasure. "Wait," he said, rolling her onto her stomach.

She gasped as he lifted the weight of her hair and kissed the nape of her neck, before trailing damp, warm kisses down the hollow of her spine. Stretching out beside her, he turned so that she was cradled against him and his fingers had free access to her breasts and belly . . . to the nest of curls on her mound.

Shannon cried out as he slipped those seeking fingers lower, stroking, rubbing, teasing. "Please . . ." she begged. Need made her brazen. She would die if he didn't quell the aching burning within her. "I want . . ."

She rolled away from him onto her back and he lowered his head and nuzzled her breast. Her nipples hardened and shivers of pleasure tugged at her loins. She opened her thighs, welcoming the length and weight of him.

He caught her nipple between his teeth and then drew it into his mouth. The sensation was beyond belief. She gasped and cried out as he kissed and laved first one nipple and then the other. She bucked against him, needing the hard thrust of his body, but still he denied her.

Nuzzling, nipping, licking, he moved lower, spreading her thighs to kiss her woman's folds. His tongue . . . She could feel his tongue . . . caressing . . . tasting . . . delving.

She climaxed in an explosion of bursting stars and a rainbow of colors, not once, but over and over. And when she thought that nothing could be sweeter, she felt him press his swollen shaft between her damp thighs.

"Yes, yes!" she cried.

There was a brief hesitation and then a sharp pain. She

felt him press deeper, and the hurt was replaced by a greater sense of urgency. She arched her hips, felt him plunge deeper, and then caught the rhythm, and they moved together. Nothing she had ever dreamed of or imagined could have captured the glory of this union. It went on and on until she thought she would shatter into a thousand points of light, until she heard him groan, his whole body stiffen, and then she felt the hot rush of his seed inside her. Once more, twice, he plunged before her own climax came in a flood of glory.

He held her then, kissing her face, her eyelids, her lips, and murmuring to her in the Cherokee tongue. She understood not a word, but it didn't matter. Exhausted mentally and physically, she fell back into the deep nest of furs and drifted first on a silver current of sheer exhilaration and finally into peaceful slumber.

Flynn's hand closed over the stock of his rifle as someone slipped under the blanket beside him. "Who's—"

"Shhh." A low giggle. "Are you cold, Truth Teller?"

The voice sounded familiar to him. "Feather Blanket?" Easily, he switched to Cherokee. "What are you doing, girl?" She slid lower, fumbling for his pizzle. He felt her warm face pressed against him and the natural response of his body to sweet woman flesh.

"Stop that, woman. Get out of there." She was as slippery as an eel.

She giggled. Near them, one of the blanket-wrapped forms chuckled.

"Feather Blanket," he whispered. "You can't do that."

She grasped him, and he felt himself harden even more.

Flynn threw off the blanket, peeled her off him, and stalked outside. Amusement rippled around the common sleeping area. He heard footsteps behind him, and felt the fool. There was no way he could get out of this without betraying his wife or giving the Cherokee something to talk about for years.

"You can't come on a man that way," he protested, fighting back his natural instinct. Damn, but she smelled good. He pushed back thoughts of her warm thighs and breasts as firm as ripe apples. "Besides, I have a wife. Oona would lift my scalp if she found I was sleeping with you."

She placed a soft hand on his cheek. "Do not be angry, Truth Teller. You know I mean no harm. Last time you came, we—"

"That was a mistake. It should never have happened."

She lay her head against him. "I did not please you? I thought I pleased you." She ran her fingers down his inner leg and his breath quickened.

"Cut it out, I say." He swallowed hard. "Yes, you pleased me," he admitted. "But I'm a married man with a grown daughter. 'Tis an example a man must set for his household. I can't be rolling in the blankets with every pretty woman I see."

"I thought you would bring me a present."

It was too dark to make out the expression on her face, but he knew she was pouting. "I did. A pair of scissors. Hardly used at all."

"I have scissors. Tallow has a mirror as big as her fist. I would like a mirror so I can see how ugly I am. Do you have such a mirror at your trading post?"

He caught one of her braids between his fingers. "You would tempt a saint, Feather Blanket. And if you're ugly, I'm a troll. But, I'm getting too old to keep more than one woman satisfied. My spear isn't what it used to be."

Her laughter tinkled in the night air. "Old lovers know how to make a woman happy. Young men care only for their own pleasure. I say your spear is a mighty one."

Flynn heard a soft thud, and Feather Blanket sighed and dropped to her knees. "None of that now. Keep your lips off my—" He broke off in midsentence as he realized she wasn't trying to blow life back into his weary pizzle.

She fell sideways and black liquid trickled from her mouth. Flynn bent to grab her arm. Something hissed past his ear.

Abruptly, a shot rang out. Screams split the air. Flynn threw himself flat on the ground and pressed his fingers to the girl's throat. She jerked away, kicked, and sprawled onto her stomach, the broken shaft of an arrow protruding from the base of her skull.

Dogs snarled. Another shot. Dark figures ran past the houses. Someone burst from a shelter. Flynn caught a glimpse of a tomahawk blade glinting in the moonlight. Shouts in Cherokee.

The hot sweet scent of blood filled the air.

Two more rifle shots blasted nearby.

"Kill'm all! Nits make lice!"

That wasn't Cherokee. It was English, damn it, Flynn thought, crawling on hands and knees toward the shelter he'd just left. That was a white man. Who, it didn't matter much. If he couldn't get to his rifle and kit pack, he'd be as dead as Feather Blanket before sides could be sorted out.

Cherokee men and boys poured out of the houses. Everywhere, individuals were fighting, and women and children were screaming. Flynn crawled faster, keeping his head down. Two figures struggled and fell to the ground an arm's length away, straining and grunting. The man on top was wearing boots; the skinny legs below, Cherokee moccasins.

Flynn leaped up, thrust his knee between the white man's shoulder blades, and seized hold of his head. With one mighty effort, he twisted the attacker's head to the left. There was a sharp crunch, and he went limp. Flynn yanked the body aside.

"Spawn of a soul sucker," gasped the old man.

"Are you hurt?" Flynn asked. He knew the elder by his wheezing voice. He was a councilman named Walks His Elk.

The old man moaned and pushed himself to a sitting position. "Better now." Blood oozed from a gash on his forehead and one wrist hung as though broken. He reached over with his good hand and snatched a hunting knife from the dead white man's fingers.

"Stay down," Flynn advised. "Play 'possom. I've got to get to my gun."

"Bear shit!" Walks His Elk grabbed a lean-to post for support and pulled himself to his feet. "I may be old, but I'm not dead yet." Swaying, knife in hand, he staggered off, uttering a thin Cherokee war cry.

Inside the sleeping shelter, all was pandemonium. Panicked people ran headlong in all directions, snatching up children and hunting for weapons. Belongings were scattered everywhere, and it was hard for Flynn to reckon just where he'd left his stash.

Someone had thrown a fur over the fire pit to douse the light, leaving the hut in total blackness. The fur scorched on the coals, sending up choking clouds of smoke. Frantically, Flynn scrambled through discarded blankets for his rifle and powder horn.

Pain ripped across the palm of his hand. Cursing, he reached down with his right hand and came up with a bone-handled skinning knife. The hilt was cut in an X pattern, and he recognized it at once. No wonder it sliced through his hand so easily. The blade was tempered Spanish steel, one he'd sold last spring to a woman named Painted Turtle. The cut was deep. He could feel blood running down his palm and wrist, but he had no time to bind it up.

Not if he wanted to live long enough to see sunlight. . . .

More shots came from outside in the street. Flynn twisted to peer in that direction, and as luck would have it, he saw the big man in buckskin running at him an instant before the rifle barrel flashed. Flynn flung himself sideways, grabbed the rifle as the rifleman's charge took him halfway through the shelter, and twisted it from his opponent's hands. The man tripped over something on the dirt floor, swore, and went down. Flynn reversed the rifle and brought the butt down across his head, splitting it like a melon.

"Shame on ye, to use such language when you're about to meet your maker," Flynn said.

Winded, he sat down hard. His heart was pounding and his head didn't feel too good either. He put a hand up to his temple, and his fingers came away wet. He didn't know what he'd done to make him so tired. He leaned over and vomited. Damn if his right arm was feeling numb and heavy, his fingers all tingly. The arm ached something fierce, and he wondered if that rifle ball had struck him after all.

Another shot rang out, but it sounded farther away. Most of the yelling had stopped. There was a strange buzzing in his ears, loud as a nest full of hornets. His breathing was still off too. Seems like he had to struggle to take a breath.

It was then that he remembered Shannon. His girl. She was here . . . someplace. She had to be. "Shannon? Shannon, darlin', where . . ."

Flynn's head sagged forward and the rifle rolled out of his limp fingers.

\* \* \*

Shannon opened her eyes. "Storm Dancer?" She felt around. He was gone. It was still dark, but the mist had closed in around their sanctuary. The moon hung low in the sky. Where was he? Why had he left her alone?

She heard several loud pops, and leaped to her feet. A dog howled. Frightened, she pulled a blanket around herself and went to the entrance of the shelter. "Storm Dancer?"

The figure of a man in a slouch hat appeared, silhouetted against the darker trees.

"There you are." She let out a sigh of relief. "I thought you'd left me here without a stitch to put on."

And then, before he uttered a word, she knew something was wrong. That wasn't a Cherokee turban. It was a white man's head covering. Her breath caught in her throat.

"Well, well, well. Ain't this pretty."

The stranger's words cut through her like ice. A strong cloud of chewing tobacco, sour sweat, and whiskey enveloped her. Whimpering in fear, she backed away, clutching her fur covering.

"Don't run away, little squaw. Simon Chew has something special fer you, gal. Something big."

# Chapter 10

"Stay where you are, gal. Don't try to run out on Simon before all the fun."

Shannon darted out the far side of the hut. The man lunged after her, grabbing the fur and tearing it away, leaving her naked. She had no time to think, only to run. Fog lay on the ground, so heavy that she couldn't see three steps ahead of her. The way was steep, downhill, and outcroppings of rock and loose scree made her footing treacherous, but she didn't hesitate.

"Come back here, you little devil!" he yelled.

A stone turned under her foot, twisting her knee, but she ignored the pain. She could hear him behind her, cursing, and sliding on rock. A pine tree loomed ahead of her. She dodged it, tripped over an exposed root, and abruptly the earth gave way.

Screaming, she tumbled through thin air.

She landed hard on her side but rolled onto her stomach, scrambled onto her hands and knees, and crawled forward into what felt like a thicket of blackberries. Seconds later, she heard her assailant cry out as he took the same plunge. She heard a heavy thud and then a groan.

Curses split the air, oaths too vigorous to come from a dead man.

Thorns cut into her skin and ripped at her hair, but Shannon crept forward until she found her way was blocked by a stump and a tangle of underbrush. Unable to move, she dropped flat on her stomach and lay motionless, a hand clamped over her mouth to hide the sound of her ragged breathing.

"You broke my leg, you red bitch!"

Mistress Klank had possessed a greater range of swearwords than either her husband or any of their rough trade, but the man in the slouch hat put her to shame with the originality of his verbal arsenal.

Shannon went cold as she heard the ominous click of a hammer and knew that the lout had cocked his gun. She pressed her face into the leaves as a long rifle blasted. The lead ball hissed through the bushes over her head, whining like an angry wasp, snapping vines and twigs, and plowing into the tree stump.

A string of rank oaths, the acrid smell of black powder, and the unmistakable sound of another ball being tamped down a gun barrel made Shannon push her body deeper into the dirt and rotting leaves.

"I'll blow your futterin' brains out!"

She clenched her eyes shut. *Holy Mary, mother of God, help me—*

Every sound, every scent seemed magnified. The earth beneath her body smelled of rotting bark and green shoots. Very clearly, she could hear the faint chatter of a squirrel and the rustle of a bird's wing. The sounds were so strangely melodic that she wondered if the rifle bullet had hit her, and if she was dead already. But the fear that had numbed her drained away so that she could feel the sting of thorns on her skin, and she knew she still lived. There was no pain in heaven.

And then, clearly, came another light thud, so stealthy that her first thought was that a great mountain cat had dropped from a tree in search of an easy meal. Gravel grated underfoot, and her attacker shrieked in alarm. His shout changed to a scream that quickly became a chilling gurgle and then silence.

She bit down on her lower lip so hard that she tasted blood. At any second she expected to hear the crunch of bone as the lion devoured his kill.

"Shannon." Storm Dancer's voice!

A flame of hope leaped in her chest. "I'm here."

"Come out."

"That man . . ."

"He will harm you no more. Come. The village is under attack."

Slowly, painfully, briars tearing at her flesh, she wiggled backward out of the thicket. Storm Dancer snatched her up from the ground and wrapped his strong arms around her, crushing her against him. "Are you hurt?"

"I'm all right," she assured him breathlessly. Her body was scratched and bleeding in a dozen spots, but it didn't matter. She was alive. "I ran. He didn't catch me." She glanced down at the dark form sprawled on the edge of the ledge and the darker pool gathering on the grass.

"You are safe?" Storm Dancer demanded, releasing her.

Faintly, from the direction of the village, she could hear shouts and screams amid the rifle shots. "Who? Why—"

"No time." He thrust a bundle into her arms. "Stay here. I must go to help my people."

"You left me. Why did—"

"I went to bring your clothes. We left them at the edge of the cornfield."

She clutched her cape and skirt against her bare breasts. "Don't leave me," she begged. "Not with him."

She glanced toward the motionless body. "I can't stay here with—"

Storm Dancer muttered something in Cherokee, walked to the corpse, and kicked it over the edge. Far below, bone crunched against rock, making Shannon wince. "Stay here," he repeated, thrusting the dead man's rifle and powder bag into her hands. "Until it is safe. I will come for you." He turned from her and scrambled back up the rocks toward the hut.

"But what if you don't?" Shannon quickly pulled on the Indian garments. "What if . . ."

She trailed off, realizing that he could no longer hear her. He was gone, perhaps forever.

Time dragged as shouts and wails drifted up from the river and cornfields. An occasional scream rose in the night. Babies cried. A woman wept, her sorrowful lament raising gooseflesh on Shannon's arms. She was terrified that something terrible had happened to either Storm Dancer or her father.

Flynn had been down in the village, probably asleep when the attack had happened. Guilt weighed heavy on her shoulders. How could she remain here while the two people who meant most to her in the world might be injured or even dead? And what of the others? Little Woodpecker and sweet Dove who had shown her such kindness? Not knowing what was happening was torture. Only a coward would put her own safety first.

When she could stand it no longer, Shannon climbed the steep bluff to the hut where she and Storm Dancer had made love. It was a difficult ascent. Twice, she lost her hold and slid back. Her fingernails broke off on the rock, and gravel bit into her knees, but she wouldn't give up, and finally dragged herself over the top.

She ran around the hut and stared down the hill. To her disappointment, she could see no more from here than she could from the ledge below. How could Storm Dancer expect her to remain here when she could picture him struck down, blood spilling from his body?

The scum who had attacked her hadn't been French; he'd been English, and no soldier. His clothing, what she'd been able to see of them, had been typical frontier wear—fringed hunting jacket, leather pants. She couldn't imagine why Englishmen would attack a peaceful Cherokee village, especially since the English were so eager to have the Cherokee join their side against the French.

If Storm Dancer hadn't come in time, the man might have caught up with her. She had no illusions about what would have happened to her. Indian or not, he would have raped her, and afterward, once he knew that she was a white woman, he would have had to silence her so that she couldn't tell what he had done to her.

Her time with Storm Dancer had been the most wonderful experience of her life. She'd come to him a virgin, given him what she should have saved for her lawful husband. But she wasn't sorry. The price for this one night might be high, but what he'd given her was beyond cost. She would remember it and cherish it always.

It wasn't as if she were helpless. She had the rifle and knew how to shoot it if she had to. Could she do such a thing—to save herself—even to save someone she loved? Aim a gun at someone and pull the trigger?

She didn't know.

She wasn't a violent person. She hated fighting, couldn't remember ever hurting another human. She would make that decision when she had to. She might be soft of heart, but she was no coward, she told herself as she made her way down the steep path toward the cornfield.

Reaching the edge of the forest trail, Shannon hesitated at the edge of the trees. She listened, but heard no more shots or screams, but there were fires in the village, and she guessed that some of the houses were burning. A woman sang a heartrending lament that could only be mourning for the dead.

Cold reason settled over her, and she wondered if the rifle she carried for protection was loaded. There was only one way to tell. She pointed the gun into the air and pulled the trigger. There was a dull thud and powder flashed in the frizzen pan, but the weapon didn't fire. She would have to fix that before she took another step.

With trembling hands, she went through the motions to reload the long rifle. It was a skill she'd learned at Flynn's knee and perfected at Saturday turkey shoots held at Klank's tavern, where she'd loaded pistols and rifles for guests during competition.

Not that the tavern gave away any real turkeys as prizes. Once there had been a cantankerous one-legged goose, too old for roasting or laying eggs, but the favorite awards of the day were kegs of moonshine for the best shooters. Usually, Mistress Klank ordered her to drain off some of the whiskey for use at the bar and refill the keg with vinegar, a spoonful of pepper, and a little black powder for flavor.

Still, Shannon had no trouble reloading the dead man's rifle in pitch blackness, and that trick might save her life. "In for a penny, in for a pound," she murmured. Anyone who saw the weapon in her hands and meant her harm would assume she'd shoot, so she may as well have the option.

Armed, she straightened her shoulders, and taking a deep breath, ventured into the cornfield. She'd not gone more than twenty paces when something big crashed out of the darkness. She stopped short, certain that whoever or whatever it is must see her coming.

Holding her breath, she waited. The thing took a few steps closer. She couldn't see what it was, but it was huge and alive. Grunting, knocking down cornstalks . . . Was it a bear or a mountain lion? It was big enough. Her stomach plunged. "Stop where you are," she said.

The thing snorted, squealed, and lunged toward her.

Shannon lowered the rifle barrel. "Stop, or I'll shoot," she warned. She didn't really expect a bear or a mountain lion to heed her command, but she was long past thinking clearly. The words just spilled out of her mouth like ale from a broken pitcher.

A heartbeat later, she made out the silhouette of a horse's head in the gloom. A horse! She'd nearly shot one of the village horses. "Whoa, whoa," she soothed as she lowered the rifle.

The animal kept coming. A warm nose thrust against her shoulder and shoved hard. Shannon tried to hold her balance, tripped and fell back, landing on her bottom in the soft soil. The horse made a snuffing sound, pushed his nose in her face, and sneezed.

"Ugh." She tried to push the animal's head aside, but it pushed the big head forward, knocking her flat a second time. "Go away. Stop it," she protested.

The horse nickered plaintively.

Shannon used the gun to help herself up. There was something familiar about the shape of this horse—not a horse, but a large pony. "Badger? Is that you?"

The pony nudged her again with its nose. With a sigh of relief, she hugged the animal's neck. The pony was trembling. "You're scared too, aren't you?" Badger puffed air between his slobbery lips. "Maybe you—"

"Shannon?" Storm Dancer came toward her from the direction of the river.

"Are you all right?" she demanded.

"Yes. But your father is searching for you."

Storm Dancer's voice was brusque, almost a stranger's, unlike the man who'd held her so tenderly hours ago.

"I think he's hurt."

"Is it serious?"

"Go to him. He's at the far end of the dance ground."

"Were many people hurt?"

"Too many. Eleven dead."

"Cherokee?"

"Eleven." He shook his head. "This man does not count the cowards who come at night to murder sleeping children."

"Are they still here?" She peered into the darkness. "Are you sure—"

"The warriors drove them off. We go after them now."

"You, too? Do you have to—"

He grasped her shoulders. "Go to your father, Shannon. It is not safe for you to be here now. You are English."

"And it was Englishmen who attacked the village," she finished for him.

"Yes. Return to the post and stay there."

"But we had nothing to do with this. You know that—"

"I know that those who have lost fathers and sisters will seek revenge. Go while you can. No one will harm you tonight. By tomorrow, it may be different."

"I don't understand," she persisted. "Why would Englishmen attack the Cherokee?"

He embraced her. His chest was bare, and she could feel the beat of his heart through her thin leather cape. "I do not know," he admitted. "But I know that we will follow those that did not fall. And we will kill them if we can."

"Wait. There must be some other way." She looked up into his face. "No one would expect you not to defend yourself when you were attacked, but if you follow them, if you take justice into your own hands, more English may come to avenge their deaths. The killing will go on and on."

He kissed her. For the space of a heartbeat, she thought her plea had touched him, but then he released her and stepped away. "Go, Shannon."

"I won't let you do this. What about us? What we shared?"

"One night, that was ours. It is over. You have one trail to follow. I have another."

"I know that's what we said," she answered, "but I can't let you go like this."

"It is over between us." He moved away from her. "Farewell, my heart. Live well. I will not forget you."

"Just like that? You're walking away from me?"

"Find a good man with white skin. Have him build you a home and father strong children for you, far from these mountains. Return to your own land, daughter of Truth Teller. Go before the rains here turn to blood."

"Shannon!"

Her father's shout came from the edge of the village. She turned toward the sound, and when she looked back, Storm Dancer was gone. Shaken, too numb to cry, she hurried toward Flynn. The pony followed her.

"Da?"

Flynn ran to her and wrapped his arms around her. His grip was so tight that it took her breath away. "I was afraid." He choked up. "I was afraid that you were one of the . . ." He squeezed her harder. "I couldn't find you."

"Da, I can't breathe." He released her and she inhaled deeply, her thoughts tumbling. "Badger ran into the cornfield," she stammered. "I was afraid and—" She touched his face. "Are you hurt? Someone said you were hurt."

"Ball grazed my head. Knocked the wind out of me. Ye know me, girl. I always did bleed like a stuck pig at the least scratch."

"It must have." Her father's voice still sounded strained, and his breaths were heavy. "But I'm all right. I heard the shots . . . and I . . . and I ran . . ." she said. "People were killed, weren't they? Who—"

"Aye, people died. White and red. Damn whoever conjured this devilment up to a fiery hell. The Cherokee won't sit quiet. You hear those war drums?"

She did. The beat was urgent, primitive, and unsettling, unlike the celebration earlier. There were angry cries as well.

"Calling for blood," Flynn said. "It's best we go. Now."

"But the white men who attacked the village. They could be out there. What if we come across them on the way home?"

"We take our chances. I fought beside the Cherokee tonight, but some won't remember that. A woman I knew, came to the post regular, Painted Turtle, she's dead. And that girl you saw at the river when we arrived. The one with no clothes on? Feather Blanket was her name. She died right beside me. Split Cane's old husband took a musket ball through his head. She lost a grandson, too, a wee lad."

"But maybe we could help with the wounded. If you fought for them—"

"Don't matter. All that matters now is the color of our skin. Later, maybe, cool heads will remember. For now, I want you out of here." He caught hold of the rope around the pony's neck. "You take this animal to the river." He pointed. "Let him drink, and wait for me there. Keep quiet. Speak to no one if you can help it."

"Where are you going?"

"My horse, if I can find him. They tried to run off the livestock, but two of the young lads risked their lives to scatter the lot."

"Will the other Cherokee villages rise? Will this mean war with the English?"

He shook his head. "I don't know. I—"

War hoops pierced the night. Loud shouts came from the trees. Someone cried out in pain.

"Come!" Flynn said. "Let's go while—"

Torches flared. A group of Cherokee men and women poured from the village. Several young men spotted her and her father and ran toward them. Shannon recognized Gall among them.

"You must come," he called, raising a torch high. "They have taken a white prisoner."

Flynn scowled in the firelight. "I want no part of this. My daughter and I will go and leave you to it."

One of Gall's companions said something in Cherokee. Shannon couldn't understand his words, but the meaning was clear. He brandished a spear at them.

Flynn glanced at Shannon. "Sorry I am that I brought you, darlin'. This is bad luck. I don't want you to see this, but I don't think we have a choice."

"I'll be all right," she answered. "We've done nothing wrong. We have nothing to be afraid of."

"I hope you're right."

Two more warriors joined Gall and the man with the spear. One wore a bloody head wrap; the other nursed a wounded shoulder. None seemed particularly friendly. Gall motioned toward the village. "Come now," he urged.

"What will they do with the prisoner?" Shannon asked.

Her father put an arm around her protectively.

"They will burn him," Gall said. "He will face the

council's judgment, and unless someone speaks for him, he will die."

"But that's not right," she protested. "Da? Can they just burn . . ."

"He must die," the brave with the head wound said. "And he may not die alone."

# Chapter 11

A wild-eyed woman dashed out of the darkness and grabbed Shannon's arm. Shannon tried to pull away, but an angry young man caught her other arm. Flynn roared and dove for him but two more warriors seized him, wrestled his rifle and weapons away, and began dragging him toward the village. Gall hobbled alongside, talking loudly, hopefully attempting to quench the crowd's lust for revenge. No one seemed to hear him, or if they did, to care.

The Indians were shouting in their own tongue and Shannon couldn't understand them. Someone shoved her roughly from behind and she stumbled. Only her captors on either side kept her from falling. Frantically, she looked around for Storm Dancer.

More men and women hurried from the town and joined the angry throng. One enraged youth, barely fifteen, shook his fist in the air and howled a chilling war whoop. Hostile cries rose from the shadows.

"Courage," Flynn urged. "We'll be all right." A woman spat in his face and shook a length of firewood at him. He spoke to her in Cherokee, and she lowered the weapon and began to cry.

Not knowing what they were saying was horrifying, and Shannon vowed that if they survived this night, she would learn the language. She raised her head and tried to keep from showing just how frightened she was. Where was Storm Dancer? How could he let this happen to her? He'd said he was leaving the village, but he couldn't be gone yet, could he? He must have known what would happen to her and her father.

Suddenly, the crowd around them stopped short. Indians stepped back to allow a battered old woman to approach. Shannon stared at her. One side of her face was swollen and bloody. A gash ran through her thin hair, and one leg was streaked with blood.

"Split Cane," Flynn said. "She'll put this right."

The matriarch raised a bloody walking stick. Her bearclaw necklace was gone, and the earring had been ripped from one torn earlobe. Still, the plump headwoman radiated power, causing the younger braves to shrink back. The bereaved mother holding Shannon's arm released it. Even Gall seemed intimidated.

Split Cane waved the stick. The seasoned warriors scowled but stepped away from Flynn, who nodded and touched his forehead out of respect for the headwoman. "Much obliged, my lady," he said in English, and then quickly switched to Cherokee.

Split Cane's lip was bloody, one eye swollen nearly shut and rapidly turning purple, her thin hair caked with dirt and something dark and wet, but so regal was her bearing that she might have been a Spanish queen seated on her throne. "Have shame," she rasped in English to those gathered around her. "Truth Teller is brother to Cherokee."

"His skin is white," a woman dared.

Split Cane turned a hard gaze on the speaker. "It matters not. Truth Teller's heart is Cherokee."

An old man hobbled to the circle and said something.

"Truth Teller killed one of the English dogs to save my life," Gall translated. "I saw him slay the scalp hunter."

Split Cane looked at Flynn and spoke softly.

"Take your daughter," Gall translated. "Go in peace, my friend. Return to your home and stay until I tell you it is safe. And forgive angry hearts who forget Cherokee laws of hospitality in their sorrow."

The headwoman pointed at Gall with her staff of office. "This man will guide you home," she said.

Flynn nodded. "No need. I know the way, lady."

Ignoring him, the old woman pointed at two more men and gave a command.

"Pine Martin and Black Walnut must come with us," Gall explained. "Split Cane says if one finger on Truth Teller's hand is harmed, we all pay with our lives."

Quickly, a boy led her pony, Badger, forward and Flynn motioned for Shannon to mount. To her left, Shannon saw another group dragging a battered white man toward them. "What will happen to the prisoner?" she asked her father. But Flynn had already grabbed the pony's rope and was leading her forward. Those who had been so quick to seize them now rushed toward the other captive. Gall limped beside the pony.

"Da?"

More shrieks and whoops echoed in the night air. Scowling and reluctant, Black Walnut and Pine Martin fell in behind the pony. Someone stepped from the darkness and pushed Flynn's rifle, powder horn, and shot bag into his hands.

"Will they kill the prisoner?" Shannon asked. Where was Storm Dancer? Why hadn't he come to help them? Had he already gotten so far away that he hadn't heard the angry mob?

"Don't look back," Flynn said.

A woman brought a horse, not her father's, but he mounted it and nodded his thanks. Gall and the other two braves found animals. Faster than Shannon would have thought possible, they had left the village behind and pressed on into fog-shrouded meadowlands.

High-pitched shrieks from the camp made her stomach churn. "They will kill him, won't they?" Shannon said.

"He will burn at the stake," Gall assured her. "But his dying will be slow."

"That's barbaric," she answered. She felt cold, colder than she should have been on a mild summer night. Where was Storm Dancer? Had he been part of the mob? Or was he one of the savages that would now torture and murder a helpless captive?

"Aye," Flynn agreed. "Almost as barbaric as a man who would slay innocent babes in their mother's arms. War is never pretty, girl. Skin color don't matter. It's the same everywhere. Weeping and dying."

"But why?" she demanded. "Why would anyone do this?"

"Same reason every war's been fought since Adam and Eve were thrown out of the Garden. Land. Land, girl. That's why men fight and die. Because land is life. The strongest claim it and the weak ones who lose it die."

"It's wrong," she protested. "This is Cherokee land."

"Aye. And it was Irish land the English took with steel and shot. All the same."

"What will you do, Da? What will we do?"

"Try and ride out the storm. Same as we've always done. Try and stay alive."

The journey home was fast and silent. Gall and his two Cherokee companions spoke only in their own language. Shannon's father rarely spoke at all. They drove the animals hard into dawn, and when the sun rose over Bald Mountain, they kicked their mounts into a gallop.

Hours later, Shannon caught sight of the post compound. The gates were shut, and a single thread of cooking smoke rose from the house. She glanced at Flynn. His horse's hide was streaked with sweat, and foam flew from its nostrils as he covered the final distance, pulling ahead of her by several lengths.

"Take care," Gall called.

He had remained close while Pine Martin and Black Walnut had ridden one on either side, keeping careful watch. However distasteful they had found the task of escort duty, they had done their jobs well. None of them had seen another human—hostile or friendly—on the trip.

Shannon smiled at Gall. "Thank you for riding home with us."

He reined his spotted mount close to Badger. "Don't trust him," he said.

"Who?" The pony slowed to snatch a mouthful of grass, then stopped, sides heaving. When she tried to pull up his big head, the animal mouthed the bit and laid back his ears in stubborn rebellion.

Gall rolled his eyes. "I never took you for a fool, Shannon. Storm Dancer cares nothing for you. Another woman to boast of."

She yanked at the reins but Badger kept eating. "I don't know what you mean."

"I saw you leave the camp in the night. You went to him, didn't you?"

She felt herself flush. "That's none of your business."

"He boasted to the young men that he would have you."

Anger replaced her shame. "That's not true," she flung back.

He shrugged and motioned to the two braves who sat watching them. "Ask them."

"You know I don't speak Cherokee."

"Who stood beside you in the cornfield when the villagers would have driven another stake in the dance ground for you and your father? Where was he then?"

A sour taste rose in her throat and she felt suddenly sick. "He went after the raiders. He said he—"

"You are just a white woman to him. He would never have you to wife. Never take you to his mother's house."

Tears sprang to her eyes. "How can you speak about him like that?"

"All my life he has taunted me for my French blood."

"Where's your loyalty? Storm Dancer is your cousin."

"He is my cousin, and I know him well. Better than you."

"He wasn't there. He would never have watched and done nothing."

Gall shook his head. "If you think that, you are as stupid as he believes."

"He wouldn't have left if he'd known—"

"He left you to the Englishman, didn't he? Left your bed to go to Feather Blanket's furs. Together they laughed at you."

"That's a lie. He wouldn't."

"Shannon!" Flynn had reined in and was waving to her. "Come on! Why are you stopping?"

Gall leaned down and smacked Badger on the rump with his bow. The pony leaped ahead, and it was all Shannon could do to hold her seat. By the time she caught up with her father and looked back, Gall and his friends had put heels to their mounts and were galloping away through the tall grass. She averted her face so that Flynn wouldn't see the tears streaking her cheeks.

"No sense getting complacent," he said. "Sooner we're behind the walls, the better."

She had to ask. "Before, when . . . when the Cherokee turned on us . . . did you see Storm Dancer anywhere?"

Flynn turned shrewd eyes on her. "Why?"

"He's our friend." She heeled Badger into a rough trot. "I just wondered if he—"

"Didn't see him. Not when the English attacked. Not after."

"Oh."

"I didn't see you either. Not until later—in the cornfield. You must have run when the shooting started," he said.

"A man chased me," she said, carefully trying to avoid an outright lie. "He thought I was Indian. I ran into the dark. Then I fell, and . . ."

"Thought as much," Flynn said. "Lots of confusion. The shelter where you were sleeping with the other women, it burned. Dove was killed. Did you know that?"

"Dove?" Sorrow gripped her. How could that sweet, shy girl be dead?

"You were lucky to get away." He coughed. "I was scared, girl, scared half to death. Worried that you were—"

"No, I'm good, Da. Nothing but a few scrapes and stone bruises. I hid in a blackberry thicket."

"Good thinking," he said gruffly. "Knew you had a knack for takin' care of yourself, darlin'. If anything happened to you, well . . ." He coughed again.

"Let's get on to the post. See if Oona's heard the news."

"How could she? We rode so fast, and it only happened last night."

Flynn scoffed. "Shows what you know about Oona. She may wear a white woman's dress and bake Irish soda bread, but she's pure Indian. Uncanny, the way they know stuff. You wait and see. 'Course, what she knows and what she tells us could be a different shade of horse altogether." He slapped his mount's neck with the reins and guided the animal back toward home.

Miles away, Storm Dancer knelt beside a stream and washed the blood from his hands. Four Englishmen he had found. Four who would never return to their homes and families . . . four who would never claim the bounty on the Indian scalps they carried in their saddlebags.

They had found tracks early in the day where the fleeing band of scalp hunters had split up. These four had turned east while the larger group had continued north on through the pass toward the English Fort Hood. The nine warriors from Split Cane's village had followed the larger group. He had chosen to track these men alone.

He had seen Dove's body after the murderers had taken their pleasure with her. They had committed butchery as well as rape. Feather Blanket's death had been an easy one compared to the younger girl's. Dove's mother had invited the village to a feast to celebrate her daughter becoming a woman, but she died an innocent child who had never known a man until the beasts who walked on two feet had come.

He had tracked the guilty ones and had done what must be done. He had taken them by knife and blowgun and arrow. The last he had drowned in this stream. He had dragged the louse-ridden and bearded monster into the bushes and left his body to be devoured by wolves.

Storm Dancer's conscience bore no guilt for the executions.

Who these white men were and why they had come so far into the Cherokee lands, he didn't know. Perhaps they had taken the pay of the French and attacked the Cherokee so that his people would turn against the English. Perhaps they were simply killers whose crops had failed or who would rather hunt women and children than deer or bear. It was said around the campfires that the governors of Pennsylvania and Virginia paid yellow gold for Indian scalps.

Maybe they wished to murder the Cherokee and claim the rich cornfields and hunting grounds for themselves. White men believed they could own the earth as well as the water. They thought nothing of hunting until every deer was shot and every beaver trapped. Wherever they went, they dirtied the streams, cut down the trees, and lorded it over men whose skins were a different color. What reasonable man could know why they did anything?

The scalps that the raiders had taken from the Cherokee he wrapped tenderly in a blanket. He had built a small fire and burned cedar bark and tobacco so that his prayers for the dead Cherokee would rise with the smoke. He would carry the *Tsalagi* scalps to his own village where the shaman would offer up holy rites. Later, a runner would carry the remains reverently back to their clans so they might be laid with the dead. It was right that a Cherokee enter the sky path whole.

Lastly, he pulled the saddles and bridles off the horses of the dead Englishmen and turned the animals loose. He was no thief. He wanted nothing their foul hands had touched. The rifles he smashed on the rocks and threw into the water. The knives and hatchets he buried.

As he extinguished the fire, he recited the ancient words of a potent curse his grandmother had taught him. "May you thirst and never drink. May you never see the light of sun or moon or hear the laughter of one who loves you. May your souls be lost and your names forgotten. May you never be born again so long as rains fall and the mountains stand."

When he had left the war party, he'd gone on foot as a lone wolf hunts. A man on horseback cannot travel silently, and he cannot cross the steepest mountain or swim the swiftest mountain river. A predator could not weigh himself down with weapons or with belongings. Now that his quarry was dead, he could set off for his mother's village unburdened by unimportant things that would slow his journey.

A lone wolf travels fast and far.

Among his people it was said that a warrior in his prime could run from the Cherokee heartland to the campfires of the Iroquois far above the river the whites called Hudson in the time it took the sun to pass overhead as many times as a man had fingers on his right hand. He himself had made that journey in his eighteenth year, and the sun was still high on the fifth day when he ate roasted bear among the Seneca. On this day, there was no need for such haste, but he ran in the same manner just the same.

Storm Dancer's heart was troubled, and he must speak with Cardinal, his betrothed. He must tell her what had passed between him and Truth Teller's daughter, and they must decide what course to take.

He ran without stopping for drink or rest. He ran as though his soul depended on it.

It did.

As Flynn had suspected, Oona already knew that the peace between the English and the Cherokee had been shattered. Typically silent Oona had waited until they had eaten supper before sharing more terrible news. Not only had Split Cane's village been attacked, but two others, as well.

One, a smaller Cherokee settlement, had been overrun, most of the people killed, the houses burned, and the gardens and fruit trees cut down. Water Bear's town, closest to the Green Valley and Fort Hood had been destroyed as well. There, many of the men had been on a trading expedition with tribes farther west. Their families had remained to tend the crops and were left unprotected.

Through chance, a small girl and her grandmother had been in a high valley gathering berries for making dye. When the child's keen eyes had seen the party of strange white men riding through a pass below, the older woman grew alarmed. The two built a fire and the grandmother sent smoke signals into sky, warning the town.

The people had gathered their little ones and their elderly and fled into the depths of forest. They reported only one death in the village, an English thief who ransacked the shaman's lodge and violated sacred belongings. When he had ripped open a bright colored basket tied shut with leather thongs, he'd been bitten by a tame rattlesnake that the healer used in his medical practice.

"Had the men not been away, the English would have found a different welcome," Oona finished. "None would have remained to murder *Tsalagi* at Split Cane's camp."

"Who were they?" Flynn demanded, shoving his empty plate aside. "Who could possibly be so stupid as to want to ruin our friendship with the Cherokee nation?"

Shannon couldn't keep from asking, "Were other Indian towns attacked? What about Storm Dancer's village?"

Oona had shot her a sharp look and ignored her question. "According to Ghost Elk, white militia men from Virginia came to the fort, saying that they were seeking the murderers of a planter and his family at Pine Hill."

"That was last fall," Flynn said. "Archie Whiggs's plantation. That's five days' ride east from here. And I thought everyone had agreed that the killings were committed by renegades or his own slaves."

"He was a bad master," Oona said. "He deserved to die, but not his wife and family."

"If any slaves had a reason to revolt, it was Whiggs's," her father agreed. "He was a hard man. They said he beat his people and used the women cruelly."

Oona nodded as she poured Flynn another mug of tea. "Only silver, clothing, and four horses were taken."

"Aye. They left more in the field, along with twenty head of cattle." Flynn slowly filled his pipe with fresh tobacco. "Most tellin', whoever did the killin' left the rifles. They didn't even burn the house."

"Shawnee would have taken scalps and guns," Oona agreed.

Shannon toyed with her china teacup, one of the few remaining from her grandmother's set that her mother had carried so carefully from Ireland. "Why blame the Cherokee?"

"This has more the look of men wantin' Cherokee land than justice," her father said. Oona spoke to him in Indian and he translated. "They wanted soldiers from the fort, but the major refused. Ghost Elk claimed he saw Creek Indian scouts with them."

"It's wrong," Shannon protested, looking at her father. "All that killing. It's unfair."

"The Cherokee have long memories." Flynn pushed tobacco into the bowl of his pipe. "These Virginians have lit a fire that may consume us all."

They sat late by the fire talking. It wasn't until Flynn went out one last time to make certain all was quiet that Oona turned to her. "You did not listen to me, did you? What have you done?"

"Nothing."

"Do you think your father is a fool? If he finds out that you and Storm Dancer—"

"We've done nothing!"

Oona scoffed. "Lie to a man if you wish. Do not lie to me. You have shared a blanket with Storm Dancer. Deny it if you can."

Shannon stared at the floor, unable to say anything in her own defense.

"His mother's village is deep in the mountains. Very strong. No white men could find it, let alone catch them unaware."

Shannon had felt a surge of relief. "Thank you."

"I do you no favor. And you do him no favor by forgetting who you are. Your father would kill him if he knew."

"We knew that nothing could come of it—that we are of different worlds."

"You knew, but you broke the laws just the same."

"One night." Shannon looked at her father's woman earnestly. "Was that so terrible? Are what you and Da are doing any less—"

"Is not the same!"

"You're Indian."

"Do not try to run from what you have done." Oona's gaze bored into hers. "I warned you."

"Storm Dancer—"

"Keep your voice down. Your father will be back in a moment."

"You don't understand," Shannon whispered.

"It is you who do not understand," Oona flung back hotly. "Storm Dancer, of all men, is not meant for you. He is a prince. A holy man. A man who is destined to save his nation. It will bring you nothing but pain and tears to desire him. And you may bring him death."

"It's over between us anyway. It was just one night." Shannon folded her hands, trying not to think about him, about the way he'd touched her, the way it had made her feel.

"And if you carry a red child in your belly?"

"That's not possible." The enormous implication of the risk she'd taken suddenly enveloped her. She couldn't be pregnant. Not after one night. Hadn't she seen the merry dance the maids at the tavern had done? Nan had assured her that a woman only took if she did it with the same man for weeks. Oona was just trying to scare her.

"I hope for you that what you think is true." Oona leaned over and banked the fire before looking back at her. "My child will be Indian. It does not matter that Flynn is white. In the eyes of your people, I am nothing. My child is nothing."

"I don't feel that way." She realized that it was true. Her first shock and revulsion had changed. Oona's baby would be Da's child, her brother or sister. And the color of its skin wouldn't matter. Not to her.

Oona sighed as she swept the hearth clean. "You have a heavy burden. If you have a red child, your life is over. No white door would be open to you. The English would spit on your child and call it bastard."

"I'm not with child. I can't be. Storm Dancer—"

"Speak of him no more to me. Forget him."

Shannon snatched a candle and retreated to her room, escaping before her father returned and saw that she was upset.

She closed the door and leaned back against it. What had she done? She wasn't stupid. She knew the risk a woman took when she slept with a man not her husband. Had she lost her mind that she'd forget reason for one night of desire?

Gall had said awful things. They couldn't be true, but what would make him be so cruel? The man who'd made love to her would never have mocked her among his own people.

Wax dripped down over the side of the pewter onto

her hand. Quickly, she set her candle on the table and sucked at the finger. She gazed into the mirror wondering how Oona had known. Did what she and Storm Dancer had done show on her face?

She could see no difference in her features . . . no scarlet letter branded on her forehead. On the outside, she was the same. But in her heart, in her soul, everything had changed.

Staring at her own pale face, she realized it had been a lie. She had been part of a lie.

No matter the cost, one night with him was not enough. . . .

# Chapter 12

Five days passed. No visitors arrived at the trading post, and no Cherokee came to buy goods. Flynn kept the gates locked, and when either Shannon or Oona went to the spring for water, he walked with them, eyes wary, cocked rifle on his arm.

All was quiet.

Shannon tried to keep from thinking of Storm Dancer by staying busy. She scrubbed the cabin floors, whisked away cobwebs from the rafters, and wiped, swept, and dusted every inch of her bedroom and the kitchen. When the house was spotless, she turned to the store, oiling the metal objects such as ax heads and hoes with bear grease to prevent them from rusting, and polishing the copper kettles until she could see her face in them.

Shannon girded up her skirts, rolled back her sleeves, churned butter, and started the process of making cheese. She cut grass for the cow with a scythe, brushed her pony, and cleaned and rasped his hooves. She was repairing a loose rail in the pound fence when Oona begged her to come and see what mischief her father was up to.

Shannon found him standing in a hole four feet deep

and almost six feet across, perhaps thirty paces from the end wall of the cabin. He'd stripped off his vest and worked barefoot in a white linen shirt and breeches. Three hounds sprawled nearby, watching their master with interest. The one-eared female nibbled at a back paw, and Shannon noticed that her belly was swelling with pups. The two other dogs lay at ease, tongues lolling.

"What are you doing, Da?" Shannon asked.

"What's it look like? I've had a mind to dig a well inside the compound for years. Thought this might be a good time."

Flynn's face was red; sweat beaded on his forehead and dampened the dark hairs on his forearms. The sun was high overhead, and it was too hot a day for him to be digging. If Shannon hadn't been so occupied inside the store and later with the animals, she would have noticed what he was up to earlier.

"Is what this woman says." Oona pushed a gourd of spring water into his dirty hands. "If the well he must have, better to wait until the Harvest Moon. Only a white man would work in the high sun."

Flynn grimaced, rinsed the dust from his mouth, and spat. "October. She wants me to wait until October. Shannon, if you see a war party swoopin' down on us, could you ask them kindly to wait until fall, after I put in a new well?"

"Oona's right. It's too hot out here for you to be digging in this hard ground. You know better than this. If it has to be dug, you should be working at dawn and sunset."

"Got to be done. No tellin' what we're in for, what with the Cherokee all stirred up."

"Fine." She slid down into the hole and reached for the shovel. "At least, let me take a turn."

"Have ye lost your mind, girl? Did you ever see me let

your mother do a man's work?" Drops of water ran down into his graying beard.

"Da, what good will this do? If someone attacked us, how could we defend the post? There are only three of us." And one a pregnant woman . . . She didn't say that, shouldn't have needed to. What was he thinking? This wasn't like her father. He'd always been so practical in the past.

Flynn tossed the gourd onto the grass, snatched up the shovel, and began to chip away at the hole. One of the dogs strolled over and licked at the water remaining in the curve of the gourd.

Oona's mouth tightened into a thin line. She shook her head in disapproval, rubbed at the scar on her face, and turned away. As she walked back around the cabin, she retrieved the container. The one-eared bitch rose and followed her inside.

Shannon climbed out of the hole, sat on the ground, and curled her bare legs under her. It had been too hot for stockings this morning, and she'd put on only her shift, boned linen bodice, and drawers under her oldest dress. She'd put aside the Cherokee clothing once they'd gotten home, but she had to admit that she missed the freedom of no stays and a short skirt.

The sun's rays felt warm on her face, and the sky above was cloudless. She couldn't feel the hint of a breeze. She glanced down at her father in the hole, completely exasperated with him.

"Da?"

"Aye." He was breathing hard through his mouth. Veins stood out on his temple and throat, and his knees trembled as he drove the shovel into the virgin soil. He'd tossed his hat aside along with the vest. His hair, tied into a queue, once thick and black as the devil's heart, was thinner with threads of silver. It shocked Shannon to see age advancing on Flynn O'Shea. He'd always seemed as solid and enduring as these mountains.

"Are we safe here?" she asked.

He paused, leaned on the shovel, and looked directly at her. For an instant, she caught a glimpse of uncertainty in his gaze, and that frightened her more than the lines around his eyes and mouth . . . more than anything he could have said. "I thought about sendin' you off to Green Valley, to be with the folks there," he admitted.

"What? And leave you and Oona? I wouldn't do that."

He scoffed. "You'll do as I say, girl. No place for her there, not among whites. But there's safety in numbers. You said it yourself. Three of us couldn't defend the post against a war party."

She got to her feet and came to the edge of the hole. "Then why are you doing this?"

He threw the shovel and sighed wearily. "Damned if I know. Keepin' busy, I suppose." He climbed up and out the edge and sat beside her. "Forgive my foul language. Doin' nothin', not knowin' what's comin', that's hard on a man."

"We could all go someplace together."

Flynn lifted his head. Moisture pooled in his eyes. "I've made a mess of things, Mary Shannon. I let your mother go East without me. I let you become a bond slave to strangers. And now, my lust has fathered a child that will never be welcomed among my own kind."

Despite the heat of the midday sun, a shiver spiraled down her spine. Hadn't she done the same? Given in to lust? Taken the risk of bringing a bastard child into the world, one whose skin color would always make it an outcast among civilized folk? Involuntarily, her hand went to her flat belly, and she wondered if there might be a new life flickering there.

"Don't blame yourself, Da."

"Do you hate me for lettin' you down? For leavin' your mother to die alone?" Pain grated through his thick Irish brogue. "I loved her, Shannon. I swear, I did. I just couldn't stomach the thought of livin' back East, in that little place, with the walls hemmin' me in."

"These mountains remind you of home, of Ireland, don't they?"

"Sorry, it is that you never knew the beauty of it. The sun risin' over the green hills and the sweet smell of burnin' peat in the air."

She threw her arms around him and hugged him as tightly as she could. "I could never hate you, Da. You mean the whole world to me."

He bowed his head and leaned it against her cheek. "Go on with ye, girl. You've honey on your tongue, and that's for certain." He pushed her away, clearly embarrassed by his show of emotion. "And you're right. Both you and Oona. I'm naught but an old fool to be diggin' a well when we've a good spring nearby. I'll take the horses and fetch some barrels of water, just to ease my mind."

"I can help." She got up and shook the dirt off her skirts. "And, in the fall, when it's cooler, we can find someone to help you dig that well, if you still want it."

He dusted off his hands, and one of the hounds came to nuzzle the back of his knee. He scratched the dog behind his ears. "Maybe I'm worryin' you two for nothin'," he said. "Split Cane's people have had time to cool their tempers. If the Cherokee have tolerated me all these years, we should be all right for a while longer."

"Da . . ."

"Flynn," he corrected, getting slowly to his feet.

She smiled at him. "Flynn. I've been thinking about the baby. Oona's baby. You know there are places where Indian children are educated. I think it would be the right thing to do—to send . . ."

"Aye. If it's a man child, that we will do. A girl can learn at her mother's feet, same as you."

"You don't believe in educating females?"

Flynn scoffed. "The more the better, I say. But I'd not trust her among strangers at some mission school. There's many willing to take advantage of a brown-skinned girl."

*And a white-skinned girl,* Shannon thought, but she didn't say it out loud.

"I didn't do so bad by you in learning, did I?" He crossed to the cabin porch and took down the hanging jar that held drinking water. The dogs crowded around his ankles as he dipped water into their bowl.

"No," she agreed. "You didn't."

Her father had given her a treasure of stories, history, and poetry. Her mother had taught her to read and write a fair hand, but Da had fired her imagination. He'd insisted she master math and memorize long Irish ballads and fairy tales that had been handed down for generations. She'd never spent a day in a formal school, but her education had surpassed that of the Klanks' oldest son who'd attended a secondary academy in Philadelphia. If Oona's baby was a girl, perhaps she could do the same for her new sister.

A little sister might be nice. She'd always wanted a sister or a brother. It was hard being an only child. She tried to picture the image of an Indian baby with her father's features, but all that she could think of was the small mischievous face of little Woodpecker at Split Cane's village. She hoped that he hadn't been hurt in the attack. He'd been adorable. She hoped Oona's child would be as bright and winning as Woodpecker.

"I mean to do the best by the babe. Born on the wrong side of the blanket or not, 'twill be an O'Shea. Whatever I leave behind when I go to meet my maker, I'll expect you to share and share alike."

Shannon nodded. "I'd do no less."

"You've a good heart. I can count on you to do what's right." He scooped up another dipper full of water, leaned over, and poured it over his head. "By all the saints, that feels good," he declared, grinning at her. "Any hotter, and you could fry eggs on my neck."

"Which is why we told you it was too hot for you to be working in the sun." She didn't like the dark circles under his eyes or the strained way he was breathing. Even his skin had a gray hue to it.

Flynn's mood grew serious. "If I should die before the babe is grown, Oona will manage. But if anything then happens to her and the child be orphaned, you must find an Indian family to adopt it."

She looked at him in astonishment. "Why couldn't I raise it?"

"No. 'Tis not possible." He hung the jar back on the hook and settled heavily onto the top step. "Among the tribes, it would be accepted. With the whites, both you and the little one would be outcasts. I'd not ruin both your lives by my sin."

"Da, the child would be my blood."

"Speak no more on it. What Oona and I have done is unnatural. Her babe will be Indian, no matter how light the skin." He pulled his vest back on and fished in the deep pocket for his pipe. "You'll have your own husband and children to look after," he continued. "A husband and little ones of your own kind. And there's an end of it."

"It seems cruel."

"Better a little cruelty than a lifetime of misery." He rapped the pipe sharply on the step to knock out the ash. "Here on the frontier, things are different. This post is apart from the white settlements. But half-breed children raised among the whites are treated worse than black slaves. There is no place for them but with their Indian kin."

Again, the fear that she could be pregnant rose in the back of Shannon's mind. What kind of woman was she that she could be so reckless? That her carnal nature could be so strong that she would risk bringing an unwanted child into the world to suffer?

"What do you think of Gall, Da?" she asked suddenly. "Would you trust him?"

"Oona doesn't, and that's a fact." He looked at her. "Why do you ask?"

"He said something to me, and I don't know whether to believe him or not."

"Can't say I've ever thought much about the lad one way or t'other. He's been a good customer, and he seems honest enough. What did he say?"

"Nothing important," she lied.

"Seems it must have been or you wouldn't be dwellin' on it."

Oona appeared in the open doorway. "Come and eat," she said. "The Johnny cake is hot, and there is fresh butter, thanks to the cow."

"Music to my ears," Flynn said. "Haven't had butter on my bread since St. Patrick drove the serpents out of Ireland."

Glad for the distraction, Shannon followed them into the house. She wished she hadn't mentioned Gall to her father. If the Cherokee had told the truth, she'd made a terrible mistake, but if he hadn't . . . He must be lying about Storm Dancer. But what reason would he have? She'd thought Gall was her friend. And whatever the answer, one of them had deceived her, but which one?

\* \* \*

Storm Dancer came to her in the night.

She'd been dreaming about her friend Anna. In the dream, Anna hadn't died, and the two of them were sitting at the long table in the smoky kitchen of Klank's tavern eating bread and honey. Anna's feet were bare, but she was wearing a beautiful dress and a straw hat with a red feather on it. She was drinking hard cider, a joke between them, because Anna's father had been a Mennonite and she'd promised him never to touch spirits.

Anna was laughing, and they were both coughing because of the smoke from the fireplace when abruptly, Anna pointed toward the open window. Shannon looked and saw Storm Dancer beckoning to her.

"Shan-non, come away with me," he said.

But it wasn't the window, she realized. Storm Dancer was leaning over the bottom half of the nail-studded Dutch door. The cook usually kept the top of the door open and the bottom latched to keep the pigs and poultry out of his kitchen.

She glanced back at Anna, but could no longer see her face because of the smoke. No, it wasn't smoke. Mist or a thick fog enveloped the kitchen, and the crackling of the logs on the hearth had changed to the cascade of water over a falls.

Storm Dancer waded through the hip-deep water, took her hand, and drew her deeper into the river.

"I can't leave Anna," she protested. "She's not dead."

"Anna is gone."

Shannon blinked and drew in a deep breath. The tavern had vanished along with her friend. Now, she and Storm Dancer were surrounded by tall trees and rocks on either side. She could hardly see the banks of the river because of the spray from the waterfall and the mist lying heavy on the surface of the water.

"I have to find Anna." Shannon tried to pull away, but Storm Dancer held tight to her hand.

"Do not be afraid. I will protect you."

"But Anna . . . I thought she was dead, and she . . ."

"Shh, she is safe." He pressed two callused fingertips over her lips.

Heat diffused through her cheeks and throat at his touch, and she gazed into his dark, luminous eyes. Haunting eyes . . . so black that they seemed a bottomless pool . . . so bewitching that they took her breath away.

"This is wrong," she argued. "I can't leave the tavern to be with you. My father—"

"Do you trust me?"

"You aren't real. This is a dream. This isn't happening."

He yanked her against him and kissed her fiercely. Her heart jumped as a stab of desire pierced her—desire so sharp and urgent that her protest drained away. She closed her eyes and fell into the all-consuming kiss.

If this was a dream, she wanted it to go on and on.

His mouth was demanding, hard, and sweet as raw cane sugar. Her thoughts tumbled; her muscles went weak as he gathered her up in heavily muscled arms and carried her toward the waterfall.

"Where are you taking me?" she begged.

He kissed her again, and her stomach contracted. Every inch of her skin tingled.

"We can't do this."

"We cannot do this in daylight," he said, "but this is not daylight. This is the dream world. Can you not be with me here and now?"

She locked her arms around his neck. His scent filled her head, made her drunk with desire. Nothing mattered but this man. Nothing mattered but this exquisite moment.

"A dream," she murmured. "Only a dream . . ."

His lips pressed against her throat. She felt his warm mouth on her skin, and ripples of excitement skittered through her veins. Another kiss ignited the flame in her core, and she raised her face to his.

"Where?" she begged. "Where are you taking me?" If it was

*a dream, there could be no guilt, no chance of a flesh-and-blood child with almond eyes and honey-colored skin. If this was a dream, there was no sin.*

*She felt him climbing over uneven rock. The roar of the waterfall grew louder . . . the cold spray beat against her face. If this was a dream, how could it be so real? If it was a dream, she never wanted to awaken.*

*"Do you trust me?" he repeated. Suddenly, she realized that he wasn't speaking in English, but Cherokee. Yet, she understood each word perfectly. Was it possible that what passed between them needed no translation?*

*"Heart of my heart," he said.*

*The chords of his sensual voice vibrated in her soul. "Storm Dancer." How beautiful his name was in Cherokee, she thought, how perfectly it suited him.*

*They passed through the cascade and into an echoing place beyond. It smelled of ancient rock and running water and moss, but the scents were haunting, as though she knew this place as she knew this man. As if they had lived this minute before . . . as if they had always been one through time.*

*She wondered at the strength of this golden man, the power of his corded muscles, the silken texture of his satin skin. In the daylight, he would be red and she white, but here, in this mystical spot, their skin colors blended to one.*

*The ground beneath Storm Dancer's feet no longer seemed uneven. She tilted her head back and gazed up at a vaulting ceiling overhead, faintly illuminated in unearthly shades of green and azure. Strange rock formations dripped from the ceiling, great waxen icicles thicker than her thigh and longer than the height of a man.*

*"Do you remember?" he asked.*

*An undercurrent of gossamer images flickered in the shadowy corridors of her mind. The air had taken on a steamy quality, and the chilly cavern warmed as Storm Dancer strode farther from the crashing cascade and deeper into the mountain.*

*It seemed as though he carried her for hours, but then, he stopped, stepped down, and lowered her into a warm bath. The water's odor was almost acrid, not unpleasant, but clean and sharp, almost like that of the lemon a visiting lady had once given her at the orphanage. She hadn't known what to do with the lemon; she'd kept it for a long time, until it shriveled and dried into a hard knot. She had never forgotten the scent. This pool reminded her of that precious gift.*

*She sighed as the warm water surrounded her, draining the tension and cold from her limbs, cradling and suspending her in timeless enchantment. The pool bubbled and hissed, and the rising steam filled her head and made her giddy. She leaned back and sighed with pleasure at the feel of the swirling water on her neck and scalp.*

*"What of the baby?" she asked, wondering where that question had come from.*

*"Do not trouble your heart. Anna will love and care for it."*

*"Our child?"*

*"Not ours, but one dear to you, heart of my heart."*

*"But Anna's . . ." Anna was dead, wasn't she? She had died horribly when they were both fourteen. She'd wept over Anna's dead body, hadn't she? Mourned her friend for years.*

*"She lives," Storm Dancer half whispered. "Death as you imagine it is an illusion."*

*She uttered a small cry of delight as the heat of his strong fingers moved over her throat and breasts. His mouth lingered at her throat and shoulder before trailing warm kisses down to her breasts, licking and nibbling until sweet ribbons of light unraveled through her veins and fueled the growing flames between her thighs.*

*Her own fingers were not still. She stroked and caressed him, savoring the feel of his body, tracing familiar lines and curves, muscle and hard sinew.*

*"Is this a dream?" she whispered.*

*"If you desire it so."*

*"I don't understand."*

*"The power is yours, Shan-non. You have called me up."*

*She would have asked him to explain, but he was kissing her again. He lifted her and lay her on her stomach on a bed of thick moss.*

*"Close your eyes," he commanded.*

*She could not have disobeyed if her life depended on it. Lulled by the sheer joy of his delving fingers, driven by the heat churning within her, she surrendered to his lovemaking.*

*For a moment, she felt nothing. Then, to her surprise, she became aware of the cold, smooth surface of a small object sliding across the skin of the back of her left thigh. "What is—"*

*"Shh."*

*She tried to think what the cool, hard substance could be. A stone?*

*"Do not speak, heart of my heart. Only feel."*

*He moved the stone in small regular circles, and when her body heat warmed it, he replaced it with another cooler one. He slid the object higher, massaging in soothing patterns over the back of her knee and onto her thigh. Then he leaned over, and gooseflesh rose on her arms as his tongue laved her left shoulder.*

*She moaned with pleasure, caught between the coolness of the stone and the heat of his moist tongue. Heat flashed under her skin as he first kissed her trembling flesh and then nipped her skin with his teeth. Spasms of pleasure burst in her veins.*

*She writhed beneath him and tried to turn over, but he leaned his weight on her and held her down. Her breaths came in short, quick gasps. "Please," she begged.*

*Another stone. Cold as ice . . . sliding over her left buttock, massaging, teasing. And all the while, Storm Dancer's mouth seduced her, first a kiss and then a bite . . . the nape of her neck, along her spine . . . the hollow of her back.*

*She was burning up. This was torture. She needed more. She wanted more. . . . "Please."*

*His tongue caressed the crease between her buttocks, his lean fingers holding the stone sliding lower yet, probing . . . penetrating.*

*Desire glittered under her skin. Trembling, she pushed herself up on her elbows. "I need . . ."*

*"Not yet."*

*She arched her hips and felt, not the unyielding surface of stone, but the soft, downy sensation of silken fur. "What are you . . ."*

*His sensual laughter echoed through the cavern. "Tell me, Shannon. Tell me what you need."*

# Chapter 13

"No, that's something I can't do." Storm Dancer jumped to his feet and folded his arms over his chest. "You ask too much. I'm flesh and blood, not some spirit mystic from a legend."

His mother tossed a handful of powder on the campfire and the flames flared up in blue and green, casting strange patterns on the round walls of her lodge. The two were alone, far enough from the other longhouses in his village that their heated discussion couldn't be overheard by curious neighbors.

He'd run for many hours into the mountain fastness to find his mother and settle this with her. Honor dictated that he free himself from his commitment to Cardinal before he could ask Shannon to be his.

Cardinal would have to be consulted as well, but the power of the senior women in this tribe lay with Firefly, as it had for nearly a decade, since his grandmother passed away. As befitted a noblewoman, his mother's cabin stood apart, near a bubbling spring, sheltered by towering trees that had been old when the first Norsemen landed their dragon-headed ships on the continent.

He hadn't expected that telling his mother about

Shannon would be easy, and she hadn't disappointed him. Her anger was barely concealed behind a mask of rigid dignity.

"Your fire tricks don't scare me, Mother," he said. "I helped you to grind those minerals when I was small. I can even make yellow or purple smoke, if you like."

"You should be afraid." Firefly got to her feet and fixed him with a steely glare. Her years numbered forty and six, but her cheeks were as smooth as girl's and she stood as straight and strong as a young oak. "You were born on a night that the heavens burned with fire. Born with the mark of a lightning bolt branded on your skin."

"I'm not who you think I am," he protested. "I'm just a man like any other, nothing more."

"You were born to save the *Tsalagi*."

"You're mistaken. According to the stories, Walks With Lightning was a wise man, a mystic. I could be a war leader, if I had to, but nothing more. Wouldn't I know it if I was a chosen one? You're deluding yourself."

She hissed through clenched teeth. "You speak to me like that? Don't forget who birthed you alone on a mountaintop . . . who single-handedly beat back a rogue wolf all that long night to keep you safe."

"I won't marry Cardinal."

She placed a hand on his arm. "You can't run away from your destiny."

"Are you listening to me, Mother? I love someone else."

"Love?" She sniffed dismissively. "Since when is love a reason to marry? Marriage is to strengthen a family—to provide for children."

Muscles tensed at the back of his neck, and he struggled to find the right words to make her understand. All his life his mother had been there for him, a tower of strength, an endless source of nurturing love. This decision would hurt her, and it tore him apart to oppose her in anything.

"I will choose my own life partner," he said. "I respect you and the council of women, but—"

"Who are you to choose your own wife? Who is any young man who thinks only with what dangles between his legs?"

"I know that it's tradition for you to pick a wife for me."

"Not tradition, but law. The senior women of the *Tsalagi* bear the burden of choosing mates for their children."

"Not for me." He sucked in a deep breath. "I came to tell you my decision out of respect. I'm not asking your permission."

She gripped his arm. "Would you shame me and Cardinal for a whim?"

He embraced her and kissed the crown of her head. She smelled of wild strawberries. "Mother, Mother." He gently pushed her away and gazed into her eyes. "You have to understand, what I feel for Truth Teller's daughter is more than lust."

"Whatever it is, quench it," she said. "The soul of your great-great-great-grandfather, Walks With Lightning, lives in your body. You are the embodiment of the prophesy. You may have forgotten who you are and what you will do to save the *Tsalagi*, but you know what to do when the time comes."

"Bless this house." A soft voice called from outside the door. "May I come in?"

Storm Dancer gritted his teeth. *Cardinal.* He might have known that his mother would drag her into the argument. How Firefly had summoned Cardinal without leaving the lodge and when no one else in the camp had seen him arrive, he didn't know. He was certain she'd done it. She was a master at women's magic.

"Your promised one," Firefly said. "Make love to her and you will forget the white-skinned stranger."

When his mother played a game, she could be ruthless, always no-holds-barred. He glared at her. "You don't miss a trick, do you?"

Amusement glinted in her luminous eyes. "Enter, daughter."

Storm Dancer touched his lips in respect. "Cardinal." He followed with the traditional Cherokee blessing.

"Husband."

*Not yet,* he thought. He hadn't wanted to see her tonight, but he didn't blame her. Cardinal was just as entangled in this trap as he was. The senior women did arrange the marriages, but it was well-known that every bride had a choice of several men—every bride-to-be but his.

For the first time, it struck him that she might be no happier about the engagement than he was. After all, Cardinal hadn't had a choice either. She'd been a babe at her mother's breast when the council of women— led by his mother—had proclaimed her the future bride of Walks With Lightning's latest reincarnation.

"I'll leave you two alone," Firefly said. "I know you have much to talk about. There is no reason to postpone the wedding ceremony any longer."

"Yes, lady." Cardinal nodded, then glanced up at him and smiled. "We do have much to talk about."

"Stay, Mother," he urged.

"No. I'm certain you can work out the small obstacles of your union best without me."

Storm Dancer could have sworn he heard her chuckling as she ducked out of the deerskin hanging that served as a doorway.

He heard a rustle behind him, and when he glanced back at his intended, he found that she had untied the deerskin strips that held her fringed dress at the shoulders.

Still smiling and unashamed, she let the garment fall and pool around her slim ankles.

Cardinal wore nothing but a necklace of blue and white shells and soft moccasins embroidered with porcupine quills, and her thick, blue-black hair tumbled loosely to her hips. Her waist was small enough for him to encircle with his two hands; her small breasts were high and firm. Her skin glowed fresh and sweet in the firelight, and he could smell the hint of cherry blossoms in her hair.

He groaned as a rush of blood and heat made his stones contract and his spear hard. He had forgotten how beautiful she was. "Cardinal," he began. "We—"

One dainty hand brushed the dark shadow at the apex of her thighs. "I've waited for you," she said. "No man has had me." She cupped a breast and fluttered her thick lashes. "This night, you will be the first."


Shannon fumbled in the darkness. "Storm Dancer?" Her bed . . . She was in her bed in her father's cabin. Alone.

Tears filled her eyes.

"Storm Dancer," she whispered. How could a dream be so real? She shook her head and felt around the mattress, half expecting to hear his deep laughter and have him enter her.

She was damp in her woman's cleft . . . wet . . . trembling with need. Had she imagined it all? The tavern? The river? The cavern behind the waterfall? Impossible.

Did madness run in her family? Was she losing her mind? Had they really made love on the mountain near Split Cane's camp? Or was that her imagination?

She couldn't lie still. The ache throbbed in her loins. In desperation, she rubbed at the sensitive flesh. In the past, she'd pleasured herself in the night, but this time, she could find no release.

If she believed in witchcraft, she would think that he'd cast a spell over her. But the only enchantment was his body pressed against hers . . . the sound of his heartbeat thudding in her ears and the taste of his mouth.

If Gall was right, if Storm Dancer had abandoned her, she'd wither and die. No man could ever fire such desire in her body and soul. What she felt for him was more than lust. It must be the kind of love that women were willing to die for.

She rose from the bed and drew on her shift. Her mouth was parched. Barefoot, she walked to the kitchen in search of the water bucket. It stood empty next to the hearth. One of the dogs raised his head and watched her through sleepy eyes as she opened the door and stepped out on the porch.

The night was still. No breeze stirred.

Shannon took down the hanging jug and drank from it. The water was cool and sweet, but as she savored the taste, she thought again of the waterfall and the bubbling hot spring in the cave.

In her mind, the images of the cavern were as real as the porch posts or the hand-hewn planks under her feet. How could she have imagined such a scene?

"Storm Dancer . . ." she called softly. "Where are you? I need you."

"Cover yourself." Storm Dancer turned away from Cardinal. "I can't make love to you."

"You find me flawed? I'm not beautiful enough for you? You think me unworthy?"

"Whatever my mother's told you—"

"Nothing. She's told me nothing, only to come, that

you were here and needed me. . . . That we should join as man and wife."

Cardinal sounded hurt. He'd not meant to insult her. This wouldn't be easy for her. All her life, she'd expected to become his, to bear his children. "You know I care for you," he said.

Was she crying? It sounded as though she was. He could never stand to see a woman in tears. He wanted to turn back, to look at her, but he was afraid his strength would fail. What man wouldn't accept such as gift as Cardinal's untouched body?

Only one whose soul had been snatched away. . . .

"It's all right," she said. "I won't attack you."

"Your dress?"

She giggled. "On."

At least she wasn't crying. He glanced over his shoulder to see that she was sitting down on the far side of the fire, her lovely nakedness covered.

She laughed. "You really don't want me, do you?"

"Can we talk?" He tried not to show his relief as he threw a handful of sticks on the coals and the fires flared up. "How did my mother call you? No one saw me when I entered the village."

"It's a woman thing. I can't tell you."

He nodded. He hadn't expected her to share secrets. "If I were free, Cardinal, there's no one I'd rather take to wife. But I'm not. I didn't seek this. It never occurred to me to go against the council's decision, but someone else has touched my spirit."

"A white woman."

"How did you know that?"

She sighed. "Firefly told me. I'm not nearly as good as she is, but when she . . . *speaks,* I hear her clearly."

"And she wanted us to couple. Here, tonight."

"It's not as though it would be a sin. We've been

betrothed since you were two." Cardinal drew her feet under her and looked into the fire. "I'm not a trouble-some person. I can't refuse what the women's council asks of me. If they insist I marry you, I will do as I'm told."

"Without complaint?"

"Don't you worry that they're right? That you are the rebirth of Walks With Lightning? That you put the people in great danger by shattering the pattern?" She divided her hair, smoothed out a section, and began to braid one half. "You do have the lightning bolt on your palm. I've seen it many times."

"It's a birthmark, nothing more."

"You didn't used to think that."

"I was a boy. Boys brag."

"The village will believe you found fault with me," she said shyly. "That something is wrong with me."

"I'll tell them differently. The fault's mine, Cardinal. What kind of husband would I be to you if I loved some-one else?"

She continued plaiting her hair. "What if something terrible happens—something that you could have pre-vented? Could you live with yourself?"

"You deserve a man who will love you and honor you."

She got up. Only one braid was completed. Half of her shining hair still hung over one shoulder. "If you hadn't met her, could you have taken me to wife? Fathered my children?"

He smiled at her. "I didn't choose Shannon. If I had never known her, I could have been happy with you."

"All right." She stood and went to the door. "I'm glad. I've always respected you, liked you, but there's someone else for me too. Someone I love."

"Why didn't you say so?"

She covered her mouth with her hand and chuckled. "I told you, I'm not a troublesome person."

"But you would have given yourself to me."

"I would have done my duty." She paused, toying with her braid. "And . . ."

"Yes?"

"He'll be glad too. In autumn, when the gossips have found something new to talk about, perhaps we can marry. And then he will know that we didn't take pleasure together."

"I wish you'd told me before," he said. "I wouldn't have felt so bad about refusing you."

She cast her gaze down so that he couldn't read the expression in her eyes.

"Can I know who this lucky man is?"

"No, not yet." She giggled. "I don't tell secrets. You'll find out soon enough."

She ducked through the doorway and Storm Dancer sat alone, staring into the flames. It was done, and easier than he'd believed possible. Tomorrow he would start his journey back to Truth Teller's trading post and he would do a harder thing. He would ask a white man for his daughter's hand in marriage.

It was still dark out when the dogs woke Shannon with their barking. She threw on her clothes and hurried into the kitchen to find her father was already halfway to the door, rifle in hand. Oona was right behind him, carrying his powder horn and shot bag.

"Stay inside," Flynn ordered. "Until I see what's what."

Oona threw her a look. As soon as they were out of the kitchen, Shannon took down the rifle hanging over the fireplace. She didn't need to check if it was loaded. Armed and prepared for whatever waited outside, she followed them.

It was immediately evident that whoever was at

the front gate wasn't an Indian war party. Although Shannon couldn't make out what the men were shouting, it was clear that they were white.

"Open up!"

She heard horses whinnying and the unmistakable pounding of fists on the gate.

"It's Drake Clark!"

"Let us in!" a second voice called.

Oona drifted back and slipped past Shannon into the house. "It is the men from Green Valley." She put her fingers to her lips. "Don't tell them that I'm here." The Indian woman went into her bedroom and closed the door behind her.

Shannon stepped down from the porch, the rifle cradled in her arm. Da's hounds were still barking as they circled the horses. Drake had already dismounted. Both the twins were talking at once, and she could only catch snatches of what they were saying.

". . . Hostiles hit us three nights ago," Damon said. "Cory Jakes is dead. Ben Taylor took an arrow in his leg."

"Ma's arm is broken. She fell climbing out of the loft."

Shannon took the reins of Drake's mount. In the moonlight, she could see that his horse had been ridden hard. His hide was wet, and he stood head down, sides heaving.

"We didn't know what we'd find here," Damon said. "Pa sent us to bring you back to Fort Hood. We're takin' all our women and kids there."

"Did you see any Indian sign on the way here?" Flynn demanded.

"No. Nothing." Damon ran a hand through his damp hair. "We're joining the militia soon as they call us up. The major has sent for reinforcements."

"The war party didn't get away scot-free," Drake exclaimed. "We killed two of them fer certain. Wounded more 'n that. Damon and me followed a blood trail the next day, but it petered out."

"It's not safe for you folks here alone," his brother said. "Just the two of you. Pa said you wouldn't want to leave your trading post, but stuff ain't worth your life. You've got Shannon to worry about."

"Who attacked you?" Flynn closed the gates and dropped the heavy bar into place.

"Indians," Drake replied. "Who the hell do you think we're talkin'—"

"What kind of Indians?" There was a hint of annoyance in Flynn's voice. "Shawnee? Creek? Cherokee?"

"Cherokee," Damon answered. "The one I shot was a big son'a gun. Wearin' a turban. Painted for war. Had to be Cherokee."

"Come down on us in the middle of the night," Drake said. "I heard Indians never fought at night, but these did. They set fire to Ben's house and drove off his cows, then hit our place. The dogs warned us in time to give as good as we got."

Her father glanced at her. "You tend to the animals, girl. Rub them down good, and keep them from water until they cool off." He turned back to the Clark brothers. "You're certain they were Cherokee? The dead Indian couldn't have been Shawnee?"

"Cherokee, Shawnee, Creek. What's the difference?" Damon asked. "The only good Injun is a dead one. That's what Pa says."

"I like your father, but he's wrong about the Cherokee. I've lived among them for years, and I've found a good Cherokee to be no different than a good man of any other color."

"They weren't good Injuns that raided us. I agree with Damon. What's the difference, one tribe or another when they're tryin' to kill you?"

"The difference is between us livin' to see the next harvest and not," her father answered. "Whites hit three of the Cherokee villages this past week. I know men from Split Cane's band went after the guilty ones, but they wouldn't have attacked Green Valley."

"We're tellin' you that's just what they did."

"It makes no sense," Flynn said. "You shouldn't have been able to drive them off so easily. If the Cherokee nation takes the warpath, none of us will survive."

"I'm tellin' you they were Cherokee," Damon repeated. "I know one when I see one. Murderin' devils."

Flynn shook his head. "If you killed two of them, there'll be hell to pay."

A cold chill slithered down Shannon's spine. How many times had she heard Da talk about Cherokee revenge? If Cherokee had attacked the Green Valley settlement, and people had been killed on both sides, there would be no smoothing over what had happened to Split Cane's village. The Cherokee would go to war.

She and Storm Dancer would be mortal enemies.

# Chapter 14

When his mother didn't return, Storm Dancer lay down in his accustomed sleeping spot and closed his eyes. He was bone weary; the last time he'd slept was the night before he and Shannon had made love. He didn't remove clothing or moccasins. He fell instantly into a deep and troubled slumber.

In a dream world, he ran through heavy fog . . . Shannon just ahead of him. He could hear her voice calling out to him, but he couldn't see her. The mist muffled her voice, confusing him, making it impossible to tell where she was.

"I need you," she cried. "Storm Dancer, where are you?"

"Shannon!"

"I need you." A hand shook him. "Son?"

Jerked from his dream, disoriented, Storm Dancer leaped up, reaching for his knife.

Male laughter assaulted him. "Is this how you greet your father?"

Storm Dancer's eyelids felt gritty. He shook the cobwebs from his thoughts and concentrated on the tall man standing near the fire pit. "I'm sorry, Flint. I didn't—"

"It's nothing. If I've gotten too old to keep out of your

reach when I wake you, I deserve what I get." His father chuckled. "You're tired. I should have waited until morning to come to you."

"No, no, it's all right." He rubbed his eyes. His eyelids felt weighty, and the vision lingered in his mind. He had the uneasy feeling that Shannon was in trouble, and he had to find her.

"I examined the bundle you brought."

Storm Dancer glanced toward the shrine where he'd reverently deposited the wrapped *Tsalagi* scalps he'd carried back for burial. Other sacred items, including a medicine bag and a Christian crucifix hung over a small shelf, directly across from the entranceway. Since he'd been a toddling babe, he'd watched his mother offer prayers there at dawn and dusk. She'd burned fragments of cedar bark or tobacco there, so that the smoke would carry those prayers to heaven.

"I wanted to ask Mother to send a runner to carry remains to Split Cane's village, but I thought it was best to settle the matter about my marriage first. I'll make the arrangements in the morning."

His father settled beside the fire, folding his legs under him. He removed a stick of sugar cane from his pouch, and snapped it in half. "I don't know that Firefly considers the matter settled," he said as he handed over half the sweet.

Storm Dancer bit the end of his sugar cane. He supposed the treat had been traded many times through many hands before arriving here in the Mountains of Smoke. A sweet tooth was something he and his father had always shared.

The last time Storm Dancer and Flint had both been home, the two of them had smoked a bee tree and raided the honey. Flint said that in the old days, there were no European bees and no fat caches of sweet honey. Storm Dancer thought that bees and steel were perhaps the only good thing the whites had brought to these mountains, and the bees had been an accident.

When he didn't answer, Flint continued. "Your mother is upset over your refusal to marry the woman she chose for you."

"And so she complained to you." Storm Dancer lowered himself to the mat. His father was still a handsome man in his prime, a warrior who had traveled far in his life and was considered a shrewd trader. The two pressed open palms together as Storm Dancer murmured the formal greeting, showing respect to his sire, whom he greatly admired and loved.

By Cherokee tradition, his mother's brothers were his Wolf Clan fathers, the ones to train him in the arts of hunting, fishing, and war. Since the *Tsalagi* counted bloodline through the mother and any child was born into her clan, the role of a birth father was always less important. Thus, Storm Dancer was of the Wolf Clan, as was Firefly.

Despite custom, Storm Dancer and his father, Flint, had always been unusually close. Flint was considered the best tracker and finest horseman among the Deer Clan, and he had taught his son his woods' lore and to ride, almost before he could walk. Flint had also insisted that Storm Dancer learn English and study the ways of the white invaders, a radical idea.

His parents' marriage—although rocky at times—was a strong one. Few men would have had the inner strength to go against Firefly, but Flint would if a matter was important to him. And even though his mother had never been able to carry another live child to birth, neither had ever considered divorce. More telling, Flint had never taken a second wife, an accepted practice among the *Tsalagi* when the first marriage was an arranged one.

"She won't take no for an answer, son," Flint said. "Your mother is determined that you marry Cardinal."

"You know that she is convinced that I'm the reincarnation of Walks With Lightning."

"So is half the Cherokee nation. They expect great things out of you."

He looked into Flint's lined face. "Do you?"

His father made a noncommittal sound. "What father does not expect miracles from a beloved son? These are dangerous times. It may be that what the people believe is more important than what is."

"I'm not a great leader or a mystic."

Flint chuckled. "Neither was your mother when we first shared our marriage bread and blanket." His tone changed from amused to serious. "There was someone else for me too, a girl I loved more than breath—or thought I did."

Storm Dancer tried to hide his surprise. Despite their loud and vocal disagreements, he'd thought that his parents' marriage was a love match. "No one ever told me."

"It's not something people would talk about."

"Who? Do I know her?"

"Her name was Tumbling Water. She is Split Cane's youngest daughter."

"What happened to her?"

"The women sent her north to secure a political alliance with our cousins, the Mohawk. She married a powerful chief."

"And you ended up with Mother."

"I was always destined for your mother. Like you, I never questioned the decision." Flint chuckled. "Not until the summer I met Tumbling Water and lost the power of reason."

"This is different. I knew Truth Teller's daughter when she was a child, but I never imagined that I'd feel this way about her now. I'm going to make her my wife, if she'll have me. I've already settled the matter with Cardinal. What Mother says doesn't matter."

Flint exhaled loudly. "Never think that. She can have you exiled. Or worse."

"What could be worse than to be barred from my clan, my village?"

His father shrugged. "Firefly loves you, my son. She would do anything for you, anything but risk the future of this village or the *Tsalagi* nation. She's not above eliminating your white woman, if all else fails."

Storm Dancer's gut twisted. "She wouldn't hurt Shannon. Mother likes her own way, but she's a good person. She wouldn't—"

"You may be right," Flint conceded. "You're much like her, you know. Hardheaded as an oak. But I didn't come here to warn you about your mother. I need you. Your people need you."

"You know I can refuse you nothing, Father, so long as you don't try to convince me to give up Truth Teller's daughter." He tossed a piece of chewed sugar cane into the fire. "And whatever you want me to do, it must wait until I go back and ask Shannon to be my wife."

"You've bedded her?"

Storm Dancer bristled. "That's none of your business. Or my mother's."

"You have, then. I was afraid of that. Winter Fox will be displeased. Her father is his friend."

"I did not say that Shannon and I—"

"There's a wide chasm between bed sport and a commitment to marriage. Most whites believe us soulless animals doomed to their Christ's fiery hell. Have you thought that your woman may laugh in your face? Many white women enjoy a red man in their blanket, because we are mighty lovers. But few choose a *Tsalagi* as husband. They would be shamed in the eyes of their own kind."

Storm Dancer stiffened. "You think I don't know that? But Shannon is different. She sees me as a man, not as a Cherokee."

"And if she refused your proposal?"

Flint rose, and Storm Dancer realized for the first time that he topped his father's height by half a hand. "If she refuses me, I still won't marry Cardinal. If I can't have Shannon, I'll have no wife at all."

"Not ever?"

"No," he answered stubbornly. "I'm going to her at first light."

"First, hear me out. You know about Split Cane's village, but you probably don't know that whites attacked two other *Tsalagi* camps, as well. And at the English fort, soldiers and Delaware guides gather, perhaps to march against us."

"Our alliance with the English is over, then."

"I'm afraid it might be. Your uncle, Winter Fox, has asked me to ride north with him to a parley with the French Colonel Gervais."

"You think we would get better treatment from the French?"

"The French come for furs and their black robes to spread the word of their Jesus-Who-Died-On-The-Tree."

"And the English want our land," Storm Dancer finished.

"We are like the boy on the log. On one side of the river, a hungry grizzly bear waits to tear him apart. On the other, a starving pack of wolves. And beneath him, rattlesnakes curl and hiss."

"So far, the *Tsalagi* have survived by not fighting for or against either side."

"Exactly. But it may be time for us to join the wolf pack

or to become a bear." He sucked thoughtfully on the sugar cane. "We cannot be snakes."

Storm Dancer nodded. "I'd heard that there would be a council on the Ohio."

"At the trading post of Big Pascal."

"You're going, then?"

"I'm going, and I want you at my side. Representatives will be there from many nations, among them Shawnee, Delaware, Huron, and Seneca."

Storm Dancer stroked his chin thoughtfully. "An interesting mix."

"As dangerous as fire and black powder. All the more reason we need a strong escort. We will listen to what the French king across the water has to say and bring back his offer. The *Tsalagi* must decide whether we should try to mend the alliance with the English or join their enemies. The future of our nation may depend on our decision."

"I can see why you and my uncle have to go, but why do you need me?"

"Each delegation is allowed only two handfuls of men. I expect treachery. And I trust no one at my back as I trust you. And if there's trouble, I'm gambling that you could get out with your scalp intact, and bring the news back to the *Tsalagi*."

"If I come, it would mean postponing returning to Truth Teller's daughter. Are you sure this isn't my mother's idea?"

Flint shook his head. "This has nothing to do with Firefly. Your woman will have to wait. If the two of you are meant to be together as you believe, it will happen. We need you with us now. There's a good chance the Shawnee or the French or our English allies could ambush us on the Warrior's Trail and smoke our hair on their scalp hoops before we ever reach Pascal's."

For a long moment, Storm Dancer considered his

father's request, but he knew in his heart that there could be only one answer. "When do we leave?"

Shannon pulled her knees up and settled the hot stone wrapped in rabbit skin against her belly. Oona had taken one look at her through the open bedroom door this morning, recognized her problem, and brought her a mug of herb tea and the heated stone to ease her women's cramps.

Shannon's courses had started just before dawn several hours after Drake and Damon had arrived. Although she was rarely bothered by discomfort, this time her monthly blood flow had brought intense pain. The relief that she wasn't carrying a babe was oddly tempered with an inner sadness. Her mixed feelings confused her. She didn't want a child now; she certainly didn't want one born out of wedlock. She should have been doing cartwheels, and instead, she was curled up, hiding in her bed.

The Clark brothers had slept in the outside quarters. Oona would remain hidden in her bedroom when Damon and Drake came in to eat, so Shannon knew she'd have to get dressed and serve breakfast. She didn't want to talk to them, because she was afraid that Da would relent and insist she go to Fort Hood with them. She had no desire to be shut up with Hannah Clark and the other women she'd traveled west with. And, if the Cherokee hadn't attacked her father in all these years, she might be safer here than riding off with the twins.

Reluctantly, Shannon got out of bed and dressed. The herb tea tasted awful, and she was hoping that Oona had brewed a pot of Darjeeling for Flynn. Shannon was certain there had still been real tea leaves left in the tin caddy. If she had a strong cup, she'd be better able to argue her case for staying with her father.

Oona was heaping hot coals on the iron lid on the Dutch oven. "Bread will be ready soon," she said. "There is fried rabbit, corn mush, and tea. Let them think that you cooked it."

Shannon glanced around the spotless kitchen. "Where is Flynn?" She took a cup from the shelf and went to pour herself hot tea.

"He's gone to the spring for water. He did not want the white men to see me, so I could not go."

"I'm sorry. I should have gotten up earlier," Shannon said.

"Is good that you have your moon time. The herbs will help with the pain."

"Yes, I'm sure." Shannon thought the heat from the warming stone might have been what had eased her cramps, but she did feel better. "I can take over here, but . . ." She hesitated. "Is it hard for you? Both Indians and whites have died in the fighting. Da is white, but you must feel torn."

"It is hard." Oona rubbed the burn scar on her cheek lightly. "Once I was beautiful," she said softly. "Once I had another husband and a son."

"Did you?" Shannon asked. "I didn't know."

"Far to the north it was, along the Ohio. I am Delaware, cousin to the Shawnee and Menominee. My name was not Oona then, but *Amimi,* the pigeon."

A chill ran through Shannon. She waited, teapot poised above the pewter mug, knowing that whatever Oona was going to say, it would be awful.

"We were sleeping when they came. Some were French, some Huron. My husband, my sisters, my mother all died. My little son . . . A white man pulled him from my arms and threw him against a tree. He fell broken, and they stepped over him, as if he was nothing. And when they had finished with me, a Huron warrior dragged me into what was left of my wigwam and set fire to it."

"I'm so sorry."

"I wanted to die. I should have died."

"But you didn't."

"Your father found me wandering in the forest with my little son in my arms, half-mad. He buried my baby and my heart with him. Flynn O'Shea cared for me as though I was of his clan. He took me to a village of the Shawnee and left me with my own kind."

Shannon set the teapot on the table and went to Flynn's woman, wrapped her arms around Oona and held her. Oona sobbed dry sobs, but did not cry. Shannon cried for her. Tears streamed down her cheeks, a flood of sorrow for Oona's baby and Oona's family that she had never seen.

"In time the burns healed," Oona whispered hoarsely. "The family Flynn O'Shea left me with had poor hunting. When a French priest came, they sold me to him for a mirror, and two horns of black powder."

"How did you and Da . . ."

Oona shrugged and stepped away. Her eyes were dry, the pupils large and clouded with horror. "A young woman, a strong woman has value, even one who has this." She tapped the ridged scar on her face. "I had many masters, some good, some not so good until I saw your father at a rendezvous. I begged him to buy me from the Dutchman who owned me then. He drank hard liquor and beat me too much. Sometimes, he gave me to other men for their pleasure."

Shannon's eyes widened in disbelief. "Flynn bought you?"

"No. He gave coin to a French monk who said the Jesus words over us to make me Flynn's wife. Then he beat the Dutchman and threw him into the river. He took the Dutchman's furs and horses and gave them to me for my bride price."

"He married you?"

"By book and cross. I am his wife. He is my husband. And now we will have a child, and my heart will beat again. That is what kind of man is your father. He has given me back my life, and if he is ashamed for his white friends to know, it is nothing."

"But I don't understand," Shannon said. "Why did he hide your lawful marriage? Why did he let me think that you—"

"Was his whore?" Oona shook her head. "Who knows why a man does anything? All I know is that my burned face does not matter to him. He tells me I am beautiful and he holds me in the dark when the bad dreams come."

"I'm sorry. I'm so sorry. I've been so terrible to you," Shannon said. "I never thought about why you would—"

"Shh. Your father comes." She put a finger to her lips and hurried into her bedroom, closing the door quietly behind her.

Shannon heard footsteps on the porch. One person, not three. She turned toward the sound. "Da?"

Flynn's complexion was tallow-gray. He leaned against the door frame for support and dropped a bucket on the plank floor. The bucket was empty. It fell over onto its side and rolled back and forth.

"What's wrong?" Shannon demanded. Her heart hammered against her ribs. "Are you all right?" He looked as though he'd seen a ghost.

"You!" He pointed at her. "What have you done?"

"Nothing," she protested. "I've done nothing. What do you mean?"

He crossed the floor, grabbed her shoulders, and shook her until her teeth rattled. "How could you?"

"What? What is it?" He shoved her away with such

force that she lost her balance and almost fell. "Da? Have you lost your mind?"

"No," he roared. "But you must have!" Sweat beaded on his forehead as veins bulged beneath his fair skin. "Did you think you could do such a thing and get away with it?"

"I don't understand," she wailed. "What have I done?"

"Go into your room. Pack your things. You're going to the fort with Drake and Damon."

"But why?"

"I wouldn't have believed it," he said. "Not of you." He drew the back of his hand across his eyes. "Damn it, Mary Shannon. I never thought ye such a fool." He sank down on a bench.

"Da."

"Do as I say, girl." He knotted one fist and smacked it into the palm of his other hand. "I'm not a man for striking a woman, not even his own slut of a daughter, but—"

"I'll not go a step until you tell me what this is all about!" she shouted back at him.

"At the spring. A Cherokee runner brought me a message from Storm Dancer's mother."

"What?"

"Her words, Mary Shannon. Her words, not mine. She's angry that you and her son have lain together as man and wife. Did you?"

Stunned, she opened her mouth to deny it. But the lie stuck in her throat. "Da, I think . . . Da, I love him."

"Did you or did you not give him what should have been your husband's?"

She looked away, unable to face him. "Please, Da, don't hate me."

Flynn shook his head. "Like your mother."

"My mother? What does my mother have—"

"What's done is done. I can't pretend to be a saint

myself, but I'll not stand by and watch you endanger your immortal soul. You'll bring no more shame on this house. It's over between you and Storm Dancer. Do you understand?"

She looked at him through her tears. "I can't promise you that."

"Can't you?" He rose unsteadily to his feet, one hand gripping his right arm. Pain crossed his face. "Pack your things, Mary Shannon. You'll not stay under this roof another night."

"You're sending me away?" she cried. "Da, please, don't—"

"This very morning your red lover married the woman his mother chose for him," Flynn thundered.

Storm Dancer? Storm Dancer had married someone? Pain tore through her, shattering her and leaving her numb.

"And you'll do the same," her father said. "Firefly has warned me to find you a husband of your own kind or else face the consequences."

"What does that mean?"

"Drake Clark has asked for your hand. You'll go with him, be married at Fort Hood, and make your home with him from this day forth."

"And if I don't want to marry Drake? You can't force me to marry a man I don't want."

"You'll do it, or I'll send you East for your own safety."

"I don't want to leave you."

"Too late. You broke my trust and put my friendship with the Cherokee in jeopardy, not to mention puttin' your own life in danger."

"From who? From what?"

"His mother. Firefly. Don't you realize what you've done?"

"Please . . ."

"You'll do as I say, or I'll disown you, girl. I swear on the cross, I will. You'll keep quiet what you've done, and you'll marry Drake Clark. You'll be a decent wife to him, and you'll never utter Storm Dancer's name again. You'll pretend that it never happened, or you're dead to me. And you'll never see my face again."

# Chapter 15

"I won't do this," Shannon protested as Flynn hoisted her onto her pony two hours later. "You can't force me to marry."

Drake looked on, hard-faced. He and his brother were armed and ready to ride. Each man carried a rifle strapped to his back. Drake had a long-barreled pistol thrust through his belt next to his skinning knife and extra shot bag. Damon led the cow on a rope. Her father had insisted she take Betty as part of her dowry.

"It's for the best," Drake said stiffly. "This country is no place for a maiden lady. I can protect you."

"This isn't right." She had no more tears to shed. Her eyes were dry, belying the pain in her breast. Storm Dancer had married one of his own kind. The night they'd spent together had meant nothing, and now her beloved father was insisting she marry a man she didn't love to hide her shame.

"What's wrong with me?" Drake stalked up beside her pony's withers. He wore the blue shirt this morning, which made it easy for her to tell him from his twin, Damon, in faded green. "I can provide for you," Drake continued gruffly. "Put food on the table and a roof over your head."

Her pony snatched a mouthful of grass and danced sideways. He never liked the saddle, and he was always saucy in the morning. Today, Shannon didn't feel up to dealing with his misbehavior.

"If you don't want him, take me," Damon offered as he swung into his saddle. "I'll marry you."

Damon's voice was rough, and the hungry look he gave her made a chill ripple under her skin. Damon was ambitious to be more than a farmer, and she'd always thought him the more intelligent of the two. She had more in common with him than she did solid Drake, who'd never wanted more than a hearty meal, land to till, and a field of good horses. But she'd never trusted Damon. Something about him always made her uneasy. No matter what Da threatened, she never would have considered marrying Damon.

"There's nothing wrong with either of you," she said. "I don't want any husband." Was that a lie? She didn't know what she wanted. All she could think of was that she'd never feel Storm Dancer's touch again, never lie beneath him wrapped in his arms, and never hear his voice murmuring endearments. Her stomach clenched and she felt sick. Her cramps had returned with a vengeance. "I want to stay here with you, Da. Please."

Flynn shook his head. "I'll ride as far as the English fort with you, to add my gun to theirs. But the choice is yours. Marry one of these boys or take the first escort back East." He tossed the reins of Drake's gelding to him. "Let's go if we're goin'."

Drake mounted and dug his heels into the bay's sides. The animal leaped ahead, pulling abreast of Damon's horse. Her father fell in behind him, leaving Shannon to bring up the rear. The sky was clear without a cloud, and the day promised to be a warm one.

She let the pony have his head, trotting or cantering to keep up, depending on the terrain. She didn't look back, but each mile that they rode made her sadder. And by the time the sun was high overhead and they were a long ways from the post, she was nearly undone. As they reached a level stretch and the horses lapsed into a walk, Shannon covered her face with her hands and slumped forward in the saddle. Her head was pounding and her mouth tasted sour.

How could her father be so cruel? His own wife, Oona—whom she knew he cared for—was Indian, and he was too ashamed to claim her in public. Soon, Da would have a half-breed son or daughter, yet he treated her, his only daughter, as though she had committed a terrible sin because she looked past Storm Dancer's skin color to fall in love with the man beneath.

It would serve Da right if she asked him how he could treat her this way—if she exposed his secret to the world—but she couldn't make that leap. What if he stopped loving her? Without Storm Dancer, Flynn was all she had left in the world. She couldn't lose him too.

She clenched her jaw and gathered up Badger's reins. Would she never see her home again? Never hear Oona's soft crooning as she sewed or brewed herbs to make medicinals? Familiar images of the cabin and store . . . of the spring and the meadow tugged at her heart. Even the hounds and the bare patch of dirt in the front yard seemed endearing. What did it matter what happened to her now . . . if she did marry Drake Clark? She'd survived worse, hadn't she?

When her mother had died and her uncle had thrust her into the children's home, she'd lived through the cold, the beatings, and the hunger. She'd survived the loneliness, and when she had found Anna, they'd suffered and laughed together. Anna would never be her lifeline again. Her dear friend was dead, but if the world held a person like Anna, why not another someone like her?

She might make another good friend. In time, she might even come to love Drake. He was a good man and honest, a hard worker. And if she couldn't feel the passion for him that she did for Storm Dancer, why couldn't she be satisfied with friendship and respect? And there would be children. She could love and care for her children, and if she was a good mother, they would love her.

She would survive because she was too much of a coward to lie down and die. She loved this world too much to go willingly into the next. Still, she couldn't marry Drake with a stain on her conscience. She gathered the leathers and reined in the pony. Drake circled his own mount and rode slowly back to her.

"Now what's wrong?" He loomed over her, heavy and solid, hands the size of hams, broad brow sheened with sweat from the morning sun.

"We need to talk."

He swept off his broad-brimmed hat and raked fingers through his damp hair. "I'm listenin'."

"If we are going to marry, we need to be honest with each other," she said. Damon and Flynn had both pulled up their horses and were glaring back at the two of them. Betty raised her tail, bawled, and let loose a stream of urine.

"Come on, girl," her father called. "You're wastin' daylight."

"In a minute, Da," she answered. Turning back to Drake, she said, "You want to marry me, even if I'm not sure I want to marry you. Is that true?" She raised a brow quizzically.

"Yeah. 'Spose that's so. I liked you the first time I caught sight of you. I thought we'd make a good pair."

"And my wishes don't matter?"

He shrugged. "Women's got funny notions. You'll come around once you see it's fer the best."

"If that's true, there's something you should know. I'm not coming to you an innocent." All the breath seemed to have drained from her lungs, and her eyes misted over with tears. "There was . . ." Her mouth was dry. She struggled for the words. "I'm no virgin, Drake. If that makes a difference to you—"

"You laid down with some man?" His face darkened as he caught a section of her skirt in one giant paw and twisted it.

She tried not to shrink back. "I did. If you don't want me because of that, I—"

"Were it Damon?"

"No! It wasn't your brother."

His eyes narrowed. "Not my father nor yorn?"

"No! What do you think I am?"

"Tryin' to figure that out. It's a big thing to a man. Most figure that a woman comes to her bridal bed untouched."

"Not as often as men think." She raised her chin. "I'm trying to be fair with you." Traitorous tears filled her eyes. "It was just one night. It's no one you know, no one you'll ever know."

"And you ain't in the family way?" He peered at her midsection suspiciously. "That ain't why Flynn's suddenly so eager to be rid of you?"

She dropped Badger's reins and held up her hands, palms out. "Forget it. Obviously, you think I'm a whore. It doesn't matter. I didn't want to marry—"

"All right. All right." He spat a plug of tobacco onto the ground between their mounts. "Don't matter then,

I suppose. It's jest that my pa's a randy dog. I couldn't stand it if you'd laid up with him or my brother."

She was shaking. "This was a mistake. I'm not the one for you. Take back your cow and tell my father—"

"I reckon I could live with it, just so you understand I won't be cuckolded under my own roof. I'll stand for no sneakin' around after you take my name. And there'd better be no six-month baby. I may not read books or talk fancy, but I can count."

"I said forget it. It wouldn't have worked anyway."

Flynn wheeled his horse back toward them. "What's up?"

"Just gettin' a few things straight between us," Drake said, before she could answer.

"You still want her?" Flynn asked.

"He doesn't." She tried to pull away from them, but Drake's fist had closed over her pony's bridle and he held her fast.

"Pay no heed to her," Drake said. "We come to an agreement."

"No, we haven't," she protested. "Da, take me home, please. I'm sorry I hurt you, but—"

"Nothin' more to say to you, girl. You've heard my offer. Drake, Damon, or Virginia. I'll provide a decent dowry, so you won't go penniless to your husband, whoever he is."

"Sounds like a fair offer to me," Drake said. "I'd prefer hard coin. I've a mind to buy Jacob Baker's black bull, and he wants a pretty piece for it."

Shannon looked from one to another in disbelief as they proceeded to haggle over her bride price as though she wasn't even here. It was clear that what she wanted didn't matter. She was an object, probably worth less than a cow to either of them. It was wrong, so wrong, but what choice did she have?

Returning East and becoming a servant again was out

of the question. The sadness in her heart swelled until it nearly choked her. Maybe she should just do what they wanted. She was only a woman after all, and if she'd lost the love of her life, maybe obeying her father would make him love her again.

It was night when Storm Dancer reached Truth Teller's trading post. He left his horse and circled the log palisade. Tucked in the pouch at his waist were bits of fresh venison for the white trader's dogs. His father had taught him long ago that a dog with a full belly doesn't bark but welcomes the hunter who brings the meat.

He'd scaled this wall many times before, but tonight all his senses were alert. His heart pounded, and his mouth was dry. He had come to ask Shannon to wait for him. He intended to find out if she would leave her people and become one of the *Tsalagi*, if she would consent to be his wife. He would promise to care for her all of her days. He would pledge his life's blood and his honor to her and to her alone. And if she would have him, it would make him the happiest man alive.

Minutes later, having soothed the hounds and crossed the compound unseen and unheard, Storm Dancer tapped at Shannon's window. He hadn't brought the bone flute. It had been difficult enough to convince his uncle and father that he had to see Truth Teller's daughter before he went north with them. His father especially had not been pleased.

"You risk much," he'd warned. "You know your mother wants you to marry Cardinal."

"I told her I wanted another."

"Have you thought what danger you put your white woman in?" Flint had asked.

Winter Fox had added his words of caution to Flint's,

but nothing would turn Storm Dancer from his mission. If Shannon would have him, he would have no other. And if she agreed, he would deal with his mother.

It was his feeling that his father allowed his mother far too much power. Firefly would not decide for him. She would be angry, but she loved him too much to disown him. And once she met Shannon and saw how true her heart, his mother would relent and welcome her. Let someone else fulfill the ancient prophecy. He was a warrior of the Cherokee, nothing more.

No sound came from within the cabin. Smoke rose from the chimney. The house was not deserted. Surely his love did not sleep so soundly that she couldn't hear his knocks against her shutter. He tapped again and whispered her name. "Shannon."

"She is gone."

Storm Dancer spun to see Oona standing in the shadows, a dog silent at her knee. "You? I—"

"You should not be here," she admonished. The dog wagged his tail. Storm Dancer didn't know if it was one he'd fed or not.

"I come to speak to Shannon." They fell easily into the Cherokee tongue. "Tell her that—"

"Are you deaf that you don't hear me, or do you choose not to understand? She's gone to the English fort to marry a white man."

He felt as though an arrow had pierced him. "Married? She can't be. She didn't say anything about—"

"What did you think? That she'd pick you? A *Tsalagi*?"

He took a step back. How was it possible that Shannon had kissed him . . . lain in his arms . . . made love to him when all the while she'd planned to marry a white man?

"Ahh. So that's how it is," Oona scoffed. "Her new husband is one of the settlers from Green Valley, a man from the wagons that brought her through the mountains."

"She said nothing of another man."

"You are a fool, Storm Dancer. A fool if you believe that Truth Teller would let you have his daughter. He is ashamed of me, but he cares for me and his coming child enough to keep me in his house. For his daughter, he wants a white man. You are *Tsalagi*. She is white. You can't be together. It was a foolish dream."

Storm Dancer fought to keep his voice from cracking. "Is this marriage her father's wish or hers?"

"The man has been coming to the post to see her. The choice was hers."

"Are you certain?" he asked. "Was she forced to marry this man?"

"Go from this house," Oona said. "Do not come here again. Do not try to follow Truth Teller's daughter and ruin her life. There is nothing for you here."

"So be it. Peace to you, daughter of the Delaware." He turned and sprinted into the darkness. He was not a man for tears. He could not cry as other men did, but his eyes burned as though live coals rested in them.

He scaled the fence and crossed the open place to where he'd left his horse. Far off, an owl hooted. "I hear you, brother," he said. And he wondered if the owl called to a lost mate or if he called to herald another death.

Shannon had chosen another man over him. She had given him her body and taken his heart in exchange. She had spoken words of love, and then had returned to her father's house and betrayed him with another.

For this he had shamed his mother and broken tradition. For this he had hurt Cardinal and made her to seem of little worth in the eyes of the women. All for a yellow-haired woman who cared so little for him that she could not tell him that she had taken pleasure with him but it meant nothing to her.

So be it. He could not return to his mother and tell

her that he'd been mistaken, that he was a fool, that a white-skinned witch had cast a spell over him. That he could not do. And he could not go to Cardinal and say, "Now that she won't have me, I'll take you to wife." That he could not do, either.

He would take no wife. He would do whatever his clan and nation asked of him. If it was their wish, he would go to war against the whites. He would lay down his life in the service of his people. But he would never give his heart to a woman again. He would trust no woman and allow none to pass beneath the shield he would erect around his shattered spirit.

Oona and Truth Teller need not fear that he would follow Shannon to her new husband's lodge. He would never lift his hand in anger against her, her father, or her man. But he would do everything in his power to drive the rest of the whites back beyond the mountains, out of Cherokee land. He would do what he must to protect the land of the *Tsalagi* from the white-skinned invaders.

The pain curled within his breast, coiling and writhing like a rattlesnake. And when the pain was too great, he threw back his head and howled one great wolf cry of black and bitter anguish.

Oona heard the owl. Shortly after came the unearthly howl that raised gooseflesh on the back of her arms. The owl's call was bad luck, but the wolf cry was worse. She knew the sound was not made by any living wolf but some spirit creature. Frightened, she called the hounds inside the house and barred the door. She threw logs on the fire, despite the heat, and crouched by the hearth.

The dogs drew close around her and she stroked their heads for courage. "What could I do?" she whispered in the language of her childhood. "I said only what my good husband bade me say."

The hound bitch raised her head and gazed into Oona's eyes.

"I lied. Yes, it was a lie, but I had to do what my husband wanted."

The hound looked unconvinced.

"It is better this way. Shannon will marry one of her own. Storm Dancer's mother would never permit him to take her to wife. She would have her killed first. Either way, he would never have her."

The dog stretched out and closed her eyes.

"Does the owl call for me?" Oona murmured into the empty cabin. "Does death wait for me?" She threw another log on the hearth and sat awake all through the night staring into the coals.


On the third day, Flynn turned back. "Fort Hood is only a little way ahead," he said. "I need to return to the post."

"Take me home with you," Shannon begged. "Please, Da. Don't make me do this."

"I expect you to marry her as soon as the minister can read the words," Flynn said. "If I hear otherwise, Drake Clark, you'll have me to answer to."

"Yes, sir," Drake said. "I give you my word."

"And if I refuse, will you drag me to the priest? Force me to say the words?" she asked. In the hours and days of their journey, she'd thought she'd reconciled herself to her fate. She'd as good as given her pledge to Drake, but now, when Da was leaving, she lost her courage.

"You'll thank me for this in time, girl," Flynn said. He rode close and grasped her outstretched hand. "God go with ye, darlin'."

"Da!" She tried to hold tight to his fingers, but he pulled away. "Don't leave me."

Drake dismounted and took hold of her pony's bridle. "You take care with your hair, Flynn O'Shea," he said. "And don't worry about Shannon. Ma will see to her."

Without another word, her father slapped his horse's rump and turned the animal's head west, back into the mountains, the way they had come, leaving her as alone and desolate as she had ever been.

# Chapter 16

Shannon's forced stay at Fort Hood was every bit as miserable as she'd guessed it would be. Drake, Damon, and most of the able men had followed the soldiers on an expedition to head off a combined attack by the French and Shawnee or the Cherokee if they rose against the English. Even Nathan Clark had gone, as eager as any of the rest to kill as many Indians and Frenchmen as possible.

Shannon was left with the women and children, and nine soldiers considered too infirm, or useless, to go into the field. In command of those sorry representatives of His Majesty's finest was a young captain, fresh from England, who had never set eyes on an Indian until he'd reached the Smoky Mountains. Captain Wormwood, in Shannon's opinion, would have been of more use changing baby nappies than giving orders.

There were far too many people within the walls. The settlers, crammed with their dogs, belongings, and livestock into a muddy section of the wooden enclosure, were frightened. Worse, it had begun to rain shortly after Shannon had arrived with Drake and his brother. Rain had fallen for all but three days of the two weeks since she'd arrived. With the rain had come sickness, a plague of fleas, and running of the bowels. The stench of vomit mixed with dog droppings and cow manure. The awful smells did nothing to encourage Shannon's appetite, especially when their diet consisted of salt pork, dried peas, and hard tack riddled with weevils.

Contrary to what Drake had promised her father, he hadn't insisted that the two of them marry as soon as they reached the fort. Instead, Drake had turned Shannon over to his mother, Hannah, and rushed off to play soldier. The delay hadn't bothered Shannon, but the older woman's obvious disapproval of the betrothal made living in an eight-by-six tent with her and Jane, Cory Jakes's widow, nearly impossible.

True to her sour disposition and the lack of proper grazing, Betty the cow had caused trouble, kicking at the other cows and dogs, and providing only half her normal amount of milk. What there was, Shannon couldn't drink, not when there were hungry babies and crying children to feed.

"I don't know why my son wants to marry you," Hannah complained one evening as rain beat on the roof of the leaky tent and seeped under the walls to dampen the blankets. "You're not cut out to be a wife. You've caused trouble between my boys, and you're too forward for a woman by a long shot."

Shannon would have answered back, but she agreed with everything Hannah Clark said. She wasn't cut out to be a wife, and Drake probably did deserve better. But she didn't intend to spend the rest of her life as a servant, either.

It was "Shannon, can you clean up this young'n fer me?" And "Girl, someone needs to milk that cow." And "Fetch a bucket, I'm gonna puke." Hannah scolded and gave her orders, as did most of the married women. Jane Jakes did nothing but weep, and Alice Clayton, the only girl anywhere near to Shannon's age, turned up her nose and refused to speak to her at all.

Wind rocked the tent. A seam split, and water poured in, soaking Jane who began to wail. Hannah began to berate the woman as if she had done something to cause the tear in the roof, and Shannon could stand it no longer. Grabbing her blanket and throwing it around her, she stepped out into the blustery night.

The nearest shelter was the lean-to reserved for the soldiers' mounts, now mostly empty. Shannon ran for it, ducked into the shadowy interior, and collided with a man.

"Well, now, honey, I wondered where you were." Male arms locked around her.

The voice was either Drake's or his brother, Damon's. But even for them, the tones were rough. As her captor pulled her against his chest, she caught a whiff of rum.

"Let me—" Her protest was cut off by a hard mouth. Frightened, she struggled to pull away and bit down as the man tried to thrust his tongue between her teeth.

"Don't be like that, darling."

"Drake?" The harder she wiggled, the tighter he held her. "Are you drunk?"

"It's Damon." He kissed her again. This time she made no effort to fight him, but she kept her teeth clenched together. He grunted and nuzzled her neck. When a big hand fumbled for her breast, she stomped down on the top of his foot. "Ouch! Damn it! That's no way to treat a man."

As he hopped on one foot, she slipped free and backed away, putting a wet horse between her and Drake's intoxicated brother. "What's wrong with you?" she demanded. Anger replaced her fear. Damon wouldn't dare assault her. If she screamed, someone would hear and come running.

"Nothing. Nothing that you couldn't fix."

He grabbed for her, but she backed up until she hit the wall and her hand closed around the wooden handle of a pitchfork. "Stay away from me," she warned. "Or I'll stick you so full of holes your mother will be able to see daylight through you."

"Bitch. You're making a mistake, you know. I'm the one you should be marrying. We're alike, you and me. Drake's wrong for you."

"Did you tell him that?"

"Yeah. He didn't like it much, either." He leaned on the log post that held up the roof and rubbed his foot. "Damn, Shannon. You didn't have to do that. All I wanted was a kiss."

"Drake would rip your head off if I told him what you did." She raised the pitchfork.

"Tell away. And I'll tell him you wanted it. That you led me on. Who do you think he'd believe?"

"Are you sure?"

Damon cursed under his breath. "What? You meeting some other man out here? Some soldier? All decent women are in their tents."

"Where is Drake? And why are you back without him?" She was certain that he wouldn't try to grab her again, but she kept her weapon in case.

She was so disgusted, she was of a mind to run the pitchfork through him anyway. Would she never be done with fighting randy men off? At the orphanage, there were always hot hands reaching for unsuspecting little girls, and later, at the tavern, it was worse. Every Jack Dandy with two copper for a mug of ale thought he could tumble the serving wenches at his leisure.

"Shannon? What the hell are you doin' out here in the dark?" Drake's bulk materialized out of the rainy night.

"Don't worry, brother," Damon said. "I'm here with

her. I was just telling her that the two of us come back with George Hatapi, the Delaware scout."

"Lord in heaven, woman." Drake pushed between the horses, took hold of her shoulders, and gave her a rough kiss. "I missed you bad."

His mouth tasted of rum and tobacco, but she wasn't repelled by it. Marriage to Drake couldn't be that bad, could it? He was a simple man, with simple tastes. Surely, they could work things out between them.

The thought that Drake's kiss didn't thrill her the way that Storm Dancer's had, surfaced, but she pushed it away. Storm Dancer had married another woman. He didn't want her. He'd gotten what he wanted from her and then abandoned her. If she was going to have a life, she'd have to make one for herself.

Drake kissed her again, and Damon laughed. "Guess I'd best leave you two lovebirds alone. I'll go see what Ma has in the cooking pot. We like to starved on the trail, but we killed Shawnee. And a Frenchman. That ought to teach them a lesson."

"I hope she's got something to eat," Drake echoed. "I've had my fill of half-raw squirrel and hard tack."

Shannon forced herself to relax in Drake's embrace. Soon, she would be his wife. A husband had a right to expect certain things from a wife. "I'm glad you're safe," she said. "Is your father all right? Was anyone hurt? Any of our people, that is?"

Drake kissed her again, gave her a bear hug, and released her. "Two dead, one broke his leg fallin' off his horse when Injuns started screeching. I think we'll be safe to go back to the farm in the mornin'."

Shannon took a deep breath. "Will we be married first? The women said there was no parson or priest here. How could we—"

"Camp commander can read the words, give us a paper.

Pa asked. Then, first chance we get, we'll get it done right. Priest or minister, don't matter to me. But it wouldn't be fittin' to take you to my house without havin' some kind of ceremony. Pa wouldn't stand for it."

No priest? Not even a Protestant man of God? Shannon's gut clenched. Maybe she should refuse and go back East. Start over. But she knew she wouldn't. She knew she couldn't bear to put the mountains between her and her father—to never see her half-sister or half-brother. That would be worse than dying. She'd been alone and unwanted too long. This good man had asked for her hand in marriage, and only a fool would refuse.

"Whatever you say, Drake," she murmured. "Whatever you think best."

He laughed. "What I think best is you give me a sample of being married, here and now. Damnation, I'm hard as a poker just thinkin' about our weddin' night."

She stiffened. "No. It wouldn't be right. After the wedding, Drake. It's the right way to start off our marriage."

"Hellfire, woman, it ain't like I'm askin' fer somethin' you ain't already give some other Johnny."

She darted under a tethered horse's neck and out into the downpour. "After the wedding, Drake Clark. There'll be time enough for pinch and tickle once we're man and wife."

"Hang on, Shannon!"

"After the wedding!" she repeated. And, ignoring his pleas, she dashed back through the mud to the comparative safety of his mother's crowded tent.

Flynn O'Shea settled onto the bench on his front porch. "Drake Clark's a little rough, but he's a decent man. He'll give her a good home."

Oona bent over the cradleboard she was stitching.

"Your daughter is like you. She can find water in a rock. She will make a good life wherever she is."

The hound bitch laid her head on Oona's foot, and the woman scratched the dog behind her ears.

"It was hard to send her away."

"Yes."

"I think she'll be safe enough in Green Valley. The raiders that hit the settlement weren't Cherokee at all. One Indian they killed, the one in the turban, was a half-breed Creek. The rest may have been robbers or those runaway slaves we heard about. If there were any Shawnee, they didn't leave any proof."

"Good. The Cherokee make bad enemies."

Flynn rubbed at his right arm. The recurring ache had returned. The long spell of rain had kept him housebound, and for once he didn't mind. He just didn't seem to have the energy he usually had. All spring and into the summer he'd been short of breath. He wasn't sleeping well either, just couldn't get comfortable.

Worrying about Shannon had made his insomnia worse. She'd been so unhappy. Turning away from her tears had ripped him apart, but he had to think of her. There was no question of her being with a Cherokee, not Storm Dancer, not any of them. It was like mixing saltwater and good Irish whiskey. It could never have worked. Once the fire died back, both would have regretted it. And considering the boy's mother and what she could do, if she had a mind to, he'd done the only thing any father could. He'd chosen to send her away.

"She'll make Drake a good wife." *Like you,* he almost added. Oona had made him happier than he'd ever thought possible when he'd brought her home. He never noticed her scarred face anymore, just how pretty she was and how graceful she moved.

Had he thought his first wife was beautiful when she

carried Shannon? He couldn't remember. But Oona was beautiful. He loved the swell of her belly and the womanly way her breasts had plumped up. Best of all was the peace she brought with her. Wherever she was, nestled together in their bed, camped beside a wild tumbling stream down some high valley, or helping him in the store, it didn't matter. When they were together, life got suddenly easier to bear.

Except this thing with Shannon and Storm Dancer. . . .

"Firefly would have sent someone to kill her before she'd let my girl have her son. She's no more anxious for a white daughter-in-law than I am a red son-in-law."

Silence from Oona. The only sounds were the panting of the dogs, frogs and insects, and the whistle of a mockingbird. The rain had tapered off, and a red sunset spilled across the western sky.

"You think I did wrong, wife?"

"This woman told him to go and never return."

"Like I asked ye."

No answer.

Flynn tapped his pipe against the floor and pushed the burnt tobacco through the crack between the boards with the toe of his moccasin. "That's the thing about bein' a father. Sometimes you have to hurt a colleen to do what's best for her."

Oona raised her gaze to meet his. "Are you well? I see pain in your eyes. And you're rubbing that arm again. I've made a tea from the inner bark of black ash. If you will take it, it will ease your weariness."

He tamped Indian tobacco into the pipe bowl. Later, he would light it from the coals on the hearth. For now, he would enjoy the sensation of the stem between his lips. The pipe was nearly worn out, like him. Maybe he'd take some of the seasoned cherry wood hanging in the loft and whittle a new bowl tomorrow.

One of the dogs let out a yip. The bitch growled, low in her throat, and the hackles rose on her neck. Instantly, all three hounds sprang off the porch and ran barking toward the small gate that led to the spring path. Flynn reached for his gun.

Oona's eyes widened. "What is it?"

"Bear, maybe. Or a stray wolf."

She looked at him with knowing eyes. No wolf or bear would come within a hundred yards of the post in daylight.

"Go on go inside," he ordered. "Lock the door. If you hear shots or anything you don't like, hide." He was already down the steps and striding toward the barred gate. Then he felt the sensation of a puff of cold air on the nape of his neck.

"Go carefully, husband," Oona called after him.

He stopped and glanced back. Tiny black sparks peppered the air in front of his eyes. The pain in his chest twisted and he sucked in air. "If the worst happens, and you survive, go to Split Cane's village. She'll take you in."

"If the bad thing happens, I will go where you go."

"Damned if you will, woman. By all that's holy, if trouble comes, you look out for our coming babe. You hear me?" The dogs were snarling and throwing themselves at the palisade wall.

Flynn forced himself to turn back toward the commotion. Lifting one leg after another, running, breathing heavy, but running. A mountain lion, he told himself. Maybe a woods' buffalo. An old bull, rank and musty, horns scarred from age and combat.

In his heart, he knew he was whistling in the dark. In his heart, he knew what was waiting beyond the log fence. And he wasn't surprised when he heard the first screech of Shawnee war whoops and saw the rain of flaming arrows arc through the gathering twilight.

\* \* \*

Shannon was glad to see the last of Drake's family and neighbors . . . her family and neighbors, she realized with a start. She was no longer Shannon O'Shea, Flynn's daughter, but Shannon Clark, Hannah and Nathan's daughter-in-law. Mrs. Drake Clark. It sounded strange, but maybe she would accustom herself to it in time.

Drake hung his rifle over the hearth. It was a small, neat cabin, one room only, but the floors were plank, the log walls tightly packed to keep out rain and snow. There was a crude table and two benches, a stone fireplace with an iron bar to hang kettles, and a wide hearth to prevent sparks from igniting the floorboards.

"What do you think of the house?" Drake asked. He was pleased, both with being back on his farm and the gifts of food and blankets the settlement had provided. His mother had given them a butter churn, and Nathan promised a pair of piglets as soon as his speckled sow farrowed. "It's not big, but once the young'ns start comin', we can build on."

"It's a fine house," she agreed.

She was tired from the long day, first the brief marriage ceremony, which seemed like no wedding at all to her, and later from the packing and walk back from the fort to the valley. She could have ridden, but she had Betty to lead, and most of the women and children were on foot. It would have seemed presumptuous to ride when older women walked. Instead, she'd put two small children on her pony's back and trudged along through the mud with the others.

There was no wedding ring on her hand. Drake had promised one when he sold his first horses to the soldiers at Fort Hood and a ring could be ordered from Virginia. She'd had no bridal dress, no wedding feast, and no celebration. Her marriage had been a hasty one, practical, and fitting to her new station in life—wife of a farmer. She tried to tell herself how lucky she was, how much more this was than she had ever expected when she was scrubbing floors at Klank's tavern. So why didn't she feel joy? And why wasn't she looking forward to her wedding night?

"You hungry?" Drake took a jug from the mantel, uncorked it, and took a long swallow.

"No, thank you." She tried not to look at the wide pallet in one corner. There was no bed yet, just a grass-stuffed mattress and two feed sack pillows.

Tonight, she would allow Drake to take his husbandly privileges. He would touch and fondle her and pump himself between her legs until his passion was sated. She wondered if she would feel anything but embarrassment and discomfort. If she could allow Drake his rightful mating without feeling anything herself, it would be less painful. But experiencing the same thrill tonight that Storm Dancer had given her would be too terrible to endure.

"Come over here, woman, and pull these off for me." Drake dragged a bench over to the hearth, sat down, and thrust out one muddy boot. "The leather's soaked through." He took another sip of the spirits in the jug and put the cork back in.

She came without protest. If she was going to be a dutiful wife, she needed to learn to obey orders from her husband without putting up a fuss. Drake slapped her playfully on the behind, and she tried not to show her distaste for his touch as she took hold of the sodden boot.

Laughing, Drake caught her between his legs and pulled her in to him. He pawed her breasts and fisted a hand in her hair. When she opened her mouth to protest, he kissed her, deep and searing. The taste of raw whiskey burned her mouth.

"Shy, ain't ye?" he teased. "No need to be. Not with me. I reckon we'll set that bed on fire in a little while." He stroked the rising tumescence at his crotch.

Shannon brushed her mouth where he'd bruised it with his kiss. He'd kissed her so hard that her lip had split. It hurt, but not nearly as much as the thought that she wasn't ready for what was to come between them.

It was almost funny. She was as jumpy as a virgin. Moths tumbled in the pit of her stomach, and her mouth was as dry as cattail fluff. This was Drake. He wasn't a stranger. She'd known him for months, and now he was her lawful husband. She'd never been a foolish chit to squeal and take fright at whatever life handed her. She was still Shannon, and she'd made the choice to marry this good man with her eyes wide open. She'd fulfill her part of the bargain, no matter what.

Drake gave her a little shove and raised his foot again. She pulled, but the boot didn't give. "Damn it, girl. Put some muscle in it."

She yanked harder and the boot came off with a sucking noise. Instantly, a wave of nausea rose in her throat as a rotten stench filled her nostrils. The sock under the boot was filthy and full of holes.

"When did you last wash your feet?" She flung the nasty boot on the hearth and stripped off the sock. Drake's foot was hardly any cleaner. His toenails were so long and nasty they resembled untrimmed sheep's hooves.

"Smells some, don't it? Last fight we had with the Shawnee, I was wading in blood ankle deep. Guess I could take a little lye soap and water to these puppies before we jump between Ma's sheets."

Swallowing her distaste, she reached for the other boot. This one was even harder to get off, but when it did come free, she'd tumbled backward onto the floor with her unwelcome cargo.

Drake guffawed as she slung the second boot into the cold fireplace. "Careful there," he said. "You'll damage my trophies."

As she picked herself up off the floor, she glanced into the fireplace to see what he was talking about. It appeared to be a string of mangy animal hides, ragged and black in color, suspended from a hook set into the mortar.

"Hung 'm in there to smoke," he said. "Smoke cures'm fast. Do you have any idea how much money they'll bring back in Virginia?"

"Cures what? What are you talking about?" She stared at the pelts in disbelief. Then realization set in. Clapping a hand over her mouth, she uttered a low cry.

It wasn't animal pelts, but human scalps. Scalps dangled from the charred rope. And one trophy bore the unmistakable remains of woodpecker feathers tangled in the bloodstained hair.

# Chapter 17

The fire beside the great game trail that led north to the Ohio River had burned low. The Cherokee delegation to the meeting with the French and the Shawnee had traveled far and fast. A day earlier, they had left their horses in a secluded valley, under the care of two teenage boys eager to prove their worth, and traveled on foot due to the rough country.

If Storm Dancer had believed that his father and uncle were showing the signs of age, he soon learned differently. Winter Fox and Flint often took the lead, their moccasin-clad feet flying down the twisting path at a dead run with barely stops for water or rest.

The group from Storm Dancer's village had joined with those of Three Spears Camp, Old Woman Mountain, and Split Cane's village. Three of the representatives were female, all council members. Firefly had considered becoming part of the expedition, but the clan mothers had decided that with the threat of war imminent, she was needed more at home. Storm Dancer was one of five young men entrusted with the security of the *Tsalagi* delegation. All were notable warriors, chosen for bravery and skill at arms.

Twenty-one had set out for the parley at Big Pascal's trading post, and now that the boys had been left behind to protect the horses, there were nineteen, a formidable unit, despite the danger. Today had been an especially tough day of travel because of the constant rain. Even Storm Dancer's muscles felt the strain of the hours of running over rough ground.

Most of the party had been reluctant to linger talking around the fire, but had rolled in blankets soon after they'd broken their fast. Another day's journey would take them into enemy territory. After tomorrow, they would travel only by night and double the watch.

Tonight, Storm Dancer and a brave from Split Cane's village had taken the second shift of guard duty. They circled the camp at a distance of several hundred yards, watching and listening, a difficult task because of the wind gusts and continuing rain. The trees here were young, the underbrush thick, and it was hard to move from place to place without becoming entangled in thickets. After two circuits, Storm Dancer climbed a beech tree and settled back in a crotch of branches.

As long as he kept moving, he could keep Shannon from his mind, but the pain of losing her was too fresh to recede for long. A night like this should be spent in a man's lodge, his woman in his arms. He remembered the night they had shared in the cave together, how desirable she had been, and how much he'd wanted to leap over the fire and make love to her. If he let himself linger on her memory, he could feel her soft pale skin against his, remember the taste of her mouth and the tiny moans she made, deep in her throat, when he entered her.

Thinking about Shannon was agony. Now, of all times, he needed a clear head. But her spell was powerful. She had tossed him away for another, but she had not broken the bonds that drew him to her. Would he ever be free of wanting her . . . of listening for her laughter?

A great horned owl swooped overhead, and a rabbit shrieked. Storm Dancer came instantly alert. Motionless, he peered through the rain and strained to hear footsteps in the trees as great drops of water struck his face and ran down through his hair and over his throat.

He heard the first night hawk cry shortly after the spirit owl had warned him. He waited. A second false bird called from the left, closer to the river, along the route of a smaller deer trail—a track so narrow and twisting that a careless eye would miss it. Storm Dancer smiled into the night.

A snap of twigs under the trees drew his attention to the silhouette of a white man in a tricorn hat. As he passed by, Storm Dancer could see the dull gleam of shiny buttons on his coat. He knew the stranger was no Indian by the way he walked, even before the unmistakable odor of wet wool and French soap wafted up to his nostrils.

Like a cat, Storm Dancer sprang from the branch. He landed light as a puma, one arm around the Frenchman's throat, one knee in the small of the man's back. He didn't need his knife. The man's neck snapped like kindling. He gave one startled gasp and crumbled facedown into the wet briars.

Storm Dancer paused long enough to snatch the heavy silver gorget from the dead man's neck. He was no thief, but the insignia might identify his enemy later. Only a high-ranking French soldier would wear such an adornment. His mother would want to see it.

As he rose from a crouched position, he heard the first shots at the campsite. War cries followed, and immediately after, the screams of the injured and dying. Storm

Dancer yanked his tomahawk from his belt and plunged forward through the underbrush toward the battle.

Shannon shrank back from the gruesome trophies hanging in the fireplace, and whirled on Drake. "Where did you get those? Do you know what they are?"

His mouth gaped open like a dying fish, and he stared at her as if she'd lost her mind. "They're scalps. I told ye, a dealer back East will pay me—"

"Who did you buy them from?"

"Buy'm, hell," he sputtered. His face reddened as he rose to his feet. "I took'm fair and square. Shot and skinned them myself."

She clamped a hand over her mouth, certain she was going to be sick. The little scalp with the feathers could only belong to a child, one child in particular, the adorable little boy she'd met at Split Cane's camp. "You were there? You killed children?"

"Nits make lice."

"Murderer!" She grabbed up the nearest thing within reach, the filthy boot she'd just flung down, and threw it at Drake. It struck him full in the chest, splattering mud over his face and into his mouth and nose.

Drake cursed and lunged at her, but she snatched up a two-foot length of firewood and bounced it off his head. He howled and grabbed his bleeding temple, and she darted across the room and seized his skinning knife from the table where he'd dropped it.

"Get out!"

"Are you crazy, bitch? I'm not getting out of my own house!" He lunged at her. Shannon stood her ground and slashed at him with the knife.

"Get out before I cut your pizzle off!" She held the weapon low, the way her father had taught her. She was half his size, but she'd been butchering game animals since she was eight years old.

He hesitated, plainly trying to work up his nerve to disarm her. "You're my wife, damn it! You can't pull a knife on me! I'll beat the crap out of you!"

"Try it and you'll be singing soprano in church choir!" A nasty scum rose in her throat and she gagged. "I'll never live with a murderer . . . a monster."

"Get a hold of yerself, you lunatic woman." His bluster became a coward's whine. "Only two of them scalps is kids. One was full-grown buck. Come at me with a war club. I'm lucky I even survived."

She took a step forward, still holding the knife, ready to strike. "What were you doing there? I heard the killers were from Virginia. How did you—"

"They come through Green Valley lookin' fer volunteers."

"And you went? What kind of man are you?"

"Yer hysterical. Injun lover, just like yer pa. Can't you see? It's the only way. This country won't be fit for God-fearin' folk until we rid these mountains of them savages."

"You're a fool, Drake. You've put every man, woman, and child in this valley in danger. If Split Cane's people knew you were part of that raiding party, they'd wipe out this settlement."

"And who's gonna tell?" he demanded. "Not you. Not my lovin' wife, crazy as a Virginia politician!"

He tried to grab her, and she slashed the blade across the back of his palm. Blood welled up. "Now you done it!" he roared. "Now I'm gonna—"

Whatever Drake intended to threaten was lost in the crash of the cabin door. Damon burst in. "What the hell?" Drake's twin was dressed for travel and had a long rifle in one hand.

"Grab her, brother! She's lost her mind!"

"Stay out of this!" Shannon said.

Damon stared from one to the other.

"Grab her, damn it!" Drake repeated.

Shannon glared at Damon. "Come near me, and I'll give you the same."

Damon threw up his hands. "I'm not getting between a man and his bride on their wedding night."

"Then if you're not going to help, get out!" Drake said.

"Pa needs you. Captain Wormwood took out six men this morning to hunt fresh meat. They walked into an Injun ambush. The captain and four of the soldiers died. Massacred. Only one made it back to Fort Hood alive. Pa says we got to go back afore they hit here. Round up your livestock. We're leaving in half an hour."

Drake looked at her. "Did you hear that? We gotta go. But don't think I'll forget this. You're not gettin' off without—"

"I think you're both crazy." Damon leaned his rifle against the doorjamb. "You can fight anytime. Why you'd rather cut each other than make bacon on your wedding night puzzles me, but we've got to get out of here before we all end up like Captain Wormwood."

"I'm not going back to the fort," Shannon said. "I'd rather take my chances with the Indians."

Drake swore. "Told ye she was crazy, didn't I, brother?"

"You go, if you're scared," she said. "I'm never setting foot in that fort again."

"You're my wife. You'll do what I say!"

"Will I? How's that working for you so far?"

"Settle this," Damon warned. "I'm getting back to Pa's. If you stay, it's your hair."

"I'd rather stay than go one step with a child killer. Did you know about those?" she asked Damon. "They're scalps." She pointed toward the hearth. "Or were you with him? Did you murder children too?"

Damon scoffed. "Not me. I don't like Injuns any better

than the next white man, but I'm not about to risk my neck wandering around the mountains in the night. Drake did that all on his self. Pa wasn't pleased about it, neither."

"That's the first sensible thing I've heard out of your pa." She moved so that her back was to the wall, but kept her gaze on Drake. "You can tell him that this marriage is over."

"What? Ye think anybody would give ye a dee'vorce over some damned Injun scalps?" Drake asked incredulously. "Now I know you're cracked. May as well lock you in the madhouse with the rest of the loonies."

"Divorce, annulment, I don't care what you call it. I doubt if our so-called marriage is legal anyway. You run back to the fort with your family. I mean to go home to my father."

"Small chance of that," Drake said. "It's three days over the mountains. If the savages don't get you, the wolves and panthers will."

"Flynn didn't sound much like he wanted you," Damon put in. "You'd best lower your hackles and come with us."

"My father didn't know what you'd done. We were there that night; did you know that, Drake? You killed his friends. You could have killed him or me. I know he would have killed you if he'd gotten you in his rifle sights."

Drake gathered up his boots and yanked them on over his bare feet. "Leave her," he said to his brother. "She'll change her tune once she sees us movin' out."

"Will I?" she said. "Wait and see. I'll shoot you myself before I lie down in your bed."

"You're bound to leave him, then," Damon asked.

"I am. And God help anybody who tries to take me by force."

Damon shook his head. "All right. I can see you're

whipped up something fierce. Tell you what. You stay here in the valley, we'll go. If you bide here until we get back from the fort and Injuns don't massacre you—if you still want to be shut of him, I'll see you home to your pa."

"The hell you will," Drake said. He took down his rifle and grabbed his vest. "Don't come cryin' to me, bitch, if you end up dead."

Damon touched his forelock in salute. "Gotta admire you, Shannon O'Shea. You do know how to pitch a temper."

Drake sucked at the cut on his hand. "You'll be sorry for this," he promised.

"I'll wait here for you," she said to Damon, "but I won't change my mind. It was a mistake for me to marry him in the first place. No matter what happens, it can't be worse than sleeping with a murderer."

Shannon didn't sleep at all that night. Instead, she'd sat by the hearth, a rifle by her feet. Whether she dreaded Drake's return or an Indian attack more, she didn't know. Finally, at dawn, Betty's loud bawling drew her from the cabin, bucket in one hand, loaded rifle in another.

Damon had left her his own rifle, assuring her that his father would lend him one of his. Drake had tried to talk him out of it, and Shannon remembered his final words. "Whatever happens is on her own head. Let the Injuns have her. She's no good to me."

The rain had stopped, and the world seemed new and fresh as Shannon walked to the pound where the cow stood by the gate. Drake had taken his horses, and he'd driven off his cattle. Only Betty and the big-headed pony remained. Badger raised his head and nickered as he saw her coming.

Shannon wished Drake had taken the cow but was

glad he'd left her pony. Betty had to be milked morning and night or she'd become sick. Shannon wondered what she'd do with gallons of milk and no one else to use it. It seemed such a waste when she knew that the settlers' children would be hungry inside the fort walls. They'd be lucky if none of them caught typhus or the pox. Stuffing so many people in a small space without clean water and a place to dispose of waste was a recipe for disaster. She'd seen far too much of that at the children's home.

She leaned her rifle against the fence and went to the shed for grain. Both the pony and cow could use a good meal. There was grass in the pound, but not much, and the horses and cattle had churned that to a muddy stew last night.

The little cabin stood proudly in the center of a clearing. Off to the left, Drake had cleared land to put in a crop, but charred tree stumps remained scattered across the field. The other homesteads were far enough away that Shannon couldn't see them. If the neighbors had remained in the valley, she supposed smoke from their chimneys would have been visible, but this morning, the sky was clear and robin's egg blue.

She liked the solitude. As she milked the cow, dodging swishes of Betty's manure-caked tail and the occasional kick, she reveled in the sounds of birdsong and bees. A bluebird lit on a fence post and preened jewel-like feathers while a wren chattered away from the tree beside the house. She thought she could have been happy here, if it weren't for Drake. But now, any marriage with him was impossible.

She'd unknowingly married a murderer.

Not married, she told herself. There had been no priest, no mention of God. The fort commander had simply listed their names and ages and personal information on a sheet torn from a ledger and declared them husband and wife. The paper was in her apron pocket still.

Shannon stood up and set the bucket aside. She stepped far enough from the cow to keep the wicked animal from kicking over the milk, and removed her marriage lines from her pocket. Betty stretched out her neck, bared yellow teeth, and tried to snatch the paper from her hands.

*Nathanial Drake Clark, farmer, born 1730, Virginia Colony, freeman, states his intention to take to wife one Mary Shannon O'Shea, freewoman, late of Baltimore, Maryland Colony, daughter of Flynn O'Shea.*

Tears blurred her eyes as she scanned the date and the commandant's rank and signature. This wasn't a marriage license. It was a bill of sale. She might as well have been a cow.

Betty leaned back on the rope that held her to the fence and swished her tail. Her bulging eyes rolled in her head as she tried desperately to reach the creased page in Shannon's hand.

"You want this?" Shannon asked. "Have it." She fed the cow the paper and watched with satisfaction as Betty chewed and swallowed the entire thing.

Shannon tried to keep busy through the day. She hobbled both the cow and the pony to keep them from wandering too far and turned them loose to graze. She swept and scrubbed the cabin floor, strained the milk through clean linen and poured it into a flat pan to let the cream rise.

She hoed the garden, pulled a few greens and turnips, and set Johnny cake to bake in a Dutch oven on the hearth. Then she drew enough water from the well to wash her clothes. After she'd hung the garments to dry on nearby bushes, she carried more water and heated it for a bath.

She washed her hair and scrubbed herself from the crown of her head to the tips of her toes, scrubbing off every trace of Drake Clark and the filthy English fort. She doubted that hostiles would attack Green Valley, but if they did—if they killed her—she intended to stand clean at the golden gates of heaven.

When the cream rose by late afternoon, Shannon carefully skimmed it off and put it in a deep bowl. The remaining milk she poured into a crock and lowered into the well in a bucket. It was cool in the well, and the milk would keep for days. She washed her new butter churn, dumped in the cream, and made a fine batch of yellow butter to eat with her bread and greens.

Where was Storm Dancer this evening? she wondered. Were he and his new wife bathing in some mountain stream, or had they crept away to make love on a secluded bed of moss? Losing him was bitter. She knew they said that they couldn't be together, that the night they'd shared was just that. But she had never dreamed how much it would hurt to give him up. Just thinking about him made her teary-eyed.

Resolutely, she tied her drying hair back, picked up the rifle, and went to look for the cow and pony. Betty, she found just beyond the pound fence, nibbling grass. Her bag seemed full, and she was mooing to be milked, so once again, Shannon fetched the bucket and tended to the animal's needs.

But this time, just as Shannon finished milking, a rabbit hopped across the grass. The cow shied, kicked over the milk, and yanked her tether free from the fence post. Before Shannon could grab the trailing rope, Betty was out the gate and trotting through the gathering dust toward the garden.

Shannon dashed after the cow, but there was no catching her. The contrary beast kicked up her heels and ran off across the field toward the far woods. "Suit yourself!" Shannon shouted. "Be eaten by bears! See if I care!"

The pony was nowhere in sight. Shannon hadn't thought the animal would stray far from the cow, but Badger was as mischievous as Betty. The sun had already dropped below the horizon, and it would be dark soon. Shannon wasn't afraid of staying alone in the cabin, but she didn't relish the thought of roaming the forest at night in search of stray livestock.

Summer days are long in the Smoky Mountains, but night falls quickly, after sunset. And all too soon, shadows closed around the cabin. Shannon retreated to the stout walls, barred the door, and put on a kettle of water to brew tea.

She was tired. She'd worked hard all day; she'd had no sleep the night before, and little the last nights before that. She was nervous, but too exhausted to think of sitting up tonight. She would keep the rifle close beside the pallet, but she would sleep. And tomorrow, she'd hunt down the pony. If Damon didn't return in a few days, she'd set out on her own. She didn't want to drag Betty along if she didn't have to, but leaving the hateful cow with no one to milk her would tug at her conscience.

The only light in the cabin was the glow from the banked coals. She wasn't so wasteful as to go to bed with a candle burning. Candles, especially good wax ones such as Drake's, were expensive. She wanted no part of him, but she wouldn't take what wasn't hers to take. Her muscles ached as she stretched out on the mattress. It had been a long time since she'd worked this hard. Quickly, she dropped off to sleep.

She didn't know what awakened her. She sat upright and listened. From the direction of the pound came the howl of a wolf. Shannon shivered and instantly, she thought of the pony and Betty. They were out there, unprotected.

She wondered if she should light a torch and take a look. Badger or the cow might be standing outside the cabin door. If he was, she could lead him inside. It would serve Drake right to have pony or cow tracks on his new floor. But the cabin had no window. There was only the one entrance and a small slide to peep through to see who was at the door. The chances were, she'd see nothing but blackness.

She rose from the pallet, put on her shift, and went to look outside. Nothing. "Badger? Are you out there?" She went back for the rifle. What would it hurt to open the door and—

Another wolf howled, this time from the direction of the garden. Was it the same wolf or another one? She took a torch from the wall, lit it, and crept to the door.

More howling. A chill went through her. A pack of wolves. What could she do with one shot against a pack? But if the pony had come back to the house for help, how could she leave him to be eaten alive? She would have to look, at least.

Summoning her courage, whispering a prayer under her breath, she slid back the bolt and threw open the door. She raised the torch, and then screamed as a flaming arrow thrummed past her head and slammed into the cabin wall, inches from her face.

# Chapter 18

Not wolves! Hostiles! Shannon ducked back inside and slammed the door. She threw her weight against it and dropped the metal bar in place. Her heart hammered against her ribs. How could she defend the cabin alone? How many Indians were out there? Were they Cherokee or some other tribe?

She forced herself to slow her breathing. Panic would do nothing but get her killed. The door was the only way in. If she made it difficult enough for the raiding party to break through the door, they might move on to another house.

The other cabins should be empty. She was certain most or all of the settlers had returned to Fort Hood with the Clarks. If the Indians had come to loot, there were easier pickings at one of the other homesteads.

Why hadn't she gone to safety with the others? Why had she been so stupid as to open the door? For a cow that was probably roasting over an Indian campfire? For a thick-headed pony?

Now the war party knew she was in here. Her carelessness had nearly cost her life. The stink of a lock of scorched hair that hung over her eyes was proof of that.

Two inches closer, and she wouldn't have known what hit her. She shuddered at the thought of the flaming arrow piercing her temple. But she couldn't waste what time she had worrying over what she'd done wrong. She had to think of what to do now, if she had any chance of living through this. "Da," she whispered, "I wish you were here to tell me what to do."

The door was stout; the metal bar secured with solid oak, but determined men could break it down. She threw kindling on the coals and flames ignited the dry wood, illuminating the single room. She ran to the table, pushed it over, and dragged it to block the entrance. Whatever happened, she wouldn't surrender. She'd fight to her last breath. But the tiny cabin left few choices for defense. Where could she hide?

Howls rose from outside. Not two shrieking warriors, but ten, twenty. The shrill cries turned her blood to ice. She was going to die here. She was going to die with her sins weighing heavy on her soul . . . and she was going straight to hell without ever feeling Storm Dancer's arms around her again.

"Holy Mary, Mother of God," she prayed. "Be with me now in my hour of—"

Shannon jumped back as something heavy struck the door. Again! The wood splintered, and a tip of silver metal appeared in the crack. An ax! They were chopping the door down. Frantically, she scanned the room.

Along one wall, steps had been cut in the logs to form a stairway leading up to the half-loft. Better there than standing here when the Indians broke in, she thought. Clutching the rifle, shot bag, and powder horn, she scrambled up the ladder. There were no furnishings in the shadowy loft, but an oxen yoke lay on the floor. She dragged it over to use as a brace for the rifle, and dropped flat on her stomach.

The ax struck the door again and again, the blade biting into the wood. It couldn't be an Indian tomahawk. That was hard steel hacking at the oak boards. With a sinking heart, she remembered seeing Drake's ax driven into a stump at the woodpile beside the open shed. Idiot! If he hadn't the sense to bring the ax inside, why hadn't she?

A chunk of wood flew inward and clattered across the floor. A painted face appeared in the jagged opening. Shannon didn't think. She took careful aim and squeezed the trigger. The long rifle boomed. The shock of the explosion threw her back, but her bullet flew straight and true.

One agonized shriek rang out. The face was gone.

"Father forgive me," she murmured. Had she killed a man? Her pulse raced, and she clenched her teeth to keep them from chattering.

Bellows of fury reverberated from outside! More blows hammered the door. It was only a matter of time and the attackers would break through. Automatically, she removed the lid from the powder flask with her teeth, raised the rifle and dumped the right amount of powder into the barrel. She could hear her father's voice in her head.

"Slow now, slow and easy. Too much and you'll blow your head off. Too little, and your ball won't carry to your target."

"I hear you, Da." Her fingers felt as though they were made of wood as she fumbled for the patch and covered the end of the barrel with it.

"Aye, girl, that's right." Da's calm words echoed from the past. Time seemed to stand still, and she could remember the day he'd taught her how to load the long rifle perfectly. "Now, darlin', seat your patch and ram it home."

With trembling hands she used the iron ramrod to shove ball and patch down the barrel. With trembling hands, she measured fine black powder into the frizzen pan. She rested the rifle barrel on the oxen yoke and pulled back the hammer.

She held her breath, waiting for another eye to peer in through the hole. And when she saw movement, she fired again. Another shriek split the air, followed by the unmistakable sound of a body falling heavily against the door.

Scuffling, then silence.

She swallowed hard and began the process of reloading the rifle. "What do you think, Da?" she whispered into the empty loft. "Will they line up single file so I can mow them down, one by one, like birds at a turkey shoot?" She didn't think that was going to happen.

She waited.

Minutes passed. Had they given up, taken their dead or injured, and gone away? It was an optimistic thought, but she didn't believe that either. She was sorry that she had only the one rifle. She could load in a hurry, but she couldn't load fast enough to hold back a full-scale attack. If the war party came through the door, she might kill another brave, but no more than one. If they came in after her, she would be lucky to die quickly.

The kindling burned low, dimming the light in the room below. The smell of smoke rose to the loft. Odd, the fire didn't seem to be that smoky, but . . . Shannon clenched her teeth and stifled a tiny moan. The fire wasn't on the hearth; the scent of smoke was coming from outside.

The Indians had set fire to the cabin.

If she didn't go out, she would burn to death. And if she surrendered, they would give her no mercy. She'd be tortured, maybe raped, before they cut her to pieces or tied her to a stake and burned her anyway.

"Madame!" a man called out in heavily accented English. "Come out. I promise to protect you."

*A Frenchman.* Could she trust him or was this a trick? She didn't want to die here, but every instinct told her that opening that door a second time would be just as wrong a move as the first.

"Madame!"

If he was French, who were his allies? Shawnee? Huron? Cherokee? If they were Cherokee, they might let her live for Flynn's sake. But they couldn't be Cherokee, could they? Unless the Cherokee had learned that Drake had been with the cowards who had attacked the Cherokee villages. And if they were Cherokee and she was in Drake Clark's house, she would suffer the same fate as he would when they caught up with him.

Shannon rose onto her knees. If the Frenchman was telling the truth, he might take her north. She could be exchanged for French captives. That happened sometimes. She'd killed at least one of the Indians. All Indians admired courage. They might let her live . . . might even adopt her into the tribe. Anything would be better than dying, wouldn't it?

A crackling sound came from the far end of the loft. It was dark back there. She couldn't see the smoke, but she could smell it. The log walls were afire. Smoke began to seep under the door and curl upward. The smoke would rise. She would die of smoke inhalation long before the flames reached her. It was the first cheerful thought she'd had since the arrow had nearly missed her head.

"Madame." The voice seemed farther away now, less certain.

Shannon coughed. Whatever else, it was time to pray.

"I can still save you," the Frenchman said.

*Yes,* she thought, *there's still a chance I can live.* She got to her feet. She'd surrender. That was the sensible thing to do. Surrender, and hope for the best.

But as she started for the ladder, she could have sworn

she heard, not her father's voice in her head, but Storm Dancer's. His words were not in English, but in Cherokee.

"Do not go out. If you do, you will die."

She shook her head. Impossible that she would hear Storm Dancer. Impossible that she would understand his native tongue. But his warning stirred doubt, and she stopped short. She'd been a fool earlier. Was she making a worse mistake now?

French officers were known for ignoring the cruel behavior of their Indian allies, and sometimes, they were known for participating in the worst of the torture. Would the death waiting outside be even more horrible than dying here with a gun in her hand?

What would Flynn O'Shea do?

The answer came as easily as her father's smile.

"Go to hell," she whispered as she returned to her defensive position on the edge of the loft and leveled the rifle. "Show your face in that doorway and I'll send you there ahead of me."

Captain Yves De Loup turned away from the burning cabin and shrugged. "We've wasted enough time on one woman," he said to his translator. "Tell them to fire the roof."

The brave repeated the Frenchman's words in Shawnee. After several shouts and a rash of defiant grumbling, one older warrior sent a fire arrow flying. Another man followed suit, and soon the cedar shingles were ablaze.

"Maybe she will come out," the translator said.

"She will not come out," De Loup answered brusquely. He gathered his reins and swung up into the saddle. "There are other cabins in this valley. Ask them if they will stay here like old women cackling or come with me and prove their courage against men?"

He was glad the woman had not surrendered. He had no time for prisoners, and he would not have risked the ire of the Shawnee war party to save her. This way was better. The woman was just as dead and would set an example for other English settlers, but he didn't have to witness her dying. He didn't like killing civilians, especially women. He had a young wife at home. But orders were orders, and dealing with Indians was not like giving orders to civilized French soldiers.

The Shawnee followed. One man carried the Englishman's ax over his shoulder, and others carried their two dead comrades. By the time he'd ridden across the cultivated field and entered the forest road, the cabin was fully engulfed. It was a pity, really. What he'd seen of the woman had looked attractive. She'd been a blonde, and he'd always been fond of yellow-haired women.

Storm Dancer was afraid that the boys guarding the horses had been ambushed as well, but he found them at their posts, sleepy, awake, and unharmed. It might have gone so differently. If Winter Fox, Flint, and the other delegates had been sleeping in the blankets by the fire, they would be dead instead of the French Colonel Gervais, five French soldiers, and more than a score of their Shawnee allies. Instead, the quarry had become the hunters. When the enemy war party struck the camp, they had found only empty blankets stuffed with branches and the *Tsalagi* at their backs.

Those of the Shawnee who survived the initial fight had fled into the forest. Winter Fox had ordered the *Tsalagi* warriors not to follow. There would be other days to fight the Shawnee. What was important was that the council members return home alive to their respective towns to report the French treachery.

The French Colonel Gervais had called a parley and then tried to murder them. And if Gall's father, Luce Pascal, was not in on the plot, he had turned a blind eye. The trader was now as much of an enemy as the Shawnee, and he would find that the Cherokee had long memories.

There was no more honor to be found among the French than among the English. The Frenchman Gervais had paid for his perfidy with his life. Winter Fox had met the colonel before in the north and recognized not only his face but the silver gorget that Storm Dancer had taken off his body.

Storm Dancer had come to the conclusion that neither the French nor the English could be trusted. The words and the treaties of white men were useless. It was clear that the Cherokee must learn to smile and shake hands with the foreigners but believe nothing they said. The *Tsalagi* must watch and learn their ways and use it against them.

Oona had warned him never to return to Truth Teller's trading post, but Storm Dancer felt he owed his old friend a warning. The fires of war blazed hot. It was no longer safe to be a lone white man on the edge of Cherokee land. Often men had accused Storm Dancer of being a hothead, of seeking war with the English, but others were far more eager than he to drive all the whites out of Indian land. Blood would flow and men on all sides would die. If he could save Shannon's father and his Delaware wife, he would.

More importantly, he must learn if Shannon was safe. Truth Teller must tell him where Shannon's new husband had taken her. That she had chosen another man cut deep, but he could not stand aside and let harm come to her. So long as he drew breath, he would love her.

He would warn her and her man as well. She still held his heart, what was left of it, and he could not bear to think of her in danger. It would be better if her husband took her back East where the Shawnee did not prowl the night and *Tsalagi* children wept for their dead mothers.

For now, he could do nothing. He had to see his uncle, his father, and the rest of the delegation safely back to their home villages before he could go to Truth Teller's trading post. Duty came before personal desire for a warrior of the *Tsalagi*. He pushed back the growing uneasiness. Worrying about Shannon wouldn't change her fate. He must fulfill his mission and then ride hard for her father's post.

If harm came to her, the sun would no longer warm him. Water would no longer quench his thirst. He would paint his face and take up the *blood tomahawk*. He would hunt down the enemy until he drew his last breath.

The ripple of smoke under the cabin door became a cloud. Above, the roof shingles popped and hissed. The cabin below was quickly filling with black, choking smoke. Shannon coughed. Soon it would be impossible to breathe. She wondered how long it would take her to die without air.

She scanned the room below in search of some way to survive the fire. And then she saw it! Where the table had stood, the floorboards ran a different direction. How had she been so stupid?

There was a trapdoor leading to a root cellar. Drake had bragged to her father about the cellar beneath his house. Taking the rifle, shot bag, and powder horn, she climbed down the ladder and ran to the hatch. It was much harder to breathe here, and she began to choke. Her eyes stung and ran with tears. But she found the loop of leather that served as a handle, yanked it up, and took a deep gulp of the fresh air rushing up from the rock hollow below.

There was no time to hunt for a candle. She half slid, half jumped into the darkness below. The hatchway dropped shut over her head, leaving her in total darkness. She stifled a scream. The floor was farther away than she'd thought, and she fell sideways when she hit bottom. The rifle jolted out of her hand and she stuck her head against the hard-packed dirt.

Half-dazed, she sat up. Faint lines of light showed over her head. The crackle of fire had become a roar. Shannon reached out, blindly trying to find her way. It was becoming hotter. If the floor above burned, she'd be caught in the falling timbers.

Too dizzy to stand, she began to crawl. One hand brushed the cold steel of the rifle barrel, and she caught it and dragged it along with her. Abruptly, wall of rock blocked her passage. She nearly panicked, but then realized that the air on her face was still musty and earth-smelling but fresh.

The cellar must extend beyond the walls of the house.

She kept moving forward, keeping her face close to the ground. Suddenly, she realized that she could touch both sides of what must be a passageway. The wall here was crumbling dirt interlaced with what she guessed were tree roots. She couldn't guess why there would be a tunnel leading away from the house, but it was cooler here, so she kept creeping and dragging the rifle behind her.

The sound of the crackling logs and roaring fire receded. Her head hurt, and she stopped to rest. She knew she must move, that she wasn't far enough from the fire, but she was so weary. She would catch her wind and then go on. Her eyes closed, and her body went limp.

Later, she had no idea how much later, she awoke with a start. For an instant, she thought she must be dreaming. She could smell smoke, but she couldn't hear a sound. She thrust out a hand, hit a dirt wall, and cried out. Was she dead and in her grave?

"Holy Mary," she began praying softly.

Her prayer was answered almost immediately by a horse's whinny. No, not a horse, a very familiar pony. Badger! She couldn't be dead if that rascal was nearby. She got to her feet and stumbled down the passage toward the source of the sound . . .

. . . And crashed full-tilt into a wooden door.

Shaken, she pushed against the hand-hewn boards. Something was holding the door from the outside. She grabbed up the rifle, wiggled it until she held the barrel, and then slammed the butt against the wood.

The door burst open and Shannon flung herself out onto the rain. When she looked around, the first thing she saw was the remains of the cabin, three blackened walls and a stone chimney silhouetted against fire-scorched trees. She was perhaps thirty feet away, just beyond the woodpile. The outer entrance to the cellar was low, hardly tall enough for a man to stand upright, set into a mound of earth and nearly concealed by flowering shrubs.

There were no Indians, no remains of a roasted cow. Smoke still rose in waves from sodden ashes. The only signs of life were the pair of wrens in the walnut tree and the big-headed pony standing not six feet away from her and watching with white-rimmed eyes.

The rope she'd hobbled the animal with was still trailing from one leg. Cautiously, she moved close enough to grab the rope, looped it around his neck, and then untied it from his right foreleg.

No war party.

She was alive.

Shannon began to laugh. She flung her arms around the pony's neck and dissolved into great sobbing tears. Once she'd had her cry, she wiped her eyes and tried to decide what was the wisest thing to do.

She had a mount, a gun, and the means to use it. Somewhere in her panic, she'd lost the powder horn, and she had to gather her courage to crawl back into the tunnel and bring it out. Luckily, none of the precious black powder had been lost. Her shot bag was half-full, and nestled in the bottom was flint and steel for fire-making. If she could catch a fish or shoot a squirrel, she wouldn't have to eat it raw.

In the cellar had been barrels of supplies, but they had been destroyed in the conflagration. She was on her own. She knew the way to Fort Hood. That was only hours away, but she had no intention of going to Drake. Now that she had lost Storm Dancer forever, there was only one place she wanted to be.

Shannon fashioned a crude bridle out of the pony's rope, tied it around his head, and climbed up on him bareback. Her father's trading post lay three days to the west through the mountains. Hostile Indians, flooded rivers, and wild animals couldn't keep her from him. She was going home.

# Chapter 19

The problem with making the journey from Green Valley to the trading post on her own was that there were no roads, not even a trail, and Shannon had never traveled the route. When she'd last left home, she'd ridden northwest to Fort Hood. Da's post was south and west, and she had to follow the valleys and passes.

Going directly over the mountains on horseback wasn't possible, at least not for her. The way was too steep and rocky. She could easily get turned around and end up back in Green Valley or totally lost.

The first day, she traveled on nerve and high spirits. She wasn't hungry or thirsty, and she was eager to get as far from the burned cabin as possible. She wasn't certain the hostiles had left the valley, and if they had, she didn't want to be there when Drake and the other settlers returned. She wasn't waiting for Damon to guide her home. She'd find her own way. At least, she hoped she would.

That night, she was lucky enough to find a small hollow in a rock outcrop that faced south. There was a spring nearby, and a ripe blackberry patch that she feasted on until her hands were stained with juice and her stomach stopped growling. The nook wasn't deep enough to be called a cave, but the depression had three walls, and an overhanging tree that she could convince herself was a roof. The crevice gave her a feeling of security.

She tied the pony securely to a tree. He hadn't grazed, but she couldn't take the chance that he would escape in the night and leave her on foot. On the far side of the spring were a few ripe elderberries and a plant her mother had called yellow dock. The leaves were edible raw and not bad tasting.

It was the wrong time of year for nuts, but she did find a cluster of tiny white mushrooms. Oona had regularly served mushrooms with their meals, but Shannon wasn't certain enough of the variety to eat these. Some mushrooms were deadly poison, and some of the good ones and bad ones looked much the same. How she wished she'd paid more attention to Oona's advice.

Shannon hadn't expected to sleep that night, alone without so much as a blanket, but she dropped instantly into a deep and dreamless slumber. When she awakened to Badger's snorting and the stamp of his hooves, light was already breaking over the treetops. She was stiff and sore, but felt proud of herself. She'd survived one day and night, found food, and hadn't been eaten by any wild creature.

It had been her intention to shoot small game or to fish, but when she saw smoke from what looked like a campfire, to the south, she was afraid whoever was responsible might be unfriendly. After that, she was reluctant to fire the gun and signal her presence. As for fishing, she didn't come upon any spot that seemed right. She knew there were small fish, frogs, and crayfish in all the streams, but it was more important to cover ground than to spend time searching for food when Oona would have plenty to eat at home.

The second night, Shannon wasn't so fortunate. She

had to sleep in the open, and the night was damp. When Badger lay down, she was all-too-ready to curl up beside him, savoring the heat from his furry body.

By the third day, she was certain she should be coming into familiar territory, but the gullies and mountains, the rocks and expanses of hardwood forest all looked the same. She was afraid that she'd gone too far south. She hadn't eaten since she'd found a patch of wild lettuce midmorning, and she was growing light-headed.

Shannon was fast losing her nerve and wondering if she should have waited for Damon to escort her home, when Badger suddenly seemed to know which way to go. Ignoring her tugs on the rope bridle, the pony broke into a trot, plunged through a muddy creek, and turned even farther to the south.

"Do you know what you're doing?" she asked. If she didn't find the post soon, she'd have to spend another night in the woods. Her stomach hurt and she'd had a headache for most of the day. More than anything, she wanted a bath, clean clothes, and the sight of her father's smiling face.

Dusk fell, and then full darkness. The ground underfoot was rocky, and twice Badger stumbled. Once they did slide halfway down a slope. Reluctantly, she slid off the pony's back and led him. When her way was blocked by a fallen tree, she gave up. She was exhausted. They would have to venture on in search of the post in the morning.

That night was the worst. The forest around them seemed alive. The sound of a hunting pack of wolves echoed from the next mountain, and Shannon shivered at their eerie howls. *A deer,* she thought. *The wolves are after a deer. If they're on the trail of prey, they're no danger to me.*

Then, closer, branches rustled, twigs snapped, and a rumbling growl came from the nearby woods. Her pony squealed and laid his ears back. His eyes rolled back and he pawed the leaves under his feet nervously. Shannon scanned the shadows, heart thumping. Minutes passed like hours until sometime in the deepest part of the night, she saw a pair of golden eyes peering at her from a branch ten feet above the ground. And at the same instant, she became aware of an acrid feral stench in the air.

Mountain lion!

Badger snorted and reared, stretching his tie rope taut. Shannon jumped to her feet and shouted, "Go! Get out of here! Shoo!" She had the rifle ready, but she was reluctant to fire. If she missed, she would be defenseless against the big cat's charge. "Get away!" she screamed.

Pulse racing, she waited, rifle against her shoulder, as the pony kicked and snorted, trying to escape. And then, as silently as the glowing eyes had appeared, they were gone. There was only darkness.

Badger calmed down. He thrust his head against her and nickered softly. "I know," Shannon said. "I was scared too. But it's gone. Whatever it was, it's gone. We scared it away." She hoped what she'd just said was true.

It was the longest night of her life, and she'd never been so glad to see the first orange and purple rays of sunrise. As soon as the shadows faded and she could see clearly, Shannon mounted the pony and gave him his head, letting him pick the way he wanted to go.

This morning her night fears seemed far away, the mountain lion a dream. Riding alone for so long gave her time to think. Time and time again, Storm Dancer's image materialized in her mind. She couldn't help but think how different this journey would be if they'd been together.

But he was gone. She'd lost him . . . if she'd ever had him. And she would never find another man to match him. The color of his skin didn't matter anymore. For one night, she'd known passion, and that memory would have to last her for the rest of her life.

Within an hour, her decision to let Badger find his own way home proved right when they picked their way around a greenbrier thicket and came out under a giant beech tree that had been hit by lightning. "I know it," she cried. "I know that tree." Home lay to the left, just over that hill and down through a flat valley. Soon, she'd be safe in her father's arms.

Her first indication that something was wrong at the trading post was the absence of smoke from the cabin chimney. It was midmorning now, but even if Oona had cooked breakfast at dawn, she'd still have a kettle on over the coals.

Shannon told herself she was worrying needlessly, that last night's encounter with the big cat had made her jumpy. In no time at all, she'd be sitting at Da's table, telling him about her adventure. Mention of the mountain lion would bring stories from her father about other near misses from lions. They would both laugh about her choosing not to fire, but chasing the cat away by outscreaming it.

But as she rode through the meadow, she could smell smoke. The odor was strong, but she couldn't see any smoke. The front gates were closed tight, but the dogs weren't barking, and Da's horses weren't in the outer pasture. If they were still on guard against an attack, why were the hounds quiet?

Shannon kicked the pony hard in the sides, and he broke into a canter. As she neared the creek crossing, she saw a flurry of movement in the tall grass. A dozen buzzards flew into the air, startling Badger so that he leaped sideways, and she nearly fell off.

"What . . ." she cried as she locked her hands in the pony's mane and regained her balance. "What could they be . . ." A feeling of dread swept over her as she dismounted and ran toward the place where the carrion birds had been feeding.

There, in the flattened grass sprawled the remains of one of Da's hounds. Obscenely protruding from the dead dog's ribs was a black-feathered arrow.

Shannon dropped Badger's reins and ran toward the palisade wall. She cut left, intending to enter by the small gate that opened on the spring pathway, and then stopped short and stared.

A great fire-blackened hole gaped in the upright logs. In the compound, nothing was the same as it had been when she left. Da's store was gone, burned to the ground, and the house roof was missing. "No!" she cried. "No!" And then, "Da! Da! Where are you?" She climbed over the burned and fallen logs and ran toward the cabin.

Another dog lay dead halfway between the wall and the store. The grass was blackened, as though fire had raced across the entire area. The door to the house hung by one hinge; the porch, where Flynn liked to enjoy his pipe at night, had nearly been destroyed by flames. Shannon climbed over the wreckage to the kitchen.

The inside of the cabin had been stripped—every object of value smashed or missing. The charred table lay on its side, one leg shattered, a tomahawk buried in the top. Strewn across what remained of the floorboard were beads, shards of Oona's cradleboard, and a single torn moccasin.

"Da!" Shannon shouted. "Oona! Where are you?" She darted to her bedroom, but the flames had been there before her. Her beautiful carved poster bed was in ruins, her mirror cracked and blackened. Nothing remained of her blankets and bed linen, and she could see patches of sky through the shingled roof.

Her father's bedroom next. No bodies, she prayed. Please, God, no bodies. The chamber was an empty shell; one back wall gone, the floor burned through to the dirt below.

"Da," she whispered, no longer able to control her fear. "Da, please. Where are you? I'm home. It's me. Mary Shannon. I'm home."

The snap of a board at the front of the house made her whirl around, afraid to go and see, afraid not to. "Who's there?" she called. "Da?" She forced herself to retrace her steps. Whoever it was, she had to know.

Sweat broke out on her forehead. Her legs moved as though she was wading through deep mud. "Da? Is that you?"

A whine. As she reached the door, the bitch hound gave a yip and wagged her tail. "Oh, baby," Shannon said.

She dropped to her knees and embraced the dog, then realized that the bitch must have had her puppies. The dog's belly was no longer full; her ribs were visible, her teats swollen with milk. "Where's Da? Where's Oona? Are you here by yourself?" Wiggling with joy, the hound licked Shannon's face and hands.

Shannon went into the yard. She couldn't panic. She'd found nothing dead here but the two dogs. Maybe her father and Oona had been warned. Maybe they'd gotten away before the Indians attacked the post. That's what it had to be, she told herself. That's what had happened.

But even as she tried to convince herself, she knew differently. Da would never have left his dogs behind. If he and Oona had fled, they would have taken the hounds.

Dazed, she wandered aimlessly around the house and

found in Oona's garden what she'd been dreading most. There, amid what had been green corn sprouts and spreading squash plants was a mound of earth heaped high with rocks that could only be a grave.

Tears blurred her eyes as she stumbled forward. A grave didn't mean her family was dead, she told herself. It could be anyone, a stranger, someone who'd come to trade at the post and been caught in the fighting. "Who are you?" she whispered. Not her father . . . she bargained. Not Oona, who'd already suffered so much. . . .

But as she drew near to the grave, her heart sank. At the foot of the mound was a hunting knife, thrust blade first into the earth. And at the head, rose a crude cross fashioned of sticks and held together by a leather binding. And dangling from the cross was Flynn O'Shea's pipe and tobacco pouch.

Hours passed before Shannon ceased her weeping, finished her prayers, and began to think about survival. Whatever she was going to do to save herself, it had to be here. There was nowhere else to go, and it had been too long since she had eaten a full meal. She was Flynn O'Shea's daughter. She'd have to face him in heaven some day, and she'd be ashamed to admit she'd given up . . . she'd laid down and died because she was too weak to fight.

Her first thought was to find the pony, but Badger hadn't gone far. Shannon found him standing in the lean-to behind the house. She turned him into the pound, raised the bars, and tossed in an armful of hay. The water bucket stood full, thanks to the rain and no animals to drink it dry.

Now that she'd seen to the pony, she could try and find dinner. Nothing edible remained in the house, but there were young squash on a half-dozen plants that had escaped the garden's destruction. She nibbled them raw as she walked down to the creek to check Oona's fish trap.

Two trout swam in the woven cage, and Shannon lifted it gratefully onto the bank. In minutes, she had a fire, and fish cleaned and grilling. The dog came to the fire, and as hungry as Shannon was, she thought of the puppies, and shared her meal.

Tonight, she would sleep in the lean-to. There was nothing for her in the house, and the hay and an old deer hide tacked to the wall would keep her warm. The fish were small, but she devoured every bite, and scratched in the garden for wild onions and a few beans.

Tomorrow, she would have to put aside her squeamishness and hunt a rabbit or a deer. She'd have to find food for the dog as well as tend the pony. She was surprised that there were just the two fish in the trap. If no one had been here for several days, there should have been more fish. Oona usually took three or four trout from the trap on long summer days when the creek water was warm.

If she was going to stay alive until friendly Cherokee came to trade or a white man passed through, she would have to be clever. She would need to salvage what was left of the garden, tend the fish trap, and dig edible roots to roast in the coals of her campfire.

So many questions . . . What would she do without her father? Where was Oona? Had she been murdered too? Had she run away or been taken captive by the attackers? And who was responsible?

The black feathered arrow she'd seen in the dead hound hadn't been the same as the fire arrows the Shawnee had used at Drake's cabin, but that wasn't proof of who was responsible for burning the post and killing her father. She didn't know enough about the tribes to identify them by the feathering on their arrows. She'd seen no evidence that white men had been involved.

There were no horse tracks, other than her father's animals, and certainly no prints from iron-shod horses. The raiders had most certainly been Indians, probably the same Shawnee who'd attacked Green Valley.

Shannon forced herself to search the compound for anything useful, but there was nothing left but a few gourds hanging on the pound fence. Those would do to carry water from the spring. She took them and the gun and set off, but she'd gone no more than a few yards down the path, when she saw something move in the trees.

Frightened, she dropped the gourds and raised the rifle. "Who's there?" A woman's high-pitched laughter sent shivers down her spine. "Oona? Is that you?"

A ragged apparition flashed through the woods and then vanished.

Shannon crouched by the edge of the forest and waited. A half hour passed, and then an hour. She'd almost begun to believe she had imagined she'd seen and heard a woman, when she heard weeping. But as soon as she took a few steps into the trees, the crying stopped.

"Oona? It's Shannon. Are you all right?"

No answer.

Shaken, but uncertain she could catch whoever it was in the woods, Shannon hurried on to the spring, dipped her gourds into the water, and returned to the spot where she'd heard the sounds. Now all she heard was birdsong and the rustle of wind through the leaves.

"I'm here, Oona, if you need me. I'll wait for you."

All the way back to the shed, Shannon felt as if she were being watched. She gathered wood and stacked it inside the lean-to, then led the pony inside. Now that the palisade wall was down, wolves might come in the night. If she and Badger were protected by the campfire, she might feel safe enough to sleep. The hound had wandered off, perhaps to go to her puppies. Shannon hoped the dog would come back. She didn't want to be alone anymore.

She forced herself to go back into the cabin. There, at the back of the hearth, nearly hidden by ashes, she found one of her mother's small copper kettles. And high up inside the chimney, on a shelf, was a wooden container of salt.

Finding the kettle and salt raised her spirits. She could boil water for herb tea. She could make soup and salt fish for days when there was no catch. A kettle was a fine prize. This copper pot had survived a sea voyage from Ireland and an Indian attack. Having it was a comfort.

There was no sign of the woman in the woods. Shannon reasoned that it had to be Oona, but if her father's wife had survived, why hadn't she come out when Shannon called her name? What if it was someone else?

As Shannon made her preparations for the night, she tried not to think of her father, tried not to think of the grave in the garden. Tomorrow would be soon enough to remember. Tonight, she couldn't bear any more sorrow.

Sometime after dark, the hound bitch came to the campfire, a small spotted pup in her mouth. The dog dropped the puppy in the hay near Shannon's feet, licked it several times, and settled down.

"Hello, what have you got there?" The puppy wiggled and squirmed until it latched on to a nipple and began to nurse. "Are there any more?" The pup was very young. Its eyes weren't open yet. "Is it a boy or a girl?"

Shannon made no move to touch the tiny creature, but watching it made her smile. Life, she thought. New life in the midst of all these ashes. She added another log to the fire. She should have been tired. Instead, she was wide-awake.

The clouds parted, and a full moon rose high over the trees. Shannon watched and waited, for what she didn't know . . . until she heard the keening cry from the garden.

The dog's hackles stiffened and she growled. Shannon grabbed the rifle and ran out of the shed toward the sound. Crouched near the grave was a ragged figure. The spectral creature rocked back and forth as it shrieked.

Goosebumps rose on the back of Shannon's arms. "Oona?" The figure turned and hobbled away, but Shannon saw the scarred face in the moonlight. She dropped her rifle and ran after the wailing woman. "Oona. Oona, it's me." She grabbed her around the waist and found that her stepmother's stomach was flat. But that was impossible. The child wasn't expected yet. It was too soon.

The Indian woman struggled and tried to break away, but Shannon held on tight. Then she saw that Oona was cradling something in her arms, something tiny and mewing wrapped in a blanket.

"Is that your baby? Did you have the baby?"

Oona dropped to her knees and rocked back and forth. The infant whimpered, almost as the puppy in the shed had whimpered. Shannon took the woman's face in her hands. It was oddly black, smeared with ashes.

"Shhh, shhh," Shannon said. "It's all right. I'm here. I'll take care of you."

Oona clutched the baby against her breasts.

"I won't hurt . . ." Horror curled in the pit of Shannon's stomach as the blanket fell away. It wasn't a baby that Oona held so tightly, but another tiny puppy.

For a moment, Shannon was too shocked to speak. It took every ounce of her strength not to scream and run back to the fire. But Oona was staring at her so pitifully . . . staring at her in the moonlight with the eyes of a madwoman.

"Come back to the fire and get warm," Shannon said. "The baby needs to be warm."

Oona looked down at the puppy in her arms and then back at Shannon. Slowly she held out a bloodstained and dirty hand.

"That's right," Shannon said. "We'll get you warm. We'll get you both warm." Step by step, the Indian woman followed her to the lean-to.

Shannon motioned to the pile of straw where she'd been lying earlier, and Oona sank down. Shannon tried not to stare.

In the space of days, her father's wife had aged years. Streaks of white had appeared in the wildly disarrayed crow-black hair. One eye was purple ringed, and swollen. Her face and her arms were bruised and scratched. Dried blood caked on her bare legs. If it were not for the old burn scar, Shannon wouldn't have known her.

Oona held out her hands to the fire and a twisted smile appeared on her swollen lips. Shannon winced. One of her stepmother's pretty white teeth was broken. Shannon looked away.

The hound bitch whined.

Oona unwound the blanket and laid the pup tenderly next to the dog. Then she took the other puppy, wrapped that one in the blanket, and rocked it against her. As Shannon watched, Oona began to croon a wordless lullaby.

Shannon couldn't hold back her tears.

# Chapter 20

In the morning, some of Oona's sanity seemed to have returned. She allowed Shannon to return the puppy to its mother without protest. When Shannon offered her hand, Oona flinched. But she followed her to the creek and allowed Shannon to wash away the dirt and dried blood that encrusted her hair and body.

By daylight, Shannon was even more shocked by her stepmother's condition. It was obvious that she had suffered a miscarriage, but since she refused to speak a word, Shannon could learn nothing about what had happened or how her father had died. She feared the worst. If her suspicions were correct, the bruises on her arms and thighs told a dark story of rape and assault. Maybe what had happened to Oona had been too terrible to survive with her mind intact.

All that day, Oona trailed Shannon around. She followed her to the spring and to the fish trap at the creek where they found three fat trout. Oona helped to carry wood for the fire and water for the pot. And when Shannon took wildflowers to place on her father's grave and knelt to pray, Oona did the same. Again, she spoke no words, but Shannon noticed that fresh tears trailed down the Indian woman's cheeks and her eyes looked more like her old self than they had earlier in the day.

Shannon laid her hand on the fresh turned dirt. "Da?" she asked. "Flynn?"

Oona's eyes widened and her mouth trembled. Shannon jerked back out of reach as Oona snatched the knife from the earth and mimicked being stabbed. Then she hugged herself and began to rock back and forth, moaning.

"Give me the knife." Shannon held out her hand. She wasn't certain if the crazed woman would attack her, but gradually, Oona calmed and looked at her from the corner of her eye.

"Please," Shannon said.

For a moment she thought Oona would refuse to surrender the weapon, but then she smiled that strange little fey smile and passed it over, handle first. Shannon examined the weapon. It was fashioned of good steel with the stamp of a metal worker in Spain. Flynn had been proud of the knives he sold, and this one was exactly like those that had rested on the shelves of her father's store.

The knife was identical except for the handle. The plain wooden handle had been replaced with one of antler, carved with the likeness of a lightning bolt and wrapped with strips of sinew. Someone had purchased or stolen one of Da's knives and had personalized it with his or her own handiwork.

She had the strangest feeling that she knew this knife, that she had seen this particular one with the antler handle before. She glanced around to see that Oona had wandered away and was down on the ground attempting to repair a battered squash plant. "Oona," she said. "Is this the knife? Is this the knife that killed Flynn?"

The woman didn't look up. She kept patting the dirt around the plant, pulling weeds, and pinching off the dead leaves. As she worked, she smiled and hummed to herself, moving on from squash to the young shoots of corn and spreading beans.

Shannon turned the knife in her hand. Where had she seen this before? At Split Cane's village? Here at the post in the leather sheath of one of their Indian customers?

She wanted to throw the hateful thing into the creek or to bury it, to never look at it again. But she needed a knife. She knew what her father would say. "Only a fool would toss away something they needed." A good blade might make the difference between life and death in the wilderness. And it would certainly make cleaning the fish easier. Yesterday, she'd had to use a sharp rock.

When they returned to the lean-to, Oona glanced at the puppies, but made no attempt to take one and wrap it in the blanket as she had before. Shannon took that as a good sign, a sign that her stepmother was healing. She was glad. She didn't know how long she could watch Oona pretending that a puppy was a baby without losing her own mind.

That evening, a raccoon came to paw in the refuge pile where Shannon had thrown the fish bones. She swallowed her reservations and shot the raccoon. There would be meat in the pot for all of them.

To Shannon's surprise, Oona picked up the knife, skinned and dressed the raccoon, and took it to the creek to wash. When she returned, she brought a handful of cattail roots and leaves with her. As Shannon watched, the woman cut up the meat, dropped bits into the kettle, and added wild onions, the cattail, and salt. Whatever part of Oona had been lost, she remembered how to prepare and cook food.

Later, by the fire, while they ate, Shannon spoke softly to her stepmother, trying to get her to answer. But Oona didn't utter a sound, and as the shadows fell, her mind seemed to drift away once more.

In the week that followed, the two fell into a routine of working in the garden, tending the fish trap, and foraging for wild plants and herbs. The hound bitch usually followed Oona, and when the puppies' eyes opened, Oona seemed to take a child's delight in playing with them. Only when they prayed at Flynn's gravesite did Oona slip into the depths of sorrow, weeping and rocking and sometimes tearing at her hair. Shannon hoped that time would heal the wounds and make her whole again.

For herself, Shannon had quit crying over her father's death. The sadness would remain, and the violent manner of his passing would never leave her. But she had no time to dwell on her loss, painful though it was. Flynn would expect her to care for his widow. The responsibility rested heavily on her shoulders. She must keep them both alive, and when rescue came for her, she had to find a safe place for Oona.

Storm Dancer held his hand over his horse's muzzle and murmured softly into the animal's ear. A Shawnee war party passed on the game trail just above the rocks where he had taken cover. The sorrel was well trained, and had dropped onto his front knees and had lain down when Storm Dancer gave the order. So long as the horse made no sound, and the enemy warriors did not look too closely into the willows below, they would be invisible.

Twice since he'd left his uncle and father at the home village, he'd encountered bands of roving Shawnee. The first war party had been small. He had seen no white men with them, but this group was larger, at least forty men. They traveled on foot, without women, and were heavily armed. There was no reason for them to invade

*Tsalagi* territory other than to raid and take scalps in the pay of the French or the English.

Truth Teller's trading post lay four to five hours away. If these Shawnee continued in the direction they were heading, they couldn't miss it. The palisade reared from the earth in an expanse of meadow in a broad valley. Storm Dancer didn't believe that the war party would pass without attacking such a ripe plum. Reaching his friend before these men would be a near thing.

Once the warriors and their rear guard had passed, Storm Dancer signaled his horse to rise. There was a trail that led over the mountain. It was rough, but passable, and once he reached the pass on the far side, his horse's speed would give him the advantage.

"Up, friend," he murmured to the animal. "We have far to go this day." He mounted and dug his heels into the stallion's sides. First the climb and then the run. Attempting to fight so many Shawnee would be a death wish, but if luck was with him, he could warn Shannon's father. There just might be time for them to vanish into the forest before the first tomahawk flashed.

Sweat streaked Storm Dancer's bare chest and face as he led the horse up a particularly bad incline. The loose shale underfoot was dangerous for a man on foot, but doubly so for the horse. The way was narrow. One slip, and the animal or both might plunge to their death.

Three times he had seen the war party running through the woods far below. He would have missed them the last time because the trees were so thick, but a flock of wild turkeys had flown up and given away their position. So far, he was keeping pace with his enemy. That wasn't good enough. He had to move faster.

Leaving the horse behind would have gained precious

time on the mountain, but he doubted the sorrel could descend the heights without falling or being eaten by a bear or mountain lion. This mountain was no place for a horse, but Storm Dancer had brought him here. It was his duty to bring his friend down unharmed.

At last, they reached the bald crest. He knew he might be seen crossing the treeless area, but there was no time to waste. Carefully, he picked his way through the rock-strewn summit and began the equally risky way down. He was afraid that the war party would move ahead of him now, but there was no alternative. When he reached the hills that rolled down to the valley, he must ride like the wind.

Shannon and Oona were checking the fish trap when Badger raised his head and whinnied. Shannon shaded her eyes with her hand and stared across the meadow, but it was Oona who saw the rider coming first and cried out.

The rifle lay propped against a boulder several yards away from the creek, and Oona reached it first. Shannon didn't stop to dispute ownership of the gun. Both women turned and ran for the tree line, but when Shannon reached the edge of the forest, Oona was no longer beside her.

Shannon was breathing hard. She'd known there was no shelter to be had within the ruined palisade, but there was little more in this part of the forest. The trees were huge and thick overhead, but few saplings or out-croppings of undergrowth offered anyplace to hide.

"Oona! Oona!" she cried. "Run and hide near the spring." She paused to catch her wind. She didn't know where Oona had gone. How had she been almost within arm's length one moment and gone the next? She looked back at the sea of tall grass and realized that her stepmother could simply have crouched down like a quail or rabbit and become invisible.

The horseman was still coming. If he reached the edge of the trees before she found a hidey-hole, she was lost. Then, to her left, she saw a fallen tree. It lay against another chestnut, their limbs intertwined. If she climbed the downed tree, she could take refuge in the branches overhead.

She had nothing left to defend herself with but the knife, and she clung to it fiercely as she scrambled up the trunk and into the shelter of the foliage above. Heart thudding so loud she was certain her pursuer must hear it, she peered through the leaves.

She could see the Cherokee perfectly as he approached the forest edge, see the weary movement of his horse, see the proud way he sat the animal with a back as straight as an arrow. She could even see . . .

"Storm Dancer!" She screamed his name. "Here! I'm here!"

Somehow, he guided his mount among the trees. She couldn't remember him doing it. One instant, she recognized his face and called out to him, and the next, she was out of the tree, into his arms, and kissing him.

"Shannon."

He didn't ask why she was here or what had happened to Da's post. He held her for long seconds, and then seized her around the waist and set her onto his horse.

"We must go," he said. "My horse is exhausted. I can't fight all of them."

"No, we can't leave yet." She glanced around. "Oona is here."

"Shawnee come. We must be gone before they get here. There is no time."

He gripped her hand so tightly that she thought the bones would break, but she didn't care. He was here.

He'd come for her. Wife or no wife, damned or not, they were together. That was all that mattered for this moment in time.

"They are right behind me. If they catch us, I can't protect you. There are too many of them."

"But Oona . . ." In a rush of words she tried to tell him everything: the burning of Drake's house, her father's death, her stepmother's madness.

Storm Dancer shook his head. "I must get you away. Deep into the mountains. It's the only way to save you."

"I won't leave her. I can't."

He took hold of her shoulders. "Listen to me. Do you see her? If you cannot find her, they won't. And if she is truly mad, not even Shawnee would dare harm her. She is under the protection of the Creator."

"We can't—"

He vaulted onto the horse's back and put his arms around her. The horse leaped ahead, plunging through the trees.

"No!"

He urged the horse faster.

Realizing that she wouldn't be able to convince him to stay, Shannon called over her shoulder. "Run, Oona! Hide! I'll come back for you! I swear I will!"

Branches brushed her face and she closed her eyes and ducked her head, fighting tears. Before she realized it was possible, they reached the creek. There, Storm Dancer slid down.

"Stay where you are," he ordered. He led the horse into the water, first wading and then swimming.

Shannon looked back one last time, but saw no sign of Oona. For perhaps ten minutes, they followed the course of the waterway, and then Storm Dancer tugged the horse toward the far bank.

When they reached dry land, he didn't remount, but

ran beside the sorrel. Carrying only her weight, the horse seemed to shed its weariness. They crossed and recrossed a small stream that led off the creek, then doubled back and swam the wider waterway again. Then Storm Dancer remounted and they were off down a gully at a full canter.

She had given up trying to argue with him. It was too late to go back. If the Shawnee had been right behind him as he said, they would be at the post by now. She prayed that Oona had heard her warning and would remain hidden and that the hound would find a safe place for her pups. She even prayed that Badger would escape capture.

In time, she grew too tired to pray. Her eyelids grew heavy, and she sagged against Storm Dancer's hard chest. She was conscious of his powerful arms holding her, and then she sank into blessed exhaustion and slept.

Shannon did not open her eyes again until the first light of morning spilled over her face. She lay on her back on a bed of thick moss, surrounded by a curtain of evergreens. The first thing she saw was the horse, his muzzle thrust into a tiny stream bubbling out of a rock. And the second thing she saw was the man stretched out beside her, his dark eyes smiling at her, his handsome chiseled face aglow.

Shannon offered a shy smile, and he rolled onto his side and reached out to catch a lock of her hair. He rubbed it between his fingers, then leaned closer and brought her hair to his lips.

She watched him as if in a daze.

But not in a daze. Shannon knew exactly what she was doing as she reached out for him. What she wanted to do. What she would do. She might not live another day, but she would live for this moment. She would savor every second . . . every caress . . . every sensation.

Storm Dancer pressed his mouth to hers. He did not speak of his wife. He did not speak of her husband. Nothing existed beyond the evergreens towering over her and the taste of Storm Dancer, the thrust of his hard tongue, the scent of him in her head.

She molded her hips to his, returning his kisses hungrily. How many times had she dreamed this dream? Only now it wasn't a dream. Storm Dancer was here in her arms, here to touch . . . to taste.

The early morning air was cool on her skin, but Shannon was suddenly overly warm. Perspiration beaded above her upper lip. The skirt and bodice she'd slept in felt restricting. Suffocating. As he kissed her cheek, the line of her jaw, the pulse of her neck, she plucked at the ties of the bodice, frustrated that she could not untie them fast enough.

He brushed her fingertips away and nimbly untied her from the confines of the fabric, all the while gazing into her eyes.

Such warmth, such depth . . . His dark eyes seemed to reflect all that was good about the world, even in this terrible hour of catastrophe. So much tenderness in his gaze . . . such deep passion.

Shannon sat up to help him pull her shift over her head. Whatever shyness she had felt the first time they'd made love was gone. It only seemed right that she should be naked in his arms. And he naked in hers . . .

She pushed the leather vest off one wide shoulder and kissed the bronze skin. She marveled at the contours of his beautiful muscles. Overnight, she had come to love the smooth, hard planes of a man's body . . . this man's body.

Her breath came fast as she explored, and her heart thudded beneath her breast. She could already feel her need for him deep inside. So deep and fierce was that aching, that she knew she would die if she didn't have him.

Storm Dancer pushed her back down into the mossy bed they shared, and when she gazed up into his eyes, she knew she would never love a man the way she loved this man. No matter what happened, no matter where she went or how far from this forest her life took her, she would never love the way she loved at this moment.

Shannon shuddered as he caught one of her breasts in his palm and squeezed gently. Both nipples puckered in response, and she moaned, pressing her hips to his, feeling his hardness through the soft leather of his leggings.

He closed his mouth over a nipple and sucked, first gently, then harder. She threaded her fingers through his hair, cradling his head, encouraging him. Her senses soared and her need became more urgent. "Storm Dancer," she whispered.

His mouth found hers again and she strained against him.

She tried to speak against his lips. "I—"

"Shh," he whispered. "Do not speak. Do not break the dream spell."

She met his gaze, her breath ragged, her chest heaving. "This is a dream?"

"Do you wish it to be?"

She shook her head.

Again he smiled and she almost laughed. Kissing him again, she parted her thighs, and he slid his hand between them. She groaned with pleasure, rocking against him.

As they kissed, the urgency became deeper. She wanted to tell him to stop. She didn't want to waste a moment of the ecstasy so close at hand. But the words didn't come, and she couldn't stop herself. Shannon wrapped her arms around his neck and moved against his hand until her world burst into shards of pleasure.

She buried her face in his shoulder, breathing hard.

But to her surprise, her need seemed to be even greater now. Nothing would satisfy her but the feeling of him bursting inside her. "Now," she whispered, pushing down his loincloth.

She didn't know what made her so bold. Was the end of their life at hand?

Storm Dancer tore away the leather binding and sprang hard and hot against her leg. She closed her eyes, guiding him over her, into her.

A rush of relief filled her as he pressed her into the soft moss of their makeshift bed. Then the urgency began to build again. She lifted her hips to meet his thrusts, crying out in the morning air, as her muscles contracted and the very fiber of her being peaked and fell.

Shannon caressed his bare buttocks, encouraging him as he thrust hard, faster. Certain she was spent, she was shocked to feel the heat inside her flame up yet again.

This time they shuddered in unison, and at last, she felt fully satisfied as she had never felt before in her life.

# Chapter 21

Shannon lay back on the thick moss and smiled as she watched Storm Dancer bathing in the spray from the spring bubbling out of the rock wall. How beautiful he was, she thought. Her man. Surely God could not have created a more perfect mortal. Muscles rippled on his back and arms and long hard thighs beneath smooth bronzed skin. His legs were perfectly proportioned, his shoulders wide, his wet hair a cascade of black silk.

What kind of wanton was she that she could take such pleasure in a man's body when she was in mourning for her newly deceased father? Three times in broad daylight? The doors of hell must loom wide for her. She was both an adulterer and a shameless daughter.

What had passed between her and Drake—their sham marriage—counted for nothing. Not even a saint could blame her for casting off a union with a child murderer. But for Storm Dancer, it was different. He wasn't free, and that mattered more than the color of their skins or what language he spoke. Whether he was heathen or not, he had his own religion and beliefs. He was already married.

She had sinned. She had stolen what belonged to

another. There could be no lasting happiness built on another's woman's pain. No matter how much she wanted to go with Storm Dancer, to turn her back on the English world, to make his people her people, she could not. Whoever that other woman was, Storm Dancer was hers.

She couldn't blame what had happened on fear or hysteria. He had not seduced or forced her. She had given herself to him willingly. And, heaven help her, she would do it again. But when they left this glorious spot to return to the Cherokee village, she would never find ecstasy in his arms again.

Somehow, she would find her way east and begin to build her life again. For so long, that had been the fate that she'd dreaded, but now everything had changed. She could never go back to Green Valley, and she couldn't remain with Storm Dancer. She had no choice but to return to an English world that had never welcomed her.

She wasn't afraid of hard work. She could find employment in any tavern. But she would never give her heart to another man, and she would never marry. So long as she drew breath, she would consider this man her true husband. And when she passed from this world to the judgment at heaven's gate, she would gladly pay the price for her sin.

She rolled onto her back and gazed up at the sky. Eden must have been like this, she thought, so green, and fresh, the air scented with the sweet smell of violets, evergreens, and wild mint. Far above the treetops, white clouds drifted in an azure sky. When she was a child, her father had pointed out the shapes of ships and animals and angels in the snowy puffs. She'd believed Da could work magic, changing the shapes to please her. Today, she needed no fairy magic to make her heart sing. The clouds were perfect in their own form, slowly moving across a vast heaven.

She had been through hell in the last weeks. She had killed a man, possibly two, she had survived starvation and a madwoman, and she had fled from certain death. Here, she would restore herself and find the strength to do what must be done. So long as she'd had Flynn and the promise of a half sister or brother, she hadn't been alone in the world. But she had lost them. She had only herself.

She closed her eyes and might have slipped into sleep except for the brush of soft butterfly wings on her forehead and nose and cheeks. "What are you—" she began, and then broke into giggles as she saw Storm Dancer standing over her, showering her with violet petals.

Laughing, he flung himself down beside her and drew her into his arms. "What am I to do with you, woman?" he teased. "You have hair as yellow as the yolk of a duck egg and skin as white as snow. Your eyes are round, and—"

She placed her hands on his damp chest and pretended to push him away. "Are you saying I'm ugly?"

"I cannot tell. You are a witch, and it may be that you can turn into any form that you wish."

"I'm no witch."

"You must be," he insisted. "You've cast a spell over me. I cannot say if you are more beautiful than a sunset or as wrinkled as a toad. My eyes are blinded. You hold my soul in the palm of your hand."

"A toad? You've been making love to a toad?"

He caught her hand and kissed her knuckles, then turned it over to trail kisses over her palm and up the underside of her wrist. In one move, he rolled her onto her back and pinned her to the moss. "Now you are my prisoner, toad witch."

She giggled and entwined her legs with his. The heat

of his thighs warmed hers, and desire stirred. She nipped his bare shoulder with her teeth and arched against him, reveling in the length and power of his body. "I don't believe you," she said between kisses. "You are the one who has cast a spell over me."

She gasped as she felt the first caress nudging at her woman's folds. Instinctively, she opened to receive his thrust. It was wrong what they were doing. She knew it was wrong, but she couldn't help herself. She wanted him inside her so badly, needed him. And soon she could never have him again.

They moved together, giving and taking, sharing the ancient dance of love. Faster and faster, harder, deeper, until the tension inside her exploded in a cascade of shooting stars and she cried out in her sweet, sweet release. Another two powerful thrusts, and he groaned as he found his own climax. Panting, sweat sheened, he cradled her in his arms and murmured love names into her ear as they drifted back to earth together.

Later, when reason returned and she could speak again, she grasped his hand and kissed it as he had kissed her. But when she turned his lean hand over, she saw the mark on his palm and felt a rush of compassion. "A scar," she murmured. "What caused—"

He chuckled. "I was born with that. It is not an injury." He spoke in Cherokee now, as she realized he did most of the time, and most of the time, she understood. "A spirit sign."

"It looks like lightning."

"It does." He sat up, pulled his hand free, and curled it into a fist. "Much trouble that mark has brought me. It's why my mother and the council women chose Cardinal to be my wife."

Suddenly, his eyes narrowed. He reached over her and

picked up the belt and knife that lay heaped beside her clothing. "Where did you get this?"

She blinked. "What?"

"My knife. Where did it come from?"

Her mouth went dry. "Your knife? It can't be."

"I noticed it missing days ago. I must have lost it at the post when I went to find you before."

Fear and suspicion shot through her. "What do you mean? When did you come?"

He hefted the knife, turning it this way and that. "It's mine. See my mark carved into the handle? The lightning bolt."

She drew back away from him. "You lost it at Da's trading post?"

"I went to find you, to ask you to come away with me, but you had already gone to your white husband. Oona told me."

"I don't understand."

His features hardened. "Before I could find you, you had already chosen one of your own kind."

She got to her feet and began to dress hurriedly. "You've no right to accuse me. You married your Cardinal first. Was I supposed to wait for a married man?"

"Married?" He stared at her. "I have no wife."

"Don't lie to me," she flung back. "Cardinal. The woman your mother chose for you." Angry tears welled up in her eyes. "The woman you cheated on by making love to me."

He shook his head. "You are wrong, heart of my heart." He wrapped his arms around her and kissed the tears away. "Do you think I could take pleasure with you, knowing I had left a wife at home?"

"You'd not be the first husband to do so."

"No. Not me. I refused Cardinal. I told her that I could not marry her because I love only you."

"Are you telling me the truth?"

"Look into my eyes. You will see that I do not lie."

Not married? He wasn't married? She began to tremble with relief. But Flynn had told her . . . If Storm Dancer was telling the truth, had her father lied to her? But seeing him holding the knife . . . the knife that had ended Da's life sent a shiver through her. "I thought . . . I . . ." She pulled away, dropped on the soft moss, and began to tug on her shoes. "Da . . . That knife killed my father."

"You found the knife in his body?"

"No, Oona did, or she saw it."

"And she said I was responsible?"

"No, she didn't. She . . . I told you, she doesn't talk since . . . since the attack. But she told me without using words. She left the knife on his grave as a sign he had been killed by stabbing."

"And you believe that I thrust my knife into him? That I killed my friend?"

"No, no, of course not."

That wasn't possible, was it? She'd loved two men in her life. That one could have murdered the other was too cruel to accept. "It was just a shock to learn the knife was yours." She should have remembered where she'd seen the weapon before, shouldn't she? Had she deliberately not remembered something she didn't want to remember?

"I was with my father and uncle when your father was killed. I didn't know about the raid on the post," he said quietly. "We were on a peace mission to meet with the French Colonel Gervais. It was a trap. We escaped, and I had to escort the tribal representatives home. Then I came to warn Truth Teller about the Shawnee."

"And found me, instead."

"And found you." Hurt showed in his dark eyes. "I would not have you believe evil of me, Shannon."

"No, I don't. It was just . . ." A rush of guilt gripped her. "I'm sorry."

"There is no need. It was strange. A coincidence, and I do not believe in coincidences. There is more to this than I can see."

She went to the spring and washed her face and drank, and then turned to face him. "What now?" she asked.

"Have you divorced your husband so soon?"

She pursed her lips. "It was no real marriage. There wasn't a priest. No religious ceremony at all. I found out something . . ."

She hesitated, unsure whether she should tell him that Drake was a murderer. Where did her loyalty lie? To a man who could kill a child and skin him as though he was an animal? "I went with him because my father said that I had to."

Storm Dancer watched her. "And you are an obedient woman?"

"No, not particularly. But . . . I thought you had a wife, and my father found out about us. He didn't want me there with him anymore."

"Now, I must tell you that I am sorry. I never wanted to hurt you, my Shannon."

"It doesn't matter now." She hurried to tell him what she thought might matter most to a man. "Drake and I . . . We never slept together."

Storm Dancer arched a dark eyebrow. "It was never the sleeping part that worried me."

She felt her cheeks grow warm. "You know what I mean. When I found out . . . when I discovered what kind of man he was, I told him that the marriage was over."

"Did he leave your house?" His eyes grew serious. "After you argued, did he leave?"

"We did more than argue," she admitted. "I threatened to cut off his penis if he ever came near me again."

Storm Dancer laughed. "Among the *Tsalagi*, that would be a divorce."

She took both of his hands in hers. "You have to believe me. I've never been with any man but you. I've never made love to another man, and I never will."

He smiled at her. "Never is a long time."

"I mean what I say," she declared. "What do we do now? Where are you taking me?"

"Home, to my mother. I cannot stay with you. I must join my brothers to drive the Shawnee from *Tsalagi* land."

"You're joining a war party? And leaving me with your mother?"

"I have no choice. She will keep you safe."

"I don't want to go there. Can't I go to Split Cane's village instead?"

"My mother and my clan must recognize you as my wife. If there was no war, if I didn't have a duty to fight to protect the Cherokee, I would gladly go away to some distant mountain to be with you alone. But you and I cannot live like that. What happens when we have children? Is it fair that a child comes into the world without family?"

"You say I am your wife? You're talking about children. But you've never asked me to marry you." She was being foolish; she knew she was being foolish, but she felt like a feather washed along the river in a spring flood. He wasn't asking her—he was telling her. How was he any different than Flynn, than Drake Clark? "I want to be asked."

"You want words. Can't you read my heart? My soul?"

"What makes you think your mother will like me?"

He laughed again. "She won't, not at first. She will do whatever she can to make your life miserable."

Shannon stared at him in dismay.

"My mother is a fair woman. When she comes to know you, she will love you."

"What makes you so certain that she'll ever accept me—that any of the Cherokee will?"

"They will accept you because you are mine." His smile became a boyish grin. "They have to—I'm the chosen one."

Hannah Clark placed a three-legged milking stool on the ground next to the fire-scorched cabin and sat down. She shoved her head hard into the cow's belly, and began to squeeze the cow's teats. Two thin streams of milk arced into the bucket.

The house door banged open, and Hannah flinched. Heavy footsteps sounded. Hannah kept milking the cow.

Nathan swore loudly. "What do you think you're doin', woman?"

"What's it look like?" She sat back, straightened her mobcap, and scowled at him. "And I'll thank ye to watch your tongue. I'm a woman in mournin' fer her dead son."

Nathan shuffled his big feet and knotted his callused hands into fists. "It's what I'm sayin', woman. Your youngest son is laid out in his coffin with pennies on his eyes. Your other boy is in pain, in what might be his deathbed, and you're out here, calm as a dead hen, milkin' this damned cow."

"Cow needs milkin', husband." She turned back to her chore. "Sicken and die if she ain't milked."

"Have you lost your mind?"

Betty switched her tail, and Hannah slapped her belly. "Hold still, you daughter of Beelzebub."

Sometimes, she couldn't figure what the Lord had in mind, making such misery for his believers. They'd come home from Fort Hood to find their cabin standing, their barn burned to the ground. One beautiful son lost, the other with his face scarred and near blind, and this ornery beast come back. It didn't seem a fair trade.

If the house still stood, wouldn't they all have had a better chance at surviving if they'd just remained here on the farm? Maybe her son would be alive if they had never left Green Valley.

She glanced back at Nathan. "Ye think I don't know our Damon is in that pine box? Who washed him and dressed him and bound up his jaw so it wouldn't hang open? And who cut out Drake's ruined eye and sewed up his back and head? Not you."

"Women's work."

"Women's work, all right." She peered into the bucket to see how full it was. What was it about a man that they always needed to talk a thing into the ground. Hadn't it been hard enough to have her boys carried home, one dead, one half dead? "The way I see it, Nathan Clark, men make the misery in this world and women clean up the mess."

He began to huff and puff. She knew without looking at him that his face was red as a Boston beet and all swollen. "You mind how you talk to me," he warned.

"What you gonna do, Nathan? Punch me? Go ahead. I been hit before. But all the yellin' and all the hittin' won't change the fact that you dragged us out here to these godforsaken mountains. We left a good farm behind, a farm where nobody came in the night and burned your barn—where no wild Injuns drove off your livestock."

"We came for the land. Those acres were worn out. This land will—"

"I've heard enough about your land. It's my sons I'm grievin' over. Who insisted them boys to go with the redcoats? Drake and Damon are farmers, not soldiers. Soldiers get paid for huntin' hostiles. But no, you had to fire them all up. So if our Damon is dead, you can take a big share of the fault for it."

"Hannah, don't blame me."

"I do. Lord knows, I do. You never treated Damon right. He weren't the son you wanted. It was all Drake, Drake, Drake. Now, Damon's gone, I 'spose you're happy. Drake will inherit it all." She looked around. "All this."

"Let the cow be. Your son's cryin' in pain. He needs more laudanum."

"Too much will kill him just as much as them wounds. He's hurtin', sure. But I don't think he's dyin'. And folks will be here for the funeral. We'll need the milk. The cows we dragged to the fort and back won't give much."

"He was askin' for Shannon. Drake was. Couldn't tell him that she's lost too."

"They find a body?" Hannah drained the last teat. "There you go, Mistress Betty." She sat the bucket safely out of reach of the cow's hind legs, and hobbled her. "Go find some grass. There's nothin' else." The grain had burned with the barn, and unless the men cut a lot of hay, it would be a hard winter. Like as not, they'd not see spring with all the cows left alive. "I thought you said there was no sign of Shannon."

"If not killed, taken. Tortured probably. Raped, fer sure. Better off dead, a white woman with savages."

"Lord help her, but I can't help but think our Drake is better off without her."

"You're a hard woman to say such a thing. Your son's wife."

"Not much of a marriage, if you ask me. No preacher. Don't seem legal to me. Not the way my family did things."

"Where's your pity? Bad enough he loses his twin. How you gonna tell him his new wife is gone too?"

Hannah picked up the bucket. "How am I gonna tell him?" She shrugged. "Reckon, I won't. You're the head of this house, so you're so fond of sayin'. You tell him."

# Chapter 22

"I don't understand why we can't go back for Oona." Shannon swayed comfortably on the back of the horse behind Storm Dancer. "We've seen no sign of enemy campfires. Surely, we're deep enough into *Tsalagi* territory that we don't have to be afraid of attack."

"I nearly lost you once," Storm Dancer replied over his shoulder. "I won't take that chance again."

"I keep worrying about her. It was wrong to abandon her. I promised that I would—"

"These were not men who dared to raid into *Tsalagi* land. These Shawnee are like the wolverines of the North Country. They are crazed by the scent of blood. They kill for pleasure."

"I'm not afraid. I was alone in Green Valley when they attacked the cabin, but I outsmarted them."

"And so you would tempt the spirits?"

"I don't believe in your spirits."

"But I do. The Shawnee would kill you, but not until they had used you in every way they could—not until they had tortured you to satisfy the perverse pleasure of their lust. You have not seen the bodies of the dead they left in their wake. I have."

"I feel like such a coward to leave Oona," Shannon protested. Guilt troubled her conscience. She and Storm Dancer had been taking joy in each other's bodies while her stepmother might be dead or worse. . . .

"You do not understand," he said gently. "Your father's woman faced the raiders before. I don't know how she survived, but what she saw must have driven her mad. That will save her from further attack. Any of the first people—what you call Indians—would consider it taboo to lay a hand on her."

"Someone did. You should have seen what she looked like. She'd been beaten, raped, I'm sure. She gave birth too early, and—"

"She survived until you got there. And you told me that she could tend the garden and the fish trap—that she could still cook. Oona will be well. And if no one goes to rescue her, I will go myself. I give you my word, Shannon. You do not have to worry about her safety."

Late in the afternoon, they had come across three families from Split Cane's town. The headwoman wasn't with the group, but the older men, women, and children were traveling to the location of an old village high in the mountains that they used in time of danger. There had been no young braves. Shannon supposed that they had gone to join Cherokee war parties, as Storm Dancer had told her that he intended to do.

The two of them had passed on word that Oona was alone at the trading post and needed care, due to her afflicted mental condition. None of the men they'd talked with were willing to go after her until they safely delivered their families into Split Cane's care, but several promised to see that Oona wasn't forgotten.

"Why can't I go with them?" Shannon whispered privately to Storm Dancer as the older braves acting as rear guard disappeared into the forest. "I'm sure Split Cane will give me shelter. You can go back for Oona and come for me at—"

"How many warriors did you see among them? If a war party hit, there would be no contest. You are safer with me."

"You're one man. How could I be safer with—"

He pressed his fingertips to her lips. "No more argument. You belong with my mother. The village is well concealed and always protected."

"But I don't want to go to your mother," she protested. "Not without you."

"We've had this discussion over and over. You're my woman. Since you have no clan, you must learn to be one of us."

Troubled, she locked her arms around his lean waist and leaned her cheek against his back. The stallion moved easily under them, seemingly not overburdened by carrying double. Shannon had given up counting the ravines they'd descended, the creeks they'd crossed, or the times they'd dismounted to walk up steep mountainsides.

She had known these mountains were vast, but she'd had no real idea what that meant in terms of crossing them. Far from roads or white civilizations, the ancient meadows, gigantic trees, crystalline waterfalls, and tumbling, rock-strewn creeks rolled on and on into the horizon. No matter how far they rode, the Smoky Mountains stretched before them. Shannon's heart thrilled to the beauty of Storm Dancer's world: herds of deer and elk, great black bears, a rainbow of birds, fox, raccoon, and numerous smaller mammals inhabited this place.

Once, midmorning, they had paused at the edge of a high clearing to watch a gray vixen and her four little fox cubs cavorting and chasing each other, scrambling over a fallen log, and wrestling. Storm Dancer had signaled her to make no sound, and they had sat on the horse and watched the family of foxes play for a long time before finally riding on.

"A vixen is a good mother," Storm Dancer said. "She will fight wolves and mountain lions for her pups. Once, I saw an eagle swoop down to snatch a tiny one. The vixen leaped to her baby's rescue with snapping jaws."

"Did she save it?"

He chuckled. "Yes. After the vixen yanked out a few tail feathers, the eagle dropped the pup. It was probably ashamed to be seen struggling with such a fox."

She smiled. "I'm glad." She had handled many a fox pelt at Da's store, but she would never regard the animal in the same way again. She would always remember the sunny glen and the loving care the female had given her little ones. "How can you bear to kill such a beautiful animal?" she asked him.

"All creatures are our brothers. If I kill a buck or even a rabbit, I must apologize to the Creator for taking the life of one of his own. I kill to put meat in my mother's pot or to provide skins for moccasins or clothing. A man must live."

"At the tavern, where I worked, I always felt sorry for the chickens when I wrang their necks, but I never thought of them as brothers or sisters."

He covered her hand with his. They were riding up a twisting pass, so narrow that two horses could not have walked side by side. Branches brushed her head and arms, and she kept her eyes clenched to protect them.

"We are taught that all life is a circle. Each drop of water, each blade of grass is as important to the Creator as each human child. And all are related. We believe that even the trees and rocks have souls, but more primitive ones than a man or woman."

"If we were married, would it be in the Cherokee custom?"

"I would want that, but if it would please you, I could find a priest to say the words over us."

She smiled. If only it was that easy. But what priest would consent to bless the union of a white woman and a heathen warrior? "In my faith, there are rules about who can and can't be married."

"As in mine. You are not a Wolf, are you? It is forbidden for me to marry one of my own clan." He lifted her hand to his lips and kissed it. "These don't feel like wolf claws," he teased.

"I thought we'd decided I had no clan. I'm an O'Shea and Irish, if anything."

"It may be that my mother will find a way around that. She is a practical woman. When I was small, she let a black robe put water on my head."

"You were christened a Catholic?"

"As I said, my mother is practical. I was her only child. If the white man's god was more powerful than the *Tsalagi,* she wanted me protected. But you must know, as much as I respect your beliefs, I have my own. I am Cherokee, blood and bone. I will never be a white man."

Shannon sighed and hugged him. "I want you to be nothing but what you are." She wished that they could go on riding like this forever, just the two of them. "Can't we just stay like this?" she begged. "No mothers, no rules, no customs but those we want?"

"Afraid not," he said with a chuckle. He reined in the big horse and pointed through the trees. "Beyond that ridge lies my home village. Our time of being alone is over."

"Are you mad?" Firefly demanded. "You dare to bring her here? To ask me to care for her?"

His mother had been kneeling on a hard-packed section of ground. In her hand, she held a coil of wet clay, and in front of her rose what would become a large oval cooking vessel.

She leaped to her feet and flung the clay at his head. "Ungrateful wretch!"

Storm Dancer ducked and the coil slapped against a tree trunk. "Mother, calm yourself."

"You are your father's child! Not mine!" Firefly seized the half-finished pot and threw that at him.

He dodged the flying vessel.

"I'll not have her under my roof!"

"You may as well accept it." He folded his arms over his chest and stood solidly in front of her. "Shannon is going to be my wife, the mother of your grandchildren."

"I'll kill her first," Firefly hissed. "I'll use her entrails for bowstrings, her yellow hair for embroidery thread."

"How did you know the color of her hair?"

"Gall told me. But it doesn't matter. I don't want her in this village. I don't want her in these mountains. She goes."

"She stays." He softened his tone. "Mother, she has nowhere else to go. She has divorced her white husband. Truth Teller is dead, and his Indian wife has lost her mind out of sorrow."

"You would shame Cardinal by bringing this white woman here? I think you have lost your mind." She tried to move around him, but he stepped in her path.

"You will come to love Shannon. I promise you."

"And I promise you that I will not. I will skin her and—"

"Whatever you think of her as my bride, she is a guest in this village. You cannot do less than to treat her with respect and kindness." He held out a hand to her. "Would you have respect for me if I let you turn away the woman I love?"

"You shame me," she thundered.

Storm Dancer wasn't fooled. For all her bluster, his mother honored the ancient rules of hospitality. Even a bitter enemy might find food and shelter in a Cherokee village if he or she were a guest. "I'm joining the war party. I have to know Shannon is safe."

"Your father is already gone, two days ago."

"And my cousin, Gall . . . Did he ride with the war party?"

Firefly shook her head. "He was set upon by the Shawnee and wounded. He is here, in the village."

"I'm sorry to hear that. Is he hurt badly?"

"No. But he is in pain. With his bad leg, he couldn't have kept up with the other men." She raised her chin, but her eyes filled with affection for him. "When will you leave, my son?"

"At once." He crossed the distance between them and embraced her. "So, will you keep her safe for me? My Shannon?"

Firefly hesitated, but then reluctantly said, "She can stay in the village, but not in my house. You ask too much of me."

"All right." He nodded. "Someone else will open their hearth to her for the sake of hospitality."

"Warn your yellow-haired white woman to stay out of my way. If she angers me, I will cut off her ears and use them for fish bait."

He chuckled and gave her another hug. "I'll tell her that," he promised. "I'm certain it will endear you to her."

Shannon woke the following morning to the unfamiliar sounds of children laughing, old men coughing, and infants wailing. She lay on her back on the cushioned sleeping platform and stared up at the ceiling of the house. Fragments of sparkling light shone through, making her remember the shelter in Split Cane's village, the night she and Storm Dancer had first made love.

This wasn't moonlight spilling onto her face; it was sunlight. It was morning. She knew that she had to rise and make herself useful. It was important that these people accept her as a productive member of the community. She wouldn't be a burden, and she wouldn't shame Storm Dancer. She would use the time that he was gone to adapt to the Cherokee way of life.

Shannon was relieved that she was the guest of a plump woman named Snowberry, and not living in his mother's house. She had been told that Storm Dancer's mother's name was Firefly and his father Flint, but she had yet to meet either of them. And frankly, as far as she was concerned, the longer she could put off the confrontation, the better.

Watching Storm Dancer ride away to join the other warriors had been terrible. She didn't want to think of him facing the tomahawks, war clubs, knives and arrows of the Shawnee, or the guns of the British or the French. She had already lost her father. What would she do if Storm Dancer didn't come back? She had thought that it would be impossible to sleep, knowing that he was going into danger, but she had slept, and now she had to face Storm Dancer's extended family and his friends.

"In for a penny, in for a pound," she murmured, and slid off the sleeping platform. Since it was summer and warm, she'd lain down in nothing but her shift. She had folded her skirt and bodice and put them on top of her shoes and stockings. They were gone. In their place lay a pair of dainty moccasins, a doeskin skirt, and a fringed vest that tied in the front.

She considered remaining in her shift, but it was torn and dirty. Her mother would have considered it good for nothing but braiding into a rag rug. There was little Shannon could do about the color of her skin or hair, but she could adapt to the Cherokee style of dress. That she would do willingly, although the hem of the skirt was shockingly short, and more breasts and belly showed than her father would have approved of.

No one remained in the round shelter, but outside, a bubbling pot hung over a fire. A stranger, an attractive young woman, knelt before the fire, placing corn cakes on a stone to bake. She wore nothing but moccasins and a short skirt. Her shapely breasts were bare.

When Shannon greeted her in Cherokee, the woman glanced up. For a second, something flashed in her eyes, but then, just as quickly, she smiled.

"Welcome to our village. Are you hungry, or would you like to bathe before you eat?"

"Thank you. I'm Shannon." She was about to say that she would like to go to the creek before she broke her fast, but before she could go on, the Indian woman spoke again in a sweet, clear voice.

"My aunt goes to the fields early. She asked me to stay with you this morning. I am called Cardinal."

Cardinal. Shannon's mind went blank. This was Cardinal, the woman Storm Dancer was supposed to marry, her rival. What could she possibly say to her? "You . . . you are beautiful," she blurted awkwardly. "I'm sorry. I—"

Cardinal laughed. "You speak our language very well. And you have beauty too. I have never seen a woman with hair like ripe corn."

"I don't know what to say."

Cardinal's mouth tightened. "Your war is not with me or my aunt. It is Storm Dancer's mother you must worry about." She used a wooden paddle to slide a corn cake off the rock and offered the morsel.

Shannon took the cake. It was hot, and she tossed it from hand to hand to avoid burning herself. Cardinal watched her, and Shannon wondered if she was being judged. When she tasted the cake, it was delicious, much better than the ones Oona had made on the cabin hearth. "Oh, it's wonderful."

"My aunt, Snowberry, is known among the *Tsalagi* for her cooking," Cardinal said. "If you ask, she will teach you her recipe."

Shannon swallowed the mouthful of cake. It was sweet and spicy at the same time. She looked up at the stately young woman. "I'm sorry if you were hurt. I never meant to fall in love with him."

"Perhaps it is better this way. Some think the old women have too much power. It is better if young people make their own choices. I would have married him, but now . . ." She shrugged. "Now I may choose my own husband."

After Cardinal had finished baking the corn cakes, she showed Shannon to the women's bathing place in a secluded spot along the creek. No one else was there. "The sun is well up," Cardinal explained. "Most of the women are in the gardens. I would be there too, but . . ."

"Go ahead," Shannon said. "I can find my own way back to the village. It's just through those trees."

"My aunt asked me to add vegetables to the pot for the noon meal."

"I can do that for you," Shannon offered.

Cardinal regarded her coolly. "Do not let the stew burn. Snowberry would be an object of ridicule if her stew is not fit to eat."

"I won't."

Nodding, Cardinal turned and hurried along a path that led away from the village. Shannon watched her until she turned a bend and vanished in the trees. The woman had said all the right things, but Shannon wasn't certain if she liked her or not. She would try and reserve judgment until she knew her better.

Shannon bathed and washed her hair quickly, then

redressed. She didn't want to be away from the house long. Letting her hostess's meal turn to charcoal wouldn't be a way to return her hospitality.

She'd gone only a few yards along the trail when someone called her name. She glanced back to see Gall limping toward her.

"You are the talk of the village," he said, when he caught up with her. "Have you faced down the she-bear yet?"

"She-bear?"

He laughed. "My aunt. Storm Dancer's mother. She swore she would not have you here. She is a powerful enemy, my friend. Are you certain you want to go against her to be with her son?"

"I guess I am," she said. "He told me you were hurt." She looked at the bandage on his leg. "Are you healing well?"

"The bullet went through without breaking a bone. I am lucky, but not so lucky that I could go with the war party."

She said nothing.

"You will never be happy here."

She started walking back toward the village. "I love him, Gall. I think I could learn to be a good Cherokee wife."

He took hold of her arm. "When winter comes and you go without food, or when we must take up weapons against your people, you may change your mind." He squeezed. "You don't have to stay here. I could take you east to a settlement before he returns."

"Gall, you don't understand. I couldn't do that. Whatever happens, I have to work that out with Storm Dancer. I appreciate your—"

He gripped her harder. She winced, and he let go.

"I am your friend, Shannon. I was your father's friend. You forget, I'm half white, myself. Trust me. I'll take you out of here before something bad happens."

Shannon walked faster. "I appreciate your offer, but I'm never going back. I'll wait for him to return, and if the village won't accept me, maybe we'll go someplace else."

Gall's face darkened. "You will regret this decision."

"Maybe," she agreed. "But I'm here. His mother will have to deal with me. Where he goes, I go."

"Don't say I didn't warn you. It never works out. Have you thought of your children? They will be nothing. Not white. Not Cherokee. They will have no place to call home. Believe me, Shannon. I know. Of all people, I know."

"Then I'll count on you to remain my friend, and to be a friend to any son or daughter that we might have. Can you do that, Gall?"

He stood there as she walked away. She could feel his gaze on her back. First Cardinal and then Gall. Would anyone in this village truly welcome her? Or would she remain what she'd always been—the outsider.

Gall caught up with Cardinal at the edge of Firefly's cornfield. Already, thick vines of beans were sprouting and running up the sturdy stalks of corn. In the fields, women and girls laughed and called to each other. Some of the older women were singing a planting song. Gall remained hidden in the trees and called out to her.

"Cardinal."

"Who is it?" She paused and turned toward him. "Gall? What are you doing here? Is there word from the war party?"

He put a finger to his lips. "I would speak with you in private."

"I have to help plant the squash seeds."

"It's about the white woman."

She came back to join him in the shelter of the cedars. "What is it?" she asked. "What do you want to tell me?"

"It was wrong of my cousin to bring his white whore here to shame you in front of everyone," he said slyly. "He was meant for you until she lured him away. I can help you."

"Help me how?" she asked. Her eyes widened with interest.

"If she was dead, he would forget her. He would marry you. The gossips would soon forget the scandal."

She didn't answer, but she didn't turn away, either. She was interested in what he had to say.

"I will kill her for you."

"Murder a guest? Why would you do such a thing? And if you did and Storm Dancer found out, he would kill you with his bare hands."

"He will not find out. If you will bring her to me, in the forest, I will rid you of her. I will push her off Ghost Ledge. She will fall to her death, and Storm Dancer will be free to be with you as his mother wishes."

"Why? Why would you do such a thing? You do nothing without a reason, Gall. What's in it for you?"

"I think only of our village, of our safety. So long as she is here, our town will be a target for the English. It's better if we get rid of her and make it look like an accident. What do you say?" He smiled at her.

"Murder? It is a thing I must think about. I don't know if I could—"

"Consider it," he said. "But don't think too long. If we are to do this, it must be soon, before Storm Dancer returns . . . before he finds a way to make her his wife."

# Chapter 23

Shannon carefully added the vegetables to the pot, and when they had cooked through, she moved the coals aside so that the food would remain warm but wouldn't burn. She took a twig broom and swept the hard-packed area in front of the house and tidied the sleeping mats inside.

Around Shannon, the men, and women, and children went about their daily routine, pretending that they didn't see her at all. Young mothers nursed infants and older matrons sewed, gossiped together, and prepared food without glancing Shannon's way. She was certain she must be the object of curiosity, but if so, the population did an excellent job of ignoring her. Not even the village dogs paid her any mind.

Shannon seemed invisible even to the small boys playing in the sand with a toddler at a neighboring cabin or to the sloe-eyed, teenage girl alternately sewing a garment and tending to the children. The boys patiently stacked pinecones as high as they could, so that the baby could knock over the tower again and again. Each time, the barefooted toddler, clad only in a necklace of shells and matching earrings, squealed with delight. As she looked on, sadness welled up in Shannon. She couldn't help remembering an adorable little boy with woodpecker feathers in his hair, a child who would never laugh in the world again.

Across the lane, in front of another lodge, a girl, about five, with huge dark eyes, fed a tame raccoon pieces of bread under the watchful gaze of a smiling grandfather and a lad that Shannon supposed must be an apprentice toolmaker. The older man held arrow shafts over a kettle of boiling water, one by one, to harden them, and then used a stone to smooth and straighten the lengths of wood until they were identical. His assistant, a youth of ten or eleven, kept the fire hot, stacked the arrows, and swept up the shavings.

Determined to prove her worth, Shannon paid close attention to what was going on around her and noticed a dark-skinned woman lift down a clay water jar suspended in a braided rawhide webbing from a tree branch by her doorway. When the woman walked away purposefully, Shannon located a similar container and followed. A short walk through the village and down a hill led to a spring. Again, Shannon waited, and when the woman's pot was full, she filled her own.

The woman averted her eyes, but when Shannon addressed her courteously in Cherokee, the stranger registered fear. She ducked her head and hurried quickly away. Puzzled, Shannon stared after her. The woman hadn't appeared to be Indian at all, but African. Da had said that Virginia and the Carolina slave owners complained that their runaways found sanctuary with the Cherokees. Was that what had frightened her? Was the woman afraid that she would report her presence to the white settlers?

When Shannon entered the town, the woman at the spring had disappeared. She'd hoped to speak to her, to assure her that she meant her no harm. Conscious of many pairs of eyes watching her, Shannon brought back the water and replaced the jar in its leather sling where it would keep cool and free of dust.

Now she was uncertain of what to do. She refused to go into the house and hide, but, after she stirred the stew, she couldn't think of any more chores that needed her attention. The thing she dreaded most was a confrontation with Storm Dancer's mother, so that's what she decided she must do. She must face Firefly and get it over with.

She crossed the lane, went to the nearest woman, and asked where Firefly lived. The old woman chuckled, but pointed to a large lodge that sat apart from the others. When Shannon thanked her and started in that direction, her informant offered, "She may be in the cornfield at this hour."

Shannon approached Firefly's house. A dog raised its hackles and growled, but Shannon refused to be deterred and ignored the threat. "Hallo," she called. "Firefly? Are you within?" The deerskin was pushed back, an invitation to enter. "Hallo."

The interior of the cabin was dark but neat. Standing by the doorway was a water jug with a lid. Shannon looked inside and saw that the water level was low. She took a smaller jug and returned to the spring to fill it. Again, she had the feeling that she was walking a gauntlet. Everyone watched her, but pretended not to.

As she came back down the wood's path with the water, a tall, elegant beauty in an embroidered red wool dress stepped into the path in front of her. Shannon tried not to be intimidated. At the tavern, she had always been taller than any of the girls, but most of the Cherokee women topped her by inches.

"What do you think you are doing?" the newcomer demanded.

Shannon inspected her closely. Silver cones dangled from her ears, and a six-inch-long engraved silver gorget hung from a chain around her slender neck. Her hair, braided and pinned high into a coronet and decorated with elk teeth, was as black as a crow's wing, her eyes fierce and intelligent. The woman didn't look old enough to be Storm Dancer's mother, but Shannon could see a marked resemblance in the eyes and forehead.

"I have fetched cool water from the spring for you, lady," Shannon replied in her best Cherokee. She kept her expression and tone smooth.

"And why would you do that?" The yellow dog that had growled at her earlier appeared and ran to the lady, tail wagging.

"Out of respect for who you are."

"And who do you think I am?"

"The mother of the man I love."

"Love." Firefly scoffed. "What does a white woman know of love? If you truly loved him, you would return to your own people and forget you ever knew him."

Shannon hugged the water pot against her chest. Water had spilled down the sides, and the damp container felt good in the heat of the day. "I didn't want to love him. I fought against it. I even tried to marry a white man." She shook her head. "I couldn't. Your son holds my heart in his hands."

"And if the *Tsalagi* make war on the whites? Where will your place be then?"

"Where he is, I will be. His enemies will be mine."

"He was destined to marry Cardinal. My son was born to serve his clan and nation. If he takes a white-skinned wife, it will shatter the spirits' plan."

Shannon exhaled softly. "Do you always know what the spirits want?"

Firefly frowned. Her long, graceful fingers touched her throat absently. "No one can always know," she admitted.

"Then, perhaps, it is their will that I be your son's wife. Maybe that is the way the plan comes together. And we are so small, so insignificant, that we can't see the pattern until it is complete."

Storm Dancer's mother reached out for the water jar. "My son bade me keep you safe. I told him that I don't want you here, but he has entrusted me with the duty to offer you hospitality."

"I don't want to be a burden. I will do whatever you ask of me."

Firefly's eyes flashed. "And if I ask you to give him up and go away?"

"Anything but that." Shannon released the container. "I didn't want to come here any more than you wanted me. I came for love of Storm Dancer. I know you love him too."

"I am his mother. He is my only child."

"So, for his sake, we should try to get along."

"You speak well for a woman with corn hair and skin like a fish's belly. But many whites say one thing and mean another." She brushed her throat with her fingertips again. "I am not your friend, daughter of Truth Teller."

"Not yet. But it may be different in the future. If I give him a child."

Firefly nodded grudgingly. "There is a slim possibility, very slim, that I may come to accept you. It does not please me, the thought that my grandchildren will be ugly."

"What child is ugly if it is loved?"

Storm Dancer's mother dismissed her with a haughty sniff. "I will be watching you, yellow hair. If you place a foot wrong, I will know."

"My name is Shannon."

"Shan-non." She shrugged. "White names are like cornhusks blowing across a field. They mean nothing."

"Not true. My name has as much meaning as yours, lady."

Firefly's mouth twitched. Shannon wondered if she was suppressing a smile or an oath.

"What does that mean? Shan-non?"

"My father said it was *little wise one.*"

She nodded. "I liked him. He was a good man, your father. A fair trader. Let us hope he was right about that." Firefly shifted the heavy pot to her hip and pointed across the village. "The cornfields are that way. If you are indeed wise, you will join the other women in the garden. You can help most by ridding our new squash plants of bugs."

"Please . . . a question?"

"Yes." Firefly regarded her coolly. "What is it?"

"I saw a woman earlier, at the spring. Her skin is black."

"Nesting Swan. What of her?"

"She seemed afraid of me. Is she an escaped slave?"

"No. She is a free woman of the *Tsalagi.* I am surprised that your father never mentioned her. He bought her from a slave catcher for two hands of prime beaver pelts."

Shannon's stomach twisted. "My father bought a slave? He never told me. Da always said he didn't believe in slavery."

"He bought Nesting Swan out of pity. She ran from a bad master, but her luck was bad. She had been bitten by a rattlesnake. The white slave catcher thought it better to have good beaver hides than a dying woman."

"But how did she get here?"

"Winter Fox, my brother, saw her at Truth Teller's post. Your father had saved her from the snake's poison, but your mother was afraid of her. She did not want a black servant. Winter Fox offered to take her as a second wife, and so she came to us."

"If my father bought her freedom, why is she afraid of me?"

"Nesting Swan is a good woman, but she is fearful of all whites. She does not want anyone to take her from her husband or her children."

"I would never do anything to hurt her. I want only to be her friend," Shannon assured her.

Firefly nodded. "I will tell her. But do not expect much. She has good reason to mistrust whites." She glanced toward the fields. "I have much to do. If you want to help, go and find Snowberry. She will show you where you are most needed in the gardens."

"Gladly. I'm not a lazy person. I feel better when I'm useful."

"We will see," Firefly replied. "In time, we will see what is true and what is not."

Shannon was close enough to the cornfields to hear the women singing when an arm came out of the thickly hanging cedar boughs and seized her. Before she could utter a sound, someone yanked her into the shadows and clapped a hand over her mouth. She struggled, but then she heard Storm Dancer's voice close to her ear.

"Did you think a mountain lion had you?" His mouth came down on hers and she gave herself over to his kiss. Her fear melted into joy at his touch, and she opened like a flower to the thrust of his hard, seeking tongue.

Eventually, they broke for air, and she gasped, "What are you doing here? Has the war party returned? Is the danger over?"

"I wish it were." He pulled her hard against him and ran warm fingers down her back to cup her buttock. "I've missed you, heart of my heart."

"You just left." Excitement made her voice breathy.

Heat stirred in the pit of her belly, and her bones felt weak. He was a fever in her blood, this great, handsome man, and she loved him with every fiber of her being.

"Even an hour away from you is too much."

"But how are you . . ."

He lowered his head and nuzzled between her breasts. She made a small sound of desire, deep in her throat. "Come with me."

"To war?"

He laughed, caught her around the waist, and tossed her onto his shoulder. "I have until the sun sets, and then I must take my turn as guard on the pass. Until then, Winter Fox has given me leave to see if his sister has burned you at the stake or dried your hair on a scalp hoop."

Her heart leaped. "We can be together?" He was here. Why or how didn't matter. All that mattered was the feeling of his body pressed against hers. All that mattered was the smell and taste of him. "I don't want to talk about your mother."

Later she would tell him about her strange meeting with Firefly. She would tell him about Nesting Swan and her father, but not now. Now, this time, so precious, was for them alone.

He laughed. "Neither do I. There is a place nearby that I've wanted to take you."

"Put me down. I won't try to escape." She tried to wiggle free, but he clapped a hand on her bottom sharply. His scent filled her head and made her dizzy. He was warm and clean and virile. There was nowhere she would rather be than here.

"I like you better this way. My prisoner." He leaped ahead, racing through the forest at breakneck speed, and dizzy, she clung to him. Only later, when they reached a steep hill, did he lower her to the ground and clasp her hand in his.

"Trust me?" he asked.

"Yes, yes, I do." Whenever she saw him, she couldn't help being amazed at his size, at the beauty of his muscled body, at the strength in his long, hard legs and sinewy arms. Today, he wore nothing but his weapons strapped to his gleaming body and a small loincloth and high moccasins.

"Good." He charged up the incline, dragging her after him.

The way was rock strewn, the footing difficult. When they reached the top, she was breathing hard. "Where are we going?" she asked. The top of the knoll was grassy. She could see a long way over the treetops that seemed to stretch on forever.

"Close your eyes."

"Close my eyes?"

"Obey me, woman. You did just say you trusted me."

Laughing, she did as he ordered.

"Just to be sure." She gasped as he tied a length of cloth around her head, blocking her vision. He bent down and kissed her again, then whispered, "Now, hold tight. We're going to fly like eagles."

"What? Are you crazy?"

The next thing she knew, Storm Dancer had given a mighty tug on her arm. She ran after him for a few yards, and abruptly, they were falling in midair.

Down and down.

She screamed, but the air rushed by her face so fast that it was all she could do to utter a small squeal. With a great splash, they landed, feet first in water. Water closed over her head and the cloth he'd tied around her eyes slipped down around her neck and drifted away. She held her breath as they plunged deep and then kicked their way up to break the surface of an enchanted forest pool.

"How did you like that?" he shouted in her ear. "I told you we would fly."

It was hard to hear him above the great roar of tumbling water. Directly ahead of her, a waterfall cascaded from rocks a hundred feet above. The air was thick with flying drops of water, the spray so thick that it formed a curtain around them.

Shannon knew she had been in this place before. It was the magic spot of her vision. She clung to him, encircling his neck with her arms, gazing into his dark, enigmatic eyes, eyes filled now with love for her. "It was like flying," she agreed.

For a long time, they floated in the deep pool, kissing and touching each other, and then Storm Dancer swam toward the falls, bringing her with him. She knew what would come next. He would gather her in his arms and carry her into the secret cavern behind the falling water. He would carry her to a warm, bubbling pool, as he had before. And there, he would make love to her.

"My Shannon," he murmured. "Do you remember?"

"I do," she said. "I do remember." And then he swept her up and climbed the slippery rocks to the base of the cascade.

This time, she was prepared for the hush of the cavern. She kept her eyes open, taking in the beauty of the cave as he walked deeper into the earth's womb.

"You were always meant to be mine," he said, kissing her throat and trailing caresses down over her breasts. "No other woman but you."

She sighed with pleasure as he lowered her into the mineral pool. "Is this heaven?"

He laughed, stripped off his loincloth, and slid into the water beside her. Shannon paddled backward, putting space between them. "I suppose you would have me take this off." She tugged at her doeskin dress. He grinned. "I would."

"And you would have me let you touch me?" she teased, lifting the wet clothing over her head.

He moved closer.

She laughed, tossing the dress to the pool's edge, moving just out of his reach.

"And if it's not what I wish?" She tried not to smile but her joy tickled the corners of her mouth.

"Oh, you wish for it." He dove for her and she squealed with laughter and she, again, moved just out of his reach.

"Come to me, Shannon." He gestured with one hand, beckoning her.

"Come to you?" She moved through the water slowly, enjoying the moment of anticipation. "And then?"

He slid his arm around her back and drew her close. "And then this." He kissed her mouth firmly. "And this." He cupped her breast in his hand. "And this."

She watched him lower his hand beneath the water, felt its warmth along the inside of her thigh, then its heat against her woman's place.

"Let me show you," he whispered in her ear. "You will like this, what I have."

"Will I?" She giggled, enjoying the play. But as he stroked her steadily, the playfulness fell away, replaced by a white-hot heat . . . a hot need she knew no one would be able to satisfy but him.

Shannon rested her hands on Storm Dancer's shoulders and opened her legs, letting them float upward, then wrapped them around his waist. Pressing her warm wet body against his, she reveled in the feel of his steely hardness against her woman's folds. "Show me," she whispered, letting her eyes drift shut.

Storm Dancer pushed her wet hair back, smoothing it in a tender caress. "Do not close your eyes, dear one.

Look into mine as we share this union. Let me drink of you as you drink of me."

Shannon opened her eyes to look into the darkness of his, and their mouths met with a building hunger. She wanted to take it slowly, to enjoy every precious moment she had with him, but her body revolted against the idea. She wanted him. Needed him. Now. Hard. Fast.

There was little foreplay. She was already wet for him, already breathing hard. And he was well past prepared. Their mouths tangled in a kiss, Shannon reached beneath the water and boldly stroked him, guiding him inside her.

Storm Dancer resisted, but she would have her way with him. Perhaps there would be time for slow, patient lovemaking later, but right now she needed consummation. Needed to feel him fill her.

Shannon moaned as he entered her and she clung to him, her arms around his neck, her cheek against his shoulder. Catching her breath, she thrust against him, pushed back, and did it again.

Storm Dancer let out a groan of surrender and tightened his arms around her, thrusting hard and deep. Water splashed around them as he thrust again and again, and she strained to ride the waves of the tide building deep inside her.

"Like this," he groaned in her ear. "Like this, my love."

Shannon bit down on Storm Dancer's shoulder as every muscle in her body contracted and relaxed. Unable to hold back any longer, make the pleasure last another moment, she gave in to it.

She surprised herself by the scream that came from her lips as her entire body was wracked with the joy of the union. She felt him thrust one final time, then heard his groan in her ear as she relaxed in his arms, satiated . . . if only for a few moments.

# Chapter 24

It was dark and beginning to rain when Shannon entered the village and returned to Snowberry's house to find the stout older woman sitting cross-legged on a mat by the central fire pit. When Shannon entered, Snowberry glanced up, smiled, and greeted her cheerfully.

"I hope the stew was—" Shannon began.

"The food was good," Snowberry answered. "Another family joined me at the meal, but we saved you some. Also these." She held out a shallow basket containing several corn cakes. "Cardinal made them for you."

Shannon thanked her. She really wasn't hungry. She wanted more than anything to curl up on her sleeping platform and dream of Storm Dancer. Their hours together had been magical. She felt as though she'd been living a dream, one she didn't want to wake up from. But now that they were parted again, she was terrified that something would happen to him. He said that they'd not found any more Shawnee in Cherokee territory, but if they discovered fresh tracks, they would chase the offenders down, no matter where they ran.

"Please. Sit and eat."

Shannon didn't know if she could eat anything, but

courtesy demanded she make an effort. Snowberry had been kind to her. Cardinal's aunt treated her, not like an unwanted white stranger, but like a favored daughter. It would be rude to go straight to bed and not talk for a while.

She felt as though the easygoing widow was her first friend among the Cherokee, other than Gall. Back at the trading post, she'd enjoyed Gall's company, but here among the *Tsalagi*, Shannon wasn't certain if she still felt the same way. Neither Oona nor Storm Dancer trusted Gall. She wondered if she'd misjudged Gall's character. In any case, she had no intentions of going anywhere alone with him, let alone to allow him to take her away from the man she loved.

She nibbled at the cakes and ate a small bowl of the stew while Snowberry chatted on about the garden, someone's new baby, a new basket shape Cardinal was weaving, and the weather. Thankfully, the woman didn't require answers, just an interested listener. Snowberry never asked where she'd been all afternoon, and Shannon didn't volunteer the information. And by the time the fire died low and the two retired for the night, the storm had hit full force.

Gusts shook the roof and howled around the lodge while torrents of rain fell, streaming down the outside walls and running in rivulets down the town streets. The summer door covering, nothing more substantial than a deer hide, whipped in the wind, and water sluiced around the smoke hole cover in the center of the room. But most of the cabin interior, including the sleeping platforms, with their storage containers tucked underneath, remained dry.

The storm didn't frighten Shannon; oddly, she found the wind and the rhythm of the falling rain soothing. The doeskin mattress, stuffed with pine boughs, was wide enough for two and comfortable. Shannon's last thought before she dropped off to sleep, amid the soothing smells of rain and pine needles, was for Storm Dancer. She hoped he and the other men had found shelter. The villagers were snug in their cabins, but any living thing that couldn't find shelter tonight on the mountain would be in dire straits.

For three days, the rains fell. Some homes flooded and families had to take shelter with friends or relatives. Winds remained strong, tugging at roofs, knocking over tall corn grinders, and blowing away household articles that had been left outside. Shannon and Snowberry remained housebound, an island of dry in a sea of water. One evening, Nesting Swan came to visit and share bread and honey. And the following afternoon, Corn Woman dashed over with hot slices of freshly roasted venison and stewed green beans with slices of wild duck.

While the rains fell, Snowberry busied herself with basket weaving and sewing. Shannon attempted to start her own basket, but she was all thumbs. The beautifully designed containers that the Cherokee women made, some so tightly woven that they held water, seemed beyond her ability to create.

"You do not learn to weave in a day, nor in two," Snowberry advised gently. "My mother taught me, but it took years for me to make a basket that my father didn't laugh at." Even as she spoke, her callused fingers twisted the split oak strips into neat patterns. "Nesting Swan weaves the best river grass baskets. Once she has stopped being afraid of you, I'm sure she will show you some of her secrets."

"She's frightened because I'm white."

"Yes," Snowberry agreed. "Nesting Swan would rather

die than be taken back to slavery. A woman with black skin, even a free woman, is never entirely safe. If there were ever papers that proved she had been legally bought, they are long lost."

"Please tell her for me that I would never tell anyone she was here."

Snowberry nodded. "I will pass on those good words, but she may not believe you." She set aside her basket strips and removed a length of tanned deerskin from the wall.

Shannon watched as the woman marked and cut the leather in shapes to form moccasins. "When they are sewn, I will decorate them for you," Snowberry offered. "A woman can always use extra footwear."

Smiling, Shannon had to agree. Sewing leather was more difficult than stitching cloth, but again, it was something that she'd learned from Flynn. "Thank you. This I can do," she said with a smile.

The Indian woman nodded her approval. "A good heart goes far to make a good human being. If you wish to be happy among the *Tsalagi*, I believe you will."

"I want to be a good wife to Storm Dancer."

"A wife, is it? To the chosen one? Let us hope that you are lucky as well as good. Firefly will do all she can to prevent such a marriage."

"Do you agree with her?"

Snowberry chuckled. "She is my friend, but we do not always agree, and I have no son to protect." She added another cherry log to the hearth. "Firefly is a powerful opponent, but her heart is good, as well. Who knows what may happen? You might even find another man you prefer to Storm Dancer."

Shannon looked into the teasing eyes. "But you aren't against the match?"

"I should be. Cardinal is my favorite niece. She would have been his wife, if he hadn't met you."

"I don't want to hurt her, but I won't give him up. I can't. And there is no other man for me."

Snowberry pursed her lips and made a clicking sound with her tongue. "What will be, will be, child. I have learned that this is one of the joys of life. No matter how old I become, I find surprises around every turn."

The days that the storm raged passed slowly. Each afternoon, Shannon made the dash through the rain to fetch fresh water. Snowberry had dry wood aplenty, stashed beneath the sleeping platform that ran all round the lodge. Still, Shannon was relieved when the downpour finally slowed to a trickle and then stopped. Clouds parted, and a bright sun shone down on the village.

Instantly, everyone in the village was out. Children and dogs scampered and played, young mothers and older girls eagerly sought out their friends while Snowberry, Nesting Swan, and the matrons set out immediately for the gardens. Snowberry handed Shannon a hoe and motioned for her to come along.

The storm had knocked down young corn plants, flooded hills of squash, and washed away beans and other vegetables. All around Shannon, women and girls were kicking off their moccasins and wading into the muddy gardens to rescue the plants. Shannon followed Snowberry to her own planting area and began to straighten and restore the vegetables that could be saved. What couldn't be salvaged, the women deftly replanted with seeds they had carried with them to the fields.

Soon, they were all laughing and covered in mud. For the first time since coming to Firefly's village, Shannon felt as though she was accepted, not simply a guest, but part of the group. She joined in the singing and jokes, and almost before she realized it, the women were pausing for a noon meal. They didn't return to the town, but walked to the creek, washed off the worst of the mud, and devoured bread and berries and morsels of roasted meat that boys had carried from the home fires.

Shannon had just reached for another piece of quail when silence fell over the chattering gardeners. Several women stepped back, and Shannon found herself face-to-face with Storm Dancer's mother, Firefly, and two other stern-faced matrons.

"What have you done?" Firefly demanded.

"Me?" Puzzled, Shannon looked around. Snowberry's expression was strained, and Nesting Swan revealed equal distress. "I was just helping—"

"Not today," Firefly thundered. "Before the storm. What did you take from my cabin? What did you steal?"

Shannon scrambled to her feet. Had she misunderstood the Cherokee words? "Steal? I didn't steal anything from you."

One of Firefly's companions, a white-haired woman Shannon had heard others call Yellow Bead, placed a basket on the ground, removed the lid, and lifted the pieces of what appeared to be a grotesque object fashioned of dried husks, corncobs, and wood. "This. The sacred Corn Mask."

Snowberry uttered a low moan. Someone behind Shannon gasped. Another covered her eyes with muddy hands. Whispers rippled through the assembly.

"A bad omen."

"Our gardens will fail."

"She did it—the yellow hair."

"I'm not a thief," Shannon protested. "I never touched your mask, if that's what it is."

"For generations, the Wolf Clan has guarded this mask," Firefly said. "It was old when my grandmother's grandmother's mother was born. Since I was your age, it has been in my keeping. Today, we went to bring it forth, so that the spirits would see that we honored them, so that our fields would recover from the great rains."

"Not only did you steal it," Yellow Bead said, "but you shattered it."

Nesting Swan began to weep.

"I didn't touch your mask," Shannon repeated. "I've never laid eyes on it before."

"She denies it," someone murmured.

"It's broken. The power is lost."

"Our children will go hungry this winter."

"I saw you go into Firefly's cabin, with my own eyes." Cardinal stepped out of the crowd. "Days ago, before the rain, when you minded the stew pot for my aunt. I saw you enter Firefly's house while she was in the cornfield. You carried something when you came out."

Shannon took a step back. Angry faces, angry words pressed closer.

"Sacrilege," came a shout from the back of the group.

"Think carefully about your words," Firefly said. "Among the *Tsalagi,* these things are great sins: theft, desecrating a holy object, and lying about your crime."

"I told you, I didn't touch your mask," Shannon insisted. "The only thing I took from your lodge was an empty water jar." She looked around her. "You must believe me. I would never—"

Firefly's eyes welled with regret. "You will be judged, daughter of Truth Teller. The council will decide whether you are innocent or guilty."

"And if you are found guilty, the penalty is death," Yellow Bead said.

"She's guilty," someone muttered. "You can see it on her face."

"I'm innocent," Shannon repeated. "I'm not a thief.

The door flap was open. I only went into your home to see if you were there."

"If you didn't steal the sacred Corn Mask," Firefly replied, "then why did we find it hidden in the storage space under your sleeping platform?"

Gall summoned Cardinal to meet him in the dark of the night at the joining of two game trails near Ghost Ledge. He was here, ears straining for the rustle of her footsteps, and she was late. She should have been here more than an hour ago. Few sounds echoed over the meadow, save the dripping of water, the lonely hoot of a barred owl, and the chirping of crickets.

Centuries ago, in the time when the Cherokee had lived far to the east, forces of an angry earth had split this mountain. The thick forest opened on a flower-strewn meadow where Gall crouched waiting, and on the far side of the expanse of grass stood a small wedge of trees. Once, more oaks, chestnuts, and beeches had thrust their roots deep into the rich soil there, but one by one, rain and wind and cliff had claimed the trees, and they had toppled over the sheer precipice to tumble hundreds of feet to the rocky floor below.

In another time, when snows were deep and blizzards roared down from the north, early hunters had driven herds of deer to their deaths off this ledge. It was said that desperate women, whose men died young, came to this spot to leap to their deaths. Many testified that the meadow and thin line of woods were haunted, and that they had seen and heard the weeping ghosts.

Few *Tsalagi* would dare to come here, but Gall knew that Cardinal was bold and feared nothing she could not touch. It was a good place to meet without fear of others seeing and listening.

He saw her the instant she moved from the shadows of the trees. "Here," he called. "I am here." And when she came closer, he asked, "Did anyone see you? Are you certain you've not been followed?"

"No, no one saw me." Cardinal's voice came high and breathy. "I could have driven a white man's wagon through the camp, and no one would have noticed. They are all talking about her stealing the Corn Mask and desecrating it."

She had always been a quiet woman, calm, Gall thought. Perhaps she did fear this place. He rose and went to her and took her hands. "What have you done?"

"Nothing. It was her. The yellow-haired witch. She stole the Wolf Clan's mask and—"

"Save it for the council. You lied. You took the mask yourself, didn't you? Stole it and smashed it." He chuckled. "You really don't fear the spirits, do you?"

"I do."

He felt her tremble.

"I dropped it by accident. I wanted to hide the mask where it would be safe and quickly found, but it was dark in my aunt's cabin, and I stumbled over a hearth stone." She tried to pull her hands free, but he held her tightly.

"Why didn't you do as I asked? I would have thrown her off Ghost Ledge, and we would have been rid of her."

"I couldn't be a party to murder." She wiggled one hand out of his grasp. "I thought they would send her back to her own kind. She isn't one of us. I didn't think they would judge her as they would a *Tsalagi*."

He pulled her so close he could feel her breath on his forehead. She was tall, like most of the Cherokee women, taller than he was. He didn't like that. It made him feel small and less a man. "If your conscience bothers you, you should tell what you've done. Explain that it was you who stole the mask—who broke it."

Cardinal shuddered. "Then I would stand trial. This is all your fault, Gall. If it wasn't for you, I would have let him have her."

He wrapped his arms around her so quickly that she was trapped. He laid his head on her warm breasts. "What have you been doing, my pretty bird? You've been with a man, haven't you? I smell his juice on you."

"None of your business."

He slid one hand down her back to stroke her shapely buttocks. "You're still wet from having sex, aren't you?"

"No. You're mistaken. I've been nowhere but here. Let me go, Gall."

"Who was it tonight? I know you prefer married men, men who cannot sully your name. But Rattlesnake would. He's the one who had your sweet plum when you were barely thirteen. And Pine Squirrel. Such tales he tells." He caught the neckline of her vest and yanked it down so that one ripe breast glowed in the darkness.

"Stop it." She kicked his ankle hard enough to make him see stars.

He couldn't let her know that she'd hurt him. "What of Buffalo Hoof? Is he lying too?" The sight of her breast made his mouth water. He would suck it until she screamed with pleasure.

"No! Let go of me." She struggled against him. She was strong, this woman. Determined. But not as determined as he was to gain something from this meeting.

Her movements excited him, made him hard as bone. He fisted his fingers in her hair and forced her head down so that he could grind his mouth against hers.

"Stop that!"

When she opened her mouth, he plunged his tongue deep, then withdrew as she tried to catch him between her sharp teeth. She thrust an elbow sharply into his ribs and brought up a knee to strike his crotch. "Let me go!" She panted. "What do you think you're doing?"

"I'm your friend," he argued. "You owe me something if you want me to keep quiet about this. All I want is a little of what you've been giving other men so easily."

She freed one arm, brought it up, and stuck his chin a hard blow with the palm of her hand. His head rocked back. He lost his balance, staggered backward, and she broke loose from his grasp.

"How dare you?" she cried. "Dog vomit. Limping worm. Half-breed!"

"Close your mouth, woman!"

"Son of Big Pascal with the tiny root. I hear he likes it with men as well as women. Are you the same, Gall? Do you want Storm Dancer for yourself?"

"Stop!"

"I would never lie down with you," she taunted. "No decent girl in the camp would. You're the laughingstock of the village. Don't you know that? Everyone talks about you—how they'd like to be rid of you."

White-hot anger churned in his chest. "Hold your tongue or I'll cut it out of you."

But she would not be still. "Sneaking around. Betraying your cousin," she went on in the shrill, mocking voice. "Pretending you're hurt worse than you are so that you wouldn't have to join the war party with the other men!"

She turned to flee, but he ran after her and knocked her to the ground. She yanked her eating knife from her sheath and drove it into his arm. The pain shriveled his shaft, and he bit the side of his mouth to keep from crying out.

"Female dog." He twisted the knife from her hand. The wound burned like fire. He felt light-headed, but he held on to her with the tenacity of a weasel. He sunk his fingers into her shoulders and shook her until she screamed.

"You will share your thighs with me!" He ripped her skirt aside, pushed her legs apart, and slammed himself on top of her.

His shaft remained flabby. She clawed his face, as he grabbed his cock and tried to jam it in her. She was hitting him with both fists. She struck him full in the nose, and he felt the bone crunch. Pain rocked his head.

He half rose on his knees. She tried to get away, and he shoved her back so hard that her head bounced.

"Dirty whore!" he shouted.

Cardinal lay still.

He called her another name, even more vile. She didn't move. Gall got to his feet, stuffed his manhood back into his loincloth, and kicked her in the ribs.

"Get up. I didn't hurt you that bad." He leaned over her, pressed his face close to hers, and felt the stir of breath on his cheek. "I said . . ."

He shook her. She didn't respond.

He rolled her over and felt the back of her head. Had she struck a rock? It wasn't until he ran his hand lower, skimming her shoulder and back that his fingers encountered the knife handle protruding from her bleeding flesh.

Instinctively, he jerked the knife out. It wasn't a big knife. The blade was narrow and short, a woman's eating knife. No man would enter a battle with such a weapon.

Blood oozed from the hole.

Cardinal was hurt. Not dying. Hurt. If he carried her back to the village, the shaman could treat her—probably save her life.

But she would tell. Everyone would know.

Sadly, Gall gathered Cardinal in his arms and walked

through the trees to the edge of Ghost Ledge. No one could fault him. Cardinal had caused this herself, and the village would believe she'd killed herself because Storm Dancer had deserted her for a white woman.

It was the only way. . . .

# Chapter 25

Shannon, a prisoner, paced the confines of her rocky cell. Storm Dancer's mother had ordered the women to take her into a cave near the village and lower her into a deep pit in the earth.

"There you will remain until the trial," Firefly said. "You must think on what you have done. You must pray that the spirit of the Corn Mask will forgive your ignorance."

"I did nothing wrong," Shannon had repeated over and over.

"Then you will be found innocent," Firefly said. "And you have no reason to worry."

She hadn't been physically harmed in any way. The women had given her food, a blanket, water and fuel, and flint and steel to make a fire. But she was trapped here, encased in a cocoon of silence. Around her, walls of sheer rock rose. Below, stretched unfathomed depths of stone and earth. The ceiling of the cavern hovered far above, cloaked in darkness.

Shannon could hear nothing but the crackle of her fire and the pulsing of her own heart. There was no breeze, no drip of water, no human voice or footfall, although from time to time, she fancied she heard the faint flap of wings and shuddered to think she might be sharing her tomb with bats.

Her conscience was clear. She wasn't a thief. This was either a clever trap or a mistake. And, even though she had done nothing wrong, she could imagine what it would be like for a guilty man or woman imprisoned here. Fear would radiate through every drop of blood, and the walls would surely close in around them. The sheer weight of rock and mountain would crush the sanity from a guilty prisoner long before the *Tsalagi* judgment.

How had this happened to her? What would they do to her? Would she live to see Storm Dancer return? Or would he come home to find her bones already stripped of flesh by carrion eaters? And who had destroyed the Corn Mask? Could Firefly be so determined that her son marry Cardinal that she would condemn the woman he loved to death on a false charge?

The day passed and the day and night after that, the time broken only by silent visitors who lowered baskets of food and pulled up the pottery container they had provided for her bodily wastes. Her captors provided fresh water, enough to drink and to bathe, and changes of clothing, warmer garments than the skimpy skirt and vest she'd worn on the day they'd placed her here. And on the third day, someone tossed down a bearskin, so that she didn't have to sleep on the hard rock.

"I will not go as mad as Oona," Shannon vowed. "I will not." Repeating the statement every few hours seemed to help. How long she would wait for this trial, she didn't know, but when the Cherokee council women came for her, she was determined to have her wits about her. She would defend herself.

She was innocent. She was the one who had been wronged. She'd never seen the mask before they'd displayed the broken pieces at the creekside. And she had never stolen anything in her life—not a penny, not a crust of bread.

Maybe time wasn't her enemy, Shannon thought on the fourth day. If enough time passed, Storm Dancer would return. He would know that she'd been falsely accused. He would come to this place and rescue her.

He must.

He would, wouldn't he? He loved her. He'd said he loved her. Unless, it was all a lie. . . . Unless Storm Dancer had lied about losing his knife . . . unless he had been the one who killed her father. . . . Storm Dancer hadn't waited for Oona. Was it because he knew she would be safe? Or was it because he knew she could condemn him for murdering Flynn and burning the trading post?

Shannon pushed away the ugly doubts. Storm Dancer could never do those terrible things. Even imagining that he might do them was as wicked as what the council women had done to her. He was as innocent as she was. He had to be.

She kept count of the days by marking the wall with a burnt stick. She also drew pictures and wrote the lines of old Irish poems that she remembered from her childhood. She sang the lyrics of story-ballads and repeated riddles merely to hear the sound of her own voice. And she named her children, children she would have someday with Storm Dancer . . . boys and girls with skin the color of wild honey and eyes like fallen angels.

By the fifth day in her pit prison, Shannon was holding long conversations with her dead friend, Anna. Shannon hadn't lost her wits yet. She knew that Anna was dead and she was alive, but it was comforting to think about Anna and imagine that she was listening.

She told Anna all that had happened to her in the months and years since they'd been so cruelly parted. She even laughed with Anna about the antics of Betty the cow, and Badger the big-headed pony that Storm Dancer had given her. She didn't tell Anna about her father's death. Anna would know, and talking about Da would only make her sad.

She didn't tell Anna about Storm Dancer's knife either. To do so would be a betrayal of the man she loved. Anna might not understand. She might think that Shannon's fears had substance . . . that Storm Dancer could do such a terrible thing. Anna might suspect Storm Dancer of murdering Da. And so, Shannon had to keep those thoughts secret.

It was the sixth day, or perhaps the seventh. Shannon couldn't remember if she had marked the day twice or not, that the routine was broken by a small, serious face fringed in black hair peering over the edge of the pit.

"Are you there, yellow-haired ghost?"

Shannon started. Goosebumps rose on her arms. She hadn't thought to speak to Woodpecker, even though the boy was as dead as Anna. What did it mean that he'd come to her on his own? Had she lost her mind? Had she died?

"Woodpecker? Is that you?" she called.

"Yes!" he cried gleefully. "It be Woodpecker. Are you well Sha-naan-O-Say?"

"I don't think so." Shannon rubbed the base of her skull. "I'm talking to you." She added more sticks to the fire. She had carefully measured out her wood supplies every day so that there would be no chance of the fire going out, but she wanted a better look at the child's specter.

"Be happy. Do not be sad. I do not believe you are a breaker of sacred things. And my mother does not think so either."

"Your mother? I'm sorry. I didn't know she was killed."

A woman's face appeared next to his. "Do not frighten

my son with tales of dying," she admonished. "What's wrong with you? I thought you were his friend."

Shannon felt light-headed. She sat down on the bear-skin and tilted her head back to look at the woman. She was a stranger. Why would the ghost of a woman, one she'd never met in life, come to talk to her? "I don't understand. Aren't you dead too?"

The boy laughed. "My mother is here. She be Blue Sky of the Paint Clan. I am holding her arm. Why do you say my mother is dead?"

Shannon took a deep breath. Maybe the water they'd been bringing her was poisoned. Or the food . . . "You're dead, though. A white man killed you the night the village was attacked. I saw the feathers in your scalp."

"Stop it," Blue Sky ordered. "Stop frightening Wood-pecker or we will go away. No one else will talk to you. I've only come because my aunt asked me to bring you word."

"Your aunt? Who is your aunt?"

"Snowberry. She is my cousin's mother on my father's side, not really an aunt since she is Deer Clan and not of my mother's Paint Clan. But Snowberry has no family left, but Cardinal and her mother, Corn Woman. And Cardinal has run away with Gall."

"Snowberry sent you?"

"Yes!" Woodpecker cried. "Aunty Snowberry. She likes you."

Blue Sky continued. "She wanted me to tell you that your little mother, called Oona, is here in this village. She knows you were worried about her."

"But how?" Shannon demanded. "We left Oona at my father's trading post, many days' travel away."

"Whistler and his wife found her near Turkey Gap. They brought her to our new village."

"We are of Split Cane's town," Blue Sky explained. "My mother, Story Woman, knew Oona as the wife of Truth

Teller, your father. But Oona was not sick in her head the last time she saw her."

"My grandmother heard from Sings Twice that Storm Dancer was bringing you here. So—"

"So we brought Oona to you," Blue Sky finished for her son. "Oona is not *Tsalagi*. She is Delaware. Split Cane feels that it is your duty to care for Oona, since she is sick, whether your father is dead or not."

"If you don't want her, we will keep her," Woodpecker said. "We like her. She has two puppies, and she lets me play with them. I think she will give me one when they are old enough to leave the mother."

"Oona is here?"

"Are you slow-witted?" Woodpecker's mother asked. "My son is alive and well and so am I. Some were killed on that dark night, but we survived. It is bad luck for you to keep saying—"

"I'm sorry," Shannon said. "I thought . . . I saw a child's scalp with black and white woodpecker feathers—"

"Ahhh." The woman nodded. "Now, I understand. It was my son's friend, Tadpole. He was struck down and scalped by white barbarians. It was his hair that you saw, not my Woodpecker's."

Shannon closed her eyes. The child wasn't dead. The little boy staring down at her was alive. Emotion made her tremble. "I didn't know."

Woodpecker sniffed. "Tadpole wanted to tease my grandmother. I put the feathers in his hair as a joke. We thought she would think he was me. My old grandmother, Story Woman, does not see so good, but she makes the best sweet cakes."

"I'm sorry for Tadpole's mother and father, but I'm glad you're alive," Shannon said. "And I'm so happy that my father's wife is here. Of course, I will take care of her. Why didn't she come with you?"

"She doesn't talk," Woodpecker said. "My aunt Snowberry gave her soup and put her and the baby to sleep. She is sad, but she has a good pony. Maybe she will let me ride it."

Shannon hugged herself and chuckled. "A pony? Does he have a big head?"

"He does," the child agreed, "but his nose is very soft, and he likes sweet cakes."

"His name is Badger," Shannon said. "And he likes everything but work."

"We must go now," Blue Sky said, "but we will be back with your evening meal."

"Please, is there any word of the war party? Any news from our braves?"

"No. Nothing. We must wait to hear, and that is always hard. Is there anything you want?"

"To get out of here. I haven't done anything wrong."

"I'm sorry. We can't interfere with council business. But we will try to bring Oona with us later."

"Wait. Do you know how long they will keep me here?"

"Snowberry says she doesn't know," Blue Sky replied. "Cardinal must be here to testify at the trial, and she and Gall have run away together."

"Everyone is surprised, especially Aunt Snowberry. She didn't think that Cardinal liked him." The woman stood up and took her son's hand. "It is a great scandal in the village. Most do not think he is good enough for her. She was always meant for Storm Dancer."

"Do you think—" Shannon began.

"No, we cannot stay," Blue Sky said. "We will talk later."

"Wait!" But they were gone, and Shannon was alone once more. "Please!" she shouted. There were so many questions she wanted to ask. . . . If only Storm Dancer would return. Then, she knew, everything would be all right.

It had to be.

*  *  *

"You are getting old and fat, Luce Pascal." A knife flew by the Frenchman's face and stuck into a tree on the other side of the trail. "If I were not your son, then what?"

"Then I would be in the arms of the angels," Luce replied in French. "Come out of the bushes. Let me see you."

"As soon as you lower that rifle," Gall answered.

Laughing heartily, the little man rested the weapon across his horse's neck. "You are too late for the war. Or have you come to gather the spoils?"

"Like you?" Gall stepped out onto the path. "What are you doing this far south?"

"The sacred blood of Christ! Haven't you heard? My trading post was burned to the ground." Luce sat in the saddle smiling down at Gall from the back of his mule, but he offered no physical show of affection such as Storm Dancer's father might have done.

*Nothing ever changes,* Gall thought. *He is what he is.* "By who? Who is your enemy now, Big Pascal?"

Luce shrugged. His belly was bigger than when Gall had last seen him more than four years ago. His mustache was longer, his hair a little grayer, but his cheeks were just as red, his small eyes as sharp as a rat's. "Who can say? The British? The Shawnee? The Cherokee? Who knows what enemies a poor trader can have? If he is a poor businessman, he starves, but if he is good, men call him greedy."

Gall thought he understood most of what his father had said. His own French wasn't the best, and Luce had an accent that was unusual among most of the Frenchmen Gall had met. He slipped into a mixture of English, French, and Cherokee.

"But why are you here?"

"I heard that the Irishman was dead. Now that the Shawnee have retreated to the north, and the Cherokee have made peace with the English—"

"What? Why haven't I heard of this?"

"Who can say? Am I an eagle that I can see what you do or where you go? All I know is that Winter Fox met with the English at Fort Hood, and peace was declared between them once more."

"Were you there? Was my cousin among the warriors? Did you see Storm Dancer?"

Luce made a clicking sound with his tongue. "Him again, is it? You should stay clear of that one. A very fierce man. He will be the death of you."

"Or I will be of him," Gall replied.

Luce scoffed. "You are bitter."

"I have good reason."

His father waved his hand. "It is not good to always have hate and envy in your heart. Come with me. Help me to start again at the Irishman's crossing. You can smooth the way for me with the Cherokee."

"The *Tsalagi* do not trust you, Father."

"But you are one of them. You can help me to forge a new alliance. After all, I may be a Frenchman, but I am not political. I care not who controls these mountains, so long as I can turn a profit."

"And what makes you think the Cherokee will accept you and let you stay?"

"I can offer them something they can get nowhere else. Do you forget that I am a maker of fine whiskey? The young men will come for the fire water, no matter what the old heads say." The mule thrust its head and bared yellow teeth.

Gall smacked the animal's nose and it squealed and shied back.

"Careful," Luce warned. "His kick is worse than his bite."

"If he kicks me, he'll find himself roasting over a fire. I've heard mule is good."

"Mule is excellent with garlic, olive oil, and the right wine," his father agreed. "But today, we have only the mule, and I fear we would be disappointed."

Gall studied the older man. Luce had a good rifle, a very good knife, an Iroquois tomahawk, and two pack-horses carrying who knew what. His father was rich as well as clever. It could be that his own best interests lay in throwing in with Luce. He did not think that Firefly's village would be the best place for him now. Especially now . . .

"Will you teach me to make the whiskey?" Gall asked.

"Certainly." Luce grinned. "With such knowledge, you will always be certain of having a full purse. Help me build a new post, and I promise you enough trade goods to buy a fat wife, perhaps two."

"You are heading in the right direction for Flynn O'Shea's post. Ahead, along this trail, lies Green Valley. There is a settlement of English farmers there. They may shoot you and take all your goods."

His father chuckled. "You think me such a fool? No, Big Pascal is not." He patted the leather pouch that hung by a braided strap to his saddle. "I carry a letter from a Quaker merchant in Philadelphia telling the English that I am a fine fellow and a friend."

"And why would an English merchant give you such a paper?"

"I told him I was not French, but German."

"And he believed you? You, Big Pascal, known as a friend to the Huron, the Shawnee, and the Oneida?"

"You have much to learn, my son. I have carried this paper for two years, in case I had need of it. And now I do. I must shed my French skin and become someone else. I am no longer Luce Pascal, known as *Big Pascal*. I am Ernst Klaus, honest merchant from Lancaster in Penn's Colony. And soon, when more whites come to these mountains, and the Cherokee go west, I will send to Pennsylvania for a good Dutch wife."

"What of your French woman, the wife you left in your own country, across the sea?" Gall asked.

"Which one?" Luce laughed at his own joke. "Clotilde, the rich baker's daughter? Or Tienette, the physician's only child? Wives, my son, are easily acquired and easily disposed of."

"Like my mother?"

"Your mother was an exception. Her, I loved. But I could hardly take her or you back to France with me, could I? Here, in your own country, is where you belonged. As Clotilde and Tienette and their offspring belong in France. But this is where I shall live from now on, here in North America, and I will need a colonial wife to care for me in my old age. Do you see?"

Gall did see. His French might not be as good as his father's or any of his French-born half brothers or sisters, but he was smart. He had thought when he'd first laid eyes on Luce that he would kill him. But now he saw what advantage he might gain by accepting his rightful place as the son of German merchant Ernst Klaus.

He would take what he could get from his father, but he would never trust him, and he would never tell him about Cardinal or the other things that he had done. It would not do to give Luce Pascal knowledge to use against him. Gall knew that he was clever enough and devious enough to live in his father's world. He might even take a white name to go with his new responsibilities. Joseph. He had always favored Joseph.

"I cannot go with you to the English settlement," he said to Luce. "But if you would have their favor, tell them where one of their own can be found. In the village of

Firefly, deep in the mountains, is a captive white woman with yellow hair. She is the daughter of Flynn O'Shea and was taken captive by Storm Dancer when he burned her husband's cabin."

"This is true?" Luce demanded, suddenly shrewd. "You have seen this white captive?"

"I have seen her and spoken to her. Tell them that her hair is yellow and her name is Shannon. Tell the white farmers that the Cherokee mean to torture her as revenge for the murders at Split Cane's camp."

His father looked doubtful. "How can this be, when Winter Fox just made a treaty with these English?"

"It can be because I say it is," Gall pronounced. "And if you want my help to build a new trading post, you must carry this word to the whites. The woman was stolen by my cousin Storm Dancer, and if they do not go quickly to her rescue, she will die at the stake."

# Chapter 26

In the bottom of the pit, Shannon tossed and turned on the bearskin. She could see Storm Dancer. He was lying on the ground . . . hurt . . . bleeding. He was pale, far too pale, and his eyes were closed. If she could reach him, she was certain she could help, but no matter how hard she ran, she could go nowhere. He remained just out of reach. "Storm Dancer!" she cried. "Don't die, please don't die."

A torch flared. Abruptly, light flooded Shannon's rocky cell. She opened her eyes, half-dazed, still tangled in the dream. "What . . ."

"Can you climb up?"

Shannon recognized Snowberry's voice. "Yes," she replied. "I'm sure I can." She was on her feet as a vine ladder tumbled over the edge of the pit. She seized it in both hands.

"Come up, daughter of Truth Teller," Firefly called. Storm Dancer's mother appeared at the rim above her.

The climb was difficult; the flimsy vine twisted and sagged under her weight, and Shannon slammed her fingers against the rock wall every time it swayed. Ignoring the pain, she forced her way up the ladder, one rung at a time. At the top, Woodpecker's mother, Blue Sky, offered her hand and helped Shannon up.

Shannon dropped onto her knees to catch her breath and looked around. Other women crowded behind Firefly and Blue Sky. One was the scowling councilwoman, Yellow Bead, who had been so quick to condemn her. The old woman no longer seemed angry, only grief-stricken. Beside her stood another council member, a wrinkled bird of a matron with gray eyes whose name was Corn Woman.

Snowberry, Cardinal's aunt, the kindly woman in whose home she'd been living before they tossed her in this hole, came forward to take Shannon's hand. "Poor little one," she murmured.

Snowberry's eyes were red; her broad face was smeared with ashes, her gray hair chopped raggedly. It was obvious to Shannon that she'd been crying.

"What's wrong?" she asked.

For a moment, Snowberry hesitated, and her lower lip quivered, and then the older woman hugged her tightly. "Be strong," she said.

"Why are you crying?" Shannon asked.

"Our Cardinal, she is gone." Snowberry's voice cracked. "We have lost her forever. My only niece." Fresh tears welled up in her brown eyes. "My pretty Cardinal."

"I don't understand," Shannon said.

Firefly motioned to her. "You must come with me," she ordered. "Quickly. There is no time for talk. Storm Dancer lies at the edge of the hereafter."

Still confused, Shannon tried to understand what Firefly meant by *edge of the hereafter,* and then the images from her dream came rushing back. "He's hurt? Storm Dancer is hurt?" Fear constricted her throat. "What's happened to him?"

His mother's face reflected the terror and uncertainty

Shannon felt. "He calls for you," Firefly said. Strain showed on the woman's face. She seemed both older and slighter than Shannon remembered, not nearly as intimidating.

"Take me to him." In spite of the way Firefly had acted toward her, Shannon felt sympathy for Storm Dancer's mother. He was her only child, and it was clear that she loved him.

"Follow me," Firefly said. Even her tone was less commanding. "Please. He may be dying, even now."

Blue Sky fell in beside Shannon and took her arm as they made their way out of the cave and down the hill toward the village. "We found Cardinal's body near Ghost Ledge," the young Indian woman whispered.

"An accident?"

Blue Sky shrugged. "Who can say? She fell or jumped. She must have survived the fall, and then been devoured by wolves. The pack won't eat dead things unless they are starving."

Cardinal dead in such a horrible way? It didn't seem possible. But Shannon had no time to ponder the young woman's fate if Storm Dancer was in danger. "But how was Storm Dancer hurt? You said Cardinal had run away with Gall. I don't understand what one has to do with the other."

Blue Sky shook her head. "No one has seen Gall, but the warriors found Storm Dancer a day's travel from the village. He had left the others to bring home the message that peace had been declared between us and the English once more."

"My husband would never have found our son, if it wasn't for buzzards circling overhead," Firefly said. "Waiting for his death."

"They carried him home on a litter," Blue Sky explained. "He took a poisoned arrow in his thigh."

"How bad is it?" Shannon demanded. "Will he live?"

"Who can say?" Firefly replied. "Shawnee poison is very powerful."

Storm Dancer's mother led the way into the village and down the street to her home. A gray-haired woman stooped through the low doorway and left the cabin. "Is my son alive?" Firefly demanded. "Is there any change?"

"He burns with fever from the poison," the woman said. "I am not the healer in our village. I have never treated a poison arrow wound before. Who can say if he is strong enough to survive? It lies with the Creator."

Firefly pointed to the doorway. "Go in to him," she said. "He calls your name, over and over."

Shannon rushed in. The lodge was brightly lit by the fire and stank of death. Not infection or bodily wastes, but death. She hurried past the hearth stones to the sleeping platform where the man she loved lay naked on his back. "Storm Dancer," she cried. "It's me. It's Shannon."

She touched his face. Heat radiated from his body. His skin felt dry, his lips pale. His high, chiseled cheekbones stood out against sunken cheeks. Dark, damp hair spread unbound around Storm Dancer's head, and his eyes were closed. When she clasped his hand, his eyelids fluttered.

"Shan-non." Her name rustled like dry cornstalks in the wind.

"I'm here, my love."

Opening his eyes seemed an impossible task. His lids flickered. She could see him struggling to focus on her face. "Ma-ry Shan-non."

"Shh, save your strength." She cupped his face in her hands, kissed his dry lips, and then scanned his bruised and battered body for injuries. A poultice covered the arrow wound on his right thigh, but it was instantly apparent that he had taken more than one injury. A jagged gash ran from his left eyebrow into his scalp, and another bandage on his left arm was soaked through with blood.

Poison, she thought. That's what Blue Sky had said. Storm Dancer had been struck by a poison arrow. Only poison or blood loss could have brought him to this point. The head injury was nasty, and she didn't know how bad the wound on his arm was, but it must be the leg that had made him so sick and brought on the fever.

Her heart raced. This was bad, very bad. She could clean minor wounds, bandage, even stitch gashes and clean boils, but Storm Dancer's condition seemed beyond her level of skill to deal with. She leaned close and kissed his forehead. "I'm here. I'm here," she repeated. "You're going to get better. I swear it."

She turned back to look at his mother. "Who is caring for him? Is there a doctor?" She corrected herself. "A shaman?"

"Our medicine woman has gone to Split Cane's village to help deliver a baby that is turned the wrong way," Firefly said. "I have sent for her, but it will be hours before she can get back. I do not know if he will live so long." Her tone softened. "I cannot deny his wish to see you. If his spirit—"

"No!" Shannon snapped. "No. His spirit is strong. It's only his body that's weak from poison." Desperately, she tried to think of something to do. "Wait. Oona is here. Blue Sky said that my father's wife is here. She is a healer. She knows—"

"She is here," Firefly agreed. "But her mind is like a child's. She does not speak."

"She doesn't have to," Shannon insisted. "Back at the post, she didn't speak, but she remembered how to do all sorts of things. She may remember her medicine. Please bring her here. If anyone can help him, it will be Oona."

\* \* \*

Captain Sidwell stood to shake Luce Pascal's hand in dismissal. They were in Sidwell's office, a poor, makeshift structure of logs nailed against the south inner wall of Fort Hood. "Thank you," the English officer said.

Knowing that the information his son had given him was valuable, Luce had turned back to the fort and asked to see the commandant. Apparently, the sudden demise of that Englishman had left Captain Sidwell the highest-ranking officer, and Luce was shown in to see him.

"His Majesty appreciates you coming forward, *Herr* Klaus," Captain Sidwell said. "We've already received a request from a prominent settler in Green Valley, Yeoman Nathan Clark, to send an expedition to recover his daughter-in-law who was kidnapped during a raid on his son's farm. We assumed that the woman had been taken by the Shawnee."

"I don't know how this Storm Dancer got her, but he's Cherokee," Luce said. "It is my understanding that *Frau* Clark is being held in his home village."

"Which is to the better," the redcoat continued. "If it was Shawnee who had her, we could do nothing. Only hope that they might take her north to Canada, where she could be ransomed from the French. If she is a captive of the Cherokee, this changes everything. Are you certain of your informant?"

"*Ja.* Joseph's word is good," Luce assured him. "I've known him for years. A most promising young man. Half-white, I understand. He seems to have had some education and speaks English well. I intend to employ him at my new fur trading post."

"And he is willing to guide a rescue force to this Fire-fly camp where Mistress Clark is held prisoner?"

"He is."

"Excellent. I have a decent scout as well, a Delaware by the name of George *Hatapi*. Do you know him?"

*"Nein."* Luce tried not to meet the English captain's gaze directly. He hoped the man would have the decency to offer him a glass of wine. Probably not, he thought. The British were such barbarians, living like this.

A French gentleman, even one stationed on this remote frontier, would have suitable furniture in his office and would meet visitors in proper dress. This English dog hadn't even bothered to shave this morning; his boots were dirty, his coat stained, and his white shirt badly in need of ironing.

"The Delaware are relatives to the Shawnee, and he speaks their language as well as Cherokee. George has proven trustworthy. We would have lost more men than we have, if it wasn't for him."

*"Ja,"* Luce agreed. "It is necessary to have translators you can trust."

"More so, now. As you may know, Fort Hood suffered two recent blows. First, the loss of our only other captain at the hands of hostiles, and then the unfortunate death of our commandant from a fever and misery of the bowels. I hold command only until Major Cook arrives with reinforcements from Williamsburg."

"You have my condolences, *Herr Kapitan,*" Luce said, careful to maintain his German accent.

Had it been in his power, he would have consigned the entire garrison to hell. Stupid English. They were children when it came to dealing with the natives. No wonder they died like inhabitants of a plague ship. If the king would only take the Americas seriously and realize there was wealth here greater than beaver pelts, he would send enough troops to drive the British back to the sea.

The captain toyed with his dirty stock. "As much as

I would like to go to this poor woman's aid, I can't do anything until Major Cook arrives."

Luce nodded. "But I may offer hope to *Herr* Clark that help is coming." He shifted his broad slouch hat from the crook of his arm to his head. "I am on my way to Green Valley with trade goods. If I could tell these farmers that you intend to go to—"

Captain Sidwell shook his head. "Unfortunately, I can make no promises. I will press upon Major Cook the urgency of this matter, as soon as he arrives. If he permits, I will personally lead the expedition to recover the woman."

"*Ja.* I am sure that will be a great consolation to *Frau* Clark's family."

"You're certain this renegade, this Storm, hasn't taken her elsewhere?"

"Storm Dancer. He was the nephew of Winter Fox. *Nein, Herr* Captain. Storm Dancer has taken his captive nowhere else. Joseph reports that the man suffered grievous wounds in combat. After he took the *junge Frau* to his village, he and hostile Cherokee troublemakers formed a war party that threatened every white settler in these mountains. There was an incident, and this Storm Dancer died as a result."

"Well." The captain smiled. "That should make our task easier. Nothing more than simple ransom. A few copper pots, some mirrors, and a bucket of beads, and we should be able to buy the Clark woman back." He waved to an aide. "Will you take a glass of ale, *Herr* Klaus? I'm afraid our rum ration has run dry. I have nothing stronger to offer you."

Luce swallowed his disgust. "*Danke.* With pleasure," he answered. "And be certain, that if you are short of any trade items to make up the ransom, I can provide them at a fair price."

* * *

Snowberry and Blue Sky came into Firefly's cabin with another woman. It took an instant for Shannon to realize that the neatly dressed Cherokee in the deerskin dress, with a cradleboard on her back, was actually Oona.

"Sorry. She would not leave the baby," Snowberry said.

"What baby?" Shannon studied the cradleboard with apprehension, half expecting to see a puppy or even a doll in place of an infant. But, to her surprise, a gurgling, curly-haired toddler stared back with solemn round eyes.

"This is Acorn," Blue Sky explained. "She was orphaned by the attack on our village. Her mother was Creek, her father an escaped slave. Both were killed by the Virginians. Many women wanted the baby, but she grieved for her own mother until we thought she would starve herself to death. She cried all the time and would not sleep."

"Oona believes the child is her own," Snowberry said. "No one can take Acorn from her. She has cared for the baby since she first laid eyes on her."

"Acorn loves her as well," Blue Sky said. "In Oona's arms she will take food, and she sleeps. Oona's spirit has healed the child's broken one. She has given the baby back the will to live, so perhaps it doesn't matter whether she speaks or not."

"We didn't think she should bring Acorn to a sick house," Snowberry repeated. "But no one could get her to leave the baby."

"Oona," Shannon said, taking her stepmother's hands. "Do you remember me?" The gaze that met hers seemed almost blank. "Oona, please. You know so much about making sick people well. Storm Dancer was shot with a poison arrow. Can you help him?"

Shannon motioned to where he lay sprawled, eyes

closed again, so still that she could hardly see his chest rising and falling with each breath. "What can we do, Oona?"

Intelligence flickered in her eyes as Oona moved to Storm Dancer's side. She touched his forehead, leaned close and smelled his breath, and pressed a palm to his throat.

"He's very sick," Shannon said.

Oona ran her fingers over his skin. She untied the bandage on his arm and inspected the injury. Fresh blood seeped out. Oona sniffed the wound, made a clicking sound, and turned to Snowberry.

"She wants something," the older woman said. "What is it? What do you need?"

Oona's mouth moved, as though she was fighting to find the words, but only unintelligible sounds came out.

"Bring what you have in your medicine chest," Firefly said.

Shannon looked around. She hadn't noticed when Storm Dancer's mother entered the cabin, but she stepped aside to allow her access to his bedside.

Firefly leaned close and whispered in his ear. He raised one hand and took hold of her wrist. "What is it, my son? What do you want?" she begged.

"Pr . . . Priest," he managed.

Firefly's eyes widened. His fingers bit into her flesh, loosened, and fell away.

"Priest."

Firefly glanced at Shannon. "I must go. Stay with him. Keep him with you. Do not let him slip away."

"I won't." Shannon took hold of his hand. "Please," she murmured. "Fight, Storm Dancer. Fight as you have never fought before."

Ignoring her presence, Oona returned to her patient

and removed the poultice that covered the inflamed wound on his thigh. Green pus oozed from the hole.

Firefly took Oona by the shoulder. "I sucked out as much of the poison as I could," she said. "But we didn't get to him in time. Now, I fear it's too late to draw the poison. I fear . . ."

Shannon knelt beside the bed. She took Storm Dancer's face between her hands as she had earlier and breathed into his mouth. "I love you," she whispered. "I love you, and I won't let you go."

Minutes passed as women moved in and out of the lodge bringing various herbs, roots, and plants. Oona built up the fire and heaped skins on Storm Dancer. She brought a gourd containing a dark liquid, pushed it into Shannon's hands, and motioned for her to give it to him.

He was so weak, he could barely swallow. Drop by drop, using a bit of hollow reed to drip it between his lips, Shannon administered the foul-smelling concoction. All the while, she prayed silently for God to let this good man live. She would do anything to save him; she would pay any price.

When the gourd was empty, Snowberry offered a basin of water and a bit of cloth. "Wipe him down," she instructed. "We must get his fever to drop."

There was a stir in the doorway, and two men entered with Firefly. "This is Flint," she said to Shannon, "Storm Dancer's father."

Shannon looked up into the sorrowful gaze of a tall, handsome man with features much like those of his son. "Flint," she said in acknowledgment.

"And this man is Travels Far," Firefly said.

Shannon glanced at the short, broad-faced Cherokee in the yellow turban, fringed hunting shirt, and leggings. She was about to greet him courteously, when she saw something unusual in his appearance. His eyes were not the walnut brown of the Indians, but a steely blue, and the shape was all wrong. And when she looked more closely, she saw that beneath the tan his skin was as fair as her own. "Are you a white man?"

He smiled. "Long ago, I was. An imperfect one." His English was measured and heavily accented, as if it had been a long time since he'd used it. Reaching inside his shirt, Travels Far pulled out a chain with a silver crucifix suspended from it. "Once I was called Father Luke. Men knew me as a priest in Charles Town in the South Carolina Colony."

"A holy father?" Shannon asked in disbelief.

"Long ago, I left that life. For many years, I have considered myself to be *Tsalagi*. I am a poor sort of priest. I have a Cherokee wife and children. But since my holy father in Rome never stripped me of my office, I believe I still hold the authority to marry you to this man. If it is what you wish."

"Marry us?"

"My son is dying," Flint said. "He wishes to make you his wife, so that if you carry a child, none can say that it has no name."

"I don't understand," Shannon stammered. "I thought that all children born to the Cherokee were legitimate. I thought . . ."

"For your sake," Firefly said. "My son has his own religion. But for you, for your belief, he wishes to make you his wife in the Christian faith. He was christened in the Jesus religion as a babe. He should be acceptable to your—"

"If you wish to become the wife of this man, he is most acceptable," Travels Far said. "I have known him since he was a child. There is no better man."

"The question is, do you want to marry him?" Firefly asked.

"Of course, I do," Shannon said. "But he isn't going to die. I won't let him."

"Let us begin at once," Travels Far said. "Knowing you are united in holy matrimony may give him the strength to fight the poison, but it will also join you to him so long as you live."

"Do you love my son enough to enter into this union?" Flint asked.

"I do," Shannon said. "Yes, I do."

Travels Far hung a beaded silk sash around his neck and took a small wooden case from a pouch on his belt. "First, I will give him last rites," he said. "In case the Creator has other needs for him."

"He's not going to die," Shannon repeated. "He can't die." She turned to Oona. "Tell me that he's going to get better!"

Oona took a deep breath and shook her head. Her expression spoke louder than words to Shannon. Oona had lost all hope of saving him.

Shannon crossed her arms over her chest and knotted her fists. If she let the tears flow, there would be no stopping them. She felt empty, already dead inside, but she knew she had to remain strong for him. And she would not give up hope. So long as Storm Dancer drew breath, she would fight for his life.

"Is there any chance you could be carrying his child?" Firefly demanded.

Shannon felt her cheeks grow warm. "Yes, but—"

"Then the sooner the two of you are man and wife, the better."

"I thought you hated me," Shannon said. "You believed that I was a thief and—"

"You must still stand trial before the council," Firefly replied. "But that can wait. What matters now is that you ease my son's spirit. He has asked me to see that you become his, and I cannot deny what may be his last wish."

"My daughter?" Travels Far said. "If you would take his hand."

And silently, Shannon did. And there, in the smoky lodge, in a Cherokee village deep in the mountains, in the shadow of death, she became the true wife of Storm Dancer, the man she loved more than life itself.

# Chapter 27

Shannon spent her wedding night wiping Storm Dancer's fever-racked body with cool cloths, and dripping water and Cherokee medicine between his lips, one drop at a time. Outside Firefly's cabin, the mournful cadence of Cherokee drums and the chanting of women offering prayers for Storm Dancer's life filled the fog-shrouded streets of the village.

Sometime in the night Egret Hatching, the village healer, returned, conferred with Oona, brought additional herbs to add to the kettle, and then, obviously exhausted, retired to her own home. Although Oona and the aging medicine woman exchanged no words, Shannon could see that the Cherokee wise woman approved of Oona's care of the patient.

Through the long hours, Oona remained at Shannon's side, always silent, keeping the fire hot, placing hot poultices on Storm Dancer's thigh wound and brewing medicine to strengthen his heart and ease his breathing. Reluctantly, Oona had allowed Blue Sky to take little Acorn to Snowberry's lodge. The baby fretted at being parted from her, but Oona seemed to understand that the child would be better away from Storm Dancer's sickbed.

All the while, Shannon talked to him, telling him how much she loved him, promising that they would be together, and urging him to fight the poison in his system. Twice, Shannon was certain she had lost him. At dawn, his breathing had become so labored that Oona had placed blankets beneath his head and shoulders to elevate his head.

It was so hot in the cabin that Shannon's clothing and skin were damp with sweat. Her eyes burned, and her back ached from bending over Storm Dancer, but she would not leave him. "Live, darling," she whispered. "Live for me. Live for the children we will have together."

At midmorning, Flint entered the cabin. Oona glanced up at him and then left the house. Flint approached his son and stood looking down at him.

"He's not going to die," Shannon repeated, more for herself than for him. She should have been intimidated by this man, Storm Dancer's father, but she wasn't. She found his presence oddly comforting.

"If my son dies, you will be free to do as you wish. You may claim a home here with us, or I will take you East to your own people."

"I don't think Firefly wants me here. She's put me on trial for stealing a Corn Mask. If they find me guilty, I'll be put to death."

Flint leaned down and brushed his son's forehead with his lips. "Only if you remain with us," he said. "If you wish to go, there will be no trial. It will be the same as if you had been banished. You can never return, but no one will judge you."

"I'm innocent." She looked up into his kind face. "I don't know who did the things they accuse me of, but someone wanted me to be blamed. And that someone hid the broken mask under my sleeping pallet."

"My wife has many faults, but she would never do such

a thing. She is a good woman. Bossy, stubborn, but her heart is good. She is not your enemy."

"He's going to live."

"If you stay, you will have to face the council."

"I'll face the council, no matter what." Her insides clenched as she realized that she'd admitted that Storm Dancer might not survive, that she might lose him. She touched Flint's lean arm with a trembling hand. "I have my own honor to uphold. And I want to stay here."

He nodded. "You have found a place among the *Tsalagi,* haven't you?"

"Oona is my family, and Snowberry, Blue Sky, and little Woodpecker. I have no one to go back to in the white world. I think I could build a good life here."

"Even without my son at your side?"

She bit her lower lip and choked back a sob. "Since I've been a child, I've never belonged to anyone . . . to anywhere. I need to belong."

"We are strangers to you, daughter of Truth Teller."

"Not strangers," she answered softly. "I see how much family means to the Cherokee."

"Do you want to remain out of duty? To care for your father's wife?"

"Yes, that's part of it, but more than that, my spirit calls to these mountains, to your people."

"And to my son."

"Yes. To my husband." And he was her husband, she thought. There might have been no church, no ring, and no marriage lines, but a priest had blessed their union. She and Storm Dancer were man and wife in the eyes of God.

"You must be strong," Flint said. "No matter what comes. Your father was a strong man, a good man. You come from good stock." He smiled. "Even if your eyes are the wrong color for a human being."

"I'm trying, but it's hard," she admitted.

"Yes, daughter, and this will be harder still." He leaned and gathered Storm Dancer in his arms and lifted him. Even with his weight loss from his illness, Storm Dancer was heavy, and muscles corded on Flint's lean body.

"Where are you taking him?" she cried. "He's alive."

Flint cradled Storm Dancer against his scarred chest as though he was a small child. "He must not die here," Flint said. "A *Tsalagi* warrior breathes his last resting on Mother Earth, with the sun shining on his face, and the mountain breeze blowing through his hair."

"No." She moved in front of Flint to block his path. "I won't let you take him. I won't let him go." But he pushed past her, crossed the room, and carried Storm Dancer out into the shimmering heat of the summer day.

His mother waited outside. Around the house stood what seemed to Shannon as every person in the village. Men and women and children, all dressed in ceremonial clothing, faces painted, and decked out in necklaces, rings, armbands and earrings. Some, including Firefly, wore elaborate engraved silver nose rings, others capes of feathers.

Shannon didn't need an explanation. Storm Dancer's friends and relatives had all come to honor him in his last minutes of life. Everyone had accepted his impending death. Standing next to his mother in all her finery, Shannon felt like a beggar in her stained skirt and vest and dirty bare feet, but she didn't care. All that mattered was her man, her beautiful husband. And no matter where they took him, she would not leave him.

The villagers formed a procession behind the four of them: Flint carrying his son, Firefly, and Shannon. Struggling under Storm Dancer's weight, Flint walked with his head high. Firefly was equally regal. No tears stained her cheeks, no emotion showed on her proud face.

Only by looking deep into her eyes could Shannon see the desolation and fear hovering in the shadows. The deep boom of a water drum echoed through the cabins, the dull clacking of gourd rattles, and the high thin piping of a bone flute wailed above the quiet sobbing of the women.

Flint reached the center of the village, laid Storm Dancer gently on a raised bed of logs cushioned with pine boughs, and took a position at the foot of the bier. Firefly moved to her son's head. Dancers swirled around them, one wearing a wolf's head mask and cap, another in antlers and deerskin robes.

Shannon recognized the healer, Egret Hatching, face painted black, naked except for an apron of white feathers, a band of otter fur covering her withered breasts, and high leather moccasins. The old woman's movements were slow and shuffling as she circled the open space where Storm Dancer rested. In one hand she carried a long stick covered with shells, and in the other, a turtle-shell rattle. Egret's thin arms and legs were covered in tattoos, her hair so thin and wispy that she appeared nearly bald, but her eyes gleamed brightly in the wizened face.

The entire scene had the appearance of a dream to Shannon. Smoke rising from the four fires around Storm Dancer was not gray, but red, blue, green, and yellow. And the fog that had covered the mountain last night had become a mist that lingered beneath the trees, hung low over the cabins, and filled the gullies. Words drifted to her ears from the chanting hymns of praise the Cherokee sang.

". . . Warrior . . . courage . . . faithful . . . honor . . ."

And through it all, Storm Dancer lay as though one already passed over. His features seemed carved of rock; his eyelids didn't flutter, and his arms lay limp at his sides. His hands—strong hands that had gripped a horse's reins . . . skillful hands that had drawn a bow . . . tender hands that had made love to her—were still as stone.

Shannon dropped to her knees, rested her head on his hand, and prayed silently for God to spare his life. Cherokee or English; it didn't matter. Skin color and language meant little. What mattered was that the Creator show mercy to this man . . . her man.

Time passed. Hours or minutes, Shannon couldn't tell. Her agony was so deep that she had lost all reference. Clouds thickened, and the pale sun vanished beneath dark thunderheads. Far off, lightning flashed. The wind picked up and it grew noticeably cooler.

The drummers and dancers did not cease their vigil. Flint and Firefly remained at their posts, unmoving. The flutes continued to play, the rattles to clack. Raindrops spattered across Shannon's arms and the back of her neck. On the far side of the gathering, Oona ran for shelter with Acorn on her back, still snug in her cradleboard. Other young mothers carried and shooed their children to shelter.

Thunder rumbled in great crashing bursts. On the next mountain, lightning struck, and a tall pine burst into flame. Shannon threw herself across Storm Dancer's chest, her tears mingling with the rain to fall on his face. "Don't leave me," she cried. "I can't live without you."

He coughed.

Shannon started up, just as a bolt of lightning flashed and trees exploded at the edge of the village, nearly deafening her. The smell of sulfur filled the air. Rain fell in sheets, cold and hard, biting into her skin.

"Are you trying to drown me?"

She stared at Storm Dancer's face. His eyes opened, eyes no longer lost in fever, but clear and bright. "You're alive?"

"Not for long," he rasped. "Not if you don't get me out of this river."

Storm Dancer's recovery took weeks. The cornstalks grew tall; pumpkins and squash blossomed and ripened. Children played hide-and-seek among the thick leaves of the climbing beans. High on the mountaintops, trees began to change the color of their leaves, and nights, which had been so hot and still, turned cooler. Summer had not yet released her grip on the land of the *Tsalagi,* but soon would give way to the rich harvest days of autumn.

Every day, Shannon cared for Storm Dancer in his mother's lodge. Firefly had moved out temporarily, so that the two of them could have privacy. At first, because Storm Dancer was too weak to walk without assistance, his father would come to help him out of the house so that he could sit in the sun and regain his strength.

Firefly brought broth and soups, and Oona came to deliver her medicinal teas and herbal remedies. But mostly, Shannon was alone with her husband, alone to talk, to share hopes and dreams, even to joke about his waking on his own funeral bier to find his wife and clan mourning his death.

Gradually, the color came back in Storm Dancer's cheeks, and his eyes took on their old sparkle, but the effects of the poison lingered. Much to Shannon's disappointment, they had not yet been able to resume their physical lovemaking. Instead, they lay naked, side by side on the sleeping platform, touching and caressing each other, all the while whispering sweet nothings.

She amused him by singing the Irish ballads her father had taught her, and Storm Dancer returned the favor by reciting Cherokee legends and stories. And when darkness fell softly over the camp, he played courting tunes on his bone flute and sang love songs to her in a deep and husky voice.

In the days of Storm Dancer's recovery, it seemed to Shannon as if she discovered a quiver full of new aspects to his personality. He was funny and serious, tender and fierce. She had fallen in love with a stranger; now she came to know and love her husband more with each sunrise.

The morning that he felt strong enough to walk as far as the village spring to drink and then bathe in the river with her made Shannon's pulse quicken with anticipation. Tonight, she was certain, they would make love again. And the weeks of forced separation would only make their coming together even more special.

"You'll not escape me tonight," he promised.

She laughed and splashed water in his face. "I've not been running all that fast."

Quick as a snake, he grabbed her and yanked her against him. A thrill went through her as they kissed, both naked as Adam and Eve in the Garden of Eden, both laughing for the joy of being alive and together. But as they walked out of the creek and up the bank, hand in hand, three women came out of the trees.

"It is time," Corn Woman said.

Yellow Bead looked solemn. "You must come with us."

The third woman was the ancient healer, Egret Hatching. "You must come," she echoed in her high, thin voice. "It is time for the judging."

Shannon's eyes widened with apprehension. "Storm Dancer, must I go with—"

He squeezed her hand. "You must. If we are to live among the *Tsalagi*, you must prove your innocence."

"Have courage, daughter," the old medicine woman whispered. "If you did not steal the mask, you will go free."

Quickly, Shannon donned her vest and skirt and thrust her feet into her low moccasins, the ones Snowberry had helped her to sew and decorate. She glanced back at Storm Dancer. "You believe me, don't you?"

He nodded. "Of course, my heart. And soon everyone will know the truth."

"Will you be all right?" she asked. "Are you strong enough to get back to the house?"

"Don't worry about me," he answered.

Reluctantly, Shannon accompanied the three down the woods path, but they didn't take the fork that led to the village as she'd expected. Instead, they took the right path, went about a hundred yards, and turned right again. There, Firefly, Snowberry, and Blue Sky waited in a grove of cedars.

"This way," Egret Hatching said.

The trail led uphill and into a tiny hollow tucked between the mountainside and a stand of red oaks. In the center of the clearing stood a low, round hut, smaller than a dwelling, formed of saplings and hides. Smoke came from a hole in the roof. Around the hut, the grass had been flattened down and patterns of white stones formed a labyrinth. More of the village women and teenage girls waited. In all, Shannon counted more than fifty.

Her heart thudded as she followed Egret Hatching down the pathway to the low opening of the hut. The women ahead of her stripped off their clothing to enter naked. Frightened, Shannon glanced at Blue Sky. She smiled and beckoned.

"It is a sweat lodge," Egret Hatching piped. "No harm will come to you there, daughter of Truth Teller."

Uncertain of what would come next, Shannon removed her clothing and followed the medicine woman inside. Instantly, a wave of moist heat hit her face. The low structure was larger inside than it had appeared from the clearing, and it seemed to be set down into the earth. Shannon descended two steps and followed Egret Hatching to a seat along the wall.

It was difficult to see because the only light came from a tiny smoke hole in the ceiling. Rocks surrounded the fire pit. A woman that Shannon didn't know poured dippers of water on the rocks, causing clouds of steam. Some women held small bundles of willow switches, and they used them to beat their bare backs. Shannon was relieved that no one offered her any willow switches.

Outside, near the far wall, a drum beat a steady, mesmerizing rhythm. Corn Woman shook a gourd rattle. Blue Sky removed a tiny wooden flute from her thick hair and began to play. Sweat poured off Shannon's skin, as the women around her began to chant. The air smelled strongly of herbs, and the swirling steam distorted Shannon's vision, so that the room seemed larger yet. Around her, it seemed that more and more women pressed close without touching her, singing, rocking back and forth in time to the drum and the flute. In the air, Shannon thought she saw tiny lights, like lightning bugs, flick on and off.

Someone passed her a gourd. "Drink," the woman said.

"What is it?" Shannon asked.

"Only water." It was Storm Dancer's mother. "Trust me," she said. "Only water."

The water was warm but clean and refreshing. Shannon drank and passed the container back.

"No, to your left," Firefly instructed.

Shannon did as she was told. The singing stopped. The drum and flute went silent. The women around her clapped, once, twice, a third time, only one clap each time.

And then Corn Woman spoke. "Spirit of Cardinal, tell us true."

Firefly joined in. "Spirit of the Corn Mask, tell us true."

Someone threw water on the rocks again. Hissing

filled the hut, and for an instant, Shannon thought she saw something blue and shapeless hovering over the fire. Then all the Cherokee women began chanting again.

Shannon wasn't certain if she fell asleep or if a great deal of time had elapsed, but someone tugged on her arm. "Come," Snowberry urged. "It is over."

"Over? What's over?"

Snowberry took her hand and led her out into the sunshine. Firefly threw a blanket around Shannon's shoulders. One by one, the others emerged from the sweat lodge. Blue Sky caught Shannon's hand.

"Come," Woodpecker's mother said. She was smiling. "Come. Now we swim." She led the way into the tall trees. After only a short distance, they reached a sandy bank. Beyond that was a pool completely surrounded by evergreens. "Come in," Blue Sky called. She threw off her own wrap and jumped in.

The water was shallow, no more than chest deep, but it felt heavenly to Shannon. All around her, the others were splashing and laughing. Even the elderly matrons seemed to join in the fun. Women retrieved small bowls of paste that made suds when they rubbed it into their hair. Someone passed Shannon a dollop and she washed and scrubbed until her skin tingled.

"Now, we are ready," Firefly said. She motioned to Shannon. Corn Woman and Snowberry waited beside her. When Shannon climbed out of the water, they dried her body with furs and rubbed sweet-smelling oils into her skin and hair.

Shannon looked into Firefly's face. "What's happening? Am I going to die?"

Firefly laughed. "We will all die someday, but not today, daughter. Not today."

"Corn Woman is my sister," Snowberry explained.

"She is the mother of Cardinal. She wants to take you as her daughter in Cardinal's place."

"Adopt you," Blue Sky explained. "You will be Deer Clan as Cardinal was. You will be the child of Corn Woman and also of Snowberry. Do you agree?"

Shannon looked around at the women. They were all smiling and nodding. "It doesn't mean I have to give up Storm Dancer, does it?" she asked.

Firefly smiled. "No, child. It doesn't. Since Cardinal was the person who testified against you, and she is no longer here, something else had to be done."

"The trial must be fair," Egret Hatching said. Her dried-apple face beamed.

"You chose to stay among us when you could have gone back to your own kind," Yellow Bead said. "You passed the test of truth. Today was only the final step."

"You are *Tsalagi* now," Blue Sky exclaimed. "Now you can wed in the *Tsalagi* way."

Firefly unfolded a white doeskin dress, fringed from the hip to the ankle. "For you, my daughter," she said, "if you will forgive me and accept this token."

Shannon nodded, too full of emotion to speak. Storm Dancer's mother lowered the dress over her head, and then other women combed out her hair and settled necklaces of shells and silver beads around her neck. Corn Woman offered a pair of moccasins adorned with tiny silver bells, and Snowberry hung shell earrings in Shannon's ears.

"You are very beautiful," Blue Sky said. "Even for one with strange colored eyes."

Children came out of the forest to shower Shannon with wildflowers as she started up the hill toward the village, surrounded by the singing women. The men came out of each house; some beat drums, others pipes or rattles. And when they reached the center of the town, where only weeks ago, Shannon had thought she would lose the man she loved, he was waiting for her.

Storm Dancer was clad as fine as she, with high fringed leggings, a butter-soft vest worked with porcupine quills, armbands of beaten copper, and a fringed loincloth. His hair was combed out long and straight, still damp and gleaming. When he saw her coming, he smiled, held out his hand, and led her into a circle of wildflowers.

Old Yellow Bead came to them and handed Shannon a cake of cornbread. She didn't have to be told what to do. She offered the bread to Storm Dancer. He smiled and whispered, "Together. We bite it together."

Laughing, they held the cake high and nibbled the edges at the same time. Then Egret Hatching handed Storm Dancer a gourd of water. He lifted the cup first to his bride's lips and then to his own. Next, Firefly approached. In her hands was a cord woven of the horse-hair and decorated with beads. She motioned to her son and he held out his left hand.

Speaking ancient words, handed down for a thousand years from generation to generation, Firefly bound Storm Dancer's wrist to Shannon's. Flint stepped forward and clapped once.

"It is done," Firefly cried.

Everyone cheered. Young girls rushed toward the bridal couple and tossed dried beans, and the village maidens began a slow circular dance around the square. Drums beat, and men and women came forward to offer gifts and food for the feast.

"Am I truly your wife?" Shannon asked. She was so happy that she wanted to pinch herself to make certain she wasn't dreaming. "Truly?"

"Truly," he answered.

"You knew, didn't you? You knew what they were going to do, and you didn't tell me?"

He smiled at her. "I couldn't. You had to face the trial alone to prove your innocence."

"You'll pay for that," she promised.

He bent and kissed her to the cheers and laughter of the onlookers. "Promises, promises," he teased.

"I hope we aren't supposed to share our lodge with your parents or all our wedding guests tonight," she said.

He laughed. "No. We go to a special place in the mountains just for newlyweds, and when we come back, you'll have a new cabin. It will be all yours. I can't even come in unless you invite me."

"Maybe you'll get lucky."

He kissed her again. "I love you, Spring Rain."

She looked up at him, puzzled. "What did you call me?"

"When you became *Tsalagi*, you shed your old name. Now you are Spring Rain, heart of my heart."

"Spring Rain. I think I like it."

"The earth would not come to life after winter without the rains of spring. And I was never alive until I found you."

She leaned her head against his chest and closed her eyes, oblivious to the laughing villagers around them. *I've come home*, she thought. *I've finally come home.*

# Chapter 28

As Storm Dancer had promised, they were able to slip away late on their wedding night. They took the horses to save him from having to walk too far, so that he could save his strength for her, he teased. Storm Dancer rode his black stallion; she was mounted on Badger. And long after they'd ridden down the valley, they could hear the drums and singing rising behind them from the village.

The moon and stars shone brightly, illuminating the forest floor where light pierced the foliage overhead and making the game trail easy for their mounts to follow. Ancient trees stretched their branches overhead, and the air smelled sweet with the odors of rich earth and pine needles. The muted clip-clop of their horses' hooves added to the merry symphony of frogs and crickets chirping in the darkness.

"Will your mother accept me now?" Shannon asked. Her voice echoed through the trees, but it wasn't a lonely sound. Rather, she felt protected by these giants, and by the man she followed.

"She will accept you. She has to." Storm Dancer reined in his horse so that she could bring the pony up beside him. The black horse pranced and arched his neck.

Badger snorted and bared his teeth at the stallion, clearly unimpressed by the taller animal. She pulled up his head. "Behave yourself," she chided the pony. "You have the manners of a goat."

"Don't worry so," Storm Dancer said. "In the eyes of our people, you have taken Cardinal's place."

"How could I take her place? Surely, her mother . . . her aunt . . ."

He shrugged and reached to lay a warm hand on her arm. "It's difficult to explain. But to my mother, you have become Cardinal. I was supposed to marry her, and in a way, I have."

"I'm not certain I like that." The pony snatched a mouthful of grass.

"You are of the Deer Clan," Storm Dancer said patiently. "You have fulfilled the prophesy by marrying me. Mother will not only accept you, she will love you as the daughter she never had."

"I'm not certain I want to be married to a prophet. It sounds painful."

He laughed. "I never said that I was a prophet or a hero. I only said my mother believes it."

He caught the end of her braid and gave it a playful tug. Blue Sky had helped Shannon to dress for her ride to the honeymoon lodge, and the Indian woman had plaited her hair into one thick braid so that it wouldn't become tangled in the tree branches.

"Somehow I find it hard to imagine your mother loving me."

"You'd be surprised. She is a woman with the weight of authority on her shoulders. First comes our village, then the Wolf Clan, then her family. She isn't nearly as intimidating as she pretends."

"So your father comes last? Your parents have a strange marriage."

"They are devoted to each other."

"But they don't live together," she protested. "I wouldn't want to be apart from you—ever. Will you leave me to live in the warrior's lodge as other married men do?" She looked at him, silhouetted in the moonlight, her big, wonderful husband, and thought how lucky she was to have found him in a most unlikely place.

He laughed. "We are different from other couples, you and me. We will make our own customs, some from the *Tsalagi* way of life, some from your Irish."

She dropped Badger's reins and leaned close to press her palm to his. "Promise me we will," she said.

"Haven't I married you in your own religion as well as my own?"

She nodded and sighed. "Both weddings were lovely, but I think I like the Cherokee one best. You were much prettier this time."

He snorted. "Pretty? Me? Storm Dancer, great warrior of the Wolf Clan?"

"Beautiful." She smiled at him. Strange that most whites believed the Indians to be dour and solemn. Most of the time, someone was joking or playing a prank on someone else, and no one enjoyed a hearty laugh more than her husband.

He pushed his heels into his stallion's sides. "It's not far now," he said. "I think you'll be pleased."

"Anywhere that we're together, I'll be happy." She hesitated, wrinkling her nose. "There's one thing I don't understand. They said I'd be tried for stealing the mask, and no one asked me any questions about it. If Cardinal hadn't been dead already, she would have repeated what she'd said. Won't people think I'm guilty and got away with it?"

He glanced back over his shoulder at her. "No. No

one believes now that you stole the mask. They accept your innocence."

"How can you be sure of that?"

"A small friend, who wears woodpecker feathers in his hair, whispered to me that his mother whispered to him that the spirit of the Corn Mask told the council of your innocence."

"The spirit told them?" She mused for a minute or two on the time she'd spent in the sweat lodge. It had been dark and hard to see, but she was certain that a blue shape had materialized. . . . No, she wouldn't think of that. It smacked too much of things that go bump in the night. "So who did steal the mask?"

"It never happened."

"Never happened? I saw it broken. They found it under my bed."

He urged his horse ahead, and she could hear his amused chuckling. "It didn't happen. Shannon doesn't exist. You are Spring Rain, wife to Storm Dancer, daughter of Corn Woman."

"But . . ."

Storm Dancer turned again to fix her with a reassuring gaze. "Never speak of it again. That act is wiped clean. If the spirit of the Corn Mask is pleased with you, then none can speak against you. Accept it, wife."

"It makes no sense to me."

"In time it will. In time our customs will seem normal. In faith, all things are not rational. They just are." He pointed through the trees. "There. There is our honeymoon home."

She kicked Badger and the pony broke into a trot. As the deer path opened up, she saw a rise with a hut built into the hillside. If he hadn't pointed it out, she never would have seen it. The roof and sides were covered in pine boughs so that the cabin blended into the mountain.

The pony quickened his trot. Just ahead, between where she was and the shelter, a tiny stream rushed and gurgled through the clearing. Thick grass reached almost to her ankles.

"It's beautiful," she said. "A fairy place."

"Our home," he said. "For the passing of a moon, four of your weeks. Women have left food and blankets inside. We will have nothing to do but watch the foxes play in the grass, sleep in the sun, and grow fat."

"And make love?"

"Yes," he agreed. "I will make love to you so often that you will beg me to go hunting, anything, so long as you can sleep."

"Never!"

He laughed. "We'll see about that, heart of my heart. We'll see."


As Storm Dancer had promised, they were entirely alone here except for the birds and animals that inhabited this mountain. They did not even keep the horses with them. The morning after they arrived, he'd stripped off the bridles and sent them trotting off home.

"Not enough grass in this valley for them," he'd explained. "When our moon of loving is up, someone will come for us and bring the horses."

"But they'll be safe? Wolves won't—"

"They are both wise and battle tested. Any wolf that comes head to head with Badger or my black stallion will go home with an empty belly and hoofprints in his side."

Storm Dancer turned, dropped the bridles, and caught her around the waist and lifted her high in the air. "And now, my yellow-haired woman, I am yours to command. So long as we remain here, my only mission is to do your bidding and bring you joy."

She raised an eyebrow mischievously. "I may prove a hard taskmistress."

"Then we'll have to do something about that." He lowered her to the ground and dropped onto his knees. She threw her arms around his neck, and, laughing, the two of them rolled over and over in the tall grass.

And, as he had promised, they made love. Neither day nor night mattered. They laughed and played together. He caught trout by lying on his stomach and dangling his hand in the cold water until a fish swam by. Then he would snatch it up and toss it into the grass. Later, they would grill them over the fire and take turns popping morsels of food into each other's mouths.

They lived on the food the women had brought them, on dried berries and honey, on fish, on squash and vegetables, and on small game. For the month of their aloneness, he would kill no deer, in honor of her clan. Shannon must do no labor, use a knife, or touch the blood of any animal. In this time, she was to be cherished, protected, and cared for by her new husband.

Once, he took her up the mountain where they could watch a sow bear playing in the hollow with her twin cubs, one black, and one russet brown. He taught her to tell the difference between hawks, to watch the young eagles hunting with their parents, and listen for the wild geese flying north.

Storm Dancer delighted in cooking for Shannon, showing her how to find edible mushrooms and greens, and how to turn leaves and blades of grass into whistles. He gathered wildflowers for her, brushed out her long blond hair, and braided it with blossoms and green leaves as adornment. He rubbed special oils into her feet and massaged her arches, then kissed his way from her toes to the crown of her head. Never, in all her life, had she felt so pampered, so spoiled.

One afternoon, when rain had kept them inside the honeymoon lodge, Storm Dancer amused her by telling her the tale of why the opossum had no fur on its tail, when she remembered something that had troubled her since she'd met him. She listened to the story, laughed in all the right places, and kissed him soundly once he was finished. Then she took his large hands in hers and asked, "Your black stallion, the one you rode here, where did you get him?"

"I raised him from a colt. My father bought a mare from—"

"I wondered," she said, cutting him off. "When we were on our way west, some white trappers passed through our camp. They had a horse that looked exactly like yours . . . and like the other animal I saw in the cave." She looked up into his eyes hopefully, wanting to be told that horses often looked alike, that she must have been mistaken.

"Bearded men," he answered. Storm Dancer's mouth became a thin, unsmiling line. "Are you certain you want to know?"

A lump rose in her throat. "Yes, I do."

"The horses were stolen. Not by me, but by the white trappers. They killed two of my friends, one only fifteen years of age. I followed them and took back the horses."

"And killed them?"

"No man, white or red, comes to *Tsalagi* land and sheds blood without paying the price." He took hold of her shoulders roughly. "Know that I will never harm a hair on your head, but I protect what is mine. I could not call myself a man if I would not fulfill my duty as a warrior of the Wolf Clan and of my nation."

She nodded. "I understand."

He enfolded her in his arms. "Do not let this stand

between us, wife. You must take me as I am. I do not take life easily. It brings me no joy to kill even an evil man."

"All right." She clung to him. "But you would never kill a good person, would you?"

"The Creator forbids it," he said. "I have killed only to defend my own life or another's, or to deliver justice to murderers."

Truth rang in the conviction of his words. Shannon sighed as she pressed her head against his chest and listened to the strong, rhythmic beating of his heart. Storm Dancer readily admitted hunting down the killers of his friends, but he could never have harmed Flynn O'Shea. She had to let that fear dissolve or let doubt destroy her own happiness.

*God help me,* she prayed silently. *I know what it means to be falsely accused.* She would accept Storm Dancer's innocence and never consider the alternative again.


They slept and ate and made love, and the time slipped away until the night air began to take on a bite and they needed to wrap themselves in furs in the early hours of the dawn. And finally, long before Shannon was ready, Flint, and Firefly, and three young warriors came riding into the clearing leading Badger and the black horse. One brave Shannon recognized as Muskrat, a second, Whistler. The third man, she didn't know by name.

"Greetings," Storm Dancer called. "What news?"

"The women are beginning to harvest the corn and the pumpkins have turned from green to orange," his mother answered. "I see neither of you has killed the other yet."

"She tried," Storm Dancer teased. "She wore my lance to a short eating knife."

The young men laughed, and Shannon blushed, but

she took it in stride. Much of the Cherokee humor was bawdy, but she'd heard plenty of that at Klank's tavern. She knew the jesting was in good humor.

"Have you made me a grandfather yet?" Flint asked, swinging down off his dappled gray.

"No more of your nonsense," Firefly said. "They need not worry about babies yet. Let them enjoy each other for a year or two."

"We're planning a great hunt," Muskrat said. "All of the men are going. The elk are fat in Beaver Valley this year. Your father wanted to go last week, but we didn't want you to miss out."

"What do you think?" Storm Dancer asked as he helped his mother down from her brown mare. "Is the time right for hunting elk?"

"Egret Hatching says that two days from now will be the best time. And your father has been scouting the herds. There are fat yearlings ready for good hunters to bring home."

Firefly handed a covered basket to Shannon. "Leave them to their talk of hunting," she said. "I've brought fresh baked bread and roast goose. Let us go inside and gather your things. After we eat, we will return to the village together."

Shannon glanced at Storm Dancer. For the first time in weeks, she wasn't the center of his attention. She sighed. Her mother-in-law was right. It was time to go home, time to help prepare food stores for the coming winter. It was time to leave this special place and return to her new life as Spring Rain.

Shannon looked around the meadow. She didn't know if they would ever come here again. If they did, it could never be quite the same. She and Storm Dancer would never be quite the same people again. But she would always carry a little of this special spot in her heart, and she could revisit whenever she wished.

"Yes," she said to Firefly. "Let's go inside. I want to hear everything that's happened in the village since we've left. How are Oona, and Blue Sky, and my new mother, Corn Woman? And how are Snowberry and her friend Nesting Swan?"

"You cannot guess," Firefly said. "Nesting Swan thought she was past the age of ever having another baby, but she is with child."

"Is she happy?" Shannon asked.

"It was her heart's greatest wish, to give Winter Fox a new son, but he is afraid for her health. Silly man, she glows with health and . . ."

Shannon smiled as Firefly chatted on. It was as if Firefly had never looked at her with angry eyes, as if she was the favored daughter. Warmth seeped through her. Perhaps Storm Dancer was right. Perhaps she and her mother-in-law could learn to live together peacefully.

Her animosity for the older woman drained away. For her husband's sake, she would try to start anew. And today seemed a good day to close the door on past unhappiness and welcome the new days and years to come.


Back at the village, Shannon eagerly settled into her new home, a cabin that the women had erected for her as Storm Dancer had told her they would. Her lodge stood at the edge of the clearing, not far from Nesting Swan's and Snowberry's houses. She had returned to find her wedding gifts installed in her house as well as stores of food.

"You'll be well provided for until I can get home with an elk for you to butcher," Storm Dancer said before kissing her good-bye. "We'll be gone three days, four at most. You'll not even notice I'm gone."

She did notice. The first night she'd slept alone in more than a month, had seemed lonely. But she rose early, eager to accomplish as much as possible in the days that her new husband was off hunting with his friends. She tidied the small cabin, cleared the sleeping platform in case she had visitors, and changed into a clean skirt and vest. Next, she hurried to the creek to bathe and wash her hair before returning to the house for a gathering basket. She'd decided to go to the gardens to help the other women and knew she might need a basket.

But, once back in her lodge, she couldn't help stopping for just a moment to survey the new home, the first she'd ever had that she could call her own. The lodge was about fifteen paces across, from the entranceway to the back wall, round as a striped melon, with a waterproof, conical roof and a hard-packed clay floor that she could sweep clean.

Strings of dried pumpkin and beans, herbs, dried fish, bags of bear fat, and smaller containers of maple sugar hung from the peeled rafters. New mats lined the floor; kindling and small logs were stacked neatly beside the fire pit, and blankets lined the sleeping platform. Along one curved side hung fishing nets, a hoe, and baskets of all shapes.

There were hooks for Storm Dancer's weapons, but the only thing that remained was a hatchet, two spears, a blowgun, and a string of fish hooks. His knives, bow, rifle, and powder horn he'd taken on the elk hunt.

"I helped make the fire pit," Woodpecker proclaimed, poking his head through the doorway. "My mother sent me to bring some of her squirrel stew. Do you like squirrel stew?"

"I do," Shannon got in before the little boy went on in a great enthusiastic burst of words.

"I brought rocks from the creek for your fire pit. Tadpole would have helped too, if he was here. I miss him a lot. He was my best friend."

Shannon took the bowl of stew, set it safely aside, and hugged the boy close. "It's hard to lose good friends," she agreed. "I'm not as much fun as Tadpole, but I'd like it if you'd be my friend."

"I will." He grinned. "And guess what? We're not going back to our old village. My mother says we are going to live here now. She wants to be near her sisters."

Shannon was delighted to hear that. Blue Sky was close to her own age, and she liked both her and her husband, Woodpecker's father.

"I have to go. Two Ponies and some of the other big boys are going swimming."

Shannon tried to hide her amusement. Two Ponies was a year or two older than Woodpecker, no more. "See, you've already found someone to play with."

"He's my cousin," Woodpecker shouted as he dashed out of the lodge.

By the time Shannon had ducked through the open doorway, the boy was already out of sight. She stopped to wave to Oona. Her stepmother was stirring a pot on a fire outside Snowberry's lodge. Shannon had thought that once she and Storm Dancer returned, Oona would come to live with them, but she found that Oona and baby Acorn were already firmly established in Snowberry's care.

"It's better this way," Corn Woman had advised. "You are newly married and need to be alone with your handsome husband. My sister needs someone to look after. She and Oona are good for each other." Corn Woman had winked. "And it doesn't matter if Oona doesn't talk. Snowberry talks enough for two women."

This morning, as Oona added pieces of pumpkin to the pot, the baby was safely tucked into her cradleboard and propped up against the side of Snowberry's cabin. Shannon supposed that Snowberry was already in the cornfield. She'd heard Snowberry say that she wanted to get an early start on harvesting her corn. Shannon thought that if Firefly didn't ask for her help, she'd offer her services to Snowberry. Next year, she'd be expected to tend her own garden, but this year she could expect a bounty of corn and vegetables from every woman in the Deer Clan.

Shannon had only gone a few steps when Nesting Swan came out of her cabin, smiled, and waved. Although the black woman was still shy, Shannon hoped that in time, they would come to be friends. Both Corn Woman and Snowberry thought the world of Winter Fox's second wife, and everyone was excited about her pregnancy.

She hurried past several other Deer Clan homes and was about to enter the path that ran through the forest to the cornfields when she heard a woman scream. Instantly, Shannon dropped her basket and turned back. The panicked cry came again.

Shannon ran as fast as she could. A few heads poked out of cabins, but the village was nearly deserted with the men away and most of the women at the harvest. The third time the scream came, Shannon knew that it was Oona.

As she rounded a long dwelling, Shannon caught sight of a boy struggling with Oona.

"You! You!" her stepmother shrieked.

Nesting Swan burst from her house. "Get away from her!" she shouted. "Let her go!"

As Shannon neared the two figures, she recognized

the boy. Not a boy, but Gall. Her eyes widened in shock. Gall had Oona by the wrist and a knife in his free hand. He stabbed at her. She twisted and kicked him hard in his bad leg.

"You!" Oona screamed again.

Shannon seized a three-foot-long wooden pestle standing in a mortar beside Snowberry's house, charged Gall, and wacked him in the head with it. He stumbled and went down on one knee, cursing in French. Oona broke free and backed away, sobbing.

"He did it! He did it! He led the attack on the post. He raped me and killed your father! Gall! He's a murderer!"

# Chapter 29

Gall scrambled to his feet and came at Shannon with his knife. Shannon swung the three-foot-long pestle at him again. This time, the heavy wooden club just missed his hand holding the weapon. He backed away, and Shannon raised the pestle. "Get out of my way," he said. "Can't you see she's dangerous? Someone has to stop her."

"What are you doing?" Shannon stepped between him and her stepmother. "Why are you trying to hurt Oona?" It all seemed so unreal, almost like a nightmare. But she was wide-awake. She could smell soup burning, hear crows cawing as they flew overhead. The sun was warm on her face, and she was threatening a man she'd believed to be her friend.

"Help!" Nesting Swan called. "Someone, help us!" She darted in to grab the baby and carry her out of danger.

"Hit him!" Oona cried. "Kill him!"

From the corner of her eye, Shannon saw Oona snatch up the knife she'd been using to slice the pumpkin for the soup pot and dart at Gall from the side.

"Murderer!" Oona accused.

Gall slashed at Oona with his skinning knife, but Shannon slammed him across the left shoulder with the pestle and the force of the blow spoiled his aim. Oona hacked at him, and then retreated, leaving Gall to stare down at his arm in disbelief. A thin red line beaded along his skin from elbow to wrist.

"George!" Gall shouted. "Where are you?" Favoring his left shoulder, he slipped a tomahawk out of his belt and swung it menacingly. "Stay out of this, Shannon. Don't listen to her. She's possessed."

From a few houses away, an old woman began to shout. Village dogs barked, and a child leading a colt let go of the lead line, and the yearling pony galloped down the path between the cabins with dogs and boy in full chase.

"Murderer! Rapist!" Oona circled Gall, and then rushed at him again.

He raised the tomahawk, ready to strike.

Abruptly, a stranger broke from the trees and blocked Oona's charge. When she tried to dodge him, he grabbed her wrist and twisted the knife from her hand. The two grappled, and Shannon attempted to go to her aid, but Gall swung the tomahawk at the back of Oona's head.

Shannon screamed and flung the club, striking Gall in the side of the face. Blood flew from his split cheek. He lost his footing and fell full length on the ground. His tomahawk went spinning out of his hand. Gall crawled away, clutching his face. Whining, he got to his feet, and ran toward the woods.

Shannon went for his discarded tomahawk, intending to use it against Oona's assailant, but before she could reach it, Oona stopped struggling and stared wide-eyed into the man's face.

"*Hatapi?*" Her voice was hoarse, but Shannon was struck by the thick emotion.

The Indian's face paled. "*Ayee,*" he said. "*Amimi?*"

Shannon took several steps toward them, the tomahawk

gripped tightly in her hands, then stopped short when she saw an expression of sheer joy spread over Oona's face. "Who is he?" Shannon demanded. "Do you know him?"

The man was obviously Indian, taller than she was and husky, but he wasn't Cherokee. His skin was several shades lighter than most of the *Tsalagi;* his features were finer, and his black hair was cut straight across. It fell at the nape of his neck, held back from his round face by a leather thong. A single eagle feather dangled at the side of his head.

Oona cried out and threw herself into the stranger's arms. He caught her and held her against him. Tears spilled down his pockmarked cheeks. *"Nemis, nemis,"* he said, over and over.

Shannon glanced back to see Gall fleeing into the trees. She lowered her weapon and cautiously approached Oona and the man. "Who are you?" she asked in Cherokee.

Oona began to weep. Her whole body trembled with the force of her crying, but she clung to the man, stroking his face and hair. "This is . . . this is my . . . my brother." Her voice was hoarse and weak, but Shannon could understand every word. "My brother lives."

"This is your brother?" Shannon asked.

"Yes," Oona said. "Yes, my only brother."

Shannon looked from one to the other. Oona was obviously upset, but she seemed perfectly sane. Something had happened to break the spell that had held her stepmother mute. Could it have been the sight of Gall? Or was it that he'd attacked her? Had his attack brought back the awful memory of what happened to her at the trading post?

"I am Strong Bow," the man said in heavily accented Cherokee. "A scout for the English redcoats. They call me George *Hatapi,* but I am Strong Bow. And this is my beloved sister *Amimi,* who I thought was long dead."

"You're not Cherokee," said Nesting Swan suspiciously. She came closer, still clutching Acorn in her cradleboard. "Are you Shawnee?"

Strong Bow grimaced and spat on the ground. "I am not Shawnee."

"He is Delaware, as I am," Oona managed, between sobs.

"We have not seen each other for many winters," he added. "My sister was taken captive long ago. I searched for her, but men told me she was dead."

Oona squeezed his hand. "I have . . . always believed that he was . . . dead too."

"You have led the English here to this village?" Nesting Swan asked. Fear filled her eyes, and she looked around nervously.

Strong Bow hugged Oona again and then pushed her gently away. "Listen to me, sister. Take the women and go into the forest. Now. Quickly. There is danger coming."

"What danger?" Shannon asked. Gall had run away. Other than the curious faces of her neighbors, she could see nothing to alarm her.

"The English soldiers," Strong Bow told Shannon. "Gall and I guided them here to trade for your release." He gave her a long appraising stare. "You do not look like a captive. You are not a captive here, are you?"

"No. I am the wife of a Cherokee. I am Cherokee," Shannon declared proudly.

Oona's brother scowled. "The redcoats will not understand. They will take you back." He pointed at Nesting Swan. "And that woman with the black skin. They will never believe she is Cherokee. If the English see her, they will seize her for a runaway slave. And her child, as well." He gestured at the brown-skinned baby in Swan's arms.

"Acorn is mine!" Oona protested. She took the child from Nesting Swan. "No one will touch my baby."

"Yours?"

"Her adopted child," Shannon explained. "The baby's parents were killed, and your sister has taken Acorn for her own."

"I did not give birth to her," Oona said, "but she is mine. The Creator has given her to me in place of my own lost infant."

Strong Bow nodded. "It is the Delaware way. A child needs a mother."

"And a mother with empty arms needs a baby," Shannon said. Strong Bow looked into her eyes, and she saw regret in his compassionate gaze.

"We were told you were stolen from your white husband."

"I wasn't. I left him." Shannon wasn't about to explain the circumstances here. "What is the danger you spoke of?"

"They are coming," Strong Bow said. "There is no time for talk. Your white husband comes with the English soldiers to buy you from the Cherokee. But they have guns, and I see no men here in this village to defend you. If they find you, they will take you, whether you wish it or not."

"He is right," Nesting Swan agreed. "And they will sell me back into slavery. Better I die here than return to that life."

"Our men are hunting," Shannon said. "They'll be back soon. And Drake Clark is not my husband. My only husband is Storm Dancer of the *Tsalagi*."

Strong Bow's thin lips parted in surprise. "I thought the great warrior Storm Dancer—the man who took you from Green Valley—was dead. Joseph, the half-breed who was with me, he told the English settlers that he killed Storm Dancer with his own hand."

"He is a lying traitor," Oona declared hotly. "His name is not Joseph, but Gall. Not only has Gall betrayed his people by leading whites to this place, but he murdered my husband, who was her father, and he dishonored me."

Strong Bow's eyes narrowed. The face which had been so open and jovial hardened to cold granite. "That man, who calls himself Joseph, he dishonored you?"

"He stabbed my husband, Truth Teller, to death," Oona insisted. "He burned our home, raped me, and beat me so badly that I miscarried our child."

Strong Bow turned to Shannon. "This is so? This Joseph-Gall has done this bad thing?"

"He told you that he killed Storm Dancer? His own cousin?" Nesting Swan asked. "He lies if he says Storm Dancer is dead. I saw him ride out to hunt elk with my husband, Winter Fox. He was as alive as you are."

"Joseph-Gall bragged to all that he shot Storm Dancer with a poisoned arrow. Joseph said he watched him die and left his body for the wolves."

Nesting Swan muttered African words and made the sign to ward off devils. "May the winds suck out his spirit and turn him to dust," she finished in Cherokee.

Strong Bow took Oona's hands in his. "Run now, sister. Go deep into the forest. Do not trouble yourself about the lame one anymore. I will make certain Gall harms no other woman or betrays no more of his kin."

"Gall? It was Gall?" Shannon asked. It was hard to accept. She'd been so certain Gall was her friend. And yet, with her own eyes she'd seen him try to kill Oona. "Are you certain, Oona? You couldn't have made a mistake? It was Gall who killed my father?"

"Yes, it was Gall," Oona said. "I do not forget that night. Not ever."

Then it was Gall, not a Shawnee brave, who had tried to murder Storm Dancer, Shannon thought. All along,

Gall had been the cowardly weasel that Oona had always believed him to be. She was sorry she hadn't brained him with the pestle. If she ever laid eyes on him again, she would strangle the bastard with her own hands.

"I have wandered these mountains for two years," Strong Bow said, "but even I did not know the location of this village. It was Joseph who led the English here. I would not have come, if I had not thought that you"— he nodded to Shannon—"were being held as a slave here. Whether he calls himself Joseph or Gall, his heart is evil. He is guilty."

Shannon nodded. "He must be. But why would he do these things? What does he have against me? Or against Storm Dancer? And why would he lead the English to his tribe's hidden valley?"

"Evil men do not need a reason," Strong Bow said.

Oona hugged the baby. "Do you think I am still mad, daughter? That I would mistake the man who tore my flesh, who stabbed the life from the man I loved, your own father?"

She spat on the ground to show her contempt, in much the same manner that her brother had done. "Gall thought I was dead too. He thought he had choked the life from me after he savaged my body." She fixed her brother with a cold stare. "Kill him for me, Strong Bow, but do not make his death easy."

"We must warn the village," Shannon said. "Grab what food and blankets you can carry. Send one of the boys to tell the women in the gardens. They will—"

A gunshot echoed through the village, followed almost at once by the strident marching cadence beat out by an English drummer boy.

"It is too late," the black woman cried. "They're here!" She grabbed Oona's butcher knife off the ground and ran for the trees.

"Go!" Shannon urged her stepmother. "Save yourself and the baby."

"I will do what I can," Strong Bow said. "If you are captured, do not tell them that we ever spoke."

"Keep yourself safe, brother," Oona said. "I would not lose you again."

"Not if I can help it." He picked a burning stick from the cooking fire and thrust it into the thatch on Shannon's house. "Forgive me," he said. "I will try to delay them long enough for you to get away."

A hunting horn sounded, and Shannon heard the thunder of horses' hooves on the village streets as she and the women dashed into the cover of the forest. Frightened by the jostling, Acorn began to wail. Oona could not run fast carrying the baby, and Shannon wouldn't leave her. Nesting Swan waited long enough for them to catch up.

When they reached a thick stand of evergreens, Shannon bade Oona leave the path. The baby was still fussing as they crawled deep beneath the hanging pine boughs. Shannon hugged her stepmother hard. "I love you," she whispered. "Remember that."

"And I you, daughter."

"Stay with her," Shannon whispered to Nesting Swan. "I'll run out. If anyone is after us, they'll follow me."

"Take care, daughter," Oona warned. Breathing hard from the run, she unlaced the baby from the cradleboard and offered the child her breast. She had no milk, but with luck, the ploy would work for a few minutes until Acorn could be calmed.

Shannon wasn't foolish enough to return to the path, but as she made her way through the thick undergrowth, she heard Acorn begin to fret again. If anyone came this way, the crying child would lead them straight to her—and to Oona and Nesting Swan. Shannon kept moving, hoping that someone had warned the women in the garden, praying that the men would return in time to help them.

Instead, she heard unmistakable shouts in English from the direction of the village, another gunshot, and another roll of the English drum. Redcoats. Gall had led redcoats to the town. Infantry. If anyone was harmed, it would mean all-out war between the Chero- kee and the whites.

Hoofbeats sounded on the game trail. Shannon parted the bushes to see Badger coming full-tilt down the path, Woodpecker clinging like a burr to the pony's neck. "Run! Run!" he shouted. "Soldiers!"

Fifty feet behind him, in hot pursuit, came a white man in buckskins on a gray horse. As Badger jumped a small stream and scrambled up the far bank, the white man reined in. Shannon could hear him cursing.

Then the baby began to cry. The man turned toward the sound and shouted. "Drake! Here! There's some of them hidin' in there."

Dread settled over Shannon. Drake was here.

Taking a deep breath, she did the only thing she could. She called out and stood up. "Drake," she yelled. "It's me. I'm here." Fighting back tears, she pushed her way through the trees into the clearing.

The first man she had seen kicked his mount. The animal leaped forward, and when they came abreast of where she stood, Ben Taylor dismounted and grabbed her by the arm. "I got her, Drake!" he shouted. "I got her!"

Shannon paid him no mind. Instead, she stared at the man she once thought would be her husband. That it was Drake Clark, there was no doubt. But he wasn't the same as the Drake who'd left her alone in the cabin to fort up with his family. Not the same at all. This Drake's hair had white streaks in it. He'd lost two stone of weight, and a puckered scar ran from his temple diagonally across the bridge of his nose and down his cheek. A patch covered one eye, and from the ridged skin on either side of the cloth, Shannon doubted that there was any eye left at all. A second scar twisted the left side of his mouth and continued down his chin to vanish in his graying beard.

Drake swung down from his horse and limped toward her, looking frail and far older than his father. "Shannon."

She nodded. "It's me."

He stopped, looking her up and down, taking in her moccasins, her short fringed skirt, and the laced vest that barely covered her breasts. "For God's sake, woman," he said, "you're half naked." He went back to his horse and pulled a coat from the roll behind his saddle. "Put this on." Drake's scarred mouth made his words come out twisted and harsh.

"I'm not naked," she protested, but he threw the coat over her shoulders.

Ben Taylor stared, and then licked his lower lip.

"Stop lookin' at her," Drake ordered. "Have the decency to turn your head until she's covered."

"There's no need—" she began.

"No, don't say nothin'," Drake said. "It wasn't your fault, what happened to ya. Folks will understand."

He leaned close, and Shannon shrank back. Drake's breath was no sweeter than it had been when she'd seen him last. He smelled of salt pork, sour sweat, and cheap whiskey.

"You're not in the family way, are ya?" he whispered.

"No," she lied. She thought there was a possibility that she was pregnant. Her courses hadn't come last month, and it was already past time again. She hadn't been nauseous, as women were supposed to be, but she was ravenous all the time, and her breasts felt tender. Whether she carried her husband's child or not was none of Drake's business. "This is a mistake," she said. "I'm not anyone's captive. I'm here of my own free will."

"Damned if you are." He caught her by the wrist and dragged her back to where his horse stood. "Now, you stand there until I get in the saddle." Once he was mounted, he offered her his hand. "Jump up behind me."

"You don't understand," she protested. From the woods, she heard Acorn wail again. Drake looked in that direction. "All right," she said, wanting to divert his attention. "I'll come back to the village with you, but we have to talk. I don't want—"

"It ain't up to you what you want," he said brusquely. "We come through hellfire and damnation to get you free from these savages and fetch you home where you belong." He yanked the horse's head around.

Ben Taylor remounted.

"Come on," Drake said. "We stay in these woods, just the two of us, we maybe get an arrow in the back."

Shannon held herself erect, trying to keep her balance behind the saddle without touching Drake. She couldn't go back to this man, couldn't go back to a life that she'd left forever. She was *Tsalagi* now. She might be carrying a Cherokee child, a dark-skinned baby that would never be accepted among Drake's family and neighbors . . . among any whites. He might even separate her from her child.

She'd heard of such practices. At the orphanage, there had been several mixed-race babies left at the doorstep in the night. But there were no mixed-race children. She'd always wondered what the authorities had done with those infants. Had they been sold into slavery . . . or worse?

As they entered the village, Shannon saw that the soldiers held a cluster of elderly men and women and several small children prisoner. A newborn wailed shrilly, and one small naked boy sobbed.

"What are they doing to them?" Shannon demanded. "Leave them alone! Those people haven't done anything wrong. Isn't there a peace treaty between the English and the Cherokee?"

"Shut your mouth," Drake said. "I got her," he called to the redcoat officer that seemed to be in charge. "This is my wife, Shannon O'Shea Clark."

"That's her, all right." Nathan Clark stepped out of one of the cabins, a long rifle cradled in the crook of his arm. "That's Drake's woman."

Several English soldiers came out of one of the larger dwellings. They were carrying furs and other items in their arms. A young girl, no more than ten or eleven, followed, loudly berating the redcoats as robbers.

"Did you come here to break the peace?" Shannon asked. "To steal from your allies?" She counted more than a half-dozen men she knew from Green Valley. There were perhaps fifteen common soldiers, including those who'd just robbed the lodge, and one man that might be a sergeant, standing near the group of prisoners.

Red-faced, the officer shouted a command to the sergeant. He, in turn, shouted at the soldiers, and they reluctantly dropped their loot. "Your pardon, Mistress Clark," the officer said. "Captain Sidwell at your service, madam. We came here to secure your release, nothing more."

"There are runaway slaves in this camp too." Gall came around the side of Firefly's house. "I saw two blacks here this morning."

"He's lying," Shannon said. "There's no one here but Indians. If you harass these people, you'll set these mountains on fire. Are those your orders, sir?" she asked the captain. "Do you mean to fight the whole Cherokee nation as well as the French and Shawnee?"

"No, madam," the captain said. "We came here to free you, nothing more. If these Indians will stand aside and make no effort to prevent us from doing so, we will do them no harm."

"I tell you there are blacks hiding here," Gall insisted.

"We got no time to hunt down runaways," Nathan Clark said. "We got my son's wife. Nobody's hurt. Now, let's get while the gettin's good."

Captain Sidwell approached Shannon. "It's my understanding that the savage that abducted you is dead. Is that true?"

Shannon's heart pounded. She didn't know how to answer. If she said that Storm Dancer was alive, would they wait and ambush him and the returning men? She glanced at Gall. He scowled back at her.

"He is dead," Strong Bow said in English, leading the officer's horse forward and handing the reins to the redcoat. "Joseph killed him." He motioned to Gall. "The man you seek is dead."

"Good," Sidwell said. "Then we can be on our way."

"Do I have any say in this?" Shannon asked. "Or am I to consider myself a captive?"

The English captain's cheeks grew red again. "Madam, your husband, your father-in-law, my men, and your husband's neighbors have ridden far through dangerous territory to rescue you."

"And if I don't want to be rescued?" Shannon asked. "What if I want to stay here?"

"Don't listen to her," Drake said. "She's half crazed from what she's been through."

"No," she protested. "I want to remain with the Cherokee. I don't want to go back with this man."

"He's your lawful husband," Nathan Clark said. "Ain't my son been through enough, Captain? He lost his twin brother to hostiles. Look at him. He's ruined for life.

Ain't it right that his wife come home where she belongs to tend to him?"

"I don't want to go," Shannon said. "Please, sir, have mercy—"

The captain shook his head. "I only enforce the king's laws and those of the Colony of Virginia. Your duty is to go where your husband bids you. I'm sure you'll feel differently, once you're back with your own kind." He turned away and mounted his horse.

"You heard the man," Drake said. "You're comin' home with me, and that's the end of it."

"Against my will?"

"You're a woman, and you're my wife," Drake replied. "What you want or don't want don't matter a tinker's damn."

# Chapter 30

The sun was high overhead, not long past noon, when Gall and Strong Bow led the mixed troop of foot soldiers and mounted farmers out of the valley and down a narrow ravine. Shannon, riding behind Drake, was puzzled. She had come this way with Storm Dancer when they returned from their honeymoon lodge in the deep mountains. He had pointed out the directions to her. Now, she was certain that the scouts were leading them south, not north to where Fort Hood lay some five days' distance.

Drake barely spoke a word to her from the time they left the village until they stopped on a creek bank in late afternoon to rest and drink. His father rode up beside them, scowled, and tossed a bundle to Drake.

"There's a dress and shift in there. Make her put them on. There's no call for her to show her bare legs and thighs for these soldiers to ogle."

"You heard him," Drake said to her.

"Do I have any say in the matter?"

"Nope. Unless you want me to take off those Injun rags and dress you decent myself."

"Am I allowed some privacy, or do you want me to strip in front of everyone?"

"There's bushes, yonder."

Nathan scowled. "Don't try nothin' stupid. You run, and we'll ride back and burn that Injun village to the ground."

"Where could I run?" she asked. "This is all wilderness."

"Damn right, it is," Drake said.

Nathan stared at the trees on either side of the creek. "I still think we should have brought some of them kids with us as hostages," he said. "Them bucks could still come down on us before we get out of these mountains."

The English captain approached. "Gentlemen, madam, you need to mount up. My guides want to be as far from that village as possible by night."

All afternoon, they continued to zigzag south, east, and then south again. They filed up mountainsides so steep that they had to dismount and lead the horses, and she was sure they'd crossed the same creek three times. Once, they waded through a fast-running stream only a few hundred yards downriver from where they traversed it hours before.

From time to time, Shannon had the uneasy feeling that Gall was watching her with hate in his eyes, but he stayed far away. No one else in the group spoke to her, and she said nothing to any of them. She tried to memorize the landmarks they passed, but each new valley and each mountain looked the same. As the day wore on, she grew weary from traveling and only wanted to stay upright on the back of the horse.

At dusk, they crossed another valley. The trees were thick on either side of the narrow game trail. Ahead, Shannon saw Strong Bow speaking to the English redcoat sergeant. He, in turn, consulted with the captain.

Soon, she heard the word passed down the line among the soldiers.

"Not far."

"Water for the horses up ahead."

The trail ended at a sheer outcrop of stone that reared more than a hundred feet straight up. Gall and Strong Bow consulted, and then split up. Gall led the troop left down a narrow gully while Strong Bow turned right and climbed the nearly vertical wooded incline.

"What's happening?" Drake asked one of the redcoats. "I thought we were stopping soon."

"Just a few more miles," said a young recruit. From his accent, Shannon thought the lad might be Welsh. "There's a good spot by a river, and George has gone to shoot us a deer for supper."

It was full dark by the time they reached the camping place at the base of another high ridge. The hollow seemed ideal, with the river on one side and craggy ridges rising steep on either side. "A good place," Drake said. "Water's too wild to ford or swim here. Soldiers set up a watch, we can sleep tonight." He gripped Shannon's knee. "What sleepin' we do." A slow smile crossed the twisted mouth. "We got a tent, darlin'. So us married folk can be alone."

She bit back a retort and slid off the back of the horse. Whatever Drake expected, he wasn't getting it, not from her. Not tonight, and not any night this side of hell. "I need the necessary," she said.

"You can use them trees, if you have to piss," he said. "But don't get any funny ideas." His father helped him down out of the saddle, and he leaned against the horse for support as he got his balance.

*He's sick,* Shannon thought, *and weak. I can fight him off if I have to.* She pushed through a screen of young willows and sat down on a rock beside the river, wanting only a few minutes to come up with a way to protect herself from Drake until Storm Dancer could rescue her.

The current rushed and tumbled over mossy rocks, throwing sprays of water into the air and drowning the sounds of men erecting tents, shouting to each other, and building campfires. Shannon felt the sting of threatening tears, but she choked them back. She wouldn't give Drake Clark or his father the satisfaction of making her cry.

"Don't be too long or I'll come after you," Drake yelled.

"All right," she answered. She stared at the roaring, boulder-strewn cataract again, wondering if she should just jump in and take her chances. The river was more than two hundred feet wide, deep and dangerous. She could swim, but her strength was no match for this fierce, torrent of black water. She'd be sucked down or dashed against the rocks. To try and cross it would be suicide. She wasn't that desperate yet.

"I warn you, woman . . ." Drake shouted.

"Just a minute."

Male laughter. "Can't rush nature," she heard the Welshman remark.

Just as she had risen to her feet to return to the camp, a wren chirped only a few feet away. Instantly, she was alert, hoping against hope that it was Storm Dancer.

Instead, when the branches parted, it was the face of Oona's brother she saw motioning her to silence. Shannon's heart sank.

"Do not worry about the safety of your village," he whispered. "These fools could not find it again from here. Gall took eight days to lead them there from Green Valley. We brought them through cane thickets and over mountains a rabbit wouldn't climb. Even the traitor Gall did not wish the English to find their way a second time." He smiled thinly. "I will guide them another ten days through the white man's hell to reach Fort Hood. None will remember the way to my sister's sanctuary."

"Gall can show them," she said. "If he did it once, he could—"

"Leave Gall to me. And do not dare this river crossing. It would be death."

"My husband is Storm Dancer. I'll die before I give myself to another man. But they've threatened to destroy Firefly's village if I run away."

"I give you my word, the village is safe. Tell my sister I will come to her before the snow falls. And if the *Tsalagi* agree, I will make my home with them. Too long I have lived without my family."

"I have to do something."

"If you were my woman, I would come for you," Strong Bow said. "If Storm Dancer is the man they sing of—the man you believe he is—he will not abandon you. Have faith. But do whatever you must to survive until he does."

Fear made her reckless. "Help me," she begged. "Help me to escape."

"If I can," he promised. "But first, there is Gall. And he has a debt to pay my sister."


Gall left the circle of firelight to retrieve a fallen log he'd seen on the riverbank. He was no more than ten yards from the nearest sentry when he bent to lift the dry section of wood from the dirt. Without warning something heavy slammed into the base of his skull. He felt a bright flash of pain, and then he knew nothing but darkness.

When Gall began to recover consciousness, he felt movement beneath him. He realized he was being carried over a man's shoulder. Gall tried to cry out, but he found that his mouth was bound with cloth. He struggled, but found his arms and legs were tied tightly together.

What had happened? His head felt as though someone had struck him with an ax. He was sick to his stomach. Bile rose in his throat. He fought panic, sensing that with the gag in his mouth he could choke to death on his own vomit. His assailant ran on, powerful legs churning, feet hitting the earth in a strong, regular cadence.

Storm Dancer? Could it be Storm Dancer? Impossible. This man didn't even smell like a *Tsalagi*. He smelled like the Delaware. George? Why would George *Hatapi* ambush and attack him?

Abruptly, the man stopped. Gall barely had time to suck in a deep breath when his captor slammed him onto the ground. Gall's head cracked against a rock, and once again, blackness enveloped him.

This time when Gall opened his eyes, he could make out the silhouettes of tree branches above him. Stars winked in the great bowl of black sky. Gall moaned and discovered that the gag was gone. "Why did you—" he began.

"Save your voice," George said as he ripped away Gall's loincloth and hunting shirt. His voice sent ice crystals sliding down Gall's spine.

A storm of excruciating pain crashed through Gall's head. He sprawled flat on his back, and when he tried to rise, he found that rawhide thongs bit into the flesh of his wrists and ankles. "Have you gone mad?" he croaked.

"No, but you will."

George's face swam into Gall's distorted line of vision. He couldn't make out George's features in the darkness, but it seemed to him that the Delaware's teeth gleamed like a wolf.

"How does it feel to be helpless, defiler of women?"

"What are you talking about? Let me go! The English

captain will—" Gall screamed as his right knee dissolved in an agony of splintered bone and crushed nerves.

George leaned close, panting. "You dishonored my sister, the wife of Truth Teller. And you murdered him."

"No! No! That's a lie. I never—"

"Scream all you like. No one will hear you but the black bears and the foxes." George lifted another rock and smashed Gall's left knee.

He howled.

George pressed his mouth next to his ear. "My sister asked that you not die too quickly. Do not disappoint her." With a two quick slashes, he sliced the leathers that held Gall's wrists tied to the stakes in the earth. And then, before Gall could say another word, the Delaware was gone, running away into the night.

"Come back!" Gall screamed. "Don't leave me like this!"

The only answer was the echoing hoot of an owl and the death shriek of a dying rabbit.


Grumbles rose around the fires when the scout didn't appear with fresh meat for the evening meal. The soldiers and farmers from Green Valley made do with water from the river, dried salt beef, and wormy biscuits. Shannon would have had to be starving to eat such food. And she had no appetite. All she could think of was the tent that Drake had pointed out, and the hours between now and dawn she would be expected to spend there alone with him.

Gathering her nerve, she approached Captain Sidwell. "Sir, I beg you. Let me sleep alone. I have no wish to bed down with that man." She indicated Drake who was washing down his chunks of beef and biscuit with swigs from a pewter flask.

"It's not my affair," the officer replied brusquely. "I've no order to interfere between you and your family."

"But that's what I'm trying to tell you," she argued. "He's not my husband. I've left him. I'll never live with him as a wife."

Clearly embarrassed, Sidwell looked at her across the camp table where he was taking his frugal meal. "Madam, do you have a legal bill of divorce, signed by a judge?"

"No, I don't, but—"

He picked up his fork, stabbed a wiggling maggot that had escaped from a piece of bread, and flicked it off onto the ground. "According to the laws of the Virginia Colony, you are your husband's property. Short of murder, he can do with you as he pleases." He frowned at her and lowered his voice. "You'll do yourself no good by continuing in this fashion. Consider yourself fortunate that you've been rescued from those savages."

"It's getting late," Drake said loudly, stretching his arms up, making a deliberate show for the circle of men around the fire. "You'd best get into our tent, woman. I'll join ya soon as I'm done with my meat." Amos Tyler chuckled, and Drake grinned at him. "A man needs his rest after a hard day, don't he?"

Shannon walked, chin up, back straight, to the ragged tent. One pole leaned and the back was pitched higher than the front. She threw open the entrance cover and stooped to duck inside. Inside, firelight filtered through the rotten seams and the thin material of the walls. A bedroll lay in the far corner. On the ground cloth, almost blocking the doorway, Drake had thrown his saddlebags.

She was about to toss them against the wall when it occurred to her that there might be a knife or even a pistol inside. She had unbuckled the left pouch and begun to rummage through the contents when Drake came into the tent.

"Get out of my stuff." He grabbed her arm and twisted her around to face him. "What are you looking for?" He tried to kiss her and she turned her head away. "I always did like a little fight in a woman."

She smacked his face, and he pushed her down.

"We can play rough if you want to."

Frantically, she grabbed the saddlebags and threw them at him. A leather-bound book fell to the floor. A patch of light shining through the half-open door illuminated the cover, and time seemed to freeze as Shannon stared at it. *Tom Jones* by Henry Fielding. *Volume 1.*

Drake swore. "Pick that up, bitch. Do you know how much that cost me?"

He shoved her, but she ignored him. Suddenly, everything that had been troubling her about Drake Clark fell into place. The book was the key that unlocked it all. Damon was the reader. Drake Clark wouldn't know what to do with a book if it hit him in the head.

"Come here, woman." He took hold of the collar of her bodice and ripped it. Tiny buttons spun against the tent sides and slid to the floor. He fumbled with the front of his trousers. "I've been waiting for this."

"You aren't Drake, you bastard," she cried. "You're Damon."

"Shut up!"

"Damon!" she screamed as loud as she could. He grabbed for her again, but she ducked out of the tent. "He's a liar," she yelled.

"What the hell!" Nathan ran toward the tent.

"He's not Drake! He's Damon! And he's not my husband."

"What's going on here?" Captain Sidwell demanded.

"Attempted rape is what's going on!" Shannon said.

"This man isn't my husband. He's been lying to you all. He's Damon Clark, Drake's twin brother."

Nathan pushed her roughly out of the way and seized the front of Damon's shirt as he came out of the tent. "Is it true?"

Damon threw up his arm to protect his face as his father began to slap him across the face. Blubbering, he dropped to his knees. "I'm sorry, I'm sorry," he sobbed.

Nathan drove a heavy boot into his son's ribs. "Snivelin' coward. Makin' a fool out of me. You're not fit to wipe your brother's boots."

"Why?" the captain asked. "Why would you do such a thing?"

Shannon stared at the man on the ground in disgust. She was no longer afraid of him. Strangely enough, she couldn't even find it in her to hate him. "Because of him," she said, pointing at Nathan. "Because Damon always came second. And maybe, when his brother was killed, he saw a chance to be first."

"I just wanted ya to love me like you did him," Damon whined. "Drake got it all . . . and I just wanted what he'd stolen from me."

Shannon turned toward the redcoat officer. "Do you see what you've done? Now, will you do the right thing? Will you let me go free?"

Sidwell looked from her to Nathan to Damon, and then shook his head. "I'm sorry," he said. "But I can't go back to my commander and tell him that I left a white woman to the mercy of the Cherokee."

"Please," Shannon begged Nathan. "Drake is dead. You don't want me. Make him let me go."

Nathan kicked the dirt with the toe of his boot. "Wouldn't be right," he said. "You gotta come back with us. I think you're crazy in the head. But, whatever you done, whatever you are, you're one of us. You deserve better than torture and abuse by the savages."

"I haven't done anything wrong. Please, Captain. Reconsider."

"Can't do it, madam." Sidwell sighed. "It would mean my career."

Shannon lay alone in the tent with two soldiers to guard her, but she could not sleep. She guessed it to be sometime after midnight when she heard the sentry call out.

"Who goes there?"

"George *Hatapi*. I bring deer."

"That's George, all right," the sergeant said in a sleepy voice. "Why the hell didn't you get back sooner, boy? I had more worms in my biscuit than meat on my plate."

"Deer runs far. You can eat in morning."

Shannon pushed aside the door cover and saw Strong Bow deposit two venison haunches next to the fire outside her tent. Slowly, he found rope and suspended the meat high enough off the ground that varmints wouldn't disturb it between now and morning.

"George sleep now," he said.

"George do that," the stout sergeant replied. "And let me get some too."

As he walked from the circle of firelight, George, whom Shannon thought of only as Strong Bow, glanced meaningfully at her. She retreated to the back of the tent and waited.

After perhaps half an hour, a whisper came through the tent wall. "Wife of Storm Dancer?"

"Yes. I'm awake."

"There will be trouble."

She held her breath.

"When fire arrows fly, go to the place where we drew water from the river."

"Is he coming for me?"

"Tell my sister she need fear Gall no more."

"Wait. Tell me . . ."

But Strong Bow was gone as silently as he'd come. In the semidarkness, Shannon took a bag containing flint and steel, a compass, a pair of warm, wool stockings, and Drake's coat from the pile of belongings by the door. She put the fire-making tools, the compass, and the stockings in the inside pocket of the coat, and put the coat on. Locating a small hole in the tent wall, she began to unravel the threads, slowly making the tear larger.

The night breeze off the river was cool, but perspiration beaded on Shannon's forehead as an hour and then another slipped away. Had she dreamed that Strong Bow had come to bring her a message of hope? When dawn broke, would she be as much a prisoner as she had been at dusk?

A long rifle cracked suddenly in the darkness, followed almost immediately by the roar of a Brown Bess. The sergeant shouted orders, and the camp dissolved into pandemonium. Men shouted and cursed. Horses neighed in distress. A mule broke free and galloped past the entrance to the tent, braying wildly.

Shannon parted the rent in the tent wall and squeezed through. Overhead, it was raining fire arrows. Tents burst into flame. Keeping to the shadows of the trees, Shannon ran for the river.

"Shawnee!" she heard Strong Bow shout. "Take cover! They have guns!"

She glanced back to see the Delaware snatch a flaming arrow from the grass and plunge it into the roof of the officer's tent. Suddenly, beyond the camp, near the entrance to the hollow, a wall of flame ignited. Another horse pulled free from the picket line. The loose mule dragged a long rope and the blazing remains of a tent attached.

"Fire!" Captain Sidwell ordered. "Fire!"

Another gun went off, and a soldier screamed. "You shot my foot, you fool!"

Sheer panic broke out as ammunition boxes, stored under sailcloth, near where the pack animals had been tethered, began to explode. The other four mules went wild. Men dove for the ground and covered their heads with their arms as mules and riding horses kicked and bucked and plunged through the wall of fire to freedom.

Shannon stood by the river, staring in amazement as three horses leaped through the conflagration and galloped straight into the camp. Her heart leaped into her throat as she recognized the big sorrel on the right. "Storm Dancer."

In the confusion, no one seemed to notice the strange horses, until Nathan Clark yelled and pointed his rifle at the animal. Shannon screamed as the shot echoed through the camp and over her head. Then man and horse leaped the last campfire, Storm Dancer leaned from his seat on the back of the sorrel and scooped her up.

More shots rang out around them as the horse gave a great leap and landed in the raging river. Storm Dancer grabbed her hand and locked it in the sorrel's mane. "Don't let go!" he shouted in her ear. And then he released his hold on her and the horse and she lost sight of him as water closed over her head.

She clung to the horse with both hands, trying to stay on the animal's back. She could feel the powerful muscles surging beneath her, hear the terrified whinny of the beast as the water pulled them down a second time.

Storm Dancer. Storm Dancer. Her world was confined to that one thought. But she could not release her hold on the stallion's mane. He sank, he swam; he thrust his great head into the air, desperate for air.

Shannon gasped as water poured in her nose and mouth. She was blind, deaf, but she could not let go of life. And somehow, against the rush of water and the peril of the rocks, the horse fought on.

. . . Until her strength gave out, her fingers weakened, and she lost her grip on the sorrel's mane and was swept away by the force of the river.

Storm Dancer kissed her. His breath was warm on her face, his tongue rough and scratchy. Scratchy? Shannon opened her eyes and found the stallion standing over her, nuzzling her with his velvet nose.

She coughed, sat up on the sand, and vomited half a river. The horse looked on sympathetically. She could hear the roar of the river, but she couldn't see it. Low tree branches and ferns blocked her view of the waterway.

She shivered and looked down. She had only her bodice and part of her shift left. One moccasin and Drake's coat were gone. She was bruised and sore, but clearly not dead. No one who was dead could ache in so many places at once.

Vividly, memories of the fires and the plunge into the river swept over her. And then, sorrow, such as she had never known gripped her, seeping through blood and bone . . .

Storm Dancer was gone. She had lost him. He'd given his life for her. She wanted to weep, but her grief was too deep for tears. She wanted to scream, but she had given her last ounce of strength to the river.

How could she go on without him? "My love," she whispered hoarsely. "My darling husband. I will never—"

The words caught in her throat as she saw the rawhide rope around the sorrel's neck.

Someone had tied the horse to a tree. Someone had found her here and left her. Strong Bow? Had he pulled her from the river? If he had, she almost wished he hadn't bothered. . . . Better to have drowned with Storm Dancer. How could fate be so cruel . . . that her one love could save her and die in the trying.

"Storm Dancer," she whispered.

"Ma-ry Shan-non."

She stiffened. Was she losing her mind? If she was, she didn't care. Being mad was better than never hearing his voice again. "I'm here," she said.

"I would hope so."

She stared in disbelief as the branches parted and Storm Dancer appeared. Grinning. In his arms, he carried a buckskin hunting shirt, a fur blanket, and a pair of moccasins.

"How does it feel to be a dead woman, wife?"

She punched him hard in the arm, aiming for the scar he'd taken in battle against the Shawnee. "You're alive? You let me think you were dead, and you're alive?"

"Yes, I'm alive, and so are you." He raised an eyebrow. "But the English believe we are dead. It was smart of you to leave your skirt and a hank of your hair on the rocks."

"My hair?" Her hand flew to her head, to the spot that ached the most. Sure enough, she was missing a patch of hair. "My hair." Now she burst into tears, and he dropped the blankets and clothing and pulled her against him.

"Shh, shh, heart of my heart. It will grow back. And you are beautiful to me, with hair or not."

"You left me," she protested between sobs. "I thought you were drowned, and you left me."

"My stallion was here to watch over you. And I needed

to get the things I'd left on the mountain. I could not let my wife freeze, could I?"

"But I don't see how . . ." A fresh flood of tears swallowed her words.

"I have spoken with Strong Bow. He found your skirt and your hair and took them to the English captain. They believe you are dead. We are safe in these mountains, Spring Rain. Safe to live out our lives, have children, and watch them grow."

"Truly?" she asked him. "Are we really safe? Can we be together now, together forever?"

"Forever is a long time, heart of my heart." He kissed her again and he wrapped a warm fur around her. "But I will never leave you again. And if a stubborn prophet and a woman with eyes no human should possess can be happy, we will be."

She put her arms around his neck and kissed him until they both were breathless. "Take me home, Storm Dancer," she murmured when they finally broke apart and gazed into each others' eyes. "Take me home."

And he did. . . .

*And thus was the prophesy fulfilled, that a wise woman of a noble clan should wed the great warrior Storm Dancer. And that together, these two would lead the* Tsalagi *to peace and security in a time when the drums of war echoed through the Smoky Mountains.*